GROUNDED
A DRAGON'S TALE

GLORIA PIPER

228 Hamilton Ave.,
Palo Alto, CA 94301

For Donna "Bird Lady" and all others who fight
for the rights of humans and animals.

ACKNOWLEDGMENTS

Thanks to my ex landlady, Marian O'Donley, who inspired me to write *Where the Sky Ends*, the short story that eventually led to this novel. Thanks to the woods and volcanic slopes of Bidwell Park, where I hike as often as possible. And thanks to the many readers of my short story who demanded it be made into a novel. Eventually I complied and ran the early draft through Novelpro, a critique group for serious writers, where I found encouragement from Sudarshan Bharadwaj to develop the characters. And thanks to K.S. Ferguson, a great author, who read and reread my novel and gave me valuable suggestions to further improve it. As always, in thankful memory of my hubby, who gave me the space to write.

CHAPTER 1

Grounded

-1-

The sky is my home.

This morning I raise my head from under my wing to see ruby shadows beneath the pale wash of red over otherwise green leaves. Lightning stabs the air. A growl of thunder follows. I smell ozone.

"Tweekie, did you see that?"

I feel the groombug nibble along my spine, and I arch my neck to look back at him, a fist-sized ball of fur with needle claws barely visible. He hums as he polishes my scales. I sometimes pity Tweekie, who has no wings, though he says I am his wings and he is content to feel the wind on his face when I mount the air.

He releases his hold and rolls to the back of my head. How he manages without falling makes me wonder, for only a single breath. He won't slip and lose his balance; groombugs never do.

And then he scrunches himself small enough to take his seat in the pocket of my central ear, which looks no different from the ear holes on each side of my head. Except it's located at the base of my skull, in the back. A slight tickle and he settles down. His voice is soft inside my head. "The Great Mother spoke in the middle of the night. I didn't want to awaken you."

All around in the old growth redwoods, my sister dragons and I hang by our fingers and toes or lounge on a platform of boughs.

Another jab of lightning. The Great Mother's talon. Ozone permeates the forest.

They stir. Yawn, stretch, and murmur about the red sky and how the Great Mother is making new manna. Food for all dragons. Sweet and delectable.

"I want to see how she makes it," I tell Tweekie.

Briefly the membrane of my third ear vibrates, which means Tweekie is hyperspeaking to other groombugs. Whatever he tells them is too high for a dragon's hearing, and of no interest to a dragon.

And then Tweekie is again with me. "Let's go."

The trees creak and rustle as the branches come alive with the clan's movement. Most adults are first into the air. My adolescent hatch sisters grab youngsters who haven't learned yet to fly, and I snatch up Nip, who is nearest to me, with my beak on the nape of her snaky neck and sling her onto my back. Nip had lost the fingers of one wing in the pinch of two branches, so she can only grasp with one hand.

Not ready yet, I watch the others kick off and stretch their arms, which are the leading edge of their wings, so their wings fan out, and they ride the wind.

"Eehee!" Nip squeals in delight. She hooks the back of my shoulders with the fingers of her good hand and curves the wing of her bad hand over my other shoulder. She's as light as a moonbeam. I can barely feel her.

I twitch my shoulders to test her grip.

Tweekie speaks from his position in my ear. "She's holding on."

He will warn me if she starts to slip. Even so, I'll be careful not to unbalance her. I climb a trunk whose branches have multiplied and formed platforms. It's a lofty world where epiphytic bushes, ferns, and mushrooms live, along with animals that have never seen the ground. I continue up a spire, to where it creaks and bends as if to break. I dare climb no higher, and I lift my arms to open them as wings.

"Keep your eyes closed," I warn the youngling. She'll see perfectly well through her second eyelids.

"I will." She giggles.

"And protect your groombug," I yell, in case the adults indulge in a fire show.

"He's safe," Tweekie tells me. "He's in her mid-ear. I'll tell him when to hide in her mouth."

I kick off to join the flock, their wings long and sharp silhouettes against red sky. Cool air rushes against me. Red with volcanic dust. I watch through my second eyelids. I raise the steamy vapor in my nostrils to filter the air. A sea of forest stretches before us, green stretching into black.

Tweekie sets my ear to buzzing. Pleasant, almost hypnotic.

I glide. The wind whips us. Tosses the scent of wetness, bruised leaves, volcanic dust. And on the wind I hear a distant moan and hoots. Dreamy. And then closer, my sister dragons blast forth their chorus of jubilation. A whoop builds in my depths and passes up my insides and spews from my throat in a mighty crow of joy, my contribution to the chorus. From my back the baby Nip adds a descant. We soar and sing, soar and sing with all the sisters who have joined me in the sky. Between our choruses we pause and listen to the distant answering song. We answer. Oh, the blessing of unity! How beautiful our song, how powerful!

We are the forest clan, the Shining Ones. A flash of lightning bounces off our scales in a rainbow of colors, as if to say it is so.

All this time, Tweekie has been hyperspeaking. Possibly hyper-singing with other groombugs. Not my business or interest to know. But as we grow quiet and hear only the whip of air on wings and the distant dragon song, he scurries to the corner of my mouth and pries.

I open and he tucks himself between my cheek and the bony ridge of my beak. Within that breath of time, adults shoot out flames, and the dust in the sky catches. The odor of burning dust sweeps over us.

Well above the trees, a lacework of sparks pop and sputter. Before they burn out, more flames rush in, and soon we are bathed in fire. In and out of it we fly, stirring it and taking care not to linger too long and get singed. We perform a fire dance as the flames shoot about us in flowery patterns and starbursts.

Only the adults are allowed to shower us and the sky with fire, for they know how to perform the patterns without injuring the mighty forest or us. We adolescents race above the burn where we have permission to shoot out flames of our own without endangering our baby passengers or their groombugs.

And then the show ends, along with our dance. In the far distance I see a flash. Not lightning. "It's the cliff clan," someone cries. "Their fire show."

The sky is paler now, only faintly red. Tweekie slips from my mouth and back into my third ear. A light rain ensues and patters on our wings and on the leaves of the giant trees. The air freshens.

Nip feels warm against my back. I feel her shift and adjust her grip, as light as a gnat. Or a groombug. She twitters. "The sky, hee, hee, hee!" and croons, "The sky is my home. My home." And then she breaks off to whisper to her groombug.

So I murmur to mine. "You know what, Tweekie? I'd like to see them. The cliff dragons. Do you think they hang from the cliffs, just like we hang from trees?"

"It's what the elders say." Tweekie's voice carries well within my ear canal.

"You think they look like us?"

"More like birds, heh, heh. Big birds. Or giant lizards with bat wings."

We're the beautiful ones, my actions say, as I shift my colors back and forth between blues and greens. And my birth name says it. Manycolors. It's only a temporary name, soon to be changed to something better. All around, the flock's scales glimmer like jewels. The light rain makes them shine even more. For we are the Shining Ones.

"And you are the most beautiful of all, Manycolors," Tweekie says. "When the Naming Ceremony for you and your hatch mates comes, choose Brightwing for yourself. To me, you are already Brightwing."

I love Tweekie. Bonded to me from hatch to death, he is mine alone, unchanging and comfortable. He smells almost of cedar and manna. Sweet.

I turn our conversation again to the cliff clan. "Do you think they ever wonder about us?"

"Probably. And I expect they follow the same rules we do. *Stay with the flock*, so how can they know how great we are? Besides, forest dragons have it much better than the cliff clan."

"Stay with the flock," I mutter. *"Don't wander off alone. It's dangerous.* That's what the elders say. How is it dangerous? They never tell us."

Tweekie doesn't answer. I don't expect him to.

When the flock turns back, I follow and land on my two feet among the others where branches have merged into a broad platform that trails among the treetops. Far below, the ground hides. Nip hops off running. The platform creaks beneath our weight. We are on the fire-etched path, which will lead us to the gathering spot that towers among the biggest trees. The hatchling races ahead to join her hatch sisters. They remind me of birds running along, wings folded or partially outspread. The knob on the back of each head looks like a natural extension of the skull, but it's each one's groombug. Some groombugs have the sense to alter their color and appearance to match their dragon's. Others are slow learners, pale fuzz balls easily recognized. I snicker at their innocence. The younglings are so cute in their awkwardness and so sweet. Nip is my favorite, and my responsibility until she learns to fly. In a way I feel guilty for not keeping a close watch over her. I might have prevented the accident. Some sisters have whispered it, along with a couple elders. Tweekie says her accident was unavoidable, and I take comfort from that. I also take comfort that Nip hasn't let the loss of her fingers hamper her from climbing or rejoicing in play.

"Her fingers are growing back," Tweekie says.

Are they? I stretch my neck to catch sight of her, but she's lost among the others.

We enter the gathering area, careful to avoid stepping on tails. Some thrash a warning. The slap of an adult's tail can knock a youngster off the platform. I've been disciplined before, and it's not only painful to batter your way toward the ground but embarrassing.

The elders crouch on their tails and face the congregation. They are larger than the rest of us. Their colors are muted now, so they fade into anonymity. Except for Fetidbreath. Her scales, normally green, brighten, so we know she will be in charge today.

Her breath steams in the light rain. It sizzles. Her voice rumbles like the purr of distant thunder. "In the time before time, the Great Mother spoke. And the world came into being. And she breathed and entities took form. Rooted entities. Free ranging entities. Legged entities, and those with wings. And with her breath of fire, she made us Shining Ones. And gave us an inner fire. She creates and replenishes the manna belt that spans our skies and sustains all dragons. Look up at the belt and see how it sparkles like pristine jewels. There is enough for all, wherever clans dwell."

Her colors fade, and Shiningsnout now vibrates a bright orange. Her voice is a deep honk, a blat of irritation. The pupils of her eyes are cold slits. She sweeps her glance over us, and I'm not alone in shying back into a bed of moss and the whimper of branches that support the platform. She will recite the duty roster, which doesn't worry me. I know in advance that the babies will attend lessons on fire etiquette. Adults will tend the hidden nest or teach or tell the great myths or learn secrets from the elders. Most who can fly will carry the babies to the manna belt and show them how to feed properly if they are hungry. Duties seldom change. I'm content with mine. What worries me is her announcement of any punishments. Since Nip's mishap, I don't think I've done anything wrong. Nevertheless I feel an inner cringe. Did I weaken the trail the last time I fire-trimmed it? Have I unknowingly insulted an elder? Has a sister complained about me? Shiningsnout is talking, but I'm too busy searching myself for faults to listen—until Tweekie nudges me.

"Manycolors, listen."

I jerk my head upright.

"She is the most agile among us," Shiningsnout says.

"She's talking about you," Tweekie whispers.

"Note how she keeps Nip safe when in flight. Have we not marveled?"

Complimenting me. And as stern as ever.

"Manycolors is the strongest of the adolescents. She launches into flight from the flimsiest of structures. Her aerobatic skills are confident, equal to those more mature. And so we have decided."

"A reward!" Tweekie whispers, quivering in delight from the top of my head.

I stand tall, feeling agile, strong, deserving.

"Highflyer can no longer carry Batwing."

I freeze, at first confused, then suddenly cold. Highflyer is one of the adults. My throat closes for I know what is coming.

"Highflyer has grown too big for Batwing to safely hold on any longer. Her arms are too short. Therefore we are forced to switch Batwing to a smaller flyer, one of her hatch mates. One who is strong enough to carry her. Manycolors."

My colors pale, and I sneak looks over the backs of those about me. And there, there is Batwing, a fellow hatchling.

My mouth is parched. "What…what of Nip?" I croak.

Shiningsnout has a wicked gleam in her eye. "Batwing won't need to be watched as closely as you failed to watch Nip. She can avoid getting her fingers caught in cross branches. And weren't you among those who teased Batwing when she was younger?"

"Punishment," Tweekie says in disgust.

Shiningsnout turns from me. The older dragons receive their assignments, but I'm not listening. Instead, I crouch and wish Batwing away.

Contrary to what Shiningsnout says, Batwing's arms are long enough but they form wings too tiny. As for the jokes, they have long faded. *Batwing, which bat did you trade with? Batwing, are those wings or decorations? Batwing, where'd you leave your wings?*

No one teases her any more. The elders grant her favors the rest of us must earn. I avoid looking at her, but the image of her grabs my thoughts. It seems inconceivable that she started out looking normal. So, why didn't her wings develop properly? We may have teased her, but the adults didn't help by crooning over her cuteness when she was small and waddled about with stunted wings, never accomplishing anything beyond making a nuisance of herself. Well, maybe she does fire trim the platform trail, but so do others. What's worse, Batwing grew up and out, in all directions.

Don't think of her, I tell myself. I squeeze my eyes shut and edge away.

The assembly breaks up. It is time to fly. Adolescents sling babies onto their backs, and I snatch at Nip.

"You!"

The word strikes at me, and I know what it means. I feel the heat of it. My attention rivets on Elder Shiningsnout. She is pulsing waves of angry orange, and she is looking right at me.

"You."

Her eyes are as cold as stones. "You will carry Batwing, starting today."

I can't help but pale. "I'd rather …I was planning…Maybe tomorrow?" It is hard to argue with an elder, particularly before the penetrating gaze of my sisters, their jaws tight. Some hug their wings against their body, as if my assignment might shift to them. They needn't worry. Highflyer pulls Nip from my back to hers.

"Perform your duty," the elder says.

I look at the other elders, who remain silent and pale. None will contradict Shiningsnout.

A steamy sigh, and I signal Batwing with a tilt of my head to come hither.

"Nice try," Tweekie murmurs in my ear, his tone sarcastic.

What can I say? Around me I sense the relaxation of my sisters. They leave with their young passengers while Batwing approaches me. My innards shrivel at the sight of her.

"What a ball of fat!" Tweekie mutters.

It makes her wings look even smaller and more useless.

"At least my wings will grow more powerful from supporting her," I whisper.

"One way of looking at it. Do you realize what it means, her coming from the same clutch of eggs as you? She'll only get larger, so anyone younger won't be expected to carry her about. And she'll never learn to fly."

I don't want to consider the possibility of transporting her all my life.

"She'll kill you," Tweekie says. "Eventually she'll kill you. And where will that leave me? Dragonless. As good as dead. There must be some alternative."

I shudder. Shake my head. I don't want to talk about it.

-2-

After a couple days of carrying Batwing, I feel disheartened and hang with Tweekie in the shade of branches for a good mope. The day, what remains of it, may have been fragrant with a cooling breeze—I didn't notice. Hatchmates may have played games of catch-the-babies in the air or sang to them—I didn't care. The only thing I focus on is Nip's joy at being on Highflyer's back, not that Nip hadn't felt less joyful when I was her transport.

"Highflyer has wing sprain." Tweekie speaks around his nibbles at the scales near my eye.

"Who told you?"

"Batwing's and Highflyer's groombugs. Batwing caused it. Too heavy."

I explode a breath of fire. "What about my wings? I'm only a half-grown! So unfair!"

Flames lick my lips as I seethe. Tweekie lingers near the safety of my eyes. He croons in his wispy voice until my nerves calm. And then he settles atop my snout, puffs himself into a gossamer ball of fur and stretches his barely exposed arms and legs. I love the sight of him, as beautiful as thistle down with two soulful black eyes nearly half his size.

"They can't be completely unfair," he says at last. "Who says we have to transport her every day? Only when it's necessary, so you get plenty of rest in between."

"Like when?"

"On a feeding day. At the manna belt. How often do dragons feed?"

"You know. It depends. Sometimes I go two hands and two feets worth of days before I eat."

"That's three and three and five and five. Sixteen days."

"Sixteen days of not carrying Batwing." My insides cool. My mood mellows. I emit a sigh of relief.

Tweekie fixes me with a tentative look. "Ole fatty. She may eat more often."

"But still." Even if she eats every one hand and one foot of days, it would still be endurable.

The next morning I fan my wings on the platform, ready to mount the dawn air when Batwing hustles up a branch to my side. I shove her so she cringes. "Go away."

"You're supposed to take me."

"Do you feed today?"

"No. Tomorrow."

"Good, then go away. I don't have to take you until it's absolutely necessary, and it isn't necessary except when you need to visit the manna belt."

Batwing huffs at me, and her breath escapes in heat waves. "You are to transport me every day."

"Says who?"

"Says the elders!"

I glance about for them and see youngsters and oldsters taking to the air. No elders among them yet, thank the Great Mother. I don't want to seek out the elders, lest they should agree with Batwing. Nevertheless, I must know. "Tweekie?"

He's hiding in my mid-ear where I feel a vibration of his hyperspeaking to other groomsbugs. And then he sighs. "It's true. One of the elder groombugs says we carry her for a time every day so she'll feel part of the clan."

I want to scream, to kick and beat my wings against the trees, to roll in the air in agony. Instead, I allow myself a few sputters. And then I clear my throat and force myself to appear unconcerned, an obvious lie. I kneel, an invitation for her to clamber onto my back. Oof!

With her aboard, I labor through the air, after I manage to get off the platform, and she squirms, challenging my balance. I pump my wings to rise into the sky.

"Sit still," I say.

"I need to go." She pants, wriggles.

"What?"

"I need to go."

"We just started."

"I don't care."

"Why didn't you go before we left?'

"I didn't need to then."

"By the Great Ancestors!"

"I need to go."

"Fine. We'll touch down, and the ride's over." I glide downward toward the platform.

"No, it's not." She nearly throttles my neck. "You can't decide to carry me for mere pulse beats."

"Then I won't land. Not if I have to force myself into the air with you two times in a row." I flap harder and rise up again.

"Dump her," Tweekie mutters.

And earn a tail thrashing from Elder Shiningsnout? One hit is bad. She'd give two and shame me before the congregation, perhaps send me to a baby class on fire etiquette.

Batwing sticks her rear over my shoulder and wiggles. I tense, afraid she will miss and soil me. Tweekie's warmth in my third ear reminds me of his support. Ever constant. I don't know where Batwing's groombug is. Not in her third ear, unless he is scrunched down with his hairs laid flat. He could well be, or anywhere else on her scales, adapting his color to hers. How does he tolerate her? Probably because he has no choice.

"Why didn't you go before we went up?"

"I didn't need to."

Her toe jabs my eye. I shy sideways and leaves flash by.

Unbalanced, I just miss a tree.

She slips and grabs my neck, nearly dislocating it. Leaves slap. I snag a talon in a branch and almost flip. We all turn pale.

Tweekie hiccups. Batwing shrieks against my cheek so my ears ring.

I thrash to regain my balance and roll sideways.

Tweekie braces himself to keep aboard while Batwing claws at my scales and gases me with her stench of fear.

That does it!

Somehow I manage to right myself. Pulsing red, I swoop low, scrape her off through a dense growth of trees, and lift myself high into the thermals.

There I wheel with other dragons, vultures, and pterodactyls, high above the dimpled forest canopy. Bright scales from sister dragons twinkle in the sun. They ignore me, and my shortened breaths become longer, more leisurely.

My inner furnace cools.

"That was close," Tweekie says after a while. "It took you a good slam to dislodge her."

Which rouses my thoughts. "Her hands are strong. So her wings must be just as strong."

Tweekie hums. I feel him swell to where he can look beyond his seat in my ear pocket. "She's climbing a tree."

"Strong," I say.

"Strong enough to reach the platform and leap on you if you fly too close."

"And I'm supposed to take her to the manna belt tomorrow? After she nearly killed me?"

"Like I warned earlier," Tweekie says. "She's dangerous."

"We need to do something."

"I agree. What?"

"I suggest we hide tomorrow. The elders will punish me, but I don't care. I refuse to take her to the manna belt. Ever!'

"Yay!"

-3-

Do not fly off alone. It's dangerous.

We are dragons. Mighty. What can endanger us? The elders never say. Actually, we wouldn't be alone. I'd be with Tweekie and he'd be with me.

The elders wouldn't be convinced. They'd come after us, bring us back, and punish us. Perhaps we'd do double duty transporting Batwing—laboring under her weight not once by twice a day.

"We'll need to hide where dragons never go," I say.

"Forbidden Mountain?"

I wish he had a better suggestion, one that wouldn't break any rules, one that would be less scary.

Stay away from Forbidden Mountain. It's dangerous. It's where the Watchers are.

I shudder at the thought. Nevertheless I put on a bold front. After all, what harm can touch a dragon? Tweekie says nothing as we set off in that direction. As we near though, I feel him tense, drawing himself small and hard as a nut in my ear pocket.

"We'll just fly over and then hide in the vicinity."

His tension eases minutely.

The woods open up, and below, Forbidden Mountain rises in a series of steps. It looks harmless enough. Still I sense an alien presence there.

Tweekie raises enough to look out. "It doesn't look dangerous, but the elders must know."

He shivers.

His fear plays on mine. "We can't stay here."

"Where'll we go?"

I soar across the mountain and around it. "We can't go back."

"Double duty, I bet. And a few tail whacks."

I continue to circle. We've already broken two rules. Three by ignoring Batwing. Before the day is over, the elders will come looking for us.

"You think they might consider that Batwing is bigger than you and that you, too, could get wing sprain?"

I feel sorry for catching Tweekie in my messes. Nevertheless I snort. "You heard their reasoning. I'm strong, I'm agile…" I'm stuck.

Unless…

"Tweekie, let's run away."

"Alone?"

"There's other clans. When we sing, the cliff clan answers us. So it's not like we'd be complete strangers. They'd welcome us. I'm sure of it." Actually I'm not, but Tweekie relaxes.

"Yay, let's do it."

His exuberance strengthens my resolve.

I set off, strong, confident. I want to hoot a greeting to the cliff clan, as far off as they are. They'd hear. So would our forest clan.

We've never flown beyond our forest. We've never seen the cliffs. We know where they are from the sound of their songs. They are silent now, and the only music we hear are the wind through the treetops, the chatter of birds, and the flutter of air in my wings.

Throughout the day, I alternate soaring and flapping. I ignore other high flyers, as they ignore me. Great vultures, winged dinosaurs, fox-faced fruit bats. We enter a great plain where herds of antelope and deer roam. In the distance lie the cliffs, a long, low ridge that looks mostly pink.

Tweekie spent the early part of the day grooming me along my back and legs. He settles on my head. "What if the cliff sisters don't welcome us?"

Was his resolve weakening?

"I'm sure they will."

"And if they don't?"

"We move on. We'll keep going until we find a clan we can join."

By midday groups of trees break up the plain. Wind sweeps up cliffs that are tall and sheer. Scrub clings to an otherwise stark surface. I soar along the edge, along dark hollows on a rocky surface. And there, there are the cluster of hanging bodies along its face. Dragons. Tweekie is in my mid-ear, stretching in curiosity. The dragons turn their heads to follow us. Otherwise, none move. My soaring turns into wing flaps. I should greet them. I should land nearby. But the cliffs are barren. There is no sweet smell of leaves. No sound of creaking tree trunks. No gentle sway of a lofty trail woven and fire-groomed among the treetops.

We leave the cliff clan behind, and I turn in a large circle to pass over the plain.

"Where are we going?" Tweekie seems merely curious.

"I don't know."

"I wouldn't have liked it there," he says.

We follow the cycle of the sun. As it lowers, we hear a low moan, as if from the bowels of the planet.

"What's that?" Tweekie says.

I soar through forest, my mouth open in an effort to enhance my hearing. The air vibrates with the moan. And then the trees open and I know. A great peak rises where trees are forbidden to thrive. A long path of broken rock leads to a mouth, which glows red. "The Great Mother."

Having never seen her, I recognize her. And feel honored. Honored. As if I am an elder, worthy of her mystery.

Ohh. Ohh.

"You hear it, Tweekie?"

"It says…"

Ohh. Ohh. As if taking a breath between moans. Hot.

And we are breathless, hardly able to speak above a whisper. But I know Tweekie's thoughts and am aware he knows mine.

"It…it's…" he stumbles.

"It-it's telling us to—" I stumble in return.

"Go home," Tweekie finishes.

Ohh. Ohh. Gooo. Hommme.

"Go home," we echo in unison.

I circle around the volcano, feeling its hot breath, feeling blessed. Who can argue with the Great Mother? And yet I continue to circle.

Tweekie says what I dread. "You think they'll punish us?"

It's not his fault I get him into these messes. Besides, groombugs are never punished. They are not even considered in the scheme of dragon rules and etiquette. They have their own society, each bonded to his own dragon. So Tweekie needn't worry. More likely, he worries about me.

"If we tell them about meeting the Great Mother, they couldn't possibly punish us," he says.

Honored by the Great Mother's message, I feel enlarged, boisterous. "I'm not afraid."

Tweekie latches onto my exaltation, for haven't we shared in the sacred experience? "Yay! Bring it on, bring it on!

My circle straightens into a course for home. Singing and laughing, we travel through darkness, flapping along for most of the way, as most thermals sleep for the night. Eventually we continue only to the sound of wingbeats. Tweekie is soon buzzing with the sleep of innocence. I want to hold on to euphoria, but with each hour into night and with each wing stroke, I feel euphoria sink into a pool of dread. A simple tale won't sway the elders. I must offer something more. My thoughts churn in preparation for when we arrive, weary, and I try to convince the elders to spare me pain and embarrassment.

-4-

I had hoped to sneak back and be ignored by my clan sisters. It is not to be. The elders are waiting in a group. Soon as I land on the platform, they surround me, so I can't see beyond their forms. As far as I can tell, the rest of the clan are going about their own business, as if our confrontation doesn't exist. Possibly they are too polite or afraid to pay attention. My punishment will be severe. Perhaps my sisters will set a precedent and banish me from the clan.

Before any can speak, I blurt, "I couldn't do it, I just couldn't, so I was running away to some other clan, and the Great Mother sent me back, I saw her, she spoke to me, she said go home, only it was goo… hoommme, and I couldn't disobey, so…so…" My breath comes in gasps.

Shiningsnout stops midway in raising up, wings spread, bright colors pulsing. Her sternness mixes with uncertainty. After a moment, she lowers herself, so she looks no more threatening than the other elders. They wait without expression. Among them, Wily seems as distant as usual, but thoughtful. Fetidbreath alone possesses a natural warmth that passes as approachable. I focus on her.

"I-uh. I-uh know…I broke some rules. Never fly alone. And-and-and not feeding Batwing. B-but…I won't do it. No matter what you do to me, I won't!" I must look white with fear. I clear my throat and my breath sizzles in my nostrils. "I won't," I whisper, almost too short of breath to speak.

"We ask too much of you," Fetidbreath says. "Is that it?"

She may be sympathetic, but I can't be sure. I press my case. "It's hard enough carrying Batwing. If I take her to the manna belt, it's impossible. The manna, you know how slick and sticky it is. It takes special maneuvering to feed, and with Batwing on my back, I can't maneuver properly. We'd get all sticky and slippery, and she wouldn't be able to hold on. And there, you have it."

"What would you propose?" The question lacks warmth because it comes from Wily. Better than coming from Shiningsnout.

I swallow a hard knot in my throat. "Let me carry someone lighter on that day. Like Nip. And I'll carry Batwing any other day"

The elders looked unconvinced.

I plunge on. "In fact, if I don't have to take her to the manna belt, I'll teach her to fly."

"Indeed!" Shiningsnout leads the elders in a burst of laughter. "What the young don't come up with!"

After shaking her sides with the rest, Fetidbreath holds up a quieting hand. "Where did you come up with so creative an offer?"

At least she will listen. "Because I think I can do it. I've been thinking about it. I have a plan."

"Perhaps," Fetidbreath regards her sisters, "perhaps we should discuss this."

The elders tighten into a group that excludes me and whisper.

"What are they saying, Tweekie?"

Groombugs have excellent hearing.

"Shiningsnout wants to whack you a good one in front of the clan. I think Fetidbreath wants to give you a chance. But now, they've lowered their voices to a depth I can't hear. I think they're taking a vote."

It doesn't take long. From the cluster of elders, Wily takes on color and she raises her head to look down her snout at me. "It has been decided. Providing you teach Batwing to fly, which I doubt can happen, you will be excused from taking her to the manna belt. This doesn't excuse you for having broken rules, however, which are provided for your safety. Because circumstances warrant it, Shiningsnout will deliver one tail whack to you in the privacy of this gathering."

Before I can thank them for their leniency, I almost bite my tongue when Shiningsnout strikes without warning. I crash through branch after branch, bouncing and thrashing all the way to the ground, the odor of bruised leaves following me.

I lie, waiting for blinking lights to disappear from my vision. Once that's accomplished, I open my wings and leap upward to a heavy branch whose shade will hide my shame. It is good to hang there, with no one to bother me. I don't know where Batwing is. I don't want to know. My eyes are moist, so the leaves are blurry. Soon Tweekie is licking the moisture away. When he finishes and my vision clears, he perches in the leaves nearest my face.

"Manycolors, why did you allow them to make you promise the impossible? We're still stuck with Batwing, and how long before you have to take her feeding?"

"It'll work out. After all, Tweekie, didn't you tell me Nip is regrowing her fingers?"

"Yes."

"So if Nip can regrow fingers, Batwing can regrow her wings."

"Batwing can…Why, of course. Batwing can regrow her wings! How clever you are, Manycolors!"

"Yes! And all I have to do is teach her to fly!"

"To fly!" Tweekie wiggles with excitement, then checks himself. "Wait. How long before her wings are ready?"

I shove aside his concern and grab at the excitement. "As long as you have the structure, you have the function."

"Her structure is awfully small."

"But strong. It can grow. You saw how strong her arms are. Just think about it, Tweekie. Nip is regrowing her fingers. If someone had worked with Batwing when we were little, she could have flown with the best of us. She was much smaller then and lighter in proportion to her wings."

"As I recall, no one wanted to be inconvenienced."

"That didn't stop them from giving her all the rewards the rest of us struggle for, but we can remedy the situation, which means no more hauling her about. No more getting knocked about by her. And I know just how to do it. Exercise, that's what she needs. It will trim her down and develop those useless appendages." The mere thought of freedom from Batwing, of seeing her fly, brings bubbles of joy bursting up my throat and over my jaws in rings of steam.

"Freedom! Freedom!" Tweekie jiggles in anticipation. "Oh, you are so clever. You are my Brightwing."

"Tweekie, I almost look forward to my next turn."

He chortles. And when he nibbles away old scales around my feet and knees, he sings in a light voice.

-5-

At the new day's dawning, I tell Batwing of my intent. "If you insist on riding my wings, your payment will be flying lessons."

She grimaces in a look of disbelief, and her colors turn muddy.

"Didn't the elders tell you?" I ask. "Didn't they?"

"Highflyer told me. I thought she was lying. It couldn't be true."

"It is. Ask the elders."

Whimpering, she ceases to argue, which means she did ask.

Dragons seldom venture to the ground, but it offers privacy. We drop down to an open area where I take her to a rock and make her jump from it and flap. She leaps like something glued to the ground and flutters her wings as if they are a fly's eyelash.

"Leap."

"I am."

"No, you're not."

I shove and she collapses.

"You'll have to be more enthusiastic than that if you're going to fly."

She whimpers from her seated position on the ground.

I huff and sit on my haunches. "Very well. We'll take tomorrow off so you can think about it. Then it's back to work."

I mustn't give up. In the name of lessons and allowing her time to absorb them, I dare to skip in-between days. The elders seem not to notice. We begin with wing circles. Eventually I develop a series of exercises and affirmations for her. Every time, she appears increasingly reluctant. Could her reluctance convince the elders to rescue her from my lessons? I dare not complain to them.

But Batwing does.

They are unimpressed.

My hatch mates snort with derision. Who am I that I should escape my duty, lest they be assigned the burden of Batwing?

Into the second week of lessons, I stand on the platform, fan my wings at Batwing, and stretch to my full height. I swish my tail side to side. My nostrils steam. Tweekie swells enough from the protection of my ear canal to eye Batwing. We are two against one. Her groombug is good at hiding.

She holds back, pale.

"Get on my back," I say. "And learn to fly."

She whines. Shakes her head.

I turn broadside to her, my colors bright and pulsing. "Get on."

I back her across the platform against a spire. She half turns beneath overhanging leafy branches and reaches for the trunk, intent on climbing off the platform away from me.

I growl. "Get on."

She glances skyward and sees an elder drift over. She leaps onto my back and nearly knocks the breath out of me.

I flap. She's heavier than ever. I run along the mat to get up speed. She slips forward, lands on my head, and I fall flat. My head feels crushed, my brains squeezed. Oof! She's fat. Fat, fat, fat!

Momentarily dizzy, I roar for her to get off. She lies on the platform path, and I shake myself, and notice something. My head had cleared, but Tweekie is very still.

"Tweekie?"

I reach up, pull him from my ear. He is limp. He's not breathing. In fact he is flattened. My skull had rebounded to its natural shape. Not Tweekie though. Batwing had sat on him.

"Tweekie?"

I stroke his soft fur and feel his bones shift. His eyes are glazed.

Batwing backs away, turns, runs. I hardly notice. I can only sit there, dazed and confused.

"Tweekie?"

It's all I can say past the tightness of my throat, the clutch of my stomach.

How long I sit there, I don't know. Around me, life goes on. The trees rustle and flowers cast their scent. Overhead, youngsters hoot and play on wing. The shadows shift.

"Tweekie?"

And then a shadow settles over me. It's Elder Fetidbreath. She enfolds me in her wing, and I show her my groombug.

She takes him from me. Shakes her head.

-6-

After Tweekie's death I shun Batwing. The elders respect my mourning. In fact they even devise a duty roster for the groombugs of my hatch mates. They must take turns grooming me. I quickly lose any popularity I might have shared among my fellow adolescents. We dragons never question groombug society, for it seems hardly to exist. Only the bond between groombug and dragon is important. Unbreakable from hatching until death. As expected, no dragon wants to lend her groombug, and I'm sure no groombug wants to overstuff his gut on me so his dragon goes neglected for a day.

Actually most of the groombugs refuse to help. When I carry Nip, her groombug will skitter over my scales as I soar. He twitters in what sounds like a panic, and Nip answers him in a nervous titter. He acts as if he'll die if separated from her for even a pulse beat. He'll only groom me for as long as I carry Nip. I fly to the manna belt and fan a section of it into a windrow. Both Nip and I open our mouths as I fly down the row.

Sweet and energizing, it will satisfy our hunger for days. Nip's groombug skips about my scales, lapping up the sticky smears of manna.

And when I hang, resting in a tree, Batwing climbs toward me and extends a tiny wing. I don't want to look at her, until I notice a furry ball rolling down her wing onto me. The gesture seems kind, but her face betrays its usual reluctance. "The elders," she says.

Her groombug grunts and nibbles along my scales. Complaining, I guess. He isn't nearly as thorough as Tweekie, and nowhere nearly as entertaining. Too soon, he zips back to Batwing. He hasn't scratched my itchy spots. He missed between my toes. He tucks into Batwing's ear, and with a huff in my direction, she leaps away to another branch.

How long before the groombugs refuse to tend me?

I ache to feel the warmth of Tweekie in my third ear, tuned especially to hear him. I loved that he could hide there and sleep there, between venturing forth to clean my scales. I miss his singing as he stroked dander from my crown. Tweekie was a magnificent furry little ball who would comfort and entertain me, even as he filled his belly on the debris from the spikes along my spine.

How long can a dragon survive without a groombug? A month? Two months?

In less time than that, the new duty roster is recited, and my refusals to accommodate Batwing no longer impress anyone. I learn this when she waddles up.

"It's your turn."

My gut tightens. I scrunch up my face and make to walk away, my lips pinched, the thorny tip of my tail twitching. I would have spat flames, but Batwing's breath is hotter than mine. The fatter the dragon, the hotter the breath. Besides that, the lessons on fire etiquette are deeply ingrained. *Don't shoot flames at a fellow dragon because you might harm her groombug. Use fire to trim the platform trails and to keep the meeting area open.* And we all look forward to the day when, as older dragons, we learn to use fire in an aerial light show for ritual and celebration. A dragon who uses fire irresponsibly will be shamed by attending the baby classes on fire etiquette.

So I grit my beak beneath its fleshy lips.

She speaks over my shoulder. "The elders said."

Now that I am back on duty, I ask, "Have you been practicing?" Surely I can still accomplish the grand mission. If I can coax her to fly unaided, her success will atone for the ashes of my heart.

She looks from beneath pouting eyes. "Can't."

"Can," I say.

"Can't."

I struggle as usual beneath her weight into the air.

"I'm hungry."

The elders forced me to take her up, but no one can force me to visit the manna belt with her. Not after she sat on Tweekie.

As we soar, the cool air dissipates the steam I'd worked up getting us aloft, and I cast about for some way to convince her into the air by her own power. I'd tried gentleness. It hadn't worked.

I don't know whose groombug has agreed to spend most of the day with me, but I am grateful. He is aloof but gracious. He whispers in my third ear, "Take authority."

Yes! That's what an elder would do. Maybe he belongs to an elder.

We fly farther than usual over the ocean of forest with intermittent islands of meadows. Forbidden Mountain rises above the trees. The peak resembles the volcano of the Great Mother, but she never whispers from there. Never shakes the ground. Never spews ashes to nourish the manna belt.

Midway down the peak light glints off a dome I hadn't notice on my earlier visit. It is just short of invisible because dust and collision smears cover it. Watchers live inside the dome, and they are watching; I'm sure of it.

Batwing jabs me with her knees. "We're not supposed to be here. What if the elders find out?"

"They won't if you don't tell them."

"They're gawking at us."

"Gawking can't hurt."

"What if they try to catch us?"

"Do you really believe they would?"

Batwing answers with a mewl.

The elders' stories include the Mountain Warning: *Don't go near Forbidden Mountain. The Watchers live there. They make Shining Ones disappear.*

Actually, I've never seen a Watcher or known of any other dragon who has. Occasionally elder Shining Ones disappear, but it is normal to go off to meet the gryphon, whatever that entails, or simply to get away. There has never been any proof a Watcher has interfered.

"The Watchers admire us," I tell Batwing. "Or rather, they admire me. They would admire you, too, if you flew. Too bad you don't know the joy of flying."

"Quit picking on me."

I sigh and circle. I note in more detail than my previous visit how rough plateaus, carved by nature, form steps that run up the mountain from the base to the top, far above the Watchers' dome.

I circle lower.

"What are you doing?" Batwing tightens her grip around my neck and throttles me.

"Don't hold on so tight."

"I'm scared. We're not supposed to be here."

"Learn how to fly, and we won't have to be."

I perch on the top step and tilt her off my back. She suppresses a squawk as she slides off and yanks my head to the ground. Her groombug utters a squeak.

She hugs herself and gapes about over the tip of her tail.

"Hold your wings out and leap down the steps."

"I'll fall."

"The next step will catch you." I shove her. "Go!"

She screeches and bounces from one step to the next, descending with increasing rapidity.

"Beat those wings. Hold them out! Glide!"

She continues to scream and bounce. My assigned groombug counts each step she strikes. "One, two, three…"

She manages to grab a bush beside step twenty-one. She hugs it and snivels.

"Why didn't you beat your wings just like we practiced in those exercises?"

"Too much work."

"Stand up. You've got to try."

"No!"

I tug at her, and she tugs at the bush.

"Let go."

"No."

From below comes the sound of running. The Watchers are coming. What the elders said might or might not be true. I don't care to wait and find out.

"Quick. Onto my back."

Amazing how swift and strong Batwing can be when she wants. She hops onto my back, knocking a grunt from me. I leap into the air and wing back to the forest.

-7-

Batwing ends my attempts to teach by whining to the elders about my endangering her on Forbidden Mountain. While it brings me a chastening and a whack from Shiningsnout's tail, it doesn't remove me from duty.

The very next day I am soaring when up flies the shadow of a Batwing-laden peer, engulfing me with a chill. I can't escape. The fellow adolescent dumps her, and she falls like a boulder. I barely have time to croak when she lands on my back with crippling force, knocking me senseless. Little dots twinkle before my eyes.

Batwing's scream awakens me. The ground is rushing at us.

"Pull up! Pull up!"

The weight of Batwing and the speed of my plummet are too great. Wind whistles by. My wings flutter like a trembling heart. Today's groombug shrills in concert with Batwing's groombug.

Abruptly I learn where the sky ends.

Unforgiving ground hits me. My neck wrenches backwards, my keel bone rams into my lungs, and my legs and wings form new joints.

Batwing sustains a slight bruise.

C H A P T E R 2

Hote, the Invisible Boy

-1-

Hote wanted to shrink. Instead, he had no choice but stand beneath Chief Li's dark gaze. With no desk between them to offer relief, the long-limbed Chief bent slightly over him, giving Hote the impression of a bird of prey.

"Doctor Kellyamber worked hard to convince me to grant you permission to help with the research at the Redwood Station. Ordinarily she doesn't allow bias to interfere with her views. However she is your mother. She claims you are capable as a fifteen-year old to act responsibly. I have yet to see that. Do you have any idea of the seriousness of what you did?"

"Yessir. I knew." Hote eyed the belt on Li's green robe.

"Then why did you do it? What makes you do such things? Don't you ever think?"

"Yes, I think."

"Then why?"

Hote had no answer. He had let Amber down. He had let the other researchers down. Not for the first time. And probably not for the last. Presently he felt as if the walls of Chief's office were closing in. Along with the crazy thoughts. *There is a box, like a kit, and in it is a doll that needs to be assembled. And I can't assemble it. It belongs to Radiant.*

31

"Why did you beg to transfer to the Redwood Station?"

Hote forced his thoughts to the subject at hand. He kept his voice even, lest he sound younger than he was. After all, he no longer called Amber Mother. Just as those closest to her called her by her last name, as if it were her first, he followed suit. Those, more formal, called her Doctor Kellyamber, as if her first and last name were one. He would never do that. "The dragons. I wanted to see them close up, sir. To study them. And I thought the Redwood Station might be my best chance. They know dragons exist in the forest because their atoms show up in the air samplers. So when I saw those two playing on the mountain, and one falling, that's the first look—"

Li raised his palm to interrupt. "If not for the station's other work, that action would have closed them down. You had no right to rush out of concealment—"

"I thought one was injured."

"You had no right to expose yourself. You violated one of the prime directives. Noninterference."

"Sorry," Hote muttered. He knew the Watcher rules and agreed with them. Even as he broke them. *There is a box, like a kit.* When he first came to the station two years ago, AT (Artificial Time), Chief Li forbade him to gibber to everyone about the box. That was the first rule.

"Should I excuse you for being a brash youth? I think not."

Hote wanted to argue. After all, it was the only time dragons had been spotted since the station opened. And he was there to see them, if only from a distance. He took a deep breath and released it. At the time, he hadn't realized he was rushing into view until he found himself outside. No point in trying to explain. Chief Li, Ahmed the acting medic, and even Amber blamed his misdeeds on delusion and his physical symptoms on a powerful imagination. He'd grown weary of telling them this thing inside him was real and sometimes took control. So he said nothing.

Li crossed his arms over his chest. "By exposing yourself like that, it's very likely they will not see any dragons there for a long time. The reason we haven't closed the station is because we have a good study of gryphons going. They are scavengers, you know. Just like any other flesh-eaters on this planet. Why couldn't you have been satisfied with that? Or the other studies in progress, such as determining that some of those redwoods are 5000 years old, which gives us some idea of when this planet was terraformed?"

"I don't know, sir."

At least the Chief hadn't called him defective to his face.

"It's best you stick to maintenance and repair. Baaden expects you back today." So Watcher members would be less exposed to him, and so he would be less likely to damage their studies. Hote didn't care to complain that Baaden refused to teach him anything about repair and upkeep of station equipment. To the mechanic, he was the invisible boy, suitable only for cleaning rooms that were self-cleaning in theory, but still needed filters to be changed and recycled. Hote had to learn on his own. Chief Li probably knew this and preferred to act also as if he didn't exist.

Excused, Hote stepped into the hallway and into his crazy thoughts.

There is a box, like a kit. It has a doll that must be assembled. I can't assemble it. It belongs to Radiant.

Hote needed to calm down, to take his time resuming his apprenticeship with the Watcher Base's sole mechanic. The base had ten core members, divided equally by gender. Baaden wasn't counted among them. Neither was Hote.

He took a detour into the base museum and dawdled among its small displays of potted and dried plants, seeds, nests, and rocks. It was quiet there, peaceful. He fingered a stuffed gryphon, unicorn, pterodactyl, and other animals, some as skeletons, others embedded in plastic. He read reports on the various research products and displays, not only from Watcher Base but from the other stations posted on the planet. Ahmed took care of the museum. Hote wished he could help. He visualized himself adding to it.

Calmer, he entered the bay, a multipurpose room just off Ahmed's lab and small museum. The bay contained the maintenance area where Baaden worked.

-2-

Seeing him, Baaden's face reddened to match his freckles and brick-red tousled hair. "Oh, it's you." Baaden was struggling to understand a computer program that controlled Traveler, a dragon look-alike automaton.

Its perfect appearance, indistinguishable from a real dragon, intrigued Hote. If only he could work with it. "Can I help?"

Baaden screwed up his face. "You don't touch Traveler. There's the supply closet over there. Take an inventory."

Hote opened it to see a clutter of tools, instruments, containers of fluid. Shelves and wall brackets cried out for order. "What are some of these things?"

"Look it up. Computer pad's right there."

It took most of the day, with Baaden and Traveler gone for a large portion. Once they returned, Hote was ready to report. He waited, watching Traveler unload a video into the computer. Of flying dragons? Had Traveler gotten so close? Where?

Baaden caught Hote watching. With a command, Baaden closed the view so the report continued to download in secret.

Hote kept his expression blank. "I finished the inventory. We're missing some brushes, we're low on detergent, and we're completely out of invisipaint."

"So?"

"We need to requisition some."

"Why, you going to paint yourself invisible? Ha-ha-ha-ha-ha!"

"No, we need it to—"

"Ha-ha-ha-ha…"

Baaden's continued laughter drove Hote into the hall where he saw Hunter sauntering from the dayroom toward the work areas. The dayroom doubled as a conference room and a cafeteria. Hote smelled the sharp sweetness and heard the snap of an apple with Hunter's each chomp.

"There he is," Hunter said offhandedly. Handsome, athletic, popular, and maddeningly droll.

"Hunter, I need to file a requisition. We need invisipaint."

Without a pause or a glance in Hote's direction, Hunter's voice contained a shrug. "What color?"

"Uh…invisible."

"Not a color."

"Clear?"

"Not a color."

"Then how—?"

"Chain of command, kid. Chain of command."

Hunter stopped at a small table that held a chess set. It was a community game, where anyone could stop by, move a piece, and continue on. Hote had never played it because he doesn't feel part of the community. He turned his back on it, clenched his teeth, and surrendered to the crazy thoughts. "There is a box. Like a kit." *Stop it. Don't even think it.* "There is a box. There is…"

"What about the box?"

Hote jumped, and for the first time he noticed the seated figure of Maximus at the chess table. No, not seated. He stood nearly a meter tall. His hair was damp, as if he had just came from the gym where he frequently lifted weights.

"Nothing," Hote snapped.

"Sounded like something to me." Maximus looked directly at Hote. His look was clinical, neither friendly nor unfriendly. And so solid. So present.

The short man gestured at the game. "Want to take a turn?"

Hote started to say he was not allowed, which wasn't true. So he shook his head. "We're short on supplies in the bay, and I have to go through the chain of command to get them."

Maximus opened his mouth, realization dawning in his eyes. "Ah. Baaden"

Hote nodded. Maximus appeared disinterested, but he understood Hote's dilemma. He really understood.

"Go through Amber."

It's not the advice Hote wanted. He was nearly grown. He wanted to be treated as an adult. "I can't."

"Why not?"

"She's my mother. Why should I run to her for everything?"

Maximus's manner did not change. "Nearly everyone goes through Amber. She's the closest to Chief Li's ear. And she knows a lot."

Hote watched as Maximus closed a hand on a bishop, moved it diagonally across the board and dropped the knight into a hole. The action reminded Hote of the sense he had of being suspended over a hole, ready to drop in.

CHAPTER 3

Stubborn

-1-

I am grounded.

Days have passed since the accident.

I have no choice but to hitch along in some semblance of walking, stumbling over roots, and tangling in brush on the floor of the old growth forest. I cannot tuck my broken wings. They are permanently spread like a glider, held rigid by a brace that crosses my back. The brace is remarkable, for it is basically a sturdy branch, beautifully woven into place by Elders Wily and Rosy. They tried to convince me to allow my wings to be permanently folded against my sides so I could move with more grace—along the ground.

But I am stubborn.

Two hatch mates try to help. In an open area Longtail squats and with Greenchild's support, levers me onto her back, but I have no way to hold on with my fingers stranded at the leading edge of my wings. Once I'm balanced, Greenchild releases me and cries to Longtail, "Fly!"

Longtail staggers and I slip from her back.

She steadies herself. "Sorry. If you had your wings set at your sides, we could carry you."

Greenchild repeats it. "If only you'd had your wings strapped to your sides."

Pride makes me stubborn. "That would have made me even more helpless. At least I should be able to soar." I don't want to be like Batwing. A cripple for life.

The two give up and ascend into the trees beyond my view. I am abandoned to a strange world.

Alone.

Day in and day out.

The ground is a world I haven't known until I am forced to dwell in it. Smells crowd together and close fresh air out. Decay surrounds me, and yet sweetness pervades. The trees look different down here, their trunks red and fibrous and broad. Wider than the length of even the largest dragon. I hunch up to the trunk of the widest giant and probe the bark with my fingers. I can hook my claws in and climb, even with my wings spread in the brace. But as I pull up, pain erupts from joints not healed. I tremble and look up. The nearest branches are distant. And far above them, beyond view, the trunk divides again and again to form that upper world of platforms and trails. I cannot climb even the length of a leg. The strain in my wings is too much, and an image terrorizes me. What if I should fall on my back? How would I right myself? Would everyone laugh? Would anyone help me? Gasping, I slide down and crouch, and wait for the thunder of my heart to ease.

With no sister dragon to distract me, I notice rustles through the undergrowth. Bright butterflies drink from sprays of flowers and pools of mud. Shiny beetles vie over dragon dung as if over something precious and carry it off. Possoms, howling mice, and bright frogs converge on the ashes that drift down from dragon fire and gobble them up. Flies with lacy wings settle on me and my wooden brace. Tweekie would have shooed them away.

High above the trees, the sun's rays split into color bands in the manna belt that spans our world. In that belt the Shining Ones graze in flight on the sustaining confection. A whimper rises in my throat as I squint up at the feeding flock that turns red, blue, green and violet in the light.

Little birds flock near me and so do rabbits, squirrels, and fanged deer barely larger, to lap at the manna caught on ground and leaves. All that remain are dribbles that fall to the forest sponge and turn rancid because I hoard them lest the lappers rob me of sustenance. If I am to feed, I must hiss them to flight.

Batwing climbs down to smirk at me, and then retraces her route upward. She races and leaps through the trees, a streak of blue-green, showing off, showing me I can't do even that. I am the useless one.

My gut boils. I'll never know serenity as long as she and I share the same clan.

My tail isn't heavy enough to offset the weight of the brace, so I shove on my keel bone through the sponge and litter. Busy. Time weighs heavily, so I've taken to creating trails and clearings on the forest floor with fire. No one assigned me. I do it without being commanded. The elders watch my industry. Do they note how useful I am, or do they fear I might set the forest aflame?

As my joints knit, Shiningsnout descends before me. I wait for her to remark on my activity, even to scold me for it. With hardly a word, she stays just long enough to give me a crutch to hold in each hand, so I can toddle like a turtle. Disappointingly they strain my fingers. I can't move much beyond where dribbles of manna fall to the ground. I don't blaze any new trails.

And so the time wears on.

The groombug who was tending me without so much as a song, hops up the tree to find his dragon and to join the groombug chorus. I can hear their buzzy melodies as they polish the scales of their dragons. The song is mesmerizing. Their dragons doze. I drink in that song, surrender to its lovely lull, and nod off at the base of a tree.

I awake to find my third ear empty. No other groombug comes to fill it.

"Whose groombug is next on the roster?" I call to the hanging sisters.

They mutter among themselves, not loud enough for me to catch their words.

The mutters grow more vigorous. Arguing. A shhh. They must keep their voices down, lest I hear.

I rock back on my haunches, not daring to rise on my legs, lest I pitch forward on my face. Eventually Elder Rosy descends to the ground and sits beside me. She waits to speak, as if sorting her thoughts or dreading what to say. A brief sniff and she regards me. "The groombugs have rebelled."

"I'm not carrying Batwing anymore, so there's no danger of them being squashed."

Rosy emits a long breath. "Groombugs don't take orders well. You should know that."

"So they refuse to touch me."

"We can't force them."

No more groombug roster. What surprises me is that any had agreed to groom me. But their sympathy only goes so far, along with dragon sympathy. With a shrug of her wings, Elder Rosy rides the air up to her perch through countless layers of branches. I am dismissed.

In the days that follow, I lose my luster. I lose my enthusiasm for fire grooming the trails and the open area. Why bother? No other dragon uses them. What will happen to me?

Whispered remarks and discussions mix with the groan of trees. My ears pick up enough snippets to piece together a horrid revelation. Without a groombug to clean my scales, I will develop sores.

-2-

Soon Longtail and Greenchild descend to the ground and apologize to me for their groombugs' refusals. "We can't order them to do it," they say.

I know. Tweekie would have been insulted to be ordered around, much less to groom someone else's dragon.

"I should leave," I say, not sure I can. I want sympathy.

Longtail digs a toe into the dirt of the trail I had cleared. "You hear what the elders said?"

"No."

She exchanges a look with Greenchild as if agreeing to tell me an invented story. Here it comes.

"The elders said you should wait around to see if they can get you a new groombug."

Is it possible? All I know is when a dragon leaves the clan, she always takes her groombug along. Hatched together, they expire together. That is the clan wisdom.

Nevertheless a snippet of hope arises, and I cast a grateful glance for the lie.

Perhaps to lend credence, no one tells me to leave.

I wait around.

It isn't more than a handful of days before Nip climbs down and soars the last few dragon lengths to land beside me.

"Ee, hee, hee, hee!" She bristles with energy and carries an envelope of fresh air about her. She flaps her wings, and they raise her a little from the ground. Fledging and sharing the good news with me. Soon she will fly on her own.

I want to congratulate her and to rejoice at her new ability. Besides that, she waves her newly formed fingers at me. Their regeneration is nearly complete. She doubly deserves my good will. A honk of joy struggles up my throat, only to wobble, and my smile won't stay put. I sniffle and finally say, "I am overjoyed for you, dear Nip."

She chortles and leaps about and soars a short distance. "I can fly, I can fly, I can fly. And the sky is my home, my home."

My chortle ends in a sob.

She settles before me. "Will your wings heal?"

I manage a smile. "I expect they will."

"Good, because we can fly together. Whee!" She flies at the tree trunk, attaches, and scrambles upward. "I can fly. I can fly."

The fledging of youngsters signals the advent of the Naming Ceremony, when my hatch mates receive their adult names. They will dance an aerial ballet through arcs of light, spewed in the sky by the older dragons. They had been practicing for days. For myself, I'd chosen Brightwing. For all the good it does.

Not invited, I choose not to watch. How can I bear it? It's bad enough to hear their trumpeting. For hours they sing, and at each pause come echoes and what sounds like answering songs of the far-off clans, some of whom Tweekie and I may have seen. We dragons can sing in a bass that carries over great distances. I feel its vibrations in my teeth, my bones, my entire body. Tweekie told me once that groombugs can't hear those bass sounds, but they feel the vibrations. So they don't hesitate to add their sweet voices.

I want to pull the entire forest over me and hide. My inward furnace is a cauldron of tears.

When the fire show sputters its last, when singing and aerial displays of flips, rolls, and wing joining end, when their exuberance has cooled, my hatch mates descend in a group, probably afraid to face me singly. They form a semicircle before me and clear their throats. Their lips tremble with joy barely contained. They exalt in their new names.

I am torn between wishing for solitude and for sympathy. I struggle to stand erect. The weight of the wing brace keeps me bowed to the ground. Humiliated. Still, I arch my neck upward and eye them, boldly.

They struggle to appear serious out of consideration for my bereavement, and after flicking looks among themselves, they nudge a spokes-sister to speak.

"I am now Silverscale." She points to each sister in turn and introduces them, as if each name is a prize won.

"And this is Longclaw. And Firewing…"

Greenchild is now Greenglow. Longtail is Greattail. And so on. Glorious names to parade about.

"And I," Batwing adds, with a lift of her snout, "am Brightwing."

Brightwing. The very name I wanted.

Once my wings were highly iridescent blues, greens, and reds, shifting and blending delicately. I will not acknowledge Batwing's new unearned name.

The sisters shift and some glance away. They make as if to leave, but Silverscale stays them. They are not finished.

She looks down and then directly at me, a look of challenge. "It's been decided to kind of give you a naming ceremony of your own. You surely can't go unnamed. After all, if you're going to stick around. So we came to tell you it's been decided what to call you."

By whom, I don't know. Probably by general consensus.

"Your new name is…Rumplewing."

Rumplewing!

Before the circle breaks up, I rage at them. "You're not doing me any favors. Not you, not the elders. I'm tired of second-hand reports that I'm supposed to stick around. For what? Are they afraid to tell me to my face what I should do? I'm tired of being at your mercy, giving me a name as if I'm worn out junk. To be tossed aside and forgotten. No thanks to you. No thanks to your groombugs. And no thanks to the elders!"

I trundle away, heaving this way and that, not at all dignified.

Anger propels me to seek out an elder before fear takes hold.

Before I completely withdraw, I overhear exclamations of how I have insulted their kindness. And I overhear what sounds like snickers.

I push on down the trail I had blazed, putting thickets and trees between them and me. Stumbling over something as tiny as a redwood pinecone and snorting and finally weeping. The farther I shove forward, the more hopeless I feel. Tears stanch my inner fires. But not my resolve.

I will face the most senior of elders. Wily.

On the other talon, make that the most approachable. The one less likely to ignore or scold me. Fetidbreath. The one who, more than the others, carried me before I fledged. Gentle and beloved, she is constantly approached. Constantly busy. Many times elders warn us not to take advantage of her kindness by pestering her. And that's what I would do. Sap her kindness. Wear her out with my problems.

My momentum slows, stops. I drop my head, close my eyes, hoping to escape into sleep. Postponing what I dread.

CHAPTER 4

Bonded from Birth to Death

-1-

I want to sleep forever. But forever doesn't come. Instead I dream of music, only to awaken feeling uneasy. The music continues, solemn. What's going on up there among the spires, the platforms of the great trees? It drones on, deep, and vibrates my bones. Too sacred to interrupt.

Eventually it stops, and I call out, "What's happening?"

No one answers.

Should I leave? Stay? Mustn't bother the elders, lest they tell me directly to leave. There must be a livable alternative.

I straighten and lean back against a tree to keep from flopping forward. Even so, the brace tilts me one way and my tail the other. Is that a giggle from the branches above me? I set my jaw and would have closed my ears if that were possible.

A rustle mounts above, a kickoff from branches, a whomph of wings, a trumpet of dragons. The Shining Ones take flight for a meal in the sun. Not all. Someone scrabbles from an uppermost branch to the ground.

Elder Wily.

Never have her scales shone so brightly. Her groombug sits on her shoulder, his hair floating about him. What a magnificent pair!

She stretches her neck tall and looks down her nose at me. "I have left an egg, to start a new clutch. I am leaving to meet the gryphon."

I gaze, unable to find the appropriate words. What are they? Congratulations? Farewell? Sorry to see you go?

"What gryphon is that?" Does it dispense great knowledge and wisdom? Or it is a guide to a special land of elders? The elders never explain what this mysterious meeting is. Perhaps Wily will.

She speaks bluntly. "I am leaving to feed the hungry. The time has come to shut myself down."

"You mean…you mean…?" Never have they appeared so healthy, so alive, so beautiful. Already, the clan has dismissed them. But I haven't. "I…I…"

Why should she tell me this? Is she suggesting I, too, should follow her example? Or…?

"Are…are you offering me your groombug?"

She stiffens, tilts her head, and narrows her eyes at me. "I do not command him."

"May I ask him?"

"Suit yourself."

How do I invite an alien groombug to join me? How should I address him? As I contemplate this, he waddles along her shoulder and stops just above me. And he spits just missing me. His saliva sizzles on the path by my neck. My nostrils burn at its sharpness. A groombug secret, revealed. They can spit acid. He turns his back and ambles to her mid ear.

Wily offers no apology. "A bond from birth to death cannot be broken." Which means they both will die.

I watch her spread her great wings and lift into the sky, away from me, away from the clan.

-2-

In a few moments, Elder Fetidbreath has chosen to meet me. Fetidbreath, the most exalted of elders, and the most mysterious.

She turns a kind eye on me. "Is there anything you wish to say?"

It hurts my throat to speak of Wily leaving, along with her groombug. As much as I want to ask about my staying or leaving, I can't find the courage. It's safer to complain about something less vital. "Why did they have to name me Rumplewing? I wanted Brightwing. It's so beautiful, so noble."

Fetidbreath cocks her head. "What would you do with such a name?"

"I don't know. Enjoy it, I guess."

She arches her long neck and lowers her face to mine. "But does it teach you anything?"

"Well…" I search for an answer. "It tells others about me. It makes them respect me."

"Does it?"

"Well…"

"Did you ever wonder why my name isn't noble?"

It did seem like the worst possible name for the most beloved of dragons.

"I chose that name, myself, so every time I open my mouth, I will consider what comes out of it."

What could come out of a mouth? Fire, spit, vomit. "I don't understand."

"You will when you're older. For now, that's not your greatest worry." She touches my third ear with her finger, and I ache for Tweekie, his warmth, his voice, his beauty. His loyalty.

She beckons. "Come. I want to show you something hidden. Something sacred."

Her body takes on a near glow, as if an inner orange and yellow flame penetrates her scales. It is the glow of pleasure.

"Come."

She eases a shoulder under my brace, so my wing lies over her back. How easy to walk with her help. Gratefulness weeps through me, so my eyes leak tears. I sniff them away.

We slip among ferns, moss, and approach an immense log. The redwood had fallen long before even the oldest dragon was hatched. It seems to stretch forever among trees not tall enough to hide it. Far less than half its girth, I see at eye level a cavity in the bark. It contains a mound of leaves, moss, lichens, and bits of bark.

Elder Fetidbreath's tone is reverent. "Here is the great nest where eggs collect and the young are born. Once after many hands and feets of years, a dragon produces an egg. After that she leaves. She never lays another egg. She flies off to meet the gryphon and takes her groombug with her."

It doesn't happen often. Consequently many in the clan forget about the solemn service of singing and adorning the egg producer as if she is the most precious of the clan, and then everyone turning from her as if she is already gone. She departs, alone. The event is special; the nest hallowed. Its location known only to a few.

Fetidbreath whispers, "The eggs lie dormant until enough have accumulated, which could take several years. Certain elders watch the nest. They shift and air the eggs to keep a constant temperature. They croon and tell stories and give lessons to the eggs, so the hatchlings will not emerge in full ignorance. Can you remember your first lesson after hatching?"

"Why, yes. It was like my memory was jogged. About basic survival."

"Such as bonding with your groombug. And now the time has come. Something few are privileged to witness. The elders have agreed to grant you this privilege."

My heart stirs. They care. They really care about me.

She cocks her head. "Listen. What do you hear?"

I stretch my neck next to hers. "Little peeps."

"They're ready to hatch. Would you like to see?"

Honored to receive hidden knowledge with an elder, I shuffle closer.

Fetidbreath noses and then blows away the nest covering. The smell of dust clears and reveals a slight metallic smell. Leathery white eggs appear. Oval, the size of a foot. Waves of opalescent color sweep over them.

"Watch," she murmurs.

The eggs vibrate, their inhabitants squirming and cheeping. Then the cracking as egg beaks hammer. A dragon head emerges, stretches tall on a long neck, a shell resting like a cap on her head. As other young break through their eggs, a swarm of dark specks stampede through the nest.

"What's that?"

"Groombugs. Each finding its bond partner."

"They're so small."

One finds the first dragon hatchling and leaps onto her slime coated neck. I hear lapping.

Fetidbreath smiles at the drama. A chuckle emerges from her throat.

"Where do they come from?" I ask.

"Some say they blow in with the dust. Or from the bark of the tree. Others say they just appear. Where they come from is a mystery."

Elders study the mysteries and hoard them among themselves. I suppose they learn the mysteries when they sojourn to wherever they go, only to return sometimes days later. Only the elders may venture off like this. Sometimes they leave in pairs or in a group. Never alone. Never is any dragon alone, unless it is leaving to meet the gryphon. They teach younger dragons practicalities and myths, but they don't explain the reasons behind each lesson.

We continue to watch until the scrambling stops.

"They race to their mates. Always there are just the right number. Still…one looks for extras. And perhaps this time an extra groombug will appear."

I count. Sure enough, every groombug finds a dragon. There are no extras. No surprise. And yet… A dying hope wrenches a sigh from my mouth. I am grateful that Fetidbreath had hoped.

After a while she clears her throat. Speaks tentatively. "When a dragon's time comes to leave the clan, she always visits the nest and deposits her egg. Wily has started a new clutch, in a secret place known only to the elders."

"I don't understand why Wily and her groombug had to leave."

"They are doing the responsible thing, going to meet the gryphon."

"How is seeking death being responsible?"

Fetidbreath snaps her fingers closed, cutting me off. It is an elder event, and I must speak no more of it.

So I ask, "What of me? I am too young to produce an egg."

Elder Fetidbreath emits a small huff of steam. Her voice is gentle. "It is also tradition that ailing dragons leave. I don't suggest you go off to meet the gryphon. Rather, let's say you seek your fortune."

Whatever that may be. Clearly, I can't remain with the clan.

"Fetidbreath, was it wrong for me to go against advice and have my broken wings braced open?"

"It depends on whether you think soaring is better than being confined to the ground."

"I do want to stay aloft, providing I can get aloft. But thermals die."

"Not all winds are thermals. In the land of constant wind, you can stay aloft forever. Or so we are told."

"It's true? How do I get there? Is it really possible?"

"If you can get aloft, it's likely you can get there. You'll know the area by the long ridges where the wind sweeps upward and by the great number of those who soar."

Could I really stay aloft forever? My hope stirs. Until I catch the sadness in Fetidbreath's lessening colors. And I know there is one other question I must ask and dread to ask. "What will happen if I continue on without a groombug?"

Fetidbreath sighs, then answers so low, I strain to hear. "You will die, eventually."

"There is a possibility…" she quickly adds. "The Watchers. We don't know their purpose. Rumors vary. One suggests they may be healers, miracle workers."

Surrender myself to Forbidden Mountain? To Watchers who are also rumored to steal Shining Ones to unknown destinations, never to return?

I have received all the help I will get. I hobble off, not before I see her shake her head over me, expression doleful. "So young," she murmurs. "So young."

She gave me a gift, and it is empty.

-3-

After the Naming Ceremony, my hatch mates' activities shift. They do more than help care for the newly hatched and carry them aloft until the young should fly on their own. They remind the young of lessons taught to them in the egg. I had looked forward to these duties. Now my thoughts turn elsewhere.

No elders order me to leave. Nevertheless actions speak loud enough. Elder Shiningsnout no longer assigns me duties, not even the treetop trail upkeep, for how can I climb to the platform? I am of no use to the clan. Batwing's usefulness is limited, but she is cute. I am not. So I develop a secret plan which Fetidbreath may have guessed. I think she sees me sneaking about at night. Other youngsters, if caught sneaking about, would be questioned. Not me. She says nothing. As for other elders, I am already invisible to them.

CHAPTER 5

The Find

-1-

"Arrgh!"

"Oh, phew!"

Sounds of gagging filled the air as Watchers entered the stench in the bay. It was really a multipurpose room with movable walls. Ordinarily they closed off a repair and maintenance shop on the right side with a storage closet in the back. At the moment the wall that separated them from Ahmed's lab had been removed.

Individuals reversed their course and pushed near the door.

"Oh, gods!"

"Whew! Where's a mask?"

Eyes teared. Hands covered mouths and noses.

Just inside the entrance, Maximus, a stocky three feet tall, dug out masks and was handing them to Hunter, who passed them to grabby hands with a "Yep, yep, yep. Nope, nope, nope. Yep, yep…"

Hote joined the members at the entrance. The reek hit him. He choked. His eyes watered and his stomach clenched. Members bumped against him in their haste. Every time he reached for a mask, a hand shot out and snatched it. Hote started to hold his nose when he noticed the stench fade, so he quit trying for a mask and followed the last member into the packed room. He angled along the wall to where he could see.

Several figures in bio-suits bent over the corpse on a wooden pallet. The creature was huge, its split and oozing scales a mottled brown and tan pattern with touches of green and blue. The Watchers' automaton, Traveler, had sighted it, and the shuttle craft brought it in. Ahmed held the dragon's head in gloved arms, and Amber, likewise suited, examined it with him. Others seemed to be taking pictures and measurements.

All around, an audience peered through face masks or helmets with masks. Except for Hote. Face bare, he held his breath until he had to breathe. And even as he drew in air between his fingers, something inside him shifted, and the stink turned meaty and flavorful. Hote gulped in the fragrance. His mouth watered.

No one else seemed happy with the delectable smell. Only Hote. Because Hote was different. Feeling conspicuous and mortified, he fled out the door, along the work stations, and into the day's fresh air. Once outside, he rounded the corner of the building onto the airstrip and almost bumped into Baaden and Traveler.

"What are you doing here?" Baaden cried.

"What are you doing here?" Hote responded without thinking.

Traveler stood, unmoving, silent.

"They took over my work area! With a stinking corpse the size of a building."

Hote wouldn't have blamed Baaden for being angry, except it seemed his normal attitude.

"Maybe you can use the dayroom. Or the gymnasium. Plenty of room."

Baaden screwed his face. "Leave. I don't need your help."

Hote sighed. "I'm supposed to be your apprentice."

"Like I said before and before that and before that. I didn't sign on to being your nursemaid."

"I've been studying. I know a lot now, so you don't have to tell me everything. Just let me watch."

"Get away from me." Baaden swatted at him.

Hote backed just enough to stay out of reach.

"I'm stuck here with a bunch of weirdos. You're all weirdos. A bunch of clowns. That bobble-headed Sparky should feed you one of her incandescent mushrooms so you could make yourself visible. And then there's that dimwit Hunter who thinks he's the great joker, talking about the sex life of a bunch of rocks. I could go on."

Though they treated Hote as an outsider, he felt a need to defend them against Baaden. "At least they have a sense of humor."

"Clowns. They should be in the circus. Every one of them."

"StarCircus?" The name popped out of Hote's mouth, for Radiant and her whereabouts was never far from his mind. Baaden blinked at the name.

"My sister joined StarCircus. They have robots. They're like kits. In a box." Hote caught himself before he repeated the litany about Radiant's box. "You ever been to StarCircus?"

Baaden's features settled. "No. Never heard of it."

Hote forced his thoughts away from boxes to the greatest thing that could occupy his mind. The dead dragon. A real dragon. Here.

Not daring to return to Ahmed's lab, he left for the garden. There he would await his mother, who would satisfy his curiosity.

The compound's garden with its scent of flowers and greenery beckoned. It was a natural area, unplanned and untouched by any gardener. It couldn't have been more beautiful, with a stream running through and shrubs making way for overtowering trees. Here, no one judged the rational or irrational. Hummingbirds, quail, and rabbits were too busy with their own affairs. Yet Hote couldn't dismiss Baaden's attack on the Watchers. They were different, sure, but likable. Take Maximus. Only three feet tall, yet considered one of the most trustworthy and industrious of Watchers. One of his duties was piloting a shuttle craft, and he often flew to I.D. Express on their usual pickup errands. Reed, a shy fellow who seemed to blush over every remark, often accompanied him, as did Hunter, whose wit kept Reed permanently red. Then there was Sparky. With her heart-shaped face and razor jaw, what really set her apart was her blue hair with its sparkles. Every time she shook her head, the sparkles snapped and flashed like static electricity. And she shook her head a lot. Yet despite her silliness, she took her work seriously and always reported good results. Everyone took her quirkiness as great fun or simply ignored it. If Hote really thought about it, he realized each Watcher had some quirk. Chief Li was too serious about his role as leader, always double checking rules and procedure. Ahmed tended to take short cuts as a medic so he could get back to whatever scientific project he worked on, such as preparing found specimens that ended in the museum after being shuttled in from whatever Watcher station had made the find. As for his mother, Amber was too easy going and allowed Li to assign her administrative duties that left her little time for research. Why should he be singled out as too different? Because his difference was not acceptable.

He gritted his teeth and tensed his hands into fists against whatever possessed him.

"Steady. Steady," he whispered. And waited.

He would wait where he wouldn't do anything weird, wait for his mother to find him, and wait to learn the exciting news about the dragon.

And so he settled. To watch ducks tip bottoms up on a pond. To listen to the ripple of water. To watch the sun shimmer on it. From somewhere came the patient creak of a frog. No one brought these animals in from outside. They'd chosen to arrive, themselves, or perhaps some, like a family of rabbits, were already here when the compound wall went up around them. How else might they have gotten here? The only way in and out was over the wall; there were no doors or gates. Hote noticed part of the wall through overhanging tree branches and occluding bushes. The walls were a one-way window. From where he sat, he could see a dense forest of conifers and hardwoods. Anyone outside who tried to look into the compound would only see an opaque camouflage of what appeared to be greenery. Hote was sure he had seen this. Somehow he had seen the forests, meadows, and plains that lay beyond the compound's view. He had seen the details of leaves, flowers, and trees, and felt them, and smelled them. Not by shuttle. How, then?

An hour later Amber found him by the pond on a bench, and he sensed her excitement beneath a calm exterior. She pushed a hand through her fly-away gray hair, redid the clip above her forehead that kept her face visible, cleared her throat, and blossomed into a smile. And then a chuckle.

"Well?" Hote urged.

"It was awesome." She had spent an hour helping Ahmed tease apart tissue. What impressed her most was his discovery of a hole in the back of the dragon's head. And in the hole he found a dead creature.

"We thought originally that the organism had eaten into the back of the skull and killed the dragon. But that doesn't make sense because it was as dead and decayed as the dragon. And you know we've never found any evidence of predation on this planet."

It was true. Foods consisted of fruits, seeds, dead matter, and that honeydew like substance that came from the sky.

"Do you think I'll get a chance to examine the dragon?" Hote asked.

She hesitated. "We'll see. If Chief Li approves."

Chief Li, who directed the Watcher programs. And who kept Amber busy with legal work when she preferred to study dragons. But then everyone pulled double duty, one part research and one part support. Except for Baaden, the mechanic. And except for Hote, who was supposed to be Baaden's apprentice.

-2-

That night, Hote dreamed of tearing at dead flesh. When morning came, he emerged from his room, half awake. Outside he heard the morning greeters.

"Morning, all."

"Morning is as morning does." That was Hunter, always the wit. "There's the moon sisters, risen with the sun."

Twins barely into their twenties who were inseparable enough to share a secret language. Identical twins the color of the moon, with long flaxen braids.

"I'm Luna."

"And I'm Europa."

Predictable answers to Hunter's teasing.

Unlike the identical moon sisters, Hote was sure he and his twin sister Radiant had never been close. She'd played some sort of prank on him. He couldn't remember.

Hote felt dirty and had a bad taste in his mouth. He returned to his room. His bed clothes reeked of decayed flesh. He bundled them up to take to the digester, where they would be recycled and made into new clothes. At the door, he almost bumped into Amber. He stopped, as if caught in a crime, his face hot, his mind blank of explanation. She eyed the filthy clothes, her expression sad. She ran a hand through her bushy hair and suddenly resolute, moved past him into his room and picked up something from the floor. It was the finger bone from the leading edge of the dragon's wing. Some flesh still clung.

They both stared at it. And then she said, "I'll sneak this back to the lab."

She knew what he had done. Yes, she knew. And she would keep secret the horror of it. Hote felt the power of a mother's love and felt undeserving and grateful.

But he was not a child. He forced a reply. "I'll take it back."

-3-

The taste of rotting flesh didn't leave until Hote bathed and ate from the replicator. And then he entered the lab where Ahmed bent over his work with dissecting needles and forceps beneath a magnifier. Hote placed the finger bone on the work bench.

Ahmed looked up through his mask.

"It's…it's part of the dragon," Hote said.

"Some flesh is missing from the haunch, I noticed."

"Yeah, well-uh, I wanted to do some dissecting. Something useful." He sounded lame and wondered if Ahmed knew he lied.

"Learn anything?"

Hote fidgeted. "Yeah. That-that it's better to work in the lab instead of my room."

The suspicion never left Ahmed's face. "Uh-huh."

He returned to his dissecting, and Hote lingered nearby. A strip of skin, mottled rose and beige, hung from the specimen. Hote started to reach. "May I? I just want to feel it."

Ahmed shrugged.

The skin felt smooth, like the cover of a purse or pair of boots. Across the bay stood Traveler, its shadow like a dinosaur specimen in a museum. Closer scrutiny showed the automaton no different in appearance from a dragon. Hote crossed to it and felt its scales, not for the first time when Baaden wasn't looking. Baaden jealously kept the automaton to himself. "It feels the same as the dragon." He continued to run a hand over the machine. "It looks so real. How is it possible when we know so little about dragons?"

Ahmed sat back in his chair. "Scarlotti."

"Who?"

"Scarlotti. He designed and built it. Long before you were born."

"How?"

"Long story. Ask your mother. Amber knows more about it than anyone else around here."

"How about Baaden?"

Ahmed snorted. "Baaden? Good mechanic. Figured out how to repair and run Traveler. He'd have you believe he knows all about it. Don't bet on it. No one has uncovered Scarlotti's secrets."

It was clear he didn't like Baaden. Who could blame him? The mechanic never socialized, never showed any interest in scientific investigation, and never shared what did interest him. Hote tried not to see himself in Baaden's narrowness and lack of personality. He returned to the work bench and looked over Ahmed's shoulder. "You think I could help you here? I've read all the research on dragons. I'm ready for hands on."

"How are you?"

"What?"

"How are you doing?"

I feel like I'm about to fall through a hole.

When he first came to the base, Ahmed told him the nerves in his feet weren't fully developed, which was why he felt like he would fall through a hole. Later he was told it was his imagination.

"I'm okay."

"That's good to hear." Ahmed pivoted to face him, with eyes narrowed, as if he were looking into Hote's skull. "Doesn't the smell bother you?"

"Smell?"

"In all the time you've been here, you act like you don't notice the smell."

Hote hadn't noticed until Ahmed mentioned it. He placed his hand over his nose. "It's just so fascinating, seeing a real specimen. Do you think if I studied Traveler, I'd understand dragons better?"

Other than a shrug, Ahmed didn't respond. Like everyone else, he didn't trust Hote. Hote wasn't normal. Amber had brought him to Watcher Base after Father had dumped him on her. Hote knew Li had bent the rules to allow him here because everyone loved Amber.

CHAPTER 6

Adrift

At night the ground world pulses. It buzzes, creaks, and peeps. I hadn't noticed the volume of noise when I dwelt with my sisters in the trees. Contentment blinded me. Now, the very breath and footsteps of night follow when I venture through thinning trees and over dry, rocky soil to Forbidden Mountain, trusting that the Watchers, at least, are asleep. There I practice. At first I launch myself from the lowest steps. Gradually I work to the top, shoving myself higher and higher up the mountain until my breastbone develops calluses. My many trips have caught the attention of a family of gryphons. On an earlier trip, one gryphon watched me. The next night, there were two. On this final night, what appears to be an entire family of seven wait on their haunches. They gabble among themselves, and when I pass, they follow. They smell of death.

"Go away!" I roll a warning ball of fire from my mouth at them.

They back away. They do not leave. At least they don't climb after me as I struggle up the steps. They are content to remain down there, waiting.

That decides it. I will not return to the clan tonight and cross through the thick of this family again. I will not listen to their eager chatter nor watch them lick at their own saliva.

So I spend my final night hidden in a dip between boulders at the top of the peak, beyond sight of the Watchers and their mostly secluded dome. Nestled there, I wish I could reach to scratch. My scales itch, and I notice a growing crust along my shoulders and my breast. How long can I live without a groombug?

I wait for the sun. I am at the summit, from where I will leap and mount the thermals. Everyone—my sisters, the gryphons—will awaken to find me gone. Yes, I will catch an updraft and soar, never to touch the ground. I will soar to a country where there are no Batwings and eat and sleep on the wing. I will soar until I dry up, a dull scale wafting on the breeze.

Below, shadows cover the gryphons. Above, sky brightens. I arise, take my position on the summit. And there it is, the sun! Its rays break above the horizon and warm the air. I leap into the thermals.

The air buoys me. The ground falls away. I scream with joy. Oh, freedom! Oh, ecstasy! What do I care who might hear me? I am airborne, beyond their reach. I am mistress of the air!

The gryphons sprint to keep pace with me, until I leave them behind. I trumpet at them. *Not today, meat eaters. Not today.*

The current carries me over a diminishing forest, shrinking streams, contracting meadows. I circle and climb. It doesn't matter that the air takes me away from the glittering globules that span our world. The belt has many branches. In time, I will find one that is remote. There is no hurry. For dragons go many days between feedings. And what I want is never to meet any of the clan sisters feeding, never to see them, never to have them see me. They can pretend I don't exist; I can pretend they don't. *Good-bye, mother clan.*

So the days turn. Sun at day, moons at night. Before thermals die, I find a high point on which to land. And the next day and the next and the one beyond that, I race to find the land of constant wind. Sometimes the moons whisper invisibly to the Great Mother, and she shakes the ground. Sometimes she only mutters in return.

And then I find the ridges where the wind blows constant.

Day and night I sail. Sometimes a vulture or pterodactyl rises to greet me. Sometimes I pass flocks of smaller winged creatures. And far below is the ground with its world of inhabitants. Night and day, without stopping, I soar. I drink the rain, and afterwards when the sky is fresh, I draw in great draughts that cool my tongue.

One day, growls and yelps catch my attention. Creatures have gathered in a meadow. Foxes, lions, flies, vultures, lizards...... From below rises the stench of decay. Some squabble over something large. Some wait in ranks. Those are the flesh eaters of our world, who must wait on death for their meal. They tear at something large. Is that a tail? A dragon?

My heart lurches. Is it Wily? Or is it one from a different clan, from the cliffs or caves, or some other forest? I circle for another look, dreading the sight but needing to discern it. It is the leg of a great deer after all, half stripped. I should feel relieved. I don't. Death plays no favorites.

And later on, I notice what appears to be the remains of a dragon, prostrate, its bones white in the sun. A closer look reveals a downed tree of a peculiar type. Its skin is white instead of red. Its leaves are broad. Even trees must die.

Suddenly I feel weary. My scales itch and in some places feel sore. They are growing shaggy. Sometimes I think I detect an odor of corruption. I am breaking down. What right do I have to live? If I were responsible, I would sink down and await death and allow scavengers to tear at my carcass. It is only proper. I keep putting it off, the long, slow path. Inevitably I will lie on the plain, my dead parts plucked and quarreled over before I completely succumb to the final sleep.

"No, no, no, no!"

I almost tip over in my haste to escape, flexing my tail to speed my flight away from the scene, away from thoughts of its indignity until I achieve a kind of numbness. Perhaps it is fatigue. Perhaps hunger. It could be despair. What I need is a clean death.

Yes. Clean. How?

Even from the sky I notice the planet's shaking, the slight sway of bushes, the tumble of rocks, the troubling of lake waters. The world breathes and tugs me out of my reverie. I listen to its breath, her breath, the Great Mother's breath.

She lives deep below the surface. From there she feeds the manna belt, replenishing it so the Shining Ones can flourish. Each time she stirs, I feel comforted, knowing she lives. I met her only that once, with Tweekie. The elders speak of her as living in the depths, sometimes sleeping and dreaming, sometimes awake and stirring. She remains the greatest mystery. I will give myself to that mystery.

I fly across the waters, across a plain. Days later I fly by cliffs, careful to ignore their dragons. Leaving them and the windswept country behind, I approach the cone that opens to Great Mother's abode. She chose a burrow, for the trees and the cliffs cannot hold her. I see the steam of her breath in the dark tunnel. I smell sulfur. What would it be like to enter her burrow, to meet her? She is fire. I know that. Though she is life, she is death. My death. I don't want to dwell on it.

I hesitate on a thermal above the entrance, dip sideways, and fall. I close my eyes and remember pain. Like every other dragon, I suffered burns as a youngster, until I learned to control my flames. Burnt tongues, burnt lips. They healed as fast as I learned control.

This death will be fiery, clean, and quick. No scavengers will corrupt my corpse.

"Mother. See me. Receive me."

I fall towards darkness, and the heat rises, hotter and hotter. I close my eyes against the heat and hold my breath. Searing tears into my scales, my muscles. I feel myself smoking, eyes boiling, the brace flaming, skin peeling. It's too much! Too late to climb out. Impossible with my broken wings and heavy brace. I scream.

A rush of hot wind catches me. A puff boils to the surface. Another puff, and a release of steam. The Mother blows and lifts me. I am caught in the updraft, forbidden to enter her lair. A moan rises through the funnel's mouth, a sustained chord that rises and falls, rises and falls again. Like part of a song we dragons sing, it rises to a hoot, and I feel its vibration.

"Go," she hisses.

And I understand. *Go and live!*

CHAPTER 7

Not Quite There

-1-

Hote stood outside the closed door of Chief Li's office, listening to the conversation between Li and Amber.

"In all the time he's been here, he hasn't changed his story," she told Li.

"Of course, you being his mother, you believe him."

"No." She sounded exasperated. "Despite being his mother, I'm willing to see things from his point of view, to give him the benefit of a doubt. He's ready for more responsibility."

"Ahmed may not be a doctor, but he is a good medic. He may not have found anything wrong with your boy, but he has the sense to believe the ship's doctor, who reported that Hote suffers from fixations and delusions. We saw it then; we see it now."

"Hote hasn't complained of being possessed for over a year now. Or about passing through walls."

"Amber, he pretends to be normal, but is he? What he might have had was a parasite, not a demon, or whatever he wishes to call it. However neither the doctor nor Ahmed found any parasite. We would not have allowed him here if he were infected. You know the health regulations. Nothing of a predatory nature can be allowed on this planet."

Amber's tone was like a steel cushion. "We agreed before I brought him here that he wasn't contagious. He was traumatized by a launchpad accident, or what may have been a prank, and I think he's improved enough that we can trust him on small things."

"I doubt the launchpad ever malfunctioned. Ever since I.D. Express parked on this planet, its transport facilities have worked perfectly. If their delivery was faulty, the Academy wouldn't have allowed them here on a permanent basis. They are our one porthole to the universe, and they've never failed to import whatever the Academy has been willing to supply us. I understand your bias against them, but the Academy trusts them and so should we."

Hote rubbed his hands over his chest. That thing inside him was quiet now. He didn't want to think of the incident and his twin sister, Radiant. As siblings, they should have been close, like the moon twins here at the base. He must not think of her, except how she admired Father and strutted around pretending to be him. No, don't even think about her. And how in the beginning when they had first come under Father's care, she dared to approach Father and blurt, "I love you," only to giggle and run away. And years later, how her worship of him froze her tongue in his presence. No, don't think of her. She's gone. Gone. So arrogant. Just like Father, who forced him into a crate and sent him into the void where this thing entered him. And he awoke in his mother's arms, no longer on the ship, no longer under Father's control.

Hote frowned, eyes closed. He'd forgotten what Father had done to him. Until now. Had it really happened, or was it part of his delusion? The memory felt real.

The sound of Li's pacing carried through the wall.

"According to 2Ray1's report, which I still have a copy of, the boy has a long history of mental imbalance during the time he was under his father's care"

Amber sighed. "2Ray1 may be an excellent commander, but he is incapable of understanding children. I believe his report of Hote's imbalance to be slanted."

The voices faded. Hote held his breath so he might hear better.

"There is a line we don't cross. How old was Hote when 2Ray1 stole your children from you?"

"Six."

"How old was he when he was returned?"

"Thirteen."

"So you've hardly known him."

"I know him well enough to…"

A group of researchers approached, carrying snacks from the replicator. Pip and Reed. Pip wore a robe cross-woven with green and gold, so it glistened green or gold depending on the cloth's movement. Reed wore a green uniform with white piping, which meant he was scheduled to shuttle to I.D. Express for supplies. The uniform with its loose leggings, was handsome, but it did nothing for his appearance, long and narrow as if he'd been caught in a stretching machine.

Hote moved from the door. Pip cast him a look and sang, "Do your ears hang wide, do they swing from side to side…" She was always humming and singing.

Reed leaned toward her, jerked a thumb in Hote's direction and whispered, "There's a sniffer."

The two passed from sight.

Hunter sauntered in the opposite direction. Ordinarily in shorts, this morning he also wore a uniform, which gave him an air of authority and strength.

"Hunter, what's a sniffer?" Hote blurted.

Hunter's tone was like a shrug. "Oh, just one of those."

"Those what? A thing?"

"That's about the size of it. Sparky, light of my life!" Hunter disappeared into the dayroom, and Hote thought he caught the sound of static electricity from Sparky's hair.

-2-

Hote cut through the work area, where some researchers were already immersed in their projects and others were just settling in. Amber caught up with him in the garden. They sat at a table in a picnic area where the dominant sound was the cry of birds and the rustle of wind in the leaves. Hote stared through the compound walls at the forest beyond. For all the personality quirks among these scientists, he alone seemed inexcusably odd. They fooled around, especially Hunter, Sparky, and Pip, whom others called the Triple Clowns, but they all took their work seriously. Therefore they counted. He didn't. He didn't want to talk about his weirdness and its effect on people. Amber sat with him and they listened to the ambiance. In the distance some creature howled.

"Amber, tell me about Scarlotti and Traveler."

She smiled, and he felt the blanket of her love. Her voice sounded bell-like, like the music of birds. "What do you want to know?"

"Ahmed said Scarlotti designed and built Traveler before I was even born. Who is Scarlotti? How come he knew so much about dragons when we know so little?"

She leaned her elbows on the table. "When I was at Academy, it was Scarlotti that got me interested in dragons. He was the founder of the Watcher program. He died before I could meet him and took many secrets with him. We don't know who terraformed the planet. Perhaps he knew. He certainly knew its dragons. He designed and built Traveler. That much is known. What isn't known is the location of his schematics. It's possible he destroyed them when it appeared his plans for research might threaten the integrity of the planet. As a result we were left with an automaton that no one knew how to run. Baaden figured some of it out. Did he ever show you?"

"Mostly he ignores me."

Maybe Hote could figure it out. Would Baaden let him?

"He's difficult, I can see that. You should take the initiative. I'll make sure you get a visor, and I'll give you the access code to Baaden's maintenance records. And whatever schematics I can round up. Would you like that?"

"Very much."

Over the next few hours, between cleaning Baaden's messes and bringing him snacks from the cafeteria, Hote dropped in on Amber frequently only to find her engaged in the little time she had for research.

Just before lights out, she still hadn't slipped him access to the records and schematics, so he sat with the computer pad, trying to get into the records when he should be asleep. Crazy thoughts plagued him, and he fought for focus. *There is the box. Like a kit…* Which brought his thoughts to Radiant. She and he were twins, weren't they? Shouldn't they be as close as the moon twins? Well, maybe not that close. Nevertheless she should message him. If she would. Maybe she couldn't.

"Computer, where is Radiant? Find Radiant."

"Radiant is not accessible on this system."

"Computer, connect me to I. D. Express."

"This system cannot connect without authorization."

"Computer, where can I connect off planet?"

"This planetary system is blocked unless cleared by the proper authority."

The proper authority would be Chief Li, unapproachable. How about Amber? Surely she had authority, or did she have to go through Li? If she had authority, it was limited. Otherwise, she would have found Radiant when 2Ray1 gave Hote to her. Wouldn't she?

There is a box…

Too tired to fight the crazy thoughts, Hote surrendered to them and eventually found refuge in sleep.

-3-

Long after everyone had retired to bed Hote found himself in the bay. The stink of the corpse had faded. The walls and ceiling glowed just enough to allow him to scan the silhouettes in the room. The first thing on his mind was Traveler. He wanted to study the automaton. To have Baaden show him how to operate it. Not now though. Not in the middle of the night. Hote glanced at the door. He hadn't used it, he was sure. How did he get inside? He examined his hands, turned them, rubbed them together, and flexed his fingers. The feeling in them came and went, just as it did in his arms, his legs, his entire body. As if pieces of him were missing. The creature must be pulling him into the void. The memory of a collision in interspace flashed in his mind, an explosion in the darkness where he and an entity had beamed at the same time from different locations. That thing inside must still be partly lost in that other dimension, which is why it could pull him through solid structures. Yes, that had to be it. Rather than fall into a hole, he must be falling sideways.

He patted the wall. It felt impenetrable. He ran his hand along it and moved toward where Traveler was parked. Except Traveler wasn't there.

Hote poked among machines, the boxes of supplies, scanned past the lab. Traveler was gone. Baaden must have parked it elsewhere. Outside on the airstrip? Inside in a lab?

Even as he wondered, Hote felt a loss of solidity. He closed his eyes and opened them again to find himself in his room. He stared at his bed, its tangled blankets.

-4-

With the sun's dawning, the shuttle crew returned from I. D. Express. Hote heard the scrape and shuffle of unloading as others gathered inside for breakfast. Hote stepped into the dayroom and took a juice from the replicator. Me-steak, berries, and a sweet tea scented the air.

"Good morning," Pip sang to everyone as she entered and tapped an order from the replicator.

Hunter began the banter amid a whisper of chairs drawn up to tables. "Top of the morning, and the bottom and sides. Let's rock."

"Oh, you!" Sparky shook her head so sparks popped from her hair.

Hunter raised his arms in fake shock. "Hair on fire, hair on fire."

Sparky shook her head all the more to the accompaniment of laughter.

Hote wanted to be part of the banter, part of friendly insults. Hunter took shots at nearly everyone, some of whom delivered as good as they got.

Ignored, he ate in a rush and left in search of Baaden. He'd confront the mechanic, and make him listen. *Baaden, you have a duty to teach me mechanics and maintenance. I'm tired of being used only to clean up after you and for any unpleasant task you don't want to do. I demand better treatment. I want especially to learn to care for Traveler.*

Baaden was not in the bay where the remains of the dragon were now contained in closed tubs.

Undeterred, Hote continued out onto the airpad. There he found Maximus, their chief pilot, leaning against the craft, its door open, now emptied of its supplies. It seemed hardly invisible, more a blotchy gray translucence. The muscular dwarf looked as if he had either descended or was about to climb in, only to be distracted by something in his hand.

Hote wandered closer. It looked like a rhinoceros beetle. Black, shiny, a large horn. Suddenly it raised lacy iridescent wings and vanished.

Maximus looked up at him. "An in-and-outer."

"I scared it off."

"Not your worry. It'll be back. And if not, well, there's lots of them in the compound here. Mostly out of sight. They'll make their appearance."

"Where do they go?"

"That's the question."

"You're studying them?"

"Aerodynamics. Whatever flies." Maximus cocked his head. "You out here for a reason?"

Hote glanced around. Traveler was not on the airstrip. "I'm looking for Baaden. He's supposed to teach me. I guess he's off somewhere with Traveler. I'll have to wait until they return."

Maximus grunted. He turned toward the craft.

"Look. It could use a coat of invisipaint." Hote wanted to sound important, aware of what his duties under Baaden should be.

"The craft?" Maximus placed a hand on it.

"It's not invisible."

"Actually it's better that way. Less dangerous if you can see it a bit."

"Really?"

"Once it's up, the light will hit it so it'll resemble a cloud."

"Really? Then what's the invisipaint for?"

"It bends the light so the cloud looks more realistic, depending on the color of the paint."

"Color?"

"Yeah. Gray reflects as blue. And then there's the speckled paint that acts like special color cells that expand and contract to control the color. It's all there in the paint structure. I'm not a physicist, so I can't tell you the details."

Hote almost stammered. "Hunter had asked me what color of invisipaint I wanted to order, and I thought he was giving me a hard time."

Maximus flashed a slight smile. "Sometimes he's serious, though it's hard to tell at times. He would never try to hurt your feelings, though. Remember that."

He started to climb into the ship.

Hote didn't want their conversation to end. "Could-could you…?"

The little man looked back. "Could I what?"

"Teach me how to fly. If you're not too busy."

Maximus studied Hote. And Hote waited to be refused, to be referred to Chief Li for permission, which would be declined.

But Maximus wasn't one to pass on responsibility. He pinched his lips. "Sure." He gestured. "Climb in."

"I have lots of questions, like how do you know where to find the different Watcher stations?"

"We can radio them. Right now there's between ten or twenty. The number changes because most are temporary camps."

"So that's why we get their members cycling through the base? I know hardly any of them."

"As a core member of Watcher Base you won't be expected to."

Hote wasn't a core member, but he didn't want to call attention to his troubles.

They settled side by side in the craft, where Maximus gestured at the controls. His finger hovered over a button. "This is the on button. Touch it and all you have to do is tell the computer to set your course for a particular place and it's done."

"How about manual control? I want to learn everything."

"Then I shall teach you…."

CHAPTER 8

The Storm

I ride a breeze that cools my blisters. The sky is gentle and lets me rest in its updrafts. In the ground world, various herds range, such as antelope, tapers, elephants, and unicorns. The latter almost glow in their whiteness, their tails and manes flowing. My shadow crosses flocks of parrots. The brace creaks, and I twist my torso to adapt to the wind currents. My tail is a rudder that directs me as fast as possible back to the wind country.

There the days carry me. Good days. My blisters heal, and the breeze blows dust from my scales.

And yet, and yet.

In the distance I hear the dragon song of a stranger clan, drawn out chords. I had resolved to forget my sisters, only to find I yearn for their fellowship, to harmonize to their tunes, to drowse in groups to the buzzy music of groombugs.

I hum along. When the dragon song dies, I'm not finished. I sing my thanks to Mother. I sing for courage. To my clan I am already dead. I cannot return.

Why did Mother tell me to live?

My stomach rumbles, reminding me of my need.

A tall tree, filled with fruit, beckons. With my wings damaged, I can't negotiate the branches. And if I land on the ground to feed on fallen fruit, I see no place nearby from where I can regain the air. Fruits, seeds, roots…not normal dragon fare. I need manna.

If I sail far enough, I should come upon a loop of the manna belt. The Great Mother will provide. Yes, I will feast and sleep on the wing. She will show me how to never touch ground again, to reach the far horizon. How long can I survive without a groombug? I don't know, but living in the sky, I invite wind to groom me.

And rain.

The rain strikes full force. At first I relish its cleansing and choose to enter its center. Yes, the elements can groom me, and I can live long and prosper.

Then the wind hits.

Angry, the gale tosses me about. I tilt side to side and thrash my tail to keep upright. The storm shows no mercy. It gusts, and despite my attention to detail, it tosses rain in my eyes and down my snout, so my inner furnace sputters and steams. The elements shrill in my ears and laugh when I forget up from down. Not that it matters. I discover I cannot stay aloft. The air twists in ways I'd never noticed when my wings were limber and mindlessly adjusted to the changes. Wind seizes control, plays tricks, and spits me from the sky.

Tree limbs like upturned talons reach for me. Branches toss me from one to the next in a game. I yelp and whimper, blinded by my own steam. Only the forest sponge takes mercy on me and gives a soft landing. Even so, I end on my back, winded. The thicket tangles my wings. The rain eases and leaves me a sodden mess. The world smells musty down here.

I try to prop my wings loose with my fingers, pushing here, tugging there. I twist sideways, kick and whip with my tail. And rest. And try again. Again, until the bushes surrender their grip. I squirm free and with a kick and a flick of the tail, I somersault onto my face. And rest some more.

I awaken, covered with dew. Deer step around me and carry away fruit that have fallen and sweetened the ground. Sponge flies sop up moisture from their eyes and nostrils and from remains of fruit on their lips. The deer sniff at me and pass on. Some of their sponge flies remain long enough to lap the moisture from me. And then they, too, are gone.

They weren't as good as groombugs, but they have given me more time to live.

Staying in one place is out of the question. I shove forward through bushes and sometimes rear up to get over a troublesome branch or rock. I spend the day lunging over forest trash, jarring myself and snagging my wings repeatedly on branches and rocks, and leave behind pieces of scale and skin.

Striking out on my own proves difficult, despite the Great Mother's blessing. Troublesome thoughts cling. In the country of constant wind, the storm had cast me from the sky. How will I get airborne? How will I stay airborne? Elder lessons say I will meet the gryphon. Why should I be different from any other dragon who leaves her clan?

I plow forward, winged arms encumbered in the wide brace, legs shoving, eyes lifted to the sky. *Great Mother, show me the way.*

CHAPTER 9

Baaden's Enterprise

On an island surrounded by bog, Baaden swept a freckled hand over his brow and flicked the sweat away. He sat in shorts on a camp stool in his tent, its walls rolled up, its floor cluttered with the corpses of bugs killed by an aerosol. He tugged at the short hairs of his red beard. Frowned. One full day away from Watcher Base with its weird members and already he was bored. More than ever, he wished he had stayed with StarCircus, had never come to the dragon planet. It was a world of bogs, swamps, sulfur springs, and volcanoes. A restless world that heaved and muttered and spat hot breath. There seemed no relief from the sultry air. Yet at times a cold snap could surprise you, and you could die of hypothermia. The coldness seemed to come after a particularly violent volcanic eruption that turned day to dusk. There seemed no rhythm to the timing of eruptions. He had learned to be ready though, thanks to his time at the Watcher Base. He had extra garments in a bag in the corner of his tent. Too bad there wasn't a bio-suit among them. With a bio-suit, he would be protected against heat and cold and whatever pests the air may carry. Too bad they were expensive and required a custom fit. He could return to Watcher Base, and no one would realize he had run off.

No. He'd grown tired of enduring the gymnastics of carrying on his covert operation with the outworlders. Much easier, even in these miserable surroundings, to conduct business without the risk of Watchers finding out.

Baaden took out his earbud, squeezed it to release a cleaner. Reinserted it into his ear.

"On," he commanded.

Without compromising the view of Baaden's surroundings, Communications Officer Stilwell appeared in his mind's eye. The man's brown skullcap did nothing to improve his coarse features. The front of his uniform displayed an upside down pyramid, from shoulders to waist, with the initials I.D.E. across the top, a design Baaden found admirable. They talked mind to mind through their earbuds.

"Stilwell, you got to see this. Traveler recorded a couple of fighting dragons. Proof the Watchers are lying."

"Make it quick, Baaden. Commander wants to see me in ten."

"Won't take but a minute." Baaden fixed his gaze on an image in the round that rose before him of an elephantine dragon. It stood, wings spread and snaky neck arched over a smaller dragon. The threatening dragon pulsed, bright bands of red moving forward in waves over its body, eager to attack. Steam leaked through the nostrils of its reptilian snout that opened in a wide grin, revealing an inner scissor-edged beak. It stood on its hind legs, tail thrashing side to side. The smaller dragon shrank back, almost white in its opalescence.

"Just to let you know. Dragons are a quarrelsome lot, and over what? Food? A mate?" Not that Baaden really wanted to know. He wasn't interest in their behavior except as it might affect him, his safety and profession.

The big dragon hitched forward with a beat of its wings. The smaller dragon shot into the air and flew off. The holo faded.

"You interrupted me for this? One dragon threatens another," Stilwell said. "So what? Watcher reports say the planet is safe. A threat isn't exactly a fight."

"Don't be swayed. They're not the objective scientists they'd like you to believe. Don't think for a nanosecond that dragons are harmless. You gotta know what you're dealing with."

"Acknowledged. Tell me again about those parasites," Stilwell said.

"You finally believe me? I warned you about them when we set up our project."

"Who decided they were parasites?"

Baaden sighed. "What else could they be? I was with the Watchers when they brought in a dead dragon with their shuttle. The stench was stomach wrenching. I saw the parasite, also dead. Evidently it had eaten into the back of the dragon's head, leaving a cavity."

"You got a good look at it?"

Baaden hadn't really looked, but he had heard the reports. "Someone pulled it out of the dragon's head. Looked like a rotten clump of lint about the size of my fist. I thought it was part of the dragon, until someone said it was a separate creature. Evidently stuck in the hole it had chewed in the dragon's skull. Dug into its brain and killed it.

"Watchers think they know it all, that all creatures on the planet are sweet and cuddly. I know what I saw. I'm not stupid. Parasites are predators, pure and simple. And if they are predators, then that means other predators live on this planet."

"Like dragons," Stilwell said.

"Yessir. Like dragons."

"I'll keep that in mind."

The conversation ended.

Baaden switched his mental image to Traveler. The automaton sent a picture of what appeared to be a small herd of white glowing horses on a plain. The flash of sun off horns demanded another look. Unicorns. With flowing manes and tails. That was the crazy thing about this planet. The terraformers, whoever they were, had based their work on fancy. Expect to find anything, from dinosaurs to lightning bugs. At least with Traveler sending images, Baaden didn't have to explore on his own and risk unknown dangers. His task was to send reports. Leave it to StarCircus to reap the benefits.

"Traveler, come," Baaden commanded.

The holo extinguished. Baaden scratched his lean shoulder and looked out over the bog that surrounded his island with its small trees. He felt mostly safe here, away from the dense forest, magma caves, or basalt cliffs where dragons might hang out, dark sinister forms, their colors adjusting to their surroundings.

Baaden dug out a trail bar of dried fruit and nuts and a strip of meat jerky from a pack. What he wouldn't give for a steak. A big one.

Rare. If only he had a replicator, he could make food from whatever floated around in the air. He could even take a cheek scraping and make a me-steak. Sometimes his stomach hurt, and there was nothing like a me-steak to settle it. Made from his own cells. Such replicators were hard to come by, especially in the field. Watcher Base had one, and it was fussy. He had repaired it repeatedly and finally assigned the invisible boy to its loathsome maintenance. Traveler was much more interesting.

Hoots, whistles, an odd song of chords and syncopation arose from afar. Bird song? Wolves? Whales? Dragons, no doubt. The song was sweet, haunting. Sometimes it seemed to come from two, even three directions. Dragons were great imitators. Highly vocal. Capable of any sound you could imagine.

He wished it would stop.

Halfway through his snack, a whoosh of wings and a clatter announced the arrival of Traveler. Baaden wrapped his food and stuffed it into the pocket of his shorts. He greeted what appeared to be an adult dragon. Traveler stood head, neck, and shoulders above Baaden. It blew and flexed its wings, like a real dragon. Baaden had learned only what he needed to know about them, which wasn't much. He understood a lot more about Traveler, for Baaden was expert at robotics, the main reason he gained admittance to the dragon planet.

At his command, Traveler turned itself off. Baaden was ready for routine maintenance. Check the eye and ear sensors, the manna bay, the programming. He had to admit Traveler was beautiful, except for its eyes. Snake eyes with slit pupils. Cold, cruel eyes.

When he acquired Traveler, it was already programmed to perfection. He didn't understand the personality application, which involved dragon communication. Only that it worked very well. Leaving that in place, he had only to tweak the program to his specifications. As a result Traveler provided him transportation—uncomfortable and slippery—, brought him supplies, and collected and delivered the product that should earn him a fortune. All in all, Traveler ensured Baaden's safety and his anonymity. Other than StarCircus, no one, not even Stilwell, had ever met Baaden face to face and didn't need to. But then Baaden had never met Stilwell either, having set up business solely through earbud contact.

CHAPTER 10

The Groombug

Into the forest a lone groombug rolls and leaps. His delicate limbs with their black needle claws are meant for climbing and clinging to dragon scales. Ordinarily a groombug can spring great distances. It isn't something he can maintain. He tries to spring and then hops. And finally creeps. If the way were smooth, he could roll. For a groombug, it is the fastest form of travel. He rolls when he can. Rocks, branches, and uneven terrain interrupt, and he stops short of collision.

He looks back along his escape route. Somewhere beyond sight stands the huge vessel from the outworld. Back there, his dragon, Elder Seemor, is missing. No one will pursue the groombug or even notice his absence. He is tiny, even for a groombug, because chunks of his fur have been burned away.

His worry isn't in being captured. His worry is how to live without Seemor—his sustenance, his shelter, his companion. Until he can reunite with her, he must find a substitute, however poor. He must look for a squalid shelter in the forest and some form of nourishment.

CHAPTER 11

The Meeting

The world is restless. In the distance I see ash coloring the sky and nourishing the manna belt. By the time I crawl beneath the belt, the sky should be clear. Huffing and steaming, I reach the first dribbles. They are meager, intermittent. They waft down, to land on leaves or lose themselves in the brush. They disappear into the ground. I lick and suck, tormented by the hint of sweetness and the fear that other feeders will soon arrive. So far I have manna to myself. The driblets collect into insultingly tiny clumps, and I try to shove some into bigger piles.

I pause for a breath.

Rustling and nibbling continues. Not mine. Some other being is here. Who? A mouse, a squirrel, a tiny deer? Where? Don't they always travel in groups? This is a single being.

I resume feeding, and we form a concert of sounds.

Whatever it is, it is small. I follow the sucking, chewing, and smacking. From under a leaf, a pair of dark, elliptical eyes blink up at me. Two black, soulful eyes, up-and-down elliptical and touching in the center. Groombug eyes. These are markedly heart fetching, even for groombugs.

We exchange stare for stare.

He is alone. Impossible! She must be somewhere, behind a tree perhaps. Or high in the branches. Too high for me to see. Odd, though, that they are not together.

"Where is your dragon?" I feel strange speaking to a groombug other than my own.

He steps into view, barely visible. His darkness disappears into the darkness of the thicket, a body without edges.

"She's indisposed." The groombug's voice is deep, for a groombug.

My sight adjusts until I make out more of him through the cast shadows. I wish I hadn't.

Again we lock eyes. To be more visible, he raises his fur. The hairs float on air, which normally adds to the beauty of groombugs. This groombug is ugly. He looks plucked. Mottled gray and pink hide reveals its secrets from among patches of hair, much of it singed. Patches of skin show on his face, but his mouth is still a hidden mystery. Except for his eyes, there is nothing beautiful about this one. Was he caught in a firestorm of fighting dragons? The situation must have been desperate, for dragons resort to fire in a fight only as a last resort. A groombug's safety always comes first.

His gaze takes in my broken wings, my brace. My ears tingle for a second. He is hyperspeaking to my groombug and getting no answer.

"Where is your groombug?"

"Dead. An accident."

Again he takes in my wings, my sorry scales, my skin scrapes. And, I'm sure, the smell of my impending death. The slightest blink, more an eye twitch, indicates he's reached a decision.

"I'll groom you. If you want."

Understatement of understatements. By the Great Mother, of course I want it as much as I want to breathe! All dragons would. My color flares red; I can't control it. Nevertheless I try to meet understatement with understatement.

"Only if you wish."

He emerges in all his ugliness. Bared hindquarters reveal the nubbin of a tail. His claws, mounted on tiny feet, are as long as his stubby legs. If not for my need, I would flee in revulsion. I back with each step of his advancement.

He stops. "I'm not diseased. I, too, suffered a mishap. As did my dragon."

How silly of me. I relax and he hops aboard. Immediately he nibbles my scales, tickling and scratching away itches. His saliva soothes my scrapes and sores. Cleaning and polishing, he gives me a grand massage. I stretch, wiggle in ecstasy, and moan in delight. Ah. My whole body tingles. When he begins his buzzy melody, I choke back tears. It reminds me of the groombug chorus when we dragons would huddle together for our grooming. I think of Tweekie's thin, sweet voice. I must admit that never have I heard a more beautiful buzz than this groombug's. His voice is deeper, stronger, and more resonant. Somehow his croon resembles two voices. Is that a capability of all groombugs, something I'd never noticed before, having taken groombugs for granted? I can't take him for granted. His croon is too pleasant.

He speaks into my middle ear. "Mind, this is only a temporary arrangement. Until I reunite with my dragon."

My growing fondness for the fellow melts in the simmer of my inner furnace. Of course the arrangement is temporary! Anyone would know that. Must he remind me and ruin my pleasure? He is giving me life…for a while. I try to breathe out the hurt.

Manna drools at the corner of my mouth, and I feel a tickle as the groombug licks at it.

My eyes mist. Tweekie used to do that. How I miss him.

I hold still so this creature can move over my scales and find a treasure of crud to digest. His hum mesmerizes.

"I'm, ahem…" My voice chokes and I try again. "I am called Rumplewing."

"Mmm," the groombug purrs. Never in all my days have I heard a more beautiful voice. I focus on that.

Sure, I miss Tweekie. Not for any particular virtue. Rather it's because we were fellow hatchlings. Bonded. Dragon and groombug. Together for life. Unless some tragedy befalls one or the other, as when Batwing sat on Tweekie. I can forgive her my broken wings. I can never forgive her my loss of Tweekie.

As nearly invisible as this groombug is, particularly when he flattens his hairs, I notice how he pauses from time to time and studies the sky. He is uneasy.

"We need to go deeper into the forest."

What an abhorrent suggestion. Can't he see my condition? "We can't. My wings."

He doesn't answer. He keeps looking up. "We need to get away from here. There's danger."

For whom? A dragon? More likely he is referring to danger for himself. Groombugs are quite helpless.

"We need to get away from here."

I glance up at the manna belt. At the shiny dribbles on the leaves. "And leave all this? There's food here."

"That's why we must go. There are flying shells that appear and disappear. They carry outworlders. Beings who know dragons frequent the manna belts. We're not safe. You're not safe. That's why we need to get away."

Outworlders? Another name for Watchers? Was he talking about Forbidden Mountain? If so, then the elders' warning was right after all. Which means Fetidbreath's suggestion that they may be healers was wrong. How could an elder be wrong?

CHAPTER 12

The Watcher Craft

-1-

Hote knew something was wrong when Baaden and Traveler stayed out overnight and didn't appear the following day. Anyone other than Baaden would have messaged Base if they were late getting in. Had he met with an accident? Not sure the Chief would take him seriously, Hote told Amber. After she and others searched the compound, members gathered in the dayroom where Hunter caught their attention.

"Listen up, everyone. Reports by Sparky on her enlightening study of glowing fungi, along with Reed's ability to suck you in on the mystery of sinkholes are canceled for today in favor of a brain strain session, sponsored by our super chief, Chief Li. Our weekly info session will resume tomorrow, to which will be added my sexy study on rock formations and what causes them to lie one on top of the other."

Chief Li waved him away and stepped forward. "It has been brought to my attention that our engineer Baaden has disappeared, along with our automaton. I have selected a team to carry out an investigation."

-2-

A day after the meeting, Hote stood near the pad of the shuttle craft. Though he formed part of the group of eight Watchers—including three visitors from another station—to see the craft off, he felt his aloneness. No one acknowledged his presence. Amber looked out what appeared to be a row of windows in the sky. Once the windows closed, the shuttle she was in would resemble a wisp of cloud. And she, Ahmed, Maximus, Hunter, Reed, and Sparky would be free to search for the missing engineer and automaton, free to visit the other research stations, and free to set down at any interesting site. The shuttle seemed small, but once it set down, it would expand to three and four times its size, to become a research station and home for the crew.

Pip waved and sang, "Baa-baa-Bad-un. Good-bye, bye." Hote knew she revealed what others felt. No one wanted Baaden back. They must find him though, and the irreplaceable Traveler.

That thing within Hote tugged at him, urged him to leap aboard. Hurry! Hote pushed against it and backed a step. He strained against the urge, trembled. If he should give in, it would be another example of his weirdness.

The craft blinked in the sun. The row of windows lifted silently and hovered a few seconds. Its passengers waved back, and Amber looked out one window and blew Hote a kiss. How he wanted to accompany her! To observe in the field. To be accepted as a trustworthy scientist. Would they see dragons?

The row of windows shot up as they closed, and the craft was gone, a blue and white cloud lost in the sky of sun and clouds.

CHAPTER 13

Flying

-1-

I feel insulted at his short-sightedness. Not safe, indeed! In all the years our clan has lived near the Forbidden Mountain, we have never been molested by the so-called dangerous Watchers.

Partly to humor him so he will be content to groom me, partly to give him the sense I am protecting him, I agree to move on.

"We'll make slow progress. In case you didn't notice, my wings are broken. That's why I wear this brace of woven branches. I'm grounded. I can't fly."

"Is that so?" He makes nibbling sounds; I suppose he is thinking. "Are your shoulders broken?"

"No."

"Can you move them?"

I shrug. "Only a little. The brace is stiff."

"We need to get you out of it."

"What? No. It holds my wings in place."

He skitters about, from wing tip to wing tip, stopping now and then to sniff and probe. He disappears under my shoulders, and I feel a slight tickle. He reappears on top and smacks and then says "Your wings have knitted."

"Have they?" Healed? I hadn't thought of it.

"You need to remove the brace."

The idea that my wings are healed keeps me from answering. I'm too busy searching them for pain and unsteadiness.

"That contraption prevents you from moving your shoulders. Get rid of it."

With my thumb and fingers stranded at the end of each wing, I don't know how I can. If I do get free, my wings might collapse into useless appendages.

The groombug insists.

So I tug and shrug. He nibbles along its length, stripping away bark, tugging its edges into slivers, which do nothing to weaken the brace. Finally he yells, "Ram it against that tree. Leap at it. Crash sideways."

I bash first one side and then the other and then headlong, as he clings and yells, "Again."

Wham! I lurch and leap and ram. I can feel his front claws cling while the rest of him whips about with each lunge. It's a wonder he doesn't sail off.

"Again. Don't stop."

But stop, I do, gasping on my own fumes. I lie, exhausted. Momentarily I consider breathing upon the brace, only to picture myself enveloped in fire and killing the groombug. I can tell him to get off, but who's to say I can control where the flames would go? A dragon's scales are resistant to fire, within reason. Prolonged exposure can cause severe burns, as can flames to any cut or open sore. I shudder.

The groombug doesn't seem tired. He skitters about and tugs at the brace. "We loosened it."

"Fine, because I'm not crashing into another tree."

The groombug says nothing. I hear only the crunch of wood beneath his beak.

"Yes, it's looser. Stand and test your wings."

I gather my legs beneath me and try to lift myself up on my arms. In one brief moment, I rear just enough for my belly to clear the ground and discover that along the stiff length of my wings, my fingers can touch the ground. Splayed as my arms are, the strain is too great. I collapse on my chin.

"Raise your wings. Use your shoulders."

My wings are stiff and awkward. The brace is heavy, my shoulders weak. I rotate them. Shaky, I manage to raise my arms a hand span, but it takes strength I wouldn't need to operate normal wings. Again I collapse.

"Walk."

"Do you have to be so pushy?" Tweekie was never like that.

"Walk."

I bring my fingers down and find I could tiptoe them forward at a slant to the ground. The strain is incredible. But I can raise myself up in spurts, and in that short span of time it's a relief to get my weight off my battered breastbone. Unable to bend my elbows, I stiff-leg it forward, shaky from the effort. I suppose he expects me to be thankful. Instead I grumble.

This groombug is definitely not like Tweekie. Beautiful Tweekie.

We travel in search of a launching spot. Rather, I trundle along and the groombug rides tucked in my third ear, his warmth and weight a comfort. Knowing I can't scratch an itch, he doesn't hesitate to take care of it for me, so I welcome the ugly creature onto my scales and into my life.

-2-

We share stories. I speak of Tweekie, how the hairs rose and floated about his body and caught the sun and glistened.

Groombug counters with a story about his dragon. "Seemor is the chief elder of our clan. The wisest of the wise. And beautiful. Rosettes line her spine and encircle her neck."

"Batwing sat on Tweekie." I leap into the sad story.

Groombug says nothing.

We emerge from forest onto a meadow. Birds call from the trees and the ground. Crickets seesaw their own melody. I stop in a circle of iridescent mushrooms and rest in a cushion of tall weeds. "I'm sorry to go on about Tweekie."

"You miss him. I understand."

Groombug starts imitating the crickets, a comforting sound. He stops, says, "Sing with me."

Sing with a groombug? "Dragons and groombugs don't sing together."

"How many dragons do you see?"

"Just me."

"How many groombugs?"

"Just you."

"So we sing together."

I don't know what to say.

"It's not forbidden," Groombug adds.

No, it isn't. And I do miss singing.

Groombug imitates frogs, a soothing sound. I join in with the imitation of a bird carol. From there he and I move to other sounds and add our own in unison and harmony, and when I trumpet, Groombug joins me in equal volume. Astounding for one so small. It's like singing in a dragon chorus. Howling, hooting, wailing, trumpeting. We lose ourselves in the joy of it. And when we fade on a long note that replays as a distant echo, I want to weep for joy. So beautiful. So satisfying. Better than anything I ever did with Tweekie.

At the thought, my joy sours. Groombug had tried to make me forget Tweekie. My tears turn to rage. Never again will I sing with him. If he should try to accompany me, I will prevent him by becoming silent.

CHAPTER 14

The Conference

Weeks passed with no news on Baaden and the automaton. Hote tried not to worry about it, but life wasn't the same without Traveler. Seated on the grass against a tree with overhanging branches, he played the last recording Traveler had sent Watcher Base. Earlier Chief Li had played it for everyone, along with news from one of the stations of the discovery of fanged deer.

Still aware of his surroundings, he watched an image the visor sent. Long wings in a vermillion sky stretched through the dawn's light. Long wings of a flock in silhouette. As Traveler flew nearer, the shapes revealed outstretched tails. And a rising sun struck scaly, membranous wings, the arms of what looked like prehistoric flying lizards. And then one somersaulted, showing in startling resolution the full form of a dragon. Hote remembered how he sucked in his breath at the first sight. Again his heart quickened. Other dragons veered into aerobatics. It became apparent they were plunging through airborne sparkling globules. They were flying through it, mouths agape, feeding on a dewy substance that spread like a belt.

The dragons glistened in the light as they dove and glided through the belt, stirring it up. Their distance and activity didn't allow a more detailed look, but it was the closest and best view of dragons so far.

"Beautiful," he breathed.

They shone in the sun like polished stones. Reds, greens, blues, and other colors.

Traveler flew closer, but the flock departed. Traveler then took a sample of the dragon food for analysis at the Watcher Base. They still had samples of it, replicated in larger proportions for study.

The recording ended. All around him a flock of birds burst from the trees and bushes, their wings stubby when compared with the dragons'.

Once inside, Hote wandered across the room to where he heard voices through an office wall. A conference. He stopped, unable to move on. His feet seemed rooted. His hearing suddenly hypersensitive. Why couldn't he just move on instead of lurking like a spy? This thing inside him seemed insatiable in its need to snoop.

"You know, with Traveler gone, the only way we can find dragons is through air samples. Traveler was our only automaton; can it be replaced?" Hote recognized Ahmed's voice.

"Nope. And Baaden's gone." Hunter sounded more serious than usual.

"Baaden," Chief Li said. "We were working on replacing him. He lacked cooperation."

"Nevertheless, he was a good mechanic, good at maintenance. He understood robotics." That was Amber.

"Where did he come from?" Ahmed asked.

"Can't be from Academy." Hunter seemed very sure.

"StarCircus," Li said. "Not our usual source of employees. He wasn't hired for his personality."

Hote no longer saw clearly and realized he had sunk into the wall and froze there. By now, the sensation was familiar. "I'm in interstitial space," he mouthed. "The in-between." He surrendered and relaxed into the thing's control.

"Have we given up searching? What about air samplers?" Ahmed.

"Even if they found molecular evidence of the whereabouts, it doesn't mean Baaden would still be there." That was Li.

"You'd think someone slipped him through the void. Like he's no longer on the planet."

The void. Hote sensed its blackness, its nothingness. Some part of the entity within him was caught in the void. He felt a dreamy curiosity.

The conversation paused, and then resumed. "How could he do that?"

"Lost in one of Reed's sinkholes," Hunter quipped, which brought a brief laughter.

Amber said, "I.D. Express has a fleet of drones. Has anyone seen them?"

"Wouldn't they be invisible?"

"No. They're harvest drones. They hunt and then levitate whatever they harvest out. They can be used for spotting whatever they want to collect. It's the only way 2Ray1's crew has contact outside the ship. Everyone stays inside."

"Are you suggesting we bring I.D. Express into the search?" Chief Li.

Two or three voices crisscrossed in reply, denying a desire for such a thing.

"Could be, 2Ray1 found Baaden and Traveler and brought them onboard I.D. Express." That was Hunter.

"If that happened, we should hear from the commander by now."

Amber chuckled. "You think so?"

"We've trusted 2Ray1 for years," Li said.

"For import, yes. This is different. This has nothing to do with a business contract. And believe me, the commander of I.D. Express is not our friend."

"You think they'd hold him for ransom?"

"What would be the point?"

"They might want the automaton," Hunter suggested. "It's one of a kind, and they might find it highly useful."

Voices of dread responded. "For what? What could they use it for?"

Chief Li evidently reached for calm. "Let me assure you, our Guiding Congress will investigate. For now it's out of our hands. We carry on as usual."

A stir of chairs. The conference was breaking up. Hote felt a release, and he strode off.

CHAPTER 15

Friction

The meadow opens through a line of trees onto a prairie. I crawl forth. Late in the day we find a small hill. A knoll. A pimple on the ground. After the miserable trek across grassland, I want to rest. Before Groombug can bully me up the hill, however, I shove through resisting weeds and over harsh rocks. At the hill's crest, I flop down.

"It will take a great leap," he says. "Rest first. Build up your strength."

The wind gusts in my face. Grasses swirl in waves across the huge expanse. The breeze is strong. How long before it dies? Will it be strong tomorrow? I gather my feet under me and balance.

"Wait," he says.

I leap. And tumble down the hill.

Groombug sighs, says nothing as I whimper and force my way again to the top. Once there, I prepare again to leap.

"Wait."

"I can't wait." Because I don't want him ordering me about.

"Very well. Then leave nothing in your path. No bushes, no weeds, no rocks. When the breeze is at its fullest, I will tell you when to jump."

"I know when to jump!"

"Evidently you don't."

His criticism stings, no matter how true. And he is right. So I do what I can to clear the way, with whatever help he can offer, which is mostly telling me what to do. "Shove that bush aside. You can do it with your hand. Now use your mouth to burn away those weeds. Nose that pebble out of the way."

"It's just a pebble."

"You could twist a toe on it."

I shove the pebble down the hill. And when the way is clear of all vegetation and twigs, and leaves, and pebbles, I raise up to face the wind. And when it gusts, Groombug yells, "Jump!" and adds a little leap of his own.

And we're airborne.

"See what we can do when we work together?" he says. Most irritating.

"Just let me concentrate on getting to where the wind blows without ceasing."

Groombug settles in my third ear. "Best you concentrate on finding a higher place from which to launch tomorrow."

And then he is blissfully quiet.

Actually I feel bliss for a mere pulse beat. It's the brace. It is slippery. I tremble at keeping it level. My breath jerks.

Groombug seems not the least disturbed. He says nothing as we sail above the prairie toward distant mountains. The land folds into mounds and teases the wind. A gust catches me. The brace scoots. I capsize.

"Twist right!" Groombug yells in my third ear. "Rudder left with your tail. Left, left, left! Get under the brace. Under! Now up."

He keeps me aloft. When I level out, my relief is ruined by a lecture.

"Smooth your movements. Don't jerk. You'll make the brace slam about."

"I know."

I surrender to the wisdom of finding tall promontories from which to leap each morning. In fact we settle on the first broad one and practice launching and landing for a couple days, long enough that I become steadier in flight. Then I head for more rugged land, accompanied by Groombug's lecture on air eddies in canyons that could knock me off balance.

"I know. You don't have to tell me. When my wings were proper, it was nothing to kick off from trees. I'm a forest dragon, so I was particularly skilled at maneuvering tight spaces. It's something cliff dragons would be awkward at."

"Don't be so sure. I'm from the cave clan, and their flying ability would have been no different from any other clans', no matter the location."

I try not to grit my beak. "We forest dragons are the greatest of fliers. We angle through the great trees, and they don't always hold still for us. Branches sway, sometimes get broken. We learn how to compensate. Your cave clan wouldn't have the opportunity to learn such skills in a place that never moves."

"You think not? Sometimes the wind buffets us, and we learn to cling without being blown away."

"The same with forest dragons."

"As for the stability of our environment, let me tell you a little story. The face of the cliff is sheer, and our clan wished for a porch in front of our cave. The Great Mother knew our wish, although we never told her. One day, the ground shook, and the face split and cascaded and left a porch before the cave entrance."

"Was anyone hurt?"

"We were all away, feeding on the manna belt."

He may think he's entertaining me, but he makes me feel my youth and inexperience.

Rather than allow him to think he is guiding me, I simply drift, airborne, always within reach of a cliff.

We drift through one day and the next, during which he sees me around hidden dangers and then condescends to entertain me with songs and stories, as if I am a youngling among elders.

"You may think dwelling in a cave or hanging from a cliff is uncomfortable. It can be as pleasant a home as the forest is for your clan. For example, the dragons build cushions for themselves, and a great nest for the clan eggs."

"How can you have a good nest in the cave?"

"Easily. They weave branches together. Then they line it with twigs, then soft materials like feathers, hair, and plant down."

Very well, this groombug is older than me; it's obvious. A regular know-it-all.

But does he really know it all?

"In our clan, we have mysteries. Like sometimes the elders fly off together. After several days, they return, and they never tell us where they went or why."

The groombug doesn't hesitate. "They attend the elders' council. Elders from various clans meet and discuss important matters, such as how to solve problems that arise, or they might pass on the knowledge of new discoveries."

Not really a mystery, after all. What if I ask him about one of the mysteries, unknown even to the elders? "Where do you think groombugs come from?"

"That's easy. From dragons."

"That doesn't make sense."

"Yes, it does. Each dragon egg is born with a groombug egg attached. Which is why you have only one groombug for each dragon."

"Bonded at birth, joined until death," we both say.

How can I not help but resent his superiority? I pretend to be bored and sometimes refuse to listen to his lectures. Sometimes a fire of anger heats my innards whenever I suspect him of coddling me.

He doesn't tell me how he came to be here, or how he came to be scarred, and I don't ask. Instead, I repeat how my wings were broken and my Tweekie was destroyed.

"Tweekie was beautiful. He'd lift his fur into a great ball, so the hairs seemed to ride the air. Sometimes the light would catch him so it looked like he was rimmed in sun."

Groombug shows no pleasure in hearing this. He depresses his fur so he is nearly invisible.

I try to be fair. I acknowledge, at least to myself, he has a sweeter voice than Tweekie ever had, he's quicker to fulfill my desire to have my back scratched, he whispers encouragements, and he anticipates my hunger. Were he not so bossy, so superior, I might be grateful.

I can't bring myself to call him anything but Groombug. Tweekie and I shared a buddy bond of mischief, of mistakes, and of lessons. We were equals.

CHAPTER 16

Dragon Problems

"Stilwell to Baaden. Come in, Baaden."

Baaden stirred awake on his hammock and groaned at the midday light that entered his tent. He tapped his earbud. "Baaden, here. How goes it?"

"Bad. The dragons you sent me are coming down with some sort of skin disease."

Baaden swung his feet over the edge of his hammock and sat up. "Did you get rid of their parasites?"

"Of course. First thing we do when we bring them in is pass them through a flame. We've done that from the start, and only some of them got sick. Then we took to spraying them afterwards, to make sure they're completely clean. And now all of them are getting sick. Like their scales are rotting. We must have brought in some sort of contagion."

Baaden stretched, yawned. "How long has this been going on?"

"A long time. Enough time that it's like they're coming apart, rotting from the inside out and dying. We've been selling them fast, before it's obvious they're sick, but we've gotten complaints from customers who hold them alive too long. And we've seen it with our own stock."

"The Watchers have dragon experts. Talk to Commander. Suggest he call in a Watcher to look at them. And remember, I don't exist, understood?"

"You exist for Commander 2Ray1. What makes you think we get dragons without him knowing? He agreed to it after Mr. Star convinced him. Commander runs a tight ship. Knows everything."

"Like my location? StarCircus supplied me with a blocker."

"I realize that. Commander's thinking of hiring a sniffer to find you. Those little beasts are good at what they do. I don't know how they do it; it just takes one. StarCircus has been using them for years."

"No need reminding me of something I know. Look, you just let Mr. Star know. No sniffers, okay?"

"I'll make sure of it. Stilwell, out."

Baaden grunted, flopped back onto the hammock to resume his nap.

CHAPTER 17

Death Unchosen

"You're ready to reach the manna belt and properly feed."
It had been over a hand and a foot of days. Nevertheless I'd go longer simply to avoid telling the groombug I'm hungry. I don't want to sound like Batwing. Without another word, we head for the nearest belt.

We cross a plain, the one where I'd seen a herd of unicorns, the adults feeding or conversing, their young chasing about. They are still there, but resting in tall grasses and red and white flowers. Gryphons, foxes, and vultures move among them. Odd.

"Get lower," Groombug says.

I drop down. Putrid air hits me. The buzz of flies. I circle. Death… Death and corruption…Everyone dead…Why would an entire herd meet the gryphon? It doesn't make sense. Did they close their bodies down, so a plague could take them? A bizarre accident? What I took for flowers are the white bodies and the red of blood on each forehead. Everyone is missing its horn. I've seen enough. I could be stuck here amid this death. Caught and unable to mount the air.

I wiggle my tail and hasten away from the scene. What accident could kill entire herd?

"An evil was committed here," Groombug says. "Something lopped their lives off. For only their horns."

"Not an accident?" I can barely speak, my throat is so tight. "How can something lop your life off? Impossible."

We sail on, silent. I meditate on the scene of corpses, robbed of life, and for what?

Why?

Why?

Why?

They chose life and found death.

The wind is fresh and soon carries the scent of ferns, flowers, and moist leaves. Groombug breaks into a hum. Pampering me, I suppose. I don't mind.

When Groombug ends his song, I say, "Why didn't the Great Mother save them?"

"That's between them and her. Not for us to know."

"After I left the clan, I visited the Great Mother. I tried to enter her dwelling. She lifted me up and out, and told me to live. I don't know why."

"Where was this?" Groombug sounds deeply interested, almost urgent.

"At the volcano, of course. I traveled a great distance to meet her. She saved me. Blew me out. I came away with blisters."

"Ah." Groombug smacks, and smugness enters his voice. "You needn't have stressed yourself, except as a lesson for one so young. A few blisters can improve the memory."

"Was there an easier way?"

"The Great Mother is not limited to the volcano. She is all there is, the whole world and everything in it."

"Like she doesn't need the volcano?"

"She uses part of it to express herself, or anything she chooses. She is not limited and can be he or it, visible and invisible at the same time."

"How do you know all this; how do you learn?"

"Elders share their discoveries."

At the elder council, no doubt.

Our conversation drops off when we smell something like honey. Ahead, the manna belt glistens in multicolor, and it dribbles scraps to the ground.

Held stiffly level as my wings are, I try to follow air currents up to the belt, for I am famished for a proper feed. But the air currents don't lead me up. They die.

The brace lurches, knocks me in the back of my head and cramps a wing. Until that moment it hasn't occurred to me how Groombug must scrunch down in my third ear to avoid being knocked loose whenever the brace shifts. This time he must have been hit. I don't feel him in my third ear. Is he clinging elsewhere? Being bounced around? I try to look back, to see if he has fallen off.

Big mistake.

I twist straight to balance the brace.

"Groombug, where are you?"

No answer.

Something kicks me in the back. The brace? I judder to remain upright and try to coast to a safe landing.

Bushes rush up. Leaves part to reveal knobby branches, pointing their fingers at me, eager to jab.

I slam into them. Omph!

The crash reverberates through my innards. Stars sprinkle through my vision.

I lie, afraid to move, waiting for my brain to cease vibrating and fearing to test my bones.

After a while I wiggle and feel pain. From where? Ah, there. I can't count the bruises that line my underside, but I hear the rustle of Groombug beside me, evidently counting. He seems uninjured.

How naive to think I could sleep on the wing. When a dragon has the full use of her arms, she doesn't take into account the gusts, the gales, or the lack of wind. Tears leak down my cheeks.

"I can't do this. I can't fly. I tried to reach the manna belt, and you can see how my wings are broken. I can't stay aloft."

"Nonsense."

"You saw. You saw how I fell."

"Are your shoulders broken?"

Groombug has the wisdom and knowledge of a high elder. He was privy to everything the elders discussed in their council. All the discoveries. I feel like a hatchling.

As much as the brace allows, I shrug my shoulders. I feel no agony. No bones scrape. "No, they're not broken."

"Then we will go on."

I groan. "Tweekie would have been more sympathetic."

"Sympathy has its place, as long as it doesn't take the place of necessary action."

"I know; you don't need to tell me." I surge into action to demonstrate my unwillingness to rest on sympathy.

CHAPTER 18

The Attack

It takes some doing, but with me harvesting branches and hoisting them to Groombug, we manage to pad the brace sufficiently to keep it from sliding. The padding pokes and abrades me. Still, I prefer the discomfort of a snug brace to the danger of a loose one.

After feeding on dribbles, I trundle to a high spot and wait for the wind to pick up, which doesn't take long. Once in the air, I am gliding when Groombug gives a hiccup that sounds like, "Watch out!"

I can't twist to see without risking a fall. Something smacks me in my blind spot. Something big enough to knock me sideways. I squirm to keep upright, lest I tumble from the sky. In full view something gigantic rushes at me, the sinuous form of a dragon.

"Dodge left," Groombug commands in my third ear.

Heeding, I yell at my attacker, "Who are you?"

Repeatedly the other dragon lunges.

"What do you want?"

"Left," says Groombug. "Down."

"Why are you doing this?"

The attacker thunders, "Give me your groombug."

"Dodge right."

"Your groombug or your life!"

"Can't we discuss this?"

All this dodging isn't easy with rigid wings. The attacker catches me in a full body slam, and I hurtle to the ground where my wings crunch and shudder. I groan.

It wouldn't take much for my attacker to suck Groombug from my third ear into her mouth.

Groombug slips away and hides.

A red dragon lands beside me, flutters her wings and folds them. It's obvious why she wants my groombug. Her scales are dull. In places a lack of polish and the accumulation of detritus has led to their splitting and the development of eruptions and running sores.

"Your groombug or your life." She hops toward me.

I hiss at her and spew a mix of gas and flame. Red and orange pulse over us, back to front. I hold a fireball in my mouth, ready to hurl it. Usually quarreling dragons aim over each other's shoulders, always protective of the groombugs. Since she doesn't have a groombug, I have her at a disadvantage. Her scales are impervious to flame, but any break in her skin is not.

She backs off. Her pulsing fades.

"What happened to your groombug? Did you sit on him?" My tone is sarcastic.

My wings tremble and the brace slips a little. It threatens my balance. I try to shrug it into place and end tilted sideways. So much for dignity.

"Your groombug," comes the demand.

"Get back!" I expel a breath that ripples with heat.

The stranger settles back on her haunches, wings half lifted over her back. "If you must know, my groombug died, and I was kicked out of the clan."

When she starts to rise, I yell, "Get back!"

She settles down. "You don't look so good, yourself. Doubtful you'll last long with your wings the way they are. What happened to you?"

"My reward for an attempted good deed."

"Oh?"

"Getting landed on by a fat dragon who was too lazy to learn to fly. My wings broke, and the only way to salvage them was to have them fixed in an outstretched position. It was that or never fly again."

I glare when I hear what sounds like a snicker.

The stranger clears her throat. "No, I wasn't laughing. It would appear you won't be needing your groombug for long."

"As long as I live." I sit on my haunches from where I can hurtle at her with a thrust of my tail. For all the good that would do with arms incapable of wrestling. At least I could roast her with my breath, if I have the energy to sustain the fire. I open my jaws to display the sharp edges of my beak and hiss.

The stranger stands, ready to challenge me. Again she pulses, the colors moving from back to front with increased brilliance and speed.

I say, "You're sorry looking enough, I expect you'll be dying soon."

"Not if I have a groombug," she answers, barely above a whisper. Inside, her fires rise to a faint roar.

All I have is bluff. Fire can kill her only if it strikes broken skin. Even then it would take repeated blasts, providing she didn't dodge. I could thrash her with my tail. But she has full use of her wings, fully capable of mauling me, pinning me down, and beating me. I listen for Groombug, who stays hidden. I must try a different approach.

"My groombug is free to choose. He will not willingly leave me. If you try to take him, he may refuse to groom you, and you'll be no better off than you are now."

The stranger sighs. "I was afraid you'd say that." She directs her attention at where she thinks Groombug might be. "Listen, little one, tell me your name."

Groombug answers from beneath me. "My name is not for you to know."

"That's no way to answer. I'm not so bad. I'm strong. I can fly. Come with me, and I promise to make you happy."

Groombug crawls into view, and I am almost shocked to see his raggedy fur, filled with grime, his bare flesh running with sores, his eyes encrusted.

"Be gone," he says.

The stranger backs off. "So be it." She turns again to me. "Look. I apologize for any inconvenience I caused. I was seeking comfort." Without a groombug, her sores will fester and eventually spread to her vital organs, and her dying tissues will provide a feast for tiny scavengers. "Before I leave, I suppose I should offer you some assistance in regaining the sky. Just so you'll know I'm not by nature a thief. But, well, it appears your groombug is closing down."

"Goodbye," Groombug says.

The stranger lifts off, only to settle a few yards away. She is working up to saying something. "You're-uh…you were banished from your clan?"

"I left voluntarily. No one kicked me out."

"You won't last long on your own. Not with your wings the way they are. They can be fixed, you know. I'm sure of it." The stranger shifts forward. "In fact, I know of a place. I'll lead you there."

"Where?"

"To the south. Difficult to find unless you have a guide."

"You've been there?"

"I've seen it, and I hear it's a wonderful place. I was just going there when I met you."

"Then why did you assault me?"

The stranger doesn't answer for a while. Steam wisps from her nostrils. "It's like this," she finally says. "I was impatient. I must apologize. Come with me, and we'll both be saved. Guaranteed."

I start forward when Groombug stops me with the power of his voice. "Liar! I know where you come from. Begone. Now, or I will come at you!"

I don't know what he can do to frighten a dragon, except look repulsive or spit acid. Without a word, the stranger lifts on wing and departs. I watch her speed off on agile wings. Soon she is lost from view.

I stare at Groombug. "Are you suddenly ill?"

"No, no. It's a disguise. A bit of saliva. A bit of plant sap. Lots of dirt."

I am surprised at how swiftly he scrubs himself clean. Even so, the scars and uneven fur remain. For once, I don't tell him how beautiful Tweekie was, compared to him. But I wonder why he drove the other dragon away.

"She was going to take me to a healing place. I could've had my wings fixed." Sadness and resentment creep into my voice.

The groombug shakes his head, which makes his whole body wiggle since he seems to have no neck. "Why would she attack you and then offer to help you? She tried to steal your very life, which is me. And when that didn't work, she tried to trick you."

I snort. "How could she do that?"

"Because she is not her own master."

I try to digest that tidbit. It makes no sense.

"She was trying to lead you into a trap, which could cost you your life."

It all seems confusing to me. "You mean, take me unawares so she could steal you?"

"Or worse."

"Worse? Like what?"

"Lead you into captivity."

"I don't see how."

"That's because you're a dragon. You have no reason to fear any other creature—you think. But you do."

The only creatures we were warned against were Watchers. They had never seemed a threat. Through all those many hand and feet spans of living near the base of the Forbidden Mountain, I doubt any of us had ever seen one. As far as I knew, Watchers did nothing but watch.

After a moment of mulling, I say, "I don't fear Watchers."

The groombug doesn't answer right away. He makes nibbling sounds, and when he speaks, it is almost a whisper. "Do you recall that herd of unicorns, rotting, missing their horns? That could be you."

"I'm not a unicorn!" I don't know whether I'm angry or scared.

"Do you think the entire herd decided to shut themselves down?"

"Not likely. I don't know. Something made them shut down. I guess."

"I've been thinking about that. Vessels did that. Collectors in flying shells from another world. They don't wait for anyone to meet the gryphon before they take. They bring death. That could be you."

I swivel my head one way and then the other, wanting to close Groombug out. Wanting to silence him. He will not be silenced.

He hops to a branch level with my nose and faces me, eye to eye. "Whether you understand it or not, I just saved your life."

CHAPTER 19

Settling In

-1-

Baaden finished a trail bar and stretched out on his hammock for a quick nap when he heard something mucking about outside his tent. He hardly dared move anything but his eyes. Whatever it was, it was near. He heard its breath. Its feet sucked through the mud. Baaden's gaze swept through his tent. His thoughts scrambled for something he could grasp as a weapon. Whatever the creature was, it took its time to sniff here and there. Baaden slipped from his hammock and eased into a sideways roll that brought him to the edge of his tent. He peered out. A moose or something like a moose browsed in the bog, twenty feet away. It sounded much closer.

The creature was harmless. Supposedly the entire planet was harmless, devoid of predators or poisonous plants. Baaden didn't believe it. He could be in danger, for he might not always have Traveler to transport him to safety. He needed a decent type of footwear to slog his way through the bog. No telling what hazards it concealed. Snakes, deadly fish, parasites. He reached for his earbuds. "On."

Once he roused Stilwell, he made his demands.

"Stilwell, get me a pair of dragon hide boots."

"They're only for officers. Or the extremely wealthy. I can get you regular boots."

"No. They won't work. Dragon hide will."

"Now isn't a good time to request anything like that from Commander. He's still going on about sending a sniffer after you."

Baaden sighed. "It's not necessary. If StarCircus felt my whereabouts were important to know, they'd send a sniffer, which they won't. They gave me a blocker instead."

"I'll remind him that you're not the source of our problems."

"2Ray1's the source of his own problems. He's just trying to be difficult. Trying to test his strength against Mr. Star. We know who'll win."

"Yes."

"So get on with it. You have ways. You can get me a pair."

"That won't be easy."

"You think what I'm doing for you is easy? I need them. If Commander 2Ray1 refuses, contact StarCircus if you have to. You're Communications Officer. You can sneak a message."

"I'll see what I can do."

-2-

Ahmed picked at the remaining skeleton of the dragon. Hote stood behind the tech's shoulder, watching him separate flesh from bone into a dish. Another dish contained scraps of scaly skin. The stench was gone, replaced by a slight meaty smell and the waxy odor of a preservative. No windows existed in this lab of softly glowing ceiling and walls. Distant voices, passing footsteps, the sound of cawing infiltrated.

"Do they know why the dragon died?"

Ahmed's hand jerked. "Forgot you were watching, I was so concentrated."

Hote sighed, his irritation revealed in his breath. For a moment he flashed on Pip walking behind him, her hand probing the air as if he were only an image in it. Or the moon twins watching him from across the room, whispering behind their hands at each other and smirking.

"Hey." Ahmed didn't look up from his work, "I'm focused. Okay?"

"Okay." Hote was sorry to feel so easily slighted. It wasn't Ahmed's or anyone else's fault that he wasn't completely there.

"Just make a little noise, will you? You know. Clear your throat, shuffle your feet, snap your fingers. Anything."

"Mm."

Ahmed scraped what looked like a vertebra. "So, what caused the dragon's death? We've been puzzling that one out. With no predators, it wouldn't come under attack. Wouldn't get sick. Could have been an accident or old age."

"Starvation?"

"Nope. Too much fat residue."

"And that's it?"

Ahmed cocked his head to one side, quirked his mouth. "Well, it's not settled. You see, there's this acid they found. Right at the back of the dragon's head. It ate a hole clear through into the brain. And it's like it came from this tiny creature."

"Attacking the dragon?"

"Don't know. That little wart was as dead and decayed as the dragon. So there's the mystery. Meanwhile The Beard is studying the microbes. Says they're all scavengers."

The Beard. Hunter's name for the man with a permanent scowl of concentration, who yakked constantly about his work but refused to give a formal talk on it. The only researcher who refused to give a talk, possibly because he suffered stage fright. Hunter didn't push him.

Ahmed cracked a smile and turned just enough to cast Hote a glance. "So, how's your mechanical training coming?"

"Fine."

"It's important, you know." Support was always important, as Hote was discovering. Nevertheless, he sensed Ahmed trying to get rid of him. He wasn't ready to leave yet.

"I'm learning how to repair the replicator."

"It's broken?" Ahmed frowned. A broken replicator could be disastrous to Watcher survival.

Hote didn't want to alarm him. "A bit touchy. I'm cleaning it. Thing is, we're short on tools and equipment. I put in a requisition, which is being ignored."

"Yeah, well, we're short on funds. The Academy is stingy about giving us everything we need."

"Can we get replacement parts for the extra shuttle? It's just sitting on the airstrip, and I know I can fix it."

Ahmed turned to his work. "You'll have to see Chief Li about that. Maybe he can put in an order. We're about due for another trip to I.D. Express for another pickup from their launchpad."

Launchpad.

Radiant.

There is a box, a kit. In it is a doll that needs to be assembled. And I can't do it. It belongs to Radiant.

"There is a box…"

"What's that?"

"Nothing."

Ahmed frowned, shook his head.

"It-it's nothing," Hote repeated.

He tried to concentrate on his unwillingness to see the Chief. At least he didn't have to go with anyone to Father's ship to pick up supplies, though he would have enjoyed a ride with Maximus who piloted the Watcher craft and told him about piloting. Hunter and Reed always went along to carry anything that might be heavy or delicate. But no! Seeing Father's ship would bring on the torture of memories. He was equally thankful no one from I.D. Express visited the Watcher stations. On the other hand, had I.D. Express anything to do with Baaden's disappearance? Besides that, what of Radiant? Why was Hote confused about her?

He could mention the need for parts to Amber. But should he depend on her for every little favor? Sometimes it was necessary. Ahmed and Amber could both put in a word for him.

"Ahmed, everyone does double duty, except me. I like fixing things, but what I really want is to get close to dragons. I want to learn everything there is to know about them. You think they could give me a project?"

Ahmed leaned back in his chair. He tapped his fingers on the table and shook his head. "Maybe later. For now, perfect your skills."

"Maybe I could help you here."

He squinted at Hote, and Hote remembered the finger bone and flesh he had taken. Would he ever be trusted?

Ahmed did the predictable. "Ask your mother. She's got a lot of weight. Besides she's probably the closest to a dragon expert there is."

Hote nodded. He had been dismissed.

CHAPTER 20

The Groombug's Story

-1-

"I just saved your life," Groombug says. The gravity with which he speaks makes my thoughts swirl. I don't know whether to snort in derision or take him seriously. I am afraid to take him seriously. I rest my snout on the ground, and he stands on the end of my nose.

"That red dragon, you saw? She's been collected; I'm sure of it."

"Collected? She didn't look collected to me. She was flying free."

"What happens is that a faker attacks dragons to take their groombugs."

"Faker?"

"Automaton. Nonliving but made to resemble a dragon. By taking their groombugs, it forces dragons to accompany it to the Collectors' camp. The dragons, in order to get their grooming, must go out and bring other dragons in."

"How do you know this?"

"It happened to me."

"How?"

"Listen."

I clamp my jaws shut and listen to Groombug's tale:

-2-

I and Seemor were feasting on the manna belt with the rest of our clan when a strange dragon flew up. Her scales were dull. Her eyes desperate. She had lost her groombug and needed help to find him. Or so she said.

Seemor and others agreed to follow the strange dragon to where she said she last saw her groombug.

Instead they ran through a firewall.

I was in Seemor's third ear. Being high elder and larger than the others, she had a particularly deep ear, so I had more than the usual protection. Over the heat and the roar of flames, I heard the screams of the dying groombugs. I was badly burned. Once through the flames, a spray hit us, and Seemor yelled, "Leap off."

I did. What groombugs had been still clinging to their dragons were washed off. I fell amid their remains until I was completely covered.

The spray stunned the dragons, and they kept calling the names of their groombugs, even as they grew groggy and finally collapsed.

Outworlders in dragon skins attached hooks and ropes to the dragons and pulled them away, even as some feebly tried to resist.

Seemor managed to cry out for me to hide, before she fully succumbed.

All of my fur was burned off. I managed to pull myself aside where I could avoid being trampled. No one noticed me. I was swept up in the debris of the dead, mixed with dragon scales, offal, and mud. I rolled in the mud to protect and soothe my burned body.

I may have passed out. I was next aware of yells, not of the dragons who were unconscious but of the Collectors pulling them along. I was too weak to follow.

Again I passed out. When I came to, I searched through holes and tunnels in their ship just large enough to admit me.

-3-

Groombug's tale is too horrible to hear. Yet I cannot cease hearing. I have to know more. "What's a ship?"

"You've seen the Watcher's dome? It's really a ship, like a big shell, a vessel, a carrier that comes from a different world."

I feel queasy.

Groombug continues his story.

-4-

Once inside, I found dragons trapped in enclosures like caves. I couldn't get close enough to speak to them because walls, made of a wind too stiff to move, divide the enclosures. It's called a force field.

I found other groombugs wandering about, a lost expression in their eyes. They couldn't tell me anything I didn't already know. They were injured and grieving. And when they felt the death of their dragons, they closed their eyes, sank down, and met the gryphon.

I was the only elder, but I couldn't convince them to cling to life. What is life without one's dragon?

The Collectors were not aware of the groombugs. I spent time as I healed, spying throughout the ship. They would peel off their second skin at night. Their own skin was smooth, the color of soil in its many shades. Like the color of groombugs but unchanging.

I noticed other outworlders, who were different. They wore different skins and did not live on the ship. They seemed somehow distant, uneasy with the Collectors.

Not until I got outside did I see that the ship is invisible except where it catches the sun's glare or where the grime covers it. I was afraid. The ship is always there to collect more dragons. And to manage the fake dragon they had built to send out. An automaton, convincingly like a real dragon. To spy. That much I surmised. It's hard to tell from a real dragon, except for certain details. For example, it has no groombug and remains shiny. It gathers information through the eyes and sends it to the outworlders. It has no third ear at the base of its head.

-5-

"How did you get away?"

"When I healed sufficiently, I searched for Seemor and can only say she is gone. Where, I don't know. Since the Collectors didn't know I exist, I had no trouble fleeing their camp. Starved for manna, I sought out the belt. That's where I met you. As you see, I found you. And…" Groombug's narrative fades. He seems about to say more and doesn't. I'm sure he's keeping something to himself.

His tale leaves me numb. I can't wrap my mind around it. I don't want to think about it; or the unicorns, or the red dragon's attack. It is too horrible.

Still, if he is right, I need to show him my appreciation. The red dragon, evil as she was, had been good enough to ask the groombug his name. Can I do less? I feel ashamed for not knowing it, and the longer I've gone without knowing, the more ashamed I feel. He might think I don't care.

"You never did tell me your name."

"You never asked."

"So, I guess…"

"Balofur."

"What?"

"Balofur. That's my name."

A name befitting an elder. Would Tweekie have earned such a name later on?

If what Balofur said is true, Collectors can intrude anywhere. He is an elder after all and filled with knowledge, so surely he knows what he is talking about. Ants of anxiety crawl in my gorge and up and down my legs.

I bring my head up, and Balofur rides my snout all the way.

"We need to get out of here," I say.

"Why?"

I don't want to admit to a fear of the Collectors. "Because of the unicorns."

"Unicorns?"

"Because of the Collectors then." There's no denying it.

"That is the danger. Follow my lead." Balofur turns to face the direction the red dragon had pointed.

"Won't that lead us closer?"

"Yes, it will."

"That's stupid. I don't want to fly into the enemy's maw."

"Sometimes the best place to hide is under the enemy's nose. Trust me."

"I trust you to be my groombug. Not enough to hide under some enemy's nose."

"They won't expect us so close. We will stay within a few days of the manna belt, so you can feed, but not close enough to be spotted. Besides, the wind is more consistent and persistent there."

"No." I shake my head.

Balofur clings like a wart. "I know what I'm talking about."

Pushy, superior Balofur. My resentment boils to the surface. "You are ugly and bossy, and you're not Tweekie."

What there is of Balofur's fur rises. "Are you so beautiful? Are you so wise? Ugly and bossy though I am, I am here. Tweekie is not."

I push myself up. "Listen, I'm bigger than you, and leaving. You have to come along."

I shift forward, and the brace slips. "Ow!"

I fall back, and Balofur shies away from me onto a nearby branch.

"Get it off of you. Try rolling to the right."

Hating myself, I comply.

"Now the left."

I keep yelping, certain my wings are shattered, but it's the brace that's broken. A little hopping about, and I am completely free of it. My wings, joints still frozen, have greater movement. As much as my shoulders allow, I can lift my wings and lower them. Unfortunately I don't seem fit to fly. Not without the support of the brace. Nevertheless, I discover I can set my arms under me as legs and walk.

Balofur wins, after all, on our staying. I can't walk far because I am too bruised. We do walk, though, until we find a rise that ends in a cave with an open area before it.

"We'll stay here until we get some strength into your wings."

CHAPTER 21

If Only

-1-

Traveler had moved Baaden to an island in the middle of a lake. Bad move. A family of gryphons lived there, and when they didn't play, they quarreled. He didn't know where they found a stinky leg bone with flesh hanging from it, but the last time he looked, he saw a gryphon fighting a vulture over it. Traveler must return him to the bog island. Moose or no moose, he felt more comfortable there, if any place on this planet could be comfortable.

-2-

Hote sat at a work station, watching through the visor. He didn't mind the compromise with Amber. After her talk with Chief Li, he was allowed to open channels to the other Watcher outposts.

Lily, a plain-faced woman with large teeth, spoke to Hote from the Redwood Station. "There are very few die-offs, so even though the gryphons are scavengers, they've learned to subsist on manna."

"Manna?"

"Dragon food."

"Oh, yeah," Hote recalled. "We got some samples of it. Sort of a jelly-like substance. Clear and very sweet. Full of nutrients. We've been replicating it and using it as a sweetener."

"Yes. It dribbles to the ground. A lot of other animals depend on it, too. Also the gryphons eat fruits. They live in small family groups."

She spoke with animation, her smile constant. Hote's view strayed to the mountain steps where the two dragons had played. The steps were formed from natural fractures in the rocky face of the peak. They varied from shallow to steep. If only he hadn't run out of the station, he'd still be there with his own research project.

"Anything on the dragons?"

She gave a slight cough into a large hand. "Nothing much. Air samples did show signs of dragon activity at night near the station. That was weeks ago."

"You see anything?"

"We don't consider them a high priority. Our night scopes are trained on gryphons."

Because of the problems Hote had caused.

He scanned other channels and caught a report from a shuttle.

The voice was agitated. "…An entire herd, gone. We zeroed in on them after sighting the vultures."

The view took form in Hote's visor. Huge black birds with naked heads soared over a prairie or perched on swollen white bodies with stiff outstretched legs. Gryphons, vultures, foxes and little dinosaurs tugged at the flesh.

Chief Li appeared in Hote's view screen. "All Watchers. Meet in the dayroom immediately.

Members, grumbling or silent, pushed away from their work stations.

Li's image vanished. Before Hote dropped the visor from his eyes, he saw that the shuttle had moved into the scene of carnage for an enlarged view. The twisted form of a pale head in grass showed dried blood on the forehead.

Hote's gut clenched. Murder had come to Paradise.

He followed the others into the dayroom. Body-conforming chairs had been arranged in a circle. Watchers took their seats. Amber appeared across the room beside Chief Li. Her gaze drifted, bypassed Hote, once, twice, and then settled on him. No one else seemed to notice him, except to stumble over his legs where he sat.

Chief Li rose, tall and lean, and lifted his hand in a peace sign, a signal for the meeting to begin.

With heart-felt emphasis, propelled by the slaughter, everyone recited the Allegiance to the Guiding Congress and the Watchers' Code of Observation and Noninterference. In fact, Reed shouted it.

Then they awaited the Chief's speech. Gaze fixed in space, he seemed to focus inward for the right words before he began.

"As most of you know, the Guiding Congress has allowed outworlders limited harvesting. You have just seen an example."

Indignant cries sprang forth.

"Limited?" Sparky sputtered amid flashes from her hair. "An entire herd slaughtered, and that's limited?" She threw up her hands.

"Cool, everyone." Hunter's calm voice intruded. "Keep our cool."

They quieted enough for Li to speak. "The unicorns will soon reproduce according to the species' need for population stability. Our studies have shown that."

Amber's warm voice rose. "Let's not take this as a positive outcome, Chief Li. Outworlders have found the dragon planet too attractive because it is safe and habitable."

Li explained. "Guiding Congress allows limited harvesting because the planet is terraformed, therefore considered artificial."

A sea of remarks closed in:

"It's like an intrusion into Eden. A blasphemy."

"Slaughtered for their horns."

Pip sang a dirge. "I don't like this."

"None of us like it," Amber remarked.

Hote couldn't hold back. He raised his hand and waggled it. "What happened to the prime directive of noninterference? You got Redwood Station punished for one person exposing himself to dragons. And here, outworlders slaughter a whole herd and no one sees it?"

Hote wondered how many knew he was responsible for the station's punishment. If anyone did, they didn't let on. Various eyes caught him, and heads nodded agreement.

"We need to have the planet declared a treasure, not to be touched," someone cried.

"How many outworlders have permission?" Hunter asked.

"Just Commander 2Ray1's ship, the I.D. Express," Chief Li said. "It was part of the contract that allowed them permanent parking so we could use their launchpad for the importation of supplies from the Academy."

At Father's name, Hote gritted his teeth. He glanced at Amber and saw nothing in her expression to indicate her feelings toward the commander. The farther away from him, the better for both Hote and his mother.

"Are there other species being taken, besides the unicorns?" Hunter continued.

"Some ferns and some flowering plants," Li said. "That's all, according to the report. The crew doesn't venture outside the ship except to send their collection shuttles."

The room filled with voiced opinions.

"It doesn't speak well for a planet that's supposed to be kept pristine." This was Maximus.

"What happened to the petition Amber sent Guiding Congress to declare the planet off-limits?" Sparky asked.

Chief Li gestured toward the seated figure next to him. "Dr. Kellyamber, you want to comment on that?"

She stood, barely level with the Chief's shoulder. Her voice was like silk. "Guiding Congress responded to our petition with this statement. Because the planet is terraformed, it is considered artificial. Watchers were originally commissioned by the Academy of Sciences to study the planet and to determine the feasibility of harvesting or possibly introducing species that can be harvested."

Reed raised his hand and yelled, "That's short-sighted. Don't they realize the uniqueness of a planet without predators? There is something beyond price here that is not duplicated anywhere else."

"I agree and included that in our petition. Therefore Guiding Congress has given us these possibilities. A planet can be declared off limits if, Number 1, it is sufficiently hazardous to visitors; Number 2, its life forms are in danger of extinction; or Number 3, a sentient species owns the planet and denies permission to exploit its resources. Can you think of any way the planet, precious as it is to us, qualifies according to congressional standards?"

Some surveyed the roomful of members. Others looked down. Ahmed asked, "Who else can we petition?"

Amber didn't hesitate to reply. "I've petitioned every authority I can think of. They say they will send someone, whoever they can spare, which could take months or not even then. I'd like to get the attention of the High Arbiter."

The High Arbiter was like a god, a final authority. Hote had heard he/she was a shapeshifter. Was their situation important enough to attract an arbiter, even a minor one?

Chief Li chewed his lips, gave Amber a regretful look. "Surely we can confer directly with Commander 2Ray1, since his is the only non-Watcher ship that's been allowed onto the planet."

Other than its fleet of collection drones, Hote thought. He couldn't read his mother's expression, but he sensed her tension. She looked away from the Chief. Everyone in the room knew she wanted nothing to do with Hote's father, the man who destroys. Only a slim communication existed between I.D. Express and the Watcher Base, just enough to maintain the launch system that beamed items onto the planet—or off. Ahmed sometimes went with Maximus, Hunter, and Reed to pick up supplies.

Amid grumbling, the meeting broke up. Members filed past his mother, squeezed her shoulder, patted her arm, or gave her a nod. "Don't give up, Amber," several said.

Hote caught up with her in time to hear her ask Chief Li, "Do we have the Academy's support?"

Li nodded. "They promised to send us an extra shuttle craft, to replace Traveler until we should recover it."

"Retrieving the automaton could take a long time, if ever."

Li smiled. "The shuttle could well be a permanent loan. They're not against that.

To search for dragons, Hote wished. If only he could take part.

CHAPTER 22

Rehabilitation

While we shelter in the cave, Balofur takes it upon himself to try to rehabilitate me.

"What you need is exercise. We will begin with shoulder shrugs and circles. It will add to your flexibility and strength, so you can better negotiate air eddies."

So I stand on a cave shelf overlooking a meadow with Balofur perched on my head. We begin with shoulder shrugs, up and down, right and left. Forward rotations, back rotations. I hadn't realized there are so many ways to move my shoulders.

I groan. "I'm tired."

"Don't whine."

"Are you punishing me?"

"No. Why do you ask?"

"For insulting you."

"You have a right to your feelings."

I sound just like Batwing. I say nothing more and resume the exercise.

"Listen, Rumplewing. You feel discouraged. Remember what happened when you flew to meet the Great Mother?"

Over my exertions, I mutter, "She saved me."

"Why?"

"I don't know." I grunt with effort.

"She saved you for a purpose. We don't just exist. We each have our purpose."

I slow, stop. "What is my purpose?"

"Only you can discover that. It is not my place or anyone else's to tell you."

"Do you know your purpose?"

"Some of it. Presently it is to help you gain strength and knowledge."

I feel like disagreeing, which would be wrong and foolish. Everyone knows a groombug's purpose is to care for his dragon. Presently I am Balofur's dragon.

I throw myself into shoulder rolls.

In less time than I expect, limbering and strengthening the shoulders does help to give more maneuverability. I can remain upright during the sudden wind gusts. Yet this ability doesn't take away the fact that I am still greatly reduced in my flying ability. I can barely lower my arms below my body, and not at all above. So I lumber through the air like a mindless wisp. without pride.

CHAPTER 23

Moving

-1-

Traveler flew to Baaden with supplies, but he didn't unload them until the automaton returned him to the bog island and he put his camp in order. Once the tent was up, he unloaded the supplies and was pleased to find food, movies, a cooling fan, insect spray, and last of all, boots. Knee highs with opalescent scales. Dragon boots were so rare, so precious, no tycoon could afford them. He sat on his camp stool and slipped the boots on. He stomped about, felt the hug on his legs, the give at his ankles. Excellent. He returned to his seat where he inserted his earbuds.

"Stilwell, just to let you know, I got the boots. You said they were a gift from Commander. Thank him for me. They fit well and should provide protection for my feet in the bog—and sulfur springs and swamps. You never know what you might step into here. The ground looks solid, and then with the next step you could burn a leg off or disappear into a sinkhole."

-2-

Hote rested one hand on the shuttle the Academy had sent them. Outdated, it stood, dismissed as unreliable. Its invisibility paint had worn so thin, the craft appeared as a faint cutout against a blue sky. Insubstantial, as if half sunk into the void. Insubstantial, the way Hote felt. He ignored the feeling and scratched at a dark spot on the shuttle skin. It would need two or three coats of light-bending paint to cover the whole craft. And still, the Chief seemed to dismiss his requisition for invisipaint and other supplies.

Hote climbed aboard, took the auto-conforming seat, and picked up the headset. It adapted to his head, so it felt as snug as a sock. Hote lowered the visor over his eyes and surveyed his surroundings. The interior smelled of dust and old plastic. The control panel lit up. A scan told him the drive was disconnected. It would reset at his thought command. Did he have the mental discipline?

Chief Li had okayed his request to repair the shuttle, provided he didn't fly it out of the compound. There again, the lack of trust. Still he felt a sense of authority over the shuttle. He'd studied its structure and operation. He had spent hours each day, studying, planning, tinkering. No one would miss Baaden's expertise. Soon they would rely on Hote, master mechanic.

Eventually the drive melded, and he raised and lowered the craft to test it. The whine that would have betrayed the shuttle's presence was gone. The magnets that gave it silent flight seemed to function well. Hote raised and lowered the ship, raised and lowered it. He checked the locator that would take him to any station if he so commanded. What if he should visit the Redwood Station? Chief Li would forbid it. Suppose he flew only a few kilometers beyond Base. Or to one of the other stations?

On the other hand, maybe he could complete a task left hanging. Ruling Congress was supposed to search for Baaden and Traveler. He sensed Amber's disgust when it handed over the search to I.D. Express. As far as he could tell, his father had issued no report on their progress or that they had even searched. Perhaps it was time to do something on his own. Talk to Father. Provided the locator could be set for his ship.

"Computer, set a course for I.D. Express."

"Course set."

Course set! It worked.

The craft rose above the shuttle pad, the playing field, the buildings, the natural garden, and the compound walls. Hote sat back and let the craft carry him away from Base. It didn't take long for the grounds to shrink into the distance. His nerves tingled. What he was doing was wrong. Breaking the rules again. He should return now, and no one would be the wiser. A thrill of fear, adventure, and the possibility of becoming a hero rushed through him. Minutes fled, leaving him with a sense of freedom too powerful to challenge. He watched the craft's shadow ripple over forest, grasslands, and eventually mountains. At one point he entered patchy fog with windows of forest and plains passing beneath him.

Something struck his craft with enough force to jolt it. Hote grabbed the controls and hastened to land.

CHAPTER 24

The Outworlder's Craft

Through no fault of my own I smack into a large object, cloaked by clouds in an echo canyon. I ricochet and plummet, aware the entire time of lance-shaped trees and iron boulders that spin larger in my vision, eagerly reaching for my remains. With Balofur's calm talk and my quick reflexes, he manages to direct me to a less injurious landing that merely breaks my bones.

Right away, Balofur, disregards my shaken condition. "That's a ship. Watcher or Collector, I don't know."

"My bones are broken," I groan.

Balofur hardly checks. "Bruised. Not broken. Get up. Stand your ground. Look dignified."

It is the first time I've seen an outworlder. It pours from the ship, pauses in sun-brightened mist, and then edges toward us. I flash on the dead unicorns, the red dragon, and ships that capture dragons.

Stopping a dragon's length from us, it lifts its wingless arms midway and emits a garbled coo.

The outworlder stands more erect than us dragons because it has no tail. Its face is strangely shortened, topped by fur. Otherwise it lacks hair or even scales, except for a brown and white skin that Balofur says is removable. It conforms to its body.

"Move your mouth and pretend to speak."

"What...?"

"Never mind. I'll be your voice. It won't even notice."

Balofur contracts himself into my third ear. He knows the outworlder speech and translates it for me as he lashes out in words. The outworlder is apologetic, its voice soft. I tremble at the tone Balofur takes, roaring in a deep voice that seems incongruous with his size, accusing it not only of seeking my harm but of committing the worst of crimes toward all dragondom. Slavery, extermination, experimentation, and general embarrassment. He speaks so fast, I collect his words without full understanding.

It offers to fix my injuries; I catch that.

"No, thanks." Then just for my ears, "Leave."

I trundle onto a mound, leap into the air, and manage to gain enough height to fly. It watches us through wisps of cloud until we are gone from its sight.

I am so caught up in what happened, I pay little attention to the country we sail over. Once my understanding catches up to what had transpired, I say, "It seemed friendly enough."

"That may be true, but we can't be sure. We know Collectors are here to capture dragons, for some unknown reason. As for Watchers, I don't know their role, so how can we trust them?"

It's the first time Balofur admits any ignorance.

"That was a Watcher," I say, not with any conviction. I had never seen the Watchers of Forbidden Mountain, but they seem similar to this brown and white-clad outworlder. Besides, it felt friendly.

I am amazed at Balofur's ability to speak the outworlder's language and simultaneously translate for me.

He denies any special ability. "I was using simspeak, where I speak fast enough that it appears to be simultaneous. Really, it isn't."

"How did this come about?"

"It's something I developed. Any groombug can do it if so inclined."

I doubt Tweekie could. Besides, if Balofur were Tweekie, we would be far away from any place where an outworlder ship might appear. We'd be far, far from the Collector camp. Balofur doesn't want to leave the area. This hiding under their nose doesn't sound right to me. He is up to something. He was with the Collectors long enough to learn their language. And he should be dead since he was separated from his dragon.

Is there really a Seemor? Maybe Balofur works with the outworlders, helping to capture dragons. Maybe he is an automaton; he certainly isn't like any groombug I knew. He never sleeps, he can simspeak. I'm sure he knows things he is keeping from me.

What can I do about it? How can I confront him?

An automaton isn't alive, so it can't bleed. I will run a test.

We settle on a hill. I stretch out in the grass to relax. Balofur hums, almost lulling me to sleep. Trickery. That's what it is. I, too, can be tricky. I wait, eyes closed as he works closer to my mouth. Right to the edge. *Take a step, Balofur. Another step. That's it.*

I flick my head and snap him into my jaws. He squeaks. I chomp down just enough to pinch him and taste blood.

He screams.

I spit him out.

"Why did you do that?" He huddles in the grass beneath my snout.

"I wanted to be sure."

"About what?"

"That you were real. That you weren't guiding me into captivity."

"That's not even logical. Since when would a groombug be an automaton? How would I go about waylaying dragons and guiding them into captivity?"

"Well, you simspeak."

"I explained that."

"You never sleep."

"Of course I sleep."

"Not that I've ever noticed."

Balofur sighs. "I can sleep with half of my brain at a time, closing one eye while keeping the other open and then switching. All groombugs do this. Tweekie would have done it."

"I don't know. I was worried."

Balofur leaps to the top of my head and bores between my scales. I feel hot acid. "Ow! What are you doing?"

"I'm drilling a hole, so I can check the inside of your skull for brains."

"It hurts."

"Of course it hurts. I can make my saliva acid. All groombugs can control the potency of their saliva. Did you know that?"

"No, I never asked. Ow!" I shake my head. Then I remember Wily's groombug and how he insulted me by spitting saliva that sizzled. All because I asked him to be my groombug, since Wily was leaving to meet the gryphon.

Balofur stops his attack. "You are such a child."

"Even a child can fear capture."

Balofur calms. "Never before have I attacked a dragon. It's something groombugs don't do. I apologize." He slides down where we can meet, eye to eye.

And of course dragons don't attack groombugs. They protect them. But I had to be sure that Balofur is a groombug. I had to. So, why do I feel like a betrayer? Untrustworthy? I want to weep. "Did I hurt you very badly?"

"Not badly."

"I'm sorry. I had to know."

"Well, now you do."

"So, how did you come to know their speech?"

"Didn't I tell you I was injured and needed to recuperate? I hid and watched and learned. I looked for ways to rescue Seemor." Balofur shrugs. "But she's gone, and I needed to escape." He leaps back onto my head.

He seems too dismissive.

CHAPTER 25

The Sighting

The dragon flew off. Hote scurried into the craft, overcome with excitement. What he had witnessed was momentous. He turned on the intercom and was immediately blasted with, "Hote, return to Base. Now."

That's exactly what he intended to do. Chief Li was angry he had left the base without permission, but when he heard of Hote's discovery, he would be delighted.

"Computer, set a course for Watcher Base, top speed."

Hote rode his excitement all the way, replaying the meeting of the dragon in his mind, seeing nothing of note in his surroundings. He felt like a hero.

Amber was waiting for him at the shuttle pad. As he climbed out of the craft, she asked, "Are you all right?"

She looked troubled, yet sympathetic.

"I'm okay."

"Chief Li called a meeting and scolded us. Bantering, he said, was acceptable and even welcome, but he blamed himself for not stopping the teasing when it turned nasty. When they first called Baaden, Bad-one and then it went from there."

Huh? This had nothing to do with Hote's unauthorized flight. "What are you talking about?"

"The Chief didn't name names, but he said the guilty knew who they were. We were afraid for you when you ran away."

Hote leaned back against the ship. "What?"

"The Chief wants to talk to you."

"What—I didn't—"

She gave him a gentle shove. "I'll meet you afterwards."

Pip. Reed. It was obvious they had snickered at his expense. Maybe the moon twins, he wasn't sure. Hote ambled to the Chief's office. As soon as he entered, Li rose from behind his desk.

"Chief, I didn't—"

Li raised a hand for silence. "Hote, next time don't run away. You come straight to me, or Ahmed, or your mother."

"I didn't run away!"

"You most assuredly did."

Hote didn't mean to yell. "I was repairing the craft! I wasn't running away. I was just doing my job. And-and I took it for a test run."

Li seemed caught between a frown and a puzzled expression. His voice dropped. "You were gone a long time for a test run."

Hote had second thoughts about reporting a meeting with a talking dragon. Chief would think he was hallucinating. Maybe he was. He matched his tone to Li's. "I thought I'd look around for Traveler. Just a quick look." Still he needed to report something about the dragon; it was important. "What took so long was, well, a dragon flew into my ship."

A moment of silence fell during which Li seemed to search Hote's face for signs of what? Delusion, probably.

"Go on."

"It really shook up the ship. A loud thud. I had to check things out. Make sure nothing was broken."

"Did you take a video?"

Hote was glad he didn't go into greater detail, for he had no proof of the sighting. "Nossir. By the time I could figure out where the recorder was and how to use it, the dragon was gone."

Li grunted. "I see. Next time you want to take the ship on a test run, you ask my permission. Understand?"

"Yessir."

The two left the Chief's office together. Hote intended to pick up something to eat in the dayroom, but that was where the Chief was headed. Hote hung back until Li passed through the door. Then Hote entered, only to see Li join a group of members who were listening to a scientific report. It was just winding down when Hunter got up to introduce the next speech. "And now the moon twins will illuminate their findings for us."

"I'm Luna," one said, smiling.

"And I am Europa."

The food replicator and drink dispenser were too close to the group. Hote didn't want to be seen. Just as the twins rose to give their presentations, he fled to the garden.

"Hote, over here." Amber was already seated at a picnic table in a leafy pattern of shade. "I got you some food."

He didn't realize how hungry he was until she placed a warm vitaroll with his designated me-steak strips before him on a tray. The roll, crisp on the outside with a buttery chew on the inside, contained just enough manna to give it a delectable sweetness. He pressed the steak strip into the roll and bit down. Its flavor flowed over his tongue. "Thanks, Amber."

"It's lovely out here, isn't it?" She was giving him enough time to settle down. Something—a frog perhaps—splashed in the stream that flowed through the garden. A slight breeze cut through sultry air.

"Am I taking you away from the presentations?"

"I can catch up. Right now I'd rather be with you. Would you like to tell me what happened?"

Hote chewed halfway through his meal, picking his words. "Everyone's given up on Baaden and Traveler, haven't they?"

"It appears that way."

"Well, I was working on the shuttle, fixing it, and then I thought it might be a good idea to take it out for a while. Sort of look for Traveler."

Amber was examining her hands, rubbing them.

"And that's when I got hit by a dragon."

She looked up, with a slight intake of breath.

"So I landed and it talked to me."

"Talked? What do you mean?"

"It talked."

He recognized her look of withheld judgement. "Did it hoot, growl, moan?"

"It…" This wasn't going to be easy. Who else could he tell who would lend half an ear and half an understanding? He had to tell someone. "It spoke our language."

The expected semi-disbelief mixed with a willingness to be convinced appeared on her face.

Hote plunged on. "It was yelling, accusing me of all sorts of crimes against dragons, from kidnapping to slavery. And then it left."

"Did it use those words?"

"Either those or pretty close."

"Did you record any of this?"

"I—! No. I couldn't find the equipment until too late."

"So you have no proof." She shook her head. Started to say something, only to shake her head again. "I want to believe you. If what you experienced can be proved, it can change things for this planet. For the better."

Hote wolfed the rest of his food. Angry at himself for failure, angry at Amber for pointing it out.

Amber waited for him to finish.

Amid birdsong he swallowed the last bite and heard a distant chorus of moans. Not for the first time. What creature made those moans? Wolves? Gryphons? Dinosaurs? Dragons? He was tempted to stomp off and brood about boxes, but too much had happened. He tried to force calm into his voice, only to sound bitter.

"There's more. And you'll probably be upset. Before the dragon ran into me, I'd ordered a course for I.D. Express. No one was doing anything about Traveler and Baaden. So I decided to give it a try."

Amber rubbed her face.

"And there's more still. It's not just Traveler. It's Radiant. Somehow I feel the boxes have something to do with her. Anyway I want to find her."

"Oh, Hote." Amber gripped his hand. "I want to find her, too. I've always wanted both of you. After years of trying, I don't know why 2Ray1 suddenly seemed eager to give you to me. Why not Radiant, too?"

"I want to find her."

Amber's lips folded between her teeth. "There's something I never told you. You weren't ready. I think you are now. When your father returned you to me, he also gave me a message from Radiant. Here. I'll show you."

She passed her visor to Hote and commanded an image. In his mind Hote saw the words superimposed on air.

"Hello, Mother.

By now Father must have sent you my dimwit brother. Don't concern yourself about me. I'm where I want to be, playing the gladiator at StarCircus, slaying dragons. Don't you worry, they're robots. Not very convincing ones at that.

Goodbye, Mother. Say goodbye to Hote.

Radiant."

She had finally succeeded in sounding just like Father, a man she'd tried for most of her life to emulate. Hote returned the visor.

"Radiant is gone," Amber whispered. "I wanted both of my children back and had to settle for one."

Boxes. Hote couldn't help the crazy thought. "There was a box, a kit. In it was—"

"A doll that needed to be assembled, I know." Amber sounded impatient, but gentle. "What has this to do with anything?"

"I can't assemble it. And it belongs to Radiant."

"Oh, Hote."

She probably thought he was regressing. He was simply where he'd always been since leaving Father. "This thing inside me wants me to—"

She put her finger on Hote's lips. "Sh. Sh."

"And sometimes I feel like I'm being pulled into the void."

"I know. I know." She took both his hands in hers, as if afraid he *would* disappear. "The mind is powerful. You must concentrate on something else."

"I know." He'd heard it before from Ahmed and Chief Li, and from Amber. *Don't think of the boxes. Think of something else. Something positive.*

Amber's knuckles went white, and Hote felt the pain of her grip. Wanted to feel it.

Her voice was intense. "I could swear you look as if your soul is ripped from you and in the void, but Ahmed checked you when you first came. There is nothing inside you that doesn't belong.

Hote sighed, drew his lips into a straight line. The story hadn't changed. Neither had the remedy.

"You've got to believe what you feel isn't real. You've got to meditate on the fact that you are perfectly healthy and you must think healthy thoughts. Every time you are tempted to dwell on being interpenetrated or about something so irrelevant as a doll in a box, take a break from studying. Go to the gym. Work out. Play."

"I know. I will," he murmured. For all the good it would do.

Just before bed, Hote decided to try something new. He sat cross-legged on his cot, placed the visor on his head, and conjured a drawing program. Before him, the air vibrated, ready for his hands to form images. He took deep breaths, let them out slowly. He let his hands rise almost of their own volition. They floated like leaves in a pond and drifted. Drifted. Without conscious thought he allowed them to sketch in the air.

Squares appeared. Cubes. Boxes. Closed because something lurked inside them. Something unpleasant.

His insides quivered. He took a deep breath, and it shook as he exhaled.

This is my art project. I can have anything I want in these boxes.

He brought one box before his mind's eye and enlarged it until it filled his vision.

I will place something beautiful inside.

But what? What? Unable to conjure a positive image, he put the project away.

CHAPTER 26

The Far Country

I convince Balofur we should get as far from outworlders as possible. He agrees after I promise to learn their language. Not something I look forward to.

I fly over mountains that are craggy and full of caves. Even as I soar and flap awkwardly, covering a great distance, I grumble. "What's the point of learning something I'll never use?"

"Don't be so sure. Again, repeat after me."

I try to repeat words he taught me. They are unpronounceable. "I can't do it."

"Nonsense. You will learn. You will say the words properly."

I give a halfhearted effort, mispronouncing on purpose.

"You cannot remain an ignorant child all your life. Knowledge is power, freedom, and life."

"When am I going to use this?"

"Who can say? Should you be captured, wouldn't you rather be prepared?"

"Couldn't I just show them how I feel through color change or a tail twitch?"

"They wouldn't understand. For one thing, they don't have tails. For another, they can't change their colors. Most of their talk is through the mouth."

I huff steam through my nostrils. "How limited."

CHAPTER 27

The Assignment

-1-

Hote raced on the treadmill in the rec room, faster and faster, his breath masking the twitter of birds and the rush of a brook in the holo image that surrounded him. Imaginary dust rose from his feet on an imaginary dirt path.

Even so, he couldn't get the message out of his mind.

Don't concern yourself about me. I'm where I want to be, playing the gladiator at StarCircus, slaying dragons. Don't you worry, they're robots.

As he concentrated, his legs gradually slowed.

This message dated from the time Amber had received him back, traumatized.

Radiant was alive and happy, as proved by a message that made her sound like the father she admired. Fearless, arrogant, and cold. Now Hote saw something else, and it nearly stopped him. StarCircus used robots. Baaden and Traveler had disappeared. Could Father have kidnapped and beamed them to StarCircus? And why hadn't Radiant sent any more messages?

Hote didn't want to dwell on these questions. His pace picked up. Faster he ran, pushing his limits until he could focus on the burn in his legs, his reach for breath.

"Hote."

He slowed. The holo image of scenery faded. He stepped from the treadmill, dripping sweat.

Amber stood in the doorway. "Hote, Chief Li just asked me to his office, and I think it may concern the both of us. I want you to follow and wait outside the door."

Hote grabbed a deodorizing towel to wipe himself off and then followed her.

She left the office door open, and Chief Li didn't tell her to close it. Hote waited just out of view.

"We have some interesting news," Li said. "I. D. Express has sent us a request for two animal caretakers."

"For the unicorns?"

"For Dragons."

"Dragons? Are they planning on taking dragons?"

Hote's heart gave a rush. Had his Father captured Baaden after all and planned to use Traveler to hunt dragons?

"Looks like they already have," Li said.

Amber groaned. "Guiding Congress gave them permission?"

"Evidently so. In a way, it's an opportunity for us to find out if Baaden is there, whether willing or not, along with our automaton. We could send Ahmed and one other."

"Me." Amber sounded insistent.

Hote knew she could barely think of 2Ray1 without gnashing her teeth.

But to see dragons close up!

"As much as I don't want to go," she said, "I see the necessity. I can petition 2Ray1 to take his crew and leave, never to return."

A face-to-face confrontation. He didn't envy her that.

"It's best," Li said, "if you send a petition. You needn't see him directly. You need to stay with Hote, take care of him."

"I'll go with Amber." Hote stepped into view before the open door. "I understand my father. I'm not afraid of him; he can't hurt me. And I've always wanted to work with dragons."

Besides, Hote needed to prove dragons could talk.

Li didn't try hard to discourage them. With feigned reluctance, he agreed to shuttle Dr Kelly Amber and her son to the outworlder ship as dragon caretakers. On a temporary basis, of course.

Hote expected to steer clear of Father. As for the dragons, could he and Amber safely approach? They would threaten, but would they attack?

And would the entity that inhabited his cells behave?

-2-

Hote and Amber sat behind Maximus, the only passengers in the Watcher craft, all three dressed in green Watcher uniforms.

Hote ran over his last exchange with Ahmed before they left Base. *"Can't say I'd want to be in your place, spending any great time in I.D. Express."*

"I know what it's like."

"Do you? You haven't seen it in what? Two years?"

Amber placed her hand on the back of Maximus's pilot chair. "Is there anything we need to know?"

"We get there, it's a pretty desolate sight. Grounds are not landscaped because the crew never leaves the ship. No need when they've got drones to harvest for them."

"How long do you suppose they've been collecting dragons?"

Maximus shrugged as he concentrated on his instruments. "Don't know."

"Ever since they got Traveler," Hote said.

"If they have Traveler." Amber obviously didn't want him to reach unfounded conclusions. He must be more scientific.

"You'll want to know about the door," Maximus continued. "The door you enter is part of a larger door that allows movement of larger goods. It's all controlled by a pointer, which only a crew member can use. So if you want to enter or exit the ship, you'll need someone with the pointer, which is programmed to the door."

They fell silent and watched the passing scene.

Amber held Hote's hand and whispered, "It's been two years, since I've seen your father's ship. The day he gave you back to me. When..." She started and then seemed to collect her thoughts. "When 2Ray1 turned you over to me, you were so quiet."

If she was haunted by all this, he couldn't tell. She seemed to marvel that it had been that long ago.

Hote tried to remember but the event seemed muffled with false memory or no memory at all.

"The ship doctor had checked you over and said you were free of infection, safe to take with me. I could tell, though, that your time with your father hadn't been happy. After a week or two, you began to…say things."

Hote didn't want her to be delicate with him. He needed to show her he wasn't embarrassed by their conversation. "I was afraid of the launchpad. I don't remember why. I think Radiant played a prank, I'm not sure. I remember Father forcing me onto the pad, probably to teach me it was safe. It wasn't. He put me in a box and sent me into the void." *And someone collided with me and is now inside me.* Hote couldn't tell her that last part; it grieved her so to hear it.

"Boxes," she said. "Is that why you talk of boxes? Because 2Ray1 put you in a box?"

Hote wanted to say no. "I don't know. Maybe." There was more to it than that. Nevertheless he sensed her relief that his talk may not be entirely crazy.

"Why did you marry him?"

"Hm." She raised her eyebrows. "I guess I thought I saw something that wasn't there." She chuckled. "I had a…a certain admiration for him."

Had Father been different then? Or was he always the efficient leader who commanded respect and admiration but never love.

She released Hote's hand and shifted her gaze to the window.

A vast forest passed below them, a dark dimpled carpet. A flock of swans flashed white above a winding river that cut a silver course through the forest. And then in and out between trees, six pterodactyls glided and slipped from sight.

"I tried for years to be assigned here. Many applied but didn't make it. They have to be fit, single, and willing to never leave the planet. It's a lifetime commitment."

"You're not single."

"Funny thing. I didn't qualify until 2Ray1 stole both you and Radiant."

Hote didn't know what to say. For years, Amber had been nearby. Not once had Father told him or Radiant.

"Amber, did you know we were on the planet?"

"It was only later I found out that I.D. Express was contracted to provide our import portal. I wanted to reach you. I tried and couldn't."

Hote thought he sensed pain in those last four words. Amber smiled at him and turned away to concentrate on the landscape.

He dared ask one other question. "After that one message, did Radiant ever contact you again?"

Without looking at him, she shook her head.

"There it is," Maximus broke in. "We're touching down."

They had reached the I.D. Express, and it was invisible, a huge shimmer large enough to accommodate a fleet of small collection craft. A landing field that resembled a weedy stretch of desert played confusedly upon the ship's surface. No buildings, no crew attended the field. Unless those buildings were also invisible. Once the Watcher craft landed, a door like a dark square in the air appeared as if into another world. A flash of sun, a shimmer of air on either side and above the door was all that suggested the presence of the outworlder ship. Hote followed Amber onto the field and steeled himself to meet Father. Yet he wasn't surprised when 2Ray1 didn't appear.

Maximus nodded at a uniformed figure that stepped outside. "That's Communications Officer Stilwell. Take care." With that, he closed the shuttle door and lifted off.

Stilwell introduced himself. "Greetings, Doctor Kellyamber. Glad you could be of service. I expect you'll have our problems solved in quick time. We'll show you to your quarters."

"If we may see the dragons first..." Amber acted cordial and undisturbed.

"As you wish."

Hote could only glimpse his surroundings and mostly watched his feet. He could not reminisce over good times spent there, for he and Radiant had been confined to the nursery and a very few other rooms. Children must not be allowed to interfere with the ship's operation. Only in the company of their nanny were they allowed anywhere else, and only as quiet observers.

-3-

Stilwell led them through the entry. "A few steps in, the floor may look solid, but watch."

They stopped.

"Shaft down."

A square seam in the floor appeared beneath their feet. They stood on a service elevator that took them downward.

"Down below is where we keep the dragons."

As they descended, Amber and Hote noticed that the shaft above them remained open. Once they reached bottom and stepped out, a door slid closed behind them. They had entered a dim bay of gray walls. A weak gamy odor, mixed with a disinfectant, met their nostrils. Hote sensed a heavy presence amid the shadows.

"The elevator is now rising so it again forms the floor over us." Stilwell gestured at the closed door. "This here takes a voice command. 'Shaft down.' Step in and you say, 'Shaft up', and the elevator will take you up. Listen though. You can't leave the ship without an escort opening the door for you. You'll also need an escort to take you to the dragons."

"Are they on this floor?" Amber asked.

"Yes, separated from us by a force field that divides them into cells. Your escort will control the force field. You'll see."

Mother and son toured the cells with Stilwell. Hote was glad he hadn't seen his father. He had steeled himself against any rush of memories. Beside the dragon chambers, though, oppression struck. Hote felt uneasy looking at the captives who clustered against the far wall, watching and silent, dark shapes in subdued light. The cells consisted of a long cavern that appeared open, the visitors walking along one wall, separated from the dragons only by an invisible force field. What did he feel from them? Hate? It pressed against him, as heavy as a boulder ready to tumble. "They're so big," he whispered.

"They're infected with some sort of scale rot. It starts as sores and worsens until it invades their insides and kills them."

Amber spoke gently. "Where would they have picked it up? From the crew?"

"Definitely not," Stilwell said. "We've checked and double checked our system. They get cleaned daily with our vibra-light. Even before that, we make sure they come in clean. Despite our best efforts everyone starts showing signs."

"What of their diet?"

"They get dragon food. Brought in from the manna belt and then pasteurized. They're fed once a week. You can see that these cells are kept clean on a daily basis." Along the front of each cell were troughs and containers of water.

Hote wondered how he and Amber would minister to the dragons. Before he could ask, Stilwell said, "We will manage the force field, so you can enter and leave a cell as needed. You can begin with the tame ones. They're docile enough so as to provide no danger."

Tame ones? Hote exchanged a subtle glance with his mother. I.D. Express hadn't just started working with dragons.

"The wild ones will be gassed, to allow you time to examine them while they're unconscious. You will wear protective suits with hoods, to keep you from being gassed and the possibility of being injured."

Hote shook his head, and Amber's reply matched what he would have said. "We hope to win the dragons' trust so we won't need to rely on special suits."

By the time Stilwell returned them to the main floor and pointed them to their quarters, Hote felt a burden of sadness, over the dragons, over the past. He wanted to flee. Instead, he gritted his teeth as he and Amber stood at the entry to their barren quarters. Nothing but the built-in essentials. A cot, a stool, a sanitation stall, all in beige and white. Amber shook her head. "It's not exactly welcoming."

"Radiant and I had rooms on the garden floor, where they grow food. Most of the time we weren't allowed to leave it."

"Well, we know what 2Ray1 thinks of our being here." Her tone was dry. "Obviously we can't expect a grand tour."

"He's got secrets."

She quirked her mouth. "Definitely has things to hide."

Boxes. Secret boxes. The words jammed against Hote's teeth. He tightened his lips. He had chosen to come here. Had chosen to uncover the secrets and to get close to dragons. He must see it through.

CHAPTER 28

Traveler

We fly to an ocean. Only then do I realize I heard its roar before seeing it. Now I pay attention to how it roars, how it shimmers in the sun, and how it seems to rise into the distance as if mounting the sky. I settle on the beach, and for a while we watch the tide come in and go out, and watch the birds that follow it in and out. Strands of green and brown seaweed sprawl along the water's edge and help to create tide pools. I settle in sand and feel the refreshing rush of tide over my feet.

My brain is weary of striving to learn what is impossible and unnecessary. Besides, I'm hungry, and there isn't a manna belt in sight. Will we have to return to danger to feed? I hate the way Balofur acts like the elder of a silly child whose tantrums are best ignored. If we do return to the belt, my clan won't be far away.

"Listen, Balofur, it's clear we're not meant for each other. It might be safe enough to return to my clan, and we could each find a more suitable solution. Because I'm sure Batwing would love you."

"Why do you say that?"

"If we met my clan, the elders would give you to Batwing and let me have her groombug; I'm sure of it."

I am not. In fact I am sure they wouldn't. Of course Balofur would know that. If I hurt his feelings, he doesn't let on.

"I could no more bond with her than I can with you. She would never produce offspring."

Bonded at birth, joined until death. I hate that saying. "So what you're saying is she'd meet the gryphon if you went with her, as if she didn't have a groombug?"

"What I'm saying is, her generation would end. Her bonded groombug, by his very presence, will inspire her to produce an egg. I could never do that."

I realize the situation is the same with me. "So I will never be inspired."

"We can never be properly bonded. I am not your groombug."

I want to feel a sense of satisfaction in his statement. Instead, I feel rejected, lonely.

Before I can brood over it, Balofur says, "Your mouth isn't like the outworlders'. Therefore we will substitute sounds that can make the words recognizable."

I sigh.

Nevertheless I find relief in using glottal stops, hisses, and growls to simulate what I can't pronounce. I find no relief, though, in Balofur's treatment of me. In some ways he has withdrawn. Even as he resumes humming, he is entertaining himself. Or if he tells a story, it is restrained. It's my fault. I haven't appreciated him and have been insensitive. He is my mentor, my companion, and savior.

How thankless, how selfish I've been! While I can never be the elder Balofur craves, surely I can act less like a youngling and more like an adult. I endeavor never to hurt him again. I will be more appreciative, more understanding, more mature.

I try to make amends. "A dragon cannot live without its groombug."

"Neither can a groombug live without a dragon. To the same extent."

"We need each other."

"Indeed."

The invisible shroud I have erected between us remains. It will take time to mend the breach. To please him, I plunge into learning the language. And we prepare to visit the manna belt.

Before we depart from the ocean, I see a speck over the water. As it grows larger, it takes the form of a dragon whose scales glimmer in the sun.

Even as I fumble into the air and away from the sea, I watch her approach. Soon she is even with us and greets us with a smile. Her eyes flicker, probably reflecting the sparkles from the ocean. "Hello! Be wadda dooba doodle. Can I join you?"

"We were just heading for the manna belt."

"Let us fly together. Hicky beedle bee."

What is this gibberish? Language spoken by an alien clan? Balofur acts invisible, which is no surprise. Groombugs seldom communicate with other dragons.

"I'm Traveler. What is your name?"

I don't want to draw attention to my immovable wings. Still, there is no getting around it. "Rumplewing."

Traveler's eyes flicker again. "Where is your clan? Hooky hooky do."

"Don't tell her," Balofur whispers. I can feel him in my third ear.

"Who's to say?" I answer Traveler. "I've been away for quite some time. How about you?"

"I am alone."

Obviously. Why would a dragon be alone? Unless she's laid her egg and is shutting down. She doesn't act like she's shutting down.

I sense Balofur's alertness. Should I be on guard? This stranger isn't like the red dragon. This stranger has magnificent scales. I see no bump at the back of her skull, which means her groombug is scrunched down or elsewhere. Groombugs can be very shy and hard to notice. Traveler has strange eyes, with fixed pupils, and she aims a smiling mouth at me. And she speaks only with her mouth. No body language. Odd though she is, she is friendly and doesn't seem to mind my oddness. In fact she allows for my slow flight and is quick to point out rest stops from where I can take off again with ease. I almost weep at her thoughtfulness.

We fall into idle conversation, during which Balofur whispers for me to avoid mentioning groombugs. Which isn't difficult. I do most of the talking, with Traveler hardly saying a word. Mostly she relies on stock phrases. I try not to notice her awkward way of communicating, of not always connecting with what I say. Likely she comes from a clan with different customs.

We satisfy our hunger at the manna belt, where some Shining Ones are feeding in the distance. Traveler suggests we join them.

"No," Balofur whispers.

"I'm avoiding the clans," I say.

Traveler doesn't argue.

I listen for Balofur's whisper and hear nothing. I feel obliged to explain my lack of a clan. "My wings. I left because my wings were broken."

Traveler looks thoughtful. "Be wadda dooba doodle. Can I join you?"

I wait for Balofur to speak.

"Let us fly together. I have a cave. A good cave."

"Agree with her," Balofur whispers. "Distract her from the others."

"Okay," I answer Traveler.

Once we reach her cave, Traveler is attentive to me, not by talking much except to repeat the same odd phrases. Too attentive, really. Perhaps I am prejudiced because she comes from a different clan, but I feel edgy around her. Why is she away from her clan and not meeting the gryphon? Why is she constantly with me? Whether I shuffle farther into the cave or to its mouth, she follows me or at least watches. If she ever sleeps, it must be when I do. Balofur doesn't help by being so secretive. I hear nothing and feel nothing from him. Is he tormenting me for mistreating him? When will I earn his full forgiveness, the ugly little know-it-all?

After our rest, Traveler says she needs to fly and suggests I accompany her. I start to beg off, only to change my mind when Balofur proves his existence by whispering in my ear to go with her. "Keep her away from the clans."

We fly, Traveler making allowances for my lumbering flight. When she pulls into the lead, I notice Balofur at the corner of my mouth. He clings where saliva leaks between my lips. I should warn him away, lest he get sucked into my mouth when I speak or take a breath. If he hadn't insisted on being ignored, I would have. Besides, I am sure he is still brooding over being insulted. What can I say or do to feel again his warmth?

Sun glints off Traveler, blinding me temporarily and casting multicolored blind spots before me. Traveler trumpets, and I blink to clear my eyes, only to rush into flames.

CHAPTER 29

Betrayed

A wall of fire roars about my ears. At the same time I feel Balofur, a round furry ball, on my tongue. When had he leaped into my mouth?

Above the flames' roar, Traveler trumpets again.

The fire is gone. Musty-smelling air stings my eyes and my nostrils. Balofur is still in my mouth. I keep it shut when otherwise I might have gasped. Protect the groombug, even above self. How deeply ingrained the habit is.

I'm in a tunnel. Outworlders cocooned in strange skin surround me, and I flounder, unable to take flight. I fall on my side and my head strikes the flat ground, and it sinks and carries me down into darkness. I flash on Seemor's capture and pass out.

I revive in a cavern with a floor like shiny rock. The back wall of the cavern is dark, and the front is lighted. The sides stretch into distance and darkness. It smells of dragon dung and rancid manna. Otherwise I feel muffled, for I cannot hear my world. No sound of the Great Mother, whether in wind, water, or soil. Have my senses died?

My breath comes in pants. My heart triple times.

Across the room, shadows huddle. My eyes adjust, and they resolve into a group of dragons on the floor. Silent. Motionless. None cling to the walls. The walls are too slick. Are the dragons alive? The air holds a sense of gloom, of defeat.

I scoot away from them, toward the lighted wall. Before I can reach it, I bump against an invisible barrier. Along it are a narrow brook of water and a depression that smells of dried manna.

I trundle to one side and run into another invisible wall. And it is the same on the other side, through which I can see silhouettes of other huddled masses.

A nudge against my tongue catches my attention. I open my mouth, and a wet Balofur scurries along my face and into my third ear.

"Bal—Balofur?" I whisper. "Where are we?"

"It's called a cell, a cage, a prison. You were just led into the Collectors' camp by an imposter." His tone is matter-of-fact.

And something else. Satisfied? Does he hate me so much he is willing to sacrifice himself?

Rage tightens my throat so I can barely speak. My color flares and pulses. "You knew! You knew Traveler was a fake dragon."

"Yes."

"By the Great Ancestress!"

"Once the fake saw you, you were already captured."

"The Shining Ones. At the manna belt. We could have warned them, got them to rescue us."

"No. We had to protect the clans. We had to get the imposter away from them."

My breath comes in gasps. Until my attention snags on a rustle of wings, a snort or two. I'd forgotten to keep my voice down, and the dragons are listening.

"Who are you?" I ask them. "How long have you been here?"

"Too long," comes a sluggish reply. "Do you have a groombug?"

"How many of you are there?"

"Too many. You got a groombug?"

Their attention feels ominous and presses against me.

"Ignore them," Balofur says in my third ear.

I resume whispering to him. "We could have gotten away when Traveler was out over the ocean far away from us."

"With your wings? It would have overtaken us."

"We could have hid."

"It's best we didn't."

"You wanted to surrender, didn't you? You betrayed us. To punish me. Was it that important?"

"Not to punish you or to betray us. My elder dragon, Seemor, is alive, I'm sure of it. I had to return to find and free her before it's too late."

"If you planned to rescue Seemor, why did you leave here in the first place?"

"To get help. On my explorations of this vessel, I've noticed the outworlders are not friendly with one another. There are the Collectors and Watchers who come and visit and take stuff away, and I've noticed tension between them. I thought the Watchers might be persuaded to help the dragons, but I wasn't sure. It was worth a gamble. When I escaped, I searched for the Watcher's ship. I couldn't find it. The ships are invisible, and I couldn't cover much distance. Besides, I wasn't sure if they even knew of a groombug's existence."

"Wasn't that a Watcher craft we collided with?"

"It was."

"So we had an opportunity right there to ask for help, and you scolded it and had me leave."

"Because I'm not sure of the Watcher role. If you must know, I was afraid. That's why I went to the manna belt, not to feast but to find my clan and warn them and beg them to help me find Seemor."

I feel as if I'd been kicked in the belly. Or is it the heart? I'm not sure which hurts more. I don't mean to whimper, but I can't help it. "What of me? I thought we were a team."

"There should be plenty of orphaned groombugs here. Once we free my elder, I'm sure we might find a groombug closer to your age, temperament, and experience. This is the only place where there might be a spare groombug. You'll certainly be rid of me."

All this time, the other dragons are quiet. Their necks are erect. Listening. On the verge of action. I don't care. I'm still angry with Balofur and forget to whisper.

"Batwing would have loved you. You match her in untrustworthiness. Tweekie was beautiful. In every way."

"Are you so beautiful?"

What can I say? My wings are stiff and ugly.

The dragons shuffle. I hear a murmur of longing among them. "Groombug. She's got a groombug."

I gulp. They have no groombug. They want Balofur. Will they gang up to get him?

He isn't even mine. In a way, he's on loan. Oh, how ugly my attitude! How wrong! Sure, it hurts that Balofur would want to leave me, but he has no choice. He must seek to return to Seemor as long as she lives.

Bonded from egg to death.

These dragons have no groombug, and I feel as spoiled as Batwing. I should have died when Tweekie was killed. Tradition says I must accept Seemor and Balofur's position, no matter how I feel. It's what any groombug would do. Why should Balofur be different? Where does that leave me? If Balofur leaves and there are no orphaned groombugs, I will meet the gryphon. And the way these dragons are listening, and the way they ask if I have a groombug, I expect to find no extras here.

Yet didn't the Great Mother tell me to live? I must try again to get on Balofur's good side.

"You're right," I say. "Completely right. And I realize we need to work together if we're going to get out of this mess. I appreciate you, I really do."

"You miss Tweekie."

"Not any more. That is, not so much. I just never appreciated you like I should. And I do appreciate you. I do. You're an elder. I need your knowledge."

Balofur seems to warm toward me. "A good decision. I'll be off now, exploring. Understand that I prepared you for this. Listen and learn. Keep your knowledge secret from the outworlders."

Before Balofur can slip away, the dragons spread their wings and sidle forward. Five of them. Their voices are urgent.

"You got a groombug?"

"Let's see him."

"I want him."

"Give me your groombug."

I rear up, arch my neck, and flare my stiff wings. "Stop. He is not yours."

Some of these dragons are bigger than me. Older. They should know better.

"Give me."

"Give me."

"No," I yell. "He can't groom all of you."

They quarrel among themselves, skip over thrashing tails, bump shoulders.

"He'll groom me."

"No, he'll groom me, or else."

"I'll groom you with flame."

Breaths hiss. Fire spurts and roars about the cage. I shy back. Dragons flaming one another. Balofur leaps off me and rolls along the floor. Wings colliding, the dragons leap after him.

CHAPTER 30

The Collector Craft

-1-

I yell, "Stop! You'll hurt him."

Balofur disappears through a vent in the floor.

"Have you forgotten your flame etiquette? By the Great Ancestress, how can you do this?"

With him gone, they droop. Heads bow, wings sag. Some weep softly. Older dragons seldom heed the young, and I expect they respond more to Balofur's absence than to anything I might say. Softly they chorus, voices overlapping with nearly the same words, "Our groombugs were killed."

They fall silent, and in their silence, I speak. "I know your pain."

The chorus rings out. "How could you, you never lost your groombug, you don't know a thing!"

After a pause, a more reasonable solo speaks. "How did yours survive?"

I don't care to tell them Balofur isn't mine. Instead, I ask the dragons about themselves. They share where they came from and how long they have been held.

"We don't know why we are here or what will happen to us."

As if remembering the dignity and wisdom of their age, the dragons speak calmly and in turn.

"We've been held long enough to see Shining Ones leave and never come back, and more arrive."

"Young dragons bring unconscious captives in."

"They're corrupting the young."

"Something we older dragons would never do."

They stop speaking. They crane their necks, and I follow their gaze. The red dragon who had tried to steal Balofur earlier passes by with some Collectors. My cellmates hiss and fume. I join them.

"There goes the betrayer."

I raise up, ready to attack. Before I can launch, my cellmates rush her.

In the suddenness and fury of their attack, I crouch to avoid being trampled. I expect to see them tear into the red dragon, who dodges sideways. Wham! My cellmates strike an invisible barrier, and the Collectors shy back in reflex, slamming their backs against the side of the corridor.

"Traitor! Betrayer!"

The Collectors are safe. My cellmates can't reach their target. In response, the Collectors shout and wave their fists.

Again and again the dragons sling talons, wings, and tails at the barrier and continue the name calling. "Traitor! Rotten one!"

My anger dies when I see the red dragon shrink back. By the time the assault subsides, my ears ring. Grumbling, the dragons retreat to the far corner. Only when they quieten do I rise up and stretch until my snout touches the solid air. I run my nose along it. Trace it from wall to wall. As high as I can reach and down to the floor, there's no way around. I breathe fire to define its borders, which confirms my assessment of its solidity.

One of the dragons speaks from the corner. "Air too thick to penetrate."

"They have a pointer," another says. "A stone that makes it and dissolves it."

The red huddles on the other side, as imprisoned as we are.

The Collectors are gone. When they left, I don't know; I hadn't paid attention. She isn't alone though.

In her cell an outworlder, different from the others, remains. It doesn't wear a cocoon-like skin cover. It has on a green skin that leaves its head bare. What is it doing to the dragon? Ah. Cleaning her with something like a mass of lichen, a poor substitute for grooming. She has sores which the cleaner dabs with a clear goop. The outworlder croons and speaks in gentle tones. As long as this continues, my cellmates are silent. Resting or relishing the comfort of the sounds.

Then a Collector comes. The elders resume their threatening stances. Pulsing red, they resume the name calling.

"Traitor! Betrayer!"

The Collector brandishes a pointer and calls the cleaner out.

"She can't go on," the cleaner says. "…die…ignorant…"

Or something like that. I'm surprised I can pick out the words.

"Who asks you…" the Collector answers. "…Hote…Give a…"

Wham! The dragons rush and bash at the barrier.

Their racket fills the contained space. It is all I can do to hear over the name calling, the thump of tails.

"Be quiet," I tell them. "Listen to what they're saying."

I seem not to exist.

The barrier dissolves just enough to allow the cleaner to pass through while a fake dragon appears, to guard the cell. Traveler. Traveler stays long enough to vomit food into a depression. I can't smell it through my wall, but I recognize it as manna.

When the red dragon is finally left alone by the captors, she laps at the manna. The dragons leave off their attack, subsiding to mutters and then to silence.

"When will we be fed?" I ask.

"Probably not for days, if that."

At the moment, I am not hungry.

"We won't get cleaned," says another. "Only the traitors are pampered."

With a final poisonous glance at the red's cell, the others turn their backs on her. They cluster together and rest. As a youngster, I don't feel welcome to join them. Some stretch out. Others wrap themselves in their wings. Eventually snoring rises.

The floor is unforgiving. I raise and lower my feet against its hardness and shift my gaze to the solid wall. Nothing on its smooth surface offers a hand or foothold for support.

I focus on the Great Mother's word. *Live.* Maybe it was only a momentary command. I want to consider it a promise. Yes, a promise that despite all appearances, I will survive. Of course we all must meet the gryphon sometime. Surely my time hasn't come. I am too young. *I will live.* With that running through my mind, I drowse.

Balofur appears and leaps onto me. I come wide awake. "Where did you go?"

"Nowhere productive. I saw where waste is deposited. See the vent at the top of this room? That's for air. Fly me up there."

I flap stiff wings and leap, only to collide with the wall. I don't have the control needed to rise in so small an enclosure.

My noise awakens the other dragons. They eye me, and I steel myself for their rush.

This time they remain calm. The largest dragon says, "I will fly you up there, if you groom me."

"Done," Balofur says.

The other dragons clamor for possession of Balofur.

"Me next."

"No, me."

The much larger dragon raises her wings in a threat and hisses. The others fall back.

Balofur makes quick work of grooming the big dragon, taking shortcuts. Then he insists, "Fly me up there."

"Not until you groom me more."

"I'll spit acid on you if you don't get me up there."

Without a word of protest, the elder lifts on wing, a graceful movement of great economy, and Balofur jumps through the air vent.

One of the other dragons mutters, "I wonder what we could offer him to groom us."

More muttering and shaking of heads follow. Then a settling down. They sleep.

I awaken later to soft weeping. It is the traitor. Balofur hasn't returned yet. I move close to the wall, finding it by feel. The red dragon looks up at me.

"They made me do it," she begins. "I had no choice. They take you when you're young and train you, just like you saw the young ones dragging in the unconscious."

Having been recently dragged in, myself, I don't care to point out that I haven't seen any of the young do this. I dread to think I will be here long enough to see such abomination.

"Then they train us further to go out and trick others to come. A group of us were taught to do this. We were shown a moving scene in the midst of our prison. It showed examples of a dragon being rewarded with a cleansing and being punished with clubs and the withholding of cleansing. I didn't want to trick you. It was that or never get cleaned or fed. By going out, we can enjoy the taste and sustenance of the manna belt if we get a chance. But we must return to be cleansed, and we must return with at least one other dragon. Or be punished. The cleaning isn't as good as grooming, and the manna they bring here tastes defiled. Still, it's better than what happens to the rest of you."

"What happens to the rest of us?"

"You will be taken away and never come back. That's all I know."

I veer between pity and rage. My words are sharp. "Even if it meant death, I would not go out like that. I would not betray the Shining Ones."

She snivels.

What can I say to encourage her? Nothing! To avoid sniveling, myself, I lumber to the far side of my cell to be as alone as possible.

There is little to do in captivity except wait. Conversation with my fellow captives goes nowhere, from questioning about their fate to cursing traitors to talking about their clans. None discuss their lost groombugs. It is the closest thing to discussing one's own death. It doesn't stop them from discussing Balofur.

"Why should you with your ruined wings rate a groombug?"

What can I say? I try to change the subject. "What do you know about the Collectors?"

They exchange glances, shrug, shake their heads.

"How many of you understand the outworlder speech?" I ask.

No response. They seem struck dumb by my stupidity.

I don't give up. "You should try to learn it. We could practice together."

"What's it matter to us what they say?"

"You need to understand your enemy."

They snort, shrug me off, and dismiss me. Anything else I have to say bounces off them. I am too young, too foolish, and too inexperienced. If they know anything or have any plans, why should they share with me? So I learn nothing from them about the Collectors, the Watchers, or Traveler. Nothing. They seem more interested in muttering among themselves about ways to coerce me into giving them Balofur.

Oldsters should know better. They are superior in knowledge and wisdom. The most elder of the group should come up with a plan to help all of us, a plan for escape. But then they are not the high elders.

It's up to me to grow the outworlder speech in my brain, with only Balofur to help me.

Surely Seemor must be the highest of elders, judging from Balofur's manner. As much as he seeks to free Seemor, he doesn't dismiss me entirely. At least I hope he doesn't. I want to drum my talons while awaiting his return, but it might draw more attention to me than I want from my cellmates. What if he injures himself among the various systems in the ship? What if he gets lost? What if he is found and killed? What if he finds Seemor? He'd have no reason to return to me. I grow nervous thinking about it.

-2-

Shaky, Hote meandered along the walkway between the front force field of the prisons and the wall. He had nearly reached the end of the great room that was arranged into gigantic invisible stalls. The cages were impressive in their sanitation. At various points he sensed the tingle of a cleansing ray enveloping a captive.

Perhaps he was foolish to refuse the protective gear offered him. The heavy suits, the helmet, the boots, the gloves. But how would he win the dragon's trust? Still, he had almost swallowed his heart before the fiery rage of the dragons beside the red's cage as they crashed repeatedly against the force field inches away. The Collectors had tittered when he recoiled. But then the red dragon also had flinched. It had paled with red blotches suffused by gray reflected from the visible walls. A sickening hue. Over the drum of his heart, he had spoken soothingly.

"Don't be afraid. It's all right. You're safe. I'm here to help you."

He patted the poor beast, and hummed to it. From a distance, it seemed healthy, magnificent. Up close, he could see the ravages of captivity. Its skin was dry and dull. A closer examination revealed sores that varied from tiny scabs to raw flesh where scales seemed to be dissolving. He tried not to look at the raging captives that seemed any second to break through and shower him in flame. How could he blame them? If their condition was as bad as this red dragon's, he must do what he could to help them. They needed his lotions, oils, and salves. He must find a way to win their trust.

When the crew members came to usher him away, he couldn't help but tell them what he thought of them.

-3-

At times, Collectors drift by, eyeing the prisoners. A trio stops before my cage.

"Beautiful, aren't they?"

"This is a good lot. Look at that big one. That'll make a fierce fighter. Lots of flesh, too. I'll be going on vacation soon. If I had the money, I'd visit StarCircus and play the gladiator and slay a dragon."

I can understand the gist of their speech. Balofur has taught me well. I glance at my cellmates. Some have nodded off. Others return bored or hostile looks. I see no comprehension among the Shining Ones.

"A perfect group, except for that one with the bad wings."

"Useless as a fighter, true. You have to admit, though, that those scales are uncommonly pretty. Shiny and prismatic."

I don't know what 'prismatic' means, and I'm not sure I should be pleased that they find my skin beautiful.

"I wish we didn't have to sell it. Bad wings and all, it'll bring a premium price because of the quality of its hide. Look how those scales change from blue to white to purple or green, depending on how the light hits them. If I had the credits, I'd buy it, myself."

"It has enough luster, enough to last if we hold onto it for a while so we can feed it up."

I'm not sure what that means. It doesn't sound good. I'll have to ask Balofur.

When the Collectors leave, I ask the most elder, "Do you know what they were saying?"

"They jabber."

"I know what they said." *Most of it.*

The dragons regard me, without interest.

"Did they say when we would be released?" the eldest asks.

"No."

"Did they explain how we might escape? Or if there are any groombugs for us?"

"No."

She turns her back. "Then there is no reason to understand their jabber."

With that, the others look away.

I have to agree there is no reason to understand the fate that awaits them if they can do nothing about it. I don't care to torture them with evil knowledge.

Where is Balofur? What's taking him so long to return? Will he return?

CHAPTER 31

Isolated

Traveler appears and enters our prison through the invisible barrier that dissolves just enough to admit it.

"Squeeckle twee twirp coo. Come with me."

Traveler isn't looking at me but at the other dragons.

I edge to the side, even more out of its line of vision. My cage mates cluster, cringing or hissing and raising their wings in a threat posture. Together they lunge at the automaton. It backs until the attackers crash into the invisible barrier. Before they can pick themselves up, Traveler reenters the cage and spews a vapor from its mouth. Sickeningly bitter, with a residue of manna sweetness, the vapor fills the room. My brain fuzzes, my vision dims. Too dizzy to stand, I crouch and try to shrink from sight. As if in a dream, I watch the others toddle by on unsteady feet.

They leap at Traveler, only to fall on their sides, their wings flapping, their tails thrashing in an effort to regain balance. They shake their heads in an effort to clear them. Woozy, myself, I watch Traveler lead them away.

I am not included in the group. Why? Because of my wings? Because I am younger, therefore smaller? Because my scales are shinier from being groomed? Will I join those dragons later, or is their fate different from mine? Is the Great Mother protecting me? Surely she doesn't favor me over the others, unless their time for death has come because they are older and each has already laid an egg.

No, they didn't leave their clans. They were taken before their time. If their fate is death, so should be mine—I must not rest on the illusion that I am favored above others. However, if the Great Mother wants me to live, I will not surrender to whatever these Collectors plan for me.

For the rest of that day, I gaze through clear walls at other cages down the row as they are being filled by the unconscious, dragged in by dragons barely younger than I. I wait for cellmates to return. I wait for the red dragon to occupy the nearby cage. Mostly I wait for Balofur. At some point, I no longer wait.

Moments pass. How many, I don't know. Either I slept or was gassed. I wake up in a smaller cell away from all the others. Alone. If Balofur should wish to return, how will he find me? I pace, my winged arms acting as stiff forelegs. Awkward, perhaps comical. Pacing is my attempt to calm my nerves.

It doesn't work.

So I call out in deep tones below the hearing of groombugs and possibly Collectors.

"Sisters. Captive sisters, hear me."

Like an echo, a rumble comes from somewhere unseen. "We hear. What do you want?" The question sounds weary.

"I'm Rumplewing. From the forest clan."

"Do you have a way out? Do you have a groombug?"

The yearning in that voice tears at me. I can hardly speak. "I…just got here. I was hoping maybe you had answers."

A rougher voice answers, hoarse from suffering. "We come from various clans. The cliff, the rock, the grove, the beach, and others. Air too dense to penetrate keeps us in a hard place of slick ground and walls, a place of darkness."

It resembles my cell. "How many are you?"

Their irritation carries in the air, and with each passing pulse, I'm less sure of an answer. Then, as if from a great distance, "Our numbers vary. Some are taken away, never to return. New ones come. Each day is different. Fifteen, yes, fifteen today."

My heart thumps. "How long have you been captive?"

A snort and then the rumble. "Long enough to know we are dying."

My throat closes. I cannot answer.

To buoy my courage, I ease softly into song, a low hum. Its vibration massages my throat, but it doesn't take away the pain in my gut and mind.

"Rumplewing."

My song breaks off. I look up, and my spirit lifts. Balofur calls from the ceiling vent. He drops onto me, as light as a flower seed. Has he found Seemor? I fear to ask.

"This time my exploration was more productive."

"What did you find?"

"Collectors everywhere. I saw dragons led to a platform. They were groggy. One of the Collectors pushed something on the wall, and the platform emptied. They were sent into a void."

Gone. Never to return. What is a void like? Is it nothingness, neither dark nor light? Is it a cubbyhole, meant to hold something? Is it another world or a path to it? Is it the final destination or part of a long journey? To where? Why?

"I want to get a better look at what makes them disappear," Balofur says.

Gone.

Never to return.

It's all I can think of as Balofur rattles on.

And then I notice a tingling sensation.

"Move out of it," Balofur commands.

"What-what is it?"

"A cleansing ray. Move out from under it."

"Why?" I ask even as I sidle to one of the force field walls, so I no longer feel the tingle.

"It will dry your scales. It will remove my sustenance."

And then he's on to something else before I'm ready to absorb his warning about the cleansing ray.

I shake myself. I should pay attention to his report. He talks of finding ways to work the device to bring dragons back from the void or perhaps destroying it to prevent others from being sent away.

We need friends. "Balofur, did you see any Watchers?"

"One. A gray top of fluffy hair. Good eyes, like a groombug's. It wasn't doing anything. Waiting around. Watching."

"While you were gone, an outworlder came in to clean the red dragon and put medicine on her sores. It sang to her."

"Did it have a green skin?" Balofur asked.

"Mostly yes. Only, it had black hair on top of its head."

"It was a Watcher. If you will notice, the Watchers resemble Collectors because they are both outworlders, except they wear different fake skins and act differently toward us. The Watchers have a green one. The Collectors have a brown one. Their own skins are the color of soil. Some dark, some pale. I'm more certain now that Watchers are our friends."

"Another thing happened while you were gone," I say. "Some Collectors talked in front of me. They liked the way I looked, but for my wings. Something about feeding me. Something about me being a good product. What does that mean?"

Balofur pauses for emphasis and then says, "They will kill you."

"Kill me?" Does that mean what I think it means? I hope to be mistaken.

Balofur makes sure there is no mistake. "There is one place I didn't go when I was exploring. I'd seen it when I was here before and didn't want to see it again. There is a room below us, like a cavern. It holds great collections from our world. Containers of brilliant feathers, skins, teeth and horns, hooves and toenails. Dried plants. Seeds. Seashells. Other things I didn't recognize." His voice drops. "And in another part, behind a wall where the air was cold, I saw blood and flesh hanging. Remains of animals. They did not shut themselves down, Rumplewing. They were shut down. Killed before their time. The Collectors will kill you."

Hideous! Nothing like that exists on our planet. When death comes, the scavengers take over. Without a groombug the dragon's flesh becomes infected, not because she is being killed. She is shutting down, and the invisible scavengers are feeding off that part of her that is dead. It isn't pleasant. I'm sure dying hurts. How much more painful if she is actually killed? A weight settles on me, and I feel weak. I sag.

Balofur speaks quickly, probably to prevent my giving up. "We need the Watchers. If they really are our friends, they will help us escape. We need to talk to them. We need to learn more of their speech. We need to learn all about them."

In a way, it's a plan. In a way, I feel an upsurge of hope.

CHAPTER 32

The Watchers

Time passes. How much time, it's hard to say. A day. Two days. Three?

Two Watchers stop outside my cage. I recognize the black-haired one I'd seen with the red dragon. The other is the one that Balofur had described. It does have eyes like a groombug's. Dark, soulful, liquid eyes, but different. Not up and down elliptical. And inside the eye, white surrounds the black. Still beautiful. What adds to the beauty is something more. A feeling emanates from this Watcher that warms me and fills my world.

In a low voice it speaks to me. "What happened to you? What happened to your wings?" Though a barrier separates us, the voice is like a murmur in my ear. Intimate, tender.

"They broke them." That voice, deeper, destroys the spell.

"We don't know that," Soulful says.

Soulful has gray, fluffy hair and lined skin. An elder? This is the one who watched the dragons disappear and did nothing. Is it really a friend or a mesmerizer?

The other is smooth, except for a thin fuzz on its face. Taller, broader, with shorter hair, it exudes an aura of confused youth and a fury barely concealed beneath a fragile membrane. Without the interference of my raging cellmates, I can feel the intensity of its vibes through the barrier. It stares at me as if in recognition, its eyes briefly enlarging. I wonder if this is the one Balofur and I met when I crashed against the craft. It is certainly the one who tended the red dragon.

Soulful again concentrates on me. "Hote, look at its scales. They're perfect."

Hote leans in, anger changing to wonder and excitement. "This looks like the dragon who talked to me. I'm sure it talked. I know it sounds wild, but what if I didn't hallucinate?" It focuses on me. "Can you talk?"

Soulful turns a pitying eye on Hote. An eye on the afflicted. "Look, Hote. Concentrate on what we see now. The dragon is in prime condition, except for its wings, poor thing. Other than that, why is it not sick? What's different here?"

"This is the one." Hote jabs a finger at me. "This is the one that talks."

"Please, son, don't disappoint yourself."

Hote jitters and forms fists. In a way it does seem afflicted, as if fading. "Okay, maybe I only imagined, but don't you think it's worth looking into? Amber? Aren't we supposed to be scientific? Open minded?"

Amber sighs, nods, and touches the other's shoulder and whispers, "You're right. That's why we're here. To investigate even the wildest ideas if it will help." Both look up at me.

"Can you talk?" Hote asks.

"Do you understand?" Amber says.

Balofur, a knob at the back of my head, whispers in my third ear, "Speak to it." For trusting the Watchers to be our friends, he is certainly secretive. I don't question his attitude; it's the way of groombugs. Besides, he's an elder.

I can't find the words, so I say nothing. We exchange only looks.

Then Amber glances down the corridor. "When Stilwell comes to let us in, we can start from this end to treat dragons."

"For all the good it will do."

"The Collectors are just ignorant."

Hote's voice rises. "Because they want to be."

Amber regards Hote. "Son, you can't put them all in the same box. I'm sure we can reach some of them, soften them. Bluemont isn't comfortable with this trade in dragons. Evidently it's been going on for some time. When the others weren't listening, she admitted it to me. And she handles the doors and the launchpad."

"You think she'll help? Everyone softens around you. Except here. No one's going to rebel against Father."

"Surely some of them love dragons enough to hate all this." Amber sweeps a hand toward the cages.

"Sure, Collectors love dragons. Dragon steak, dragon-skin boots, dragon-hide capes. Bluemont included."

I can't understand every word, the way they rattle on. Each unfamiliar word slips away, so I settle on the last one. "Vot iss capes?"

The Watchers snap alert. Hote utters a quick heh-heh. "What-what—did you just speak?"

Amber presses a hand on the barrier. "You understand?"

"Some."

"See? I knew it." Hote gives a little leap. "You remember me? We met in the field; I'm sure it was you. I offered to help you then, but you were too upset. Wow."

"Vot is vow?"

"Never mind. I'm Hote, her son."

I give them a blank look. Hote talks too fast, and I have to take time to translate, with Balofur's whispered help.

Amber touches Hote on the shoulder. "It doesn't understand. Talk slowly and in simpler terms." And then to me, "I am Amber. Amber."

"Amber."

"That's right. This is Hote. Hote is my son. I am Amber, I am she. Hote is he."

Hote is a he? Given his size, how is that possible? "I am Rumpleving. I am she."

"Good." Amber motions to dragons in the other cages. "Can you tell me which are he and which are she?"

"All dragons are she."

"She? Are there any hes?"

"Our groombugs."

"Groombugs?"

"Small hes."

"Don't tell them anything more about groombugs," Balofur says.

Hote asks, "What are groombugs?"

I don't answer.

"She may not understand." Amber enunciates slowly. "Hote and I…Amber…look the same but we are not exactly the same. He is my offspring. Like-like the deer. Do you know deer?"

Balofur whispers in my third ear about the great herds we saw on the plains.

"I understand," I say. I don't.

Amber continues. "I was a bonded pair with another. A he. He and I made offspring. Together we made Hote, a he, and another, a she."

"Now that we cleared that up…" Hote tilts his head toward an approaching Collector.

Amber gives a pleasant nod. "Greetings, my dear sir."

The Collector, lean and tall, stops between Hote and Amber. "And a fair greeting to you, Doctor Kellyamber. Here's your new schedule. Commander wants you to start down at the end and work your way up to here. Is that okay?"

"That's fine, thank you."

"I'm ready," Hote says. By now, he emits so small a presence, he seems like an image without depth.

The Collector gives him a stony look. "Oh. It's you-uh, what's your name, boy? Whit?"

"Hote."

The Collector jerks his head. "You'll do cages in the other wing. Get it? You do them. And you'll need protective suits for these wild dragons."

The outworlders leave.

Left to ourselves, Balofur and I continue the conversation in an effort to make sense of it.

"Amber is bonded with someone like her and Hote." Balofur sounds very sure of himself. "The same size, like deer."

"He's like a groombug but different?" *Not small. Not a ball of fur.*

"If they are to have offspring, he must be something like a groombug because he is a he."

"What has that to do with offspring?" It's a mystery no elder dragon would be prepared to answer.

"Considering dragons, it has everything to do with offspring. All very understandable." Balofur's flippant answer reminds me of why I find him an irritating know-it-all.

I huff. "So there's no mystery in it."

"The mystery lies in how the Watchers accomplish it. We know, though, that Amber's bond mate is a he, and Amber is a she. Which means, he is a he-mother and she is a she-mother."

"I know!" Actually, it's a revelation to me. "You must think I'm dumb."

I want comfort. Instead, Balofur oozes reason. "You're not the smartest dragon."

I huff again. "How do you put up with me?"

"You're young and still learning." He sounds smug. "Besides, intelligence means little if it fills the head of a dragon who gives up."

"Have I ever given up?"

"You are uniquely stubborn."

Steam wisps from my nostrils. I can never win with Balofur. The best thing would be to take his last statement as a compliment.

As an act of rebellion, I again call out below the level of his hearing. "Sisters. Hear me. Trust the Watchers. Outworlders who wear a green skin. A he and a she. They are our friends and want to help us."

No one answers.

"Are you there?"

Are they all taken? Sent into the void? Dead in their cages? Or do they think I'm a traitor, out to trick them with false hope?

CHAPTER 33

The Launchpad

-1-

Hote awoke to the sound of a whimper. A bird? Not in his quarters where sterile walls surrounded him and his cot in silence. Despite a lack of windows, he felt as if he had looked out in a still night at the stars. The whimper didn't come again, and he realized the sound was his. He had dreamed. Yes, a nightmare? What was it? He was in darkness, in the void, or something like it. Only it wasn't completely dark, and he was on a plain. An in-between world? He had taken a different form. He was striding along on long, thin legs. Running with ease. And it felt good in the cool air. It felt so real. The alien inside him—did they switch places when he slept?

He didn't always sleep when he slipped into the space between molecules, or rather the thing inside him did, bringing him along. Hote had no choice in the matter. Was he invisible then? Was it possible he could gain control? Would the thing inside him allow it?

This room was more a cubicle, smaller but basically similar to the one he and Radiant had shared as children. Despite a lack of plants or entertainment center, it seemed soaked in memories, as when they played with toy animals. And fought each other for dominance. It was the only chance for control either of them had. Otherwise they obeyed whatever tutor followed Father's orders. They were seldom to be seen, never heard by others on ship, lest they distract crew members from their duties.

Father's controlling presence permeated the walls. Radiant's presence seemed peculiarly absent. Hote couldn't stop thinking of her.

-2-

After breakfast in his room, Hote wandered about the main floor of the ship, ignored by most and thankful he didn't see Father anywhere in the two days he and Amber had been there. The metal gray corridors and work areas felt oppressive. Not many workers occupied the main floor, where they moved their hands over computer screens or levitated various sized crates into the cavernous area near the launchpad. Hote had no idea what they held and if they were being sent or received.

Boxes. Boxes.

The crazy thoughts arose again, and he was sure Amber's revelation that these thoughts came from the trauma of Father forcing him into a box was not accurate. Otherwise, why did the thoughts still plague him? At least he might find some comfort in working on the lower floor with the dragons, aware they could talk. Mildly disappointed he couldn't work with Rumplewing, he expected to find other talkers among the dragons where he was assigned.

Some of the crew glanced at him and then went about their business, as if he were not there. He stopped by a woman in uniform who touched icons on a console beside the launchpad. Her name tag said Bluemont. This was where Maximus, Hunter, Reed, and Ahmed picked up their Watcher supplies. This is where Hote wanted to be. He shifted. Cleared his throat. Coughed. She seemed too engrossed to notice him.

"Hi," he finally said.

She glanced up at him, then continued pressing icons. A collection of boxes appeared on the pad, and she spoke into earbuds, announcing their appearance.

Boxes. Boxes.

Crew members arrived to cart the boxes away, and she pivoted in her chair to look up at Hote. "Do I know you?" Her voice was crisp.

"Uh, no. I'm…Hote. The Commander's son."

"Commander 2Ray1? I didn't know he had a son. Why haven't I seen you before?"

"Yes, well. Because I've been away, with my mother. Dr. Kelly Amber. Of the Watchers."

"Oh. Kellyamber. She's your mother? Nice lady." Bluemont softened.

"Yeah. And I need you to do me a favor."

"If I can."

"What I need is to get onto the launchpad. See, a few years ago, my sister took it to visit StarCircus, and I'm not sure, but it could have malfunctioned. Do you know anything about it?"

"It must have been before I transferred here. I've never known the pad to malfunction. Was she injured?"

"Well, I don't know. Maybe." Hote had never considered it.

"Whatever. I'm certainly sorry about your sister."

Had she been injured? Or had she played a prank on Hote and was alive and in touch with Father? If only Hote could remember. Surely Bluemont would know. "Her name was Radiant. You've never heard of her?"

"Pretty name. No. Commander keeps his personal life private. So, no. I've never heard of her."

"You've never transported her? Never sent a message or got one?"

"I'm sure Commander 2Ray1 would receive or send on a his personal channel. Unless he sent through Stilwell, which I don't see happening. Why? Don't you speak with your father?"

Hote ignored her question. "How about a dragon automaton and a guy named Baaden? Did you transport them?"

She shook her head.

"Nothing to StarCircus?"

"We ship a lot to StarCircus, but not them. Why do you ask?"

Hote shrugged. "Doesn't matter. What I was hoping for was… Well, just after my sister left—I think what happened—well, Father launched me, and I collided with someone who was being launched from elsewhere, and…I know it sounds crazy, but they're still inside me. This other being." Hote noted Bluemont's growing suspicion. He continued, "If you could focus on it, I think maybe you could separate us."

She narrowed her eyes, raised an eyebrow, and turned back to the console.

"Talk to my mother. She'll explain,"

"Sorry, I'm not authorized."

"I know it sounds impossible. Ask Father. It's no secret. He can tell you all about it, how it happened."

Bluemont sighed. "I'm sorry, kid. First of all, I can't go barging in on the Commander to ask him about something that is none of my business. And second, I can't risk tearing you apart in an attempt to separate you from some entity. Because I'm sure that's what would happen. I'd tear you apart and have to live with that my entire life. I don't want to be responsible."

That said, Bluemont went back to her work and refused to look at him.

Hote turned away. The entity tugged at him again, trying to pull him into the void or away from the launch platform. He couldn't tell. He held his fists by his sides to avoid pawing at his chest.

CHAPTER 34

The Fate of the Captives

-1-

A Collector passes by at intervals to let Amber enter and leave each cell. Eventually she reaches our cell. It's the first time she's been inside. She begins going over my body, starting at my feet.

"I see nothing here to polish or medicate." Her fingers trace along each scale, advancing slowly up one leg. "Which means you've newly arrived, haven't you?"

"Yes."

As she works more quickly, moving to my other leg, we talk, and I understand enough on my own to get the gist of her message. Balofur secretly translates what I can't understand. If he wants to remain hidden, I won't betray his presence. It means he still isn't completely sure of the Watchers, or perhaps he has an alternative plan if the Watchers don't help. Sometimes Balofur breathes a question into my ear, which I repeat aloud.

"Vhy are cullectors taking dragons?"

Amber takes a deep breath and releases it. "It's not good, and we want to stop it. Crew members have told me that some dragons are taken off world and sold to the tournaments in alternate space, to be killed eventually by some knight who knows he can't defeat a dragon on its own turf. Sooner or later they are all slaughtered for their body parts. Made into products and for food and trophies."

My imagination falls to the floor below us, the processing room where carcasses hang. In my bones, I feel the coldness, smell the decay. My mind shivers.

"Originally, so I'm told, they used robot dragons. I suppose they still do for those who want a safer contest. But…"

Why end the living before their time? These offworlders must suffer a type of decay.

She has reached my tail before I ask the next question. "Vhy are yuh Vatchers here? On our planet?"

"To understand that, you need to know the purpose of the Watchers. The why. Long before our time, terraformers planted life on this world. Our task is to watch over it and protect it from interference."

They planted life? Had they created the Great Mother? Before I can completely digest the concept, Balofur gives me the next question to ask.

"Can yuh plant life?"

Amber runs a hand along my side, moving forward until she reaches my head. "As far as I can tell, you're in excellent health."

She kneels by my face and strokes it. "We could alter your genes, but we are not the animaters. Neither were the terraformers. You say all dragons are female? Then for some unknown reason, those who populated the planet couldn't get viable male dragons. It's not unusual for some species to be all female. Aphids are an example. They reproduce by such methods as parthenogenesis."

"Par…par…?" I try to grasp what she says.

"They produce young without the use of males. How is it with you?"

"How?" It is one of the great mysteries. Unwilling to show my ignorance, I fumble for an answer. "The Great Mother—"

Balofur hushes me.

"The Great Mother?"

My tongue is stuck. Balofur is no help. Maybe he doesn't know as much as he lets on.

Amber must think my stumble is a problem I have with understanding outworlder speak, which is partly correct. "I guess I know what you mean. The great ancestress. Dragons have been around for a long time. We don't know all of what went into the genetic process because a lot of the records have not survived. So it's a matter of discovering how you evolved."

"Vot about other vorlds? They are all same?"

"Each world is different, but not like this. This is truly a unique planet. Here, the only flesh eaters are scavengers."

"Yuh made other vorlds?"

"Terraformed. Not by us. We don't know who terraformed them. We are assigned to this one. Not to change anything, but to watch and protect from outside influences. We each have our duties. Some of us study plants or rocks or weather. Hote and I study dragons. We have a center of operations, and from there we ride small, invisible ships to our various points of observation. That way, we intrude as little as possible."

Her stroking hands slow and stop. "Actually we have been forced to intrude, in that we now interact with you, as friends and protectors."

<h3 style="text-align:center">-2-</h3>

Amber comes often, so with each grooming day, our talks continue, and Balofur and I grow more adept at outworlder speech. Amber has taken to massaging my stiff wings. Eventually I tell her how they were broken. Even as she digs her fingers into my joints, I doubt this will loosen them. That she works to comfort me feels good, even if it accomplishes little other than to develop my trust. I feel it is time to ask some hard questions.

"Vy are cullectors here?"

She hesitates in her massaging. "Unfortunately they received permission to harvest certain forms of life on this world."

"How?"

"We had a ruling that forbade hunters from setting foot on the planet. They get around that by sending out drones to stun animals in the open and levitate them away. Fortunately the forests are too dense for them to penetrate."

Right away Balofur throws out questions for me to ask. I pick the last one. "Vhat give permission?"

"There is an off planet authority, a federation that—"

"This our vorld. Ve decide."

"I'm sorry. We all have to answer to it because it governs all the planets. It has laws. Rules everyone must follow, so we can all live in peace."

"Vhere are peace fer our planet?"

I am stirred up, asking my own questions. How can outsiders command us?

"We are working in your interest. Searching for ways to ban their harvesting and to prohibit their presence here. What we have succeeded in doing, so far, is to get a ban passed on the harvest of intelligent life. Unfortunately, the Collectors don't see the dragons as intelligent. Hote and I have hired on here, partly to keep an eye on the Collectors and partly to find a way to help the dragons."

"Yuh vill help us escape?"

"One way or another, yes." She gives my snout a pat. "And you have given us a weapon against the Collectors. Speak to them. Prove your intelligence."

"Easily proven." Balofur rises from my third ear so I see him from the corner of my eye. He raises his hairs and alters his color so he becomes visible, scars and all.

At the sound of his voice, Amber looks up. "Hello. Who are you?"

"A groombug."

"You groom Rumplewing?"

"For now. Each groombug has a dragon. If it is to live."

Her expression brightens. I've never seen such delight, as if she is looking at a miracle. I suppose she is.

"Are you the groombug Rumplewing mentioned?" Amber whispers.

"I am."

"Yes, it makes sense. Oh, dear groombug, battered and scarred, poor thing. How is it you are here?" She reaches to touch him, and he shrinks back, hairs flattened. Groombugs don't like to be cuddled by just anyone. She withdraws her hand. "Sorry," she murmurs.

He relaxes and stands on my snout, not far from her. He could just fit the palm of her hand if he wanted. "Call me Balofur. I had different dragon here. Elder, beautiful, wise. Seemor. She passed through flame. I burned."

"A flame? How? When?"

"A trick. A trick leads us here."

"But you survived. Are there other groombugs here?"

"No."

"What happened then?"

"I hid to heal, to learn outworlder speech. To find Seemor and save her."

"You found her?"

"No. I left to find help and saw Rumplewing. We are together. I taught her outworlder speak."

I notice Balofur says nothing about my having no groombug. Sometimes he can be incredibly selfish, thinking only of his needs.

"You know Seemor? Great elder? Orange rosettes around her neck, down her spine?"

"There are so many dragons. We'll look and let you know."

Near terror rises in me. They must not find Seemor. They mustn't.

CHAPTER 35

Revelations

Hote didn't want to listen, but his inner entity planted him in a stairwell just outside the officers' quarters. How he got there, Hote didn't know. He fought to creep away on paralyzed legs, only to give up when "Baaden…" caught his attention.

"What does he want now?" He recognized his father's deep voice.

"A replicator." The second voice was thinner.

"Stilwell, we've been through that before. It's enough that we receive his tissue samples, culture them into me-steak, and replicate them here. He gets plenty of that, plus other supplies, to keep him more than satisfied, wherever he's hiding out."

2Ray1 was definitely peeved, though in a controlled way, befitting a commander.

"He threatens, sir." Stilwell spoke cautiously.

"Does he now?" Father sounded amused.

"He says he'll withdraw the use of Traveler. He says he'll no longer send us reports of herds or anything else we can harvest if we don't give him what he wants. He's particularly upset you hired Dr. Kellyamber to take care of the dragons. He—"

"I know. I know." 2Ray1 cut him off. "He can threaten all he wants. What could he do? Complain to StarCircus? He's no longer in their employ. Rejoin the Watchers? They'd turn him in to the authorities. Let him threaten. We'll protect him as long as he is useful. When Traveler shows up, send Baaden extra me-steak. And a couple movies. Along with the regular."

Stilwell's voice grew louder as he bade the Commander adieu and announced that he was leaving to take Amber to the dragon enclosures. Hote scurried lightly down the steps. Stilwell would often escort Amber when he could have assigned someone else. Obviously the Communications Officer enjoyed her company, just as so many did.

Hote found her at the bottom of the stairs, waiting.

He spoke in a rush. "Baaden's not on the ship or at StarCircus. He reports to Stilwell, and Father knows."

Amber looked at him in surprise. "How do you know?"

Overhead, a door closed and they glanced up.

"I overheard. Father and Stilwell were talking just now. They use Traveler to send Baaden supplies, and he tells them what to harvest."

"How did you—?"

"It's that thing inside me. Making me do crazy things. Always listening to stuff, mostly things I don't want to hear. Waking me up in the middle of the night—" He stopped abruptly. Then in a hoarse whisper, "Stilwell."

"Where is Baaden?"

"Outside. No one knows where. Maybe I'll hear something about it."

The metal stairs rang with approaching footsteps.

Amber touched Hote's arm. "Be careful, my son. Don't let them catch you."

Taking Action

-1-

I need to give the other dragons hope, if they are still alive. So I rumble in secret. "Sisters, hear me. Trust the Watchers who wear green skins. A he with dark hair and a she, his mother, who has gray hair. They want to free us."

No answer.

Still I must try. "Help them to help you. Learn their language. I will tell you some of their words from time to time, if you will hear me. Can you hear me?"

Even if they are dead, there are still live dragons in the cages I can see. Surely they would respond. From what I can tell, they are young. Are the other dragons much older? Are there elders among them? Are they already dead? To salve my conscience, I take a risk. "Is there a Seemor among you?"

A small risk, really, which doesn't make me feel heroic.

"No. No Seemor."

That voice is lighter, stronger, and a bit shy. It came from one of the cells of youngsters. No matter the reply, I don't dare tell Balofur. What keeps him alive is believing Seemor is alive.

After several days of captivity, we watch Traveler belch out food in far cells, working closer and eventually burping out a mess in the trough in my cell. Balofur, of course, hides.

Once Traveler leaves, I lap up the mess and Balofur takes his share. "Not fresh," he says.

It's better tasting than the rancid dribbling I had consumed from the ground beneath the manna belt. I don't mention this. It might suggest our captivity is pleasant.

Later, water gushes over the floor of our cage, sloshing away waste into the drain. Since dragons don't eat for several days at a time, we don't leave much waste. Mainly a sack of watery and solid fecal matter. Then a cleansing ray tingles the air, and I huddle out of the way near the wall.

Afterwards Balofur gazes at the ceiling vent.

He doesn't have to tell me he wants to explore. Asking me to lift him up there in this smaller cage with my useless wings would be an insult, suggesting I am useless and a burden. I must prove I'm not. Meanwhile he waits.

My opportunity comes to prove my usefulness when three Collectors pass by. I yell at them. "Yuh! Yuh there. No kill me."

They falter, one bumping into the other. One starts to stop, but the other grabs its arm and pulls it away. The third does stop and ogles me. "What? What did you say?"

"Come on," its companions cry. "Keep going."

The three hurry away.

-2-

The usual Collector brings Amber and Hote. Or perhaps Hote just tags along. The Collector ignores him. Hote is like a shadow that slips into our cell with Amber. The Collector leaves. We can see Hote and smell him. Sometimes, however, we don't feel his presence.

Their visit enables us to learn more about one another. "Yuh say outvorlders make dragons. We look not tuh outvorlders. We look tuh Great Mother."

Amber nods. "You are spiritual. That's in your favor."

Hote fastens me with a look. "What is your Great Mother like?"

"Mountain that breathe fire and make rock like water."

"A volcano?"

Volcano. I latch onto the new word. "Volcano is our mother, life giver of our world."

The light in Amber's eyes fades. "A volcano." The sound of disappointment and tenderness enter her voice. "Still…even if it's a volcano you worship…"

"Vhat is vorship?"

"Worship? You speak to it, asking favors and giving praise."

Balofur breaks in. "You want we to pray to the Watchers?"

She takes a step back and raises both palms toward us. "No. Oh, no. No, no, no. Pray to whomever you think is sacred. If you believe in a volcano god—or goddess—it still shows you have a sense of the spiritual. Part of being intelligent."

Hote isn't so tender. "Volcanoes aren't gods."

Amber shakes her head at him. He ignores her "They're only a release valve for the molten interior of the planet."

"There's more to it than that," his mother says.

Hote will not be stopped. "Amber, the idea of a volcano being supernatural is nothing but superstitious nonsense. Dragons shouldn't believe in that. It stunts their intellectual development."

"Hote."

"They need to know the truth."

"In time."

"No, not in time."

I don't think we are so ignorant. I try to explain. "The Great Mother speak. I hear."

Hote shakes his head and ambles to the far end of the cell. I arch my neck after him.

Amber crisscrosses her hands in front of me. "It's all right. I understand. I do."

I'm sure she doesn't.

Sooner than we want, the Collector comes and escorts her and Hote away.

"Why was Hote offended?" I ask Balofur.

"He thinks he knows everything. He doesn't know what you experienced. Which doesn't mean you know everything either."

"What don't I know?"

"The Great Mother uses what she wants. The volcano for her breath. The trees for her hands. The little creatures for her eyes."

As I mull his statement, he breaks into a buzzy melody, and I feel the caress of his mouth on my scales. The loveliness takes away any sting I might have felt at his mention of my ignorance. Besides, what he said of how the Great Mother manifests herself in so many ways sounds poetic, so I bathe in the luxury of that poetry and the sensation of his grooming. And I ponder and reach for words that suggest I understand.

"The volcano is and is not the Great Mother."

"All is natural. All is sacred."

I feel rewarded at his reply.

The next time, I suppose it's the next day, Amber is escorted to our cage and gives my wings a good massage. Balofur tells her when she finishes, "I need to explore. Can you sneak me around?"

"In my pocket?"

"I can't see from there."

Amber strokes her hair and adjusts the shiny clip that holds her fluffy hair away from her forehead.

"There," Balofur says.

Amber's hands pause as he leaps onto her head and snuggles next to the clip. He slicks his hair back and blends his color to match her hair. He is nearly invisible. "I can see better from here."

Amber moves her hands sideways and gradually lowers them. "Will it work? It's fine with me if it does. I hardly feel a thing."

"I hardly see a thing," I say.

I hate being left behind. Whenever Balofur goes, I feel bereft, for I'm never sure he will return. The two Watchers haven't found Seemor, and I'm certain that's why Balofur insists on going with Amber when the Collector comes to let her out.

-3-

Amber follows her usher to the elevator, and Balofur notes his command, "Shaft down."

A door opens. They step inside.

"Shaft up."

Balofur looks up to see the open shaft above them. Once the door closes, they rise to the surface of the ground floor, and the usher leaves them.

Balofur grips Amber's hair in his claws. "Take me where the dragons disappear," he whispers.

Amber walks through corridors into work areas where she is greeted, ignored, given curious looks, or told gently the area is off limits.

She stops often to converse. "Hi, Prissy, how's your stomach? Gilmore, you're looking handsome today. Wollingston, you get that promotion yet?"

How soon she's connected with them! How they melt before her, some taking her hand, touching her arm, one even hugging her. Balofur squeezes himself as small as possible. He wants to urge Amber to hurry, but she has no third ear into which he can whisper. Impatience, however, is for the young. Besides, he can learn more as she takes her time.

"Here we are." Amber approaches a female worker with brown hair secured by a clip at the neck. "Hi, Bluemont. Care if I watch?"

"Oh, hi, Amber. Glad for the company." Bluemont strokes a console that angles from the wall.

Amber nods at a decoration on the console. "I'm surprised Commander 2Ray1 allows that."

"Oh, you mean my stick-on pop-eyed cartoon doll?" Bluemont laughs and gestures at it. "So far, I've gotten away with it. A gift from a special friend."

Its feathery tendrils trail over the console, just missing each colorful icon on the shiny brown surface. "Cute."

"Yeah, I think so."

The doll seems a caricature of a groombug. An insult. Still Balofur supposes it adds interesting texture to an uninspired flat surface.

Alongside, the wall gives way to a platform, occupied by waist tall boxes.

"What's in the boxes?" Amber asks Bluemont.

"Freight."

Balofur sniffs, trying for some clue to the boxes' contents and sensing only the plastic material from which the boxes are made. They could contain any of the collections he's seen in the bottom room. Feathers, skins, flesh. Examples of the Collectors' ugly business.

Bluemont touches a symbol on the wall, and the boxes fade and are gone.

"That's how everything is sent off, right?" Amber says.

"Right."

"How does it work?"

"See this icon next to the one I touched?" Bluemont points. "That's the I. D. drive. Interdimensional. That sends this entire craft into the void. Really not a void, but a world in between. Sometimes we enter it and use it like a cloak of invisibility. Thing is, though, we can't transmit messages when we're cloaked. Well, you can't. Not without a strong enough radio, which only special officers can use. Can't leave the ship either."

"How do you leave the ship?"

Bluemont moves her hand to a lower icon. "Touch this and it opens the ship's doors.

"Can anyone touch it?"

Ah. So far, Amber is asking the right questions.

Bluemont moves to the side. "Try."

Amber presses one icon after another. Nothing happens.

"Good security, wouldn't you say? Bars against accidents, like someone stumbling against the panel. You need the passkey. Just direct it, and the system is yours. Only me and Commander have access."

"Excellent. I'm impressed."

So is Balofur.

After thanking Bluemont, Amber strolls off. She pushes through a door into a private area with steps.

"What's this?" Balofur asks.

"Stairwell. And an elevator. They lead to the other floors. Would you like to take a peek?"

The stair steps ring beneath her feet. "These particular stairs lead only to two other levels. The crew occupies the second floor, and the officers, the top floor. It is on the top floor where Commander has his office."

They peer in at the second level. Balofur has seen all this on his exploration through air ducts, but Amber's explanations give it meaning. "What's that smell?"

"Cooking. They will be eating soon."

It smells like nothing he would call food. Vulgar. In a way, like carrion. Outworlders must be scavengers.

At the top floor the smell is similar but less concentrated. Only a few outworlders are there, each with more elaborate uniforms. "These are the high ranking, the officers," Amber says.

"Elders?"

"In a way."

On their way down, they pass an upcoming crowd. The steps ring. Voices echo. Amber reaches bottom through the growing congregation. She pushes through the door away from the stairs. Apart from the approaching workers, something catches Balofur's attention, and he gives a little jerk. His breath hits Amber's ear. "What's that on the one's feet?"

"Boots. Only the high ranking wear them."

The officer stands near the edge of the crowd. The boots are knee high and are scaled in orange rosettes against a brown, green, and blue field. Dragon skin boots? The color looks familiar.

"Get me closer." Balofur is almost panting.

They draw close enough that Balofur picks up the smell of the boots. Even with the chemical odors mixed in, he detects Seemor's scent.

"Take me back, take me back," Balofur urges.

Amber pulls away. When they are far enough removed from the others, she says, "I don't dare do anything to cause suspicion. I'll try to find a Collector to get us back to—"

Balofur collapses from Amber's hair into her hands. He lays his hairs back and shrivels.

CHAPTER 37

Stricken

Amber appears at my cage sooner than expected. The Collector drops her off and hurries on.

Face troubled, she opens her hands for me, and I see Balofur. Ordinarily he would have filled her entire hand.

"To the size of a pea," she says. "Hard, like a pebble."

I feel shaken. My breath staggers. What happened? "B-Balofur?"

"Seemor is dead." Balofur's voice chokes.

He is trembling, his eyes half closed.

"Seemor is dead," he repeats. "Goodbye, Rumplewing."

"What's happening; what did he say?" Amber doesn't understand dragon speak.

I feel a pounding in my chest. "How do you know Seemor is dead? Balofur? Balofur? How do you know?"

Balofur switches to outworlder speak. "Seemor is boots."

"B-bohts?" I don't understand.

"The boots!" Amber slaps her cheek. "So that's it. Oh, dear Balofur. I'm so sorry. So sorry."

"The bohts?" I again fumble.

Amber speaks in disgust. "An officer was wearing boots. Footwear. Made from Seemor's hide."

Like all groombugs who lose their dragons, Balofur is shutting down.

He mustn't! Doesn't he care about me? I want to rail at him for being so selfish. On the other claw, he is doing what tradition requires of him. He is doing the right thing.

My eyes sting. I want to hold Balofur, but my stiffened wings prevent it. I nuzzle the stricken groombug and warm him with my breath. "Don't shut yourself down. I can't survive without you. You are my life. I love you. I love you."

Amber sets Balofur on the floor before me. I sniffle. Tears run down my face and pool beside Balofur.

"What's happening; what did you say?" Amber asks.

"Cullectors killed Seemor. Balofur is killing Balofur."

Both of us plead in our own ways for him to live.

When the Collector comes for Amber, I hide Balofur in my mouth.

He barely clings to life. He remains in my mouth, safe from discovery. Both Amber and Hote come when they can and kneel outside the invisible wall. They whisper their concern. What else can they do? Nothing.

I keep vigil. From time to time I speak around Balofur, trying to reason with him. "Listen. I lost Tweekie, and I was going to shut myself down. Instead, the Great Mother told me to live. So I don't think it's required that you meet the gryphon. Balofur? Balofur, are you listening? If the Great Mother told me to live, how could I do it without a groombug? I think she sent you to me. I think she wants you to live, too. Balofur?"

At times I croon to Balofur, a deep massaging hum.

A group of Collectors come to my cell and try to get me to talk. I can't speak outworlder. Not with Balofur in my mouth. I'd risk exposing him. I can only stand there, mute.

They jeer in disbelief.

"No, it did talk. Three of us heard."

"If it did, it was only parroting. That's all."

"If so, it'd be useful as a novelty. Make an interesting pet or a performer."

By the third day, Balofur stirs. I release him from my mouth. He lies, wet as a newly hatched. I croon a whispered song to him, and after a while he buzzes an accompanying croon, weak. It dies and my song dies, too.

He lies beneath my chin and sleeps. After a while, he rouses and speaks, voice weak. "I now understand why you missed Tweekie so. I understand those captive dragons' preoccupation with groombugs. I feel like my innards are pulled out. Emptied of substance and energy. I understand now why other groombugs, who upon feeling their dragon's death, close their eyes, slump down, and meet the gryphon."

I want to plead some more with him, but I've pleaded enough. It is time for me to listen and allow him to make his own decision.

Instead, he sleeps, and in sorrow, I escape into sleep.

How long I've slept, I don't know. A whimper awakens me, and I see Hote inside my enclosure, pawing at his chest. He seems even more insubstantial than before. What's wrong with him?

He stands, hunch shouldered. "It's pulling me into the void. Into the void."

I crane my neck to look him full in the face. "Are yuh dying?" I sniff and detect no odor of decay.

He smooths his hands over his chest. Shakes his head. "I can't feel my feet. It's pulling me into the void."

"Vhat is pulling?"

"A living creature inside me. Pulling me into the void! It pulled me here, through the force field. And now it's…!"

"Yuh have pointer?"

Hote shakes his head several times. "No. It's the thing inside me."

A live being inside Hote?

"Yuh!" I take as commanding a position as I can, raising up. Hote starts, blinks up at me, and takes one step back. "Yuh! Come out! Come!"

Hote jitters. Indeed his feet do seem to be disappearing. I try to grab at him with my hands. My wings won't bend. So I snatch his arm in my mouth and lift him clear of what I think might be the void.

"Huh! Huh!" Hote cries. "No! No!"

Suddenly Balofur is alert. "Come out of him!"

I try to repeat it but I can't talk well with Hote's arm in my mouth. I try to shake the creature out of him.

Hote thrashes about but doesn't tell me to stop. "Come out of me!"

Back and forth Balofur and Hote yell the same command. Over and over.

"Come out of him!"

"Come out of me!"

And then Hote gets strange. "Boxes! There is a box! It's like a… Inside is a…And I can't…I can't…I…" He eases off as his feet become more substantial.

I set him down as if he were about to break. He is panting and sweating and falls against me. I can't help but feel protective. I tuck him under my armpit, and when he wraps his arms around my neck, I feel tender toward him as if he were Nip. I want to thank him for rousing Balofur. Instead I say nothing, lest it should only remind Balofur to choose death.

"It didn't come out," Balofur says.

Hote leans his face against mine. "It's resting now."

"Vhy yuh speak boxes?"

"I don't know. I guess it's because…" He struggles over what to say. "Sometimes the thing pulls me through solid objects."

"Vhy?"

"Because it's curious, I guess. It listens in on conversations. And it's partly connected to the void, so it can pull me between molecules. Into the space between solids. That's how I got here, through the force field, without a pointer."

I sense Balofur's tingle of alertness, and I share his surge of expectancy. "Vould it pull us free? From here? From this ship?"

Hote places his palm on his chest. "You mean, pull you through solid objects, like the force field and these walls?"

My colors brighten at the possibility.

"I wish," he said. "I have no control over it. A long time ago, I was sent into space and this thing crashed into me and entered me. I don't know what it is. It's alive, I know that. It would be too small, I think, to pull a dragon through anything solid. And you saw how it won't come out. It probably can't. It's too blended with my body."

We remain still, him tucked under my wing and hugging my neck. Balofur is too quiet. Hidden. We could have slept that way through much of the day. But a Collector approaches, and I nudge Hote into view. It's his chance to escape our cell.

"Hello." Hote catches the man's attention. "I'm ready to come out now."

"Oh? How'd you get in there? Thought you were working in the other area."

So the other dragons are not dead. Why won't they answer me?

"We work here and there."

The Collector opens the force field, and Hote steps through. With a glance in our direction, he whispers, "It's no use. Sorry."

Once Hote and his escort leave, Balofur seems to mutter from nowhere, "So much for depending on Watchers." Where had he been?

Though I'm tempted to sag from Hote's failure, or feel anger over being ignored by the other dragons, I wonder if Balofur is still intent on death. I'm afraid to ask. I must.

"Balofur, can I depend on you?" *Don't die.*

He stands on the floor where Hote had stood and fluffs hairs that cannot cover his scarred hind quarters. "When I was burned, I hid among the debris and survived on discarded dragon scales and left-over manna. Once I grew stronger, I searched the dragon cells for Seemor. To no avail. And I noted the gabble of the outworlder speech. I spied on them and pieced together the meanings of their speech. All in the hope of finding and rescuing Seemor. Again to no avail." He pauses, and I think he's finished. I have nothing to say. He continues, "I know now there is no turning back. You and I, by coming together, we've broken with tradition. The old ways guide us through life. Sometimes, though, the old ways no longer serve. For our survival and the survival of all dragons, we must realize that tradition is pliant and subject to necessary change. You and I are remolding the old ways."

I release a deep sigh and lay my chin on the floor to rest while he scrambles to my third ear.

"I've got to tell you, Balofur. I've been trying to connect with the other dragons. Voicing to them. They won't answer."

Balofur nibbles in thought. Then, "Don't give up. Keep trying to reach them."

His approval strengthens my resolve, and I feel as if I'd won a prize.

The following day, the Watchers return. Only Amber can come in. Hote, who glances repeatedly over his shoulder at us, is led away.

Amber looks about for Balofur. "Where is he? Is he…?" Her voice catches.

"Up here," Balofur says from my third ear.

She gazes up. When she sees Balofur, a light flicks on in her eyes, and her mouth spreads to reveal white teeth, as if she sees the most beautiful sight. I've rarely seen teeth so close.

"If you must know," Balofur tells Amber, "I came to rescue Seemor. From egg to death, I belong with her. I should be dead."

Balofur scoots from his perch and lands on my nose beside Amber's hand. I hold my head low, so she kneels before Balofur and me.

"You don't have to die. We can heal both your body and your spirit."

She turns to me and rubs my cheek. "And we can heal your broken wings, so they'll be as good as new. There is yet reason to live, reason to strive."

Is it possible? Are the Watchers healers, as Fetidbreath had suggested?

Our conversation lulls when Traveler clumps by. It occurs to me that the automaton needs no escort to allow it to enter and leave the force field. It has a built in pointer.

When it is no longer in sight, I ask, "How many automatons are there?"

"One."

"If cullectors think dragons are not intelligent, vhy does the automaton act like a dragon?"

"Because," Amber says, "a Watcher built it long ago. Traveler was designed to pick up information with its eyes and ears and send it to the Watcher Base. A Collector, who pretended to be a Watcher, stole Traveler and changed it to capture dragons."

Traveler is nearing our cage.

Balofur perks up at its approach. "Can Traveler recognize groombugs?"

"Its eye can pick up the image and send it."

"The eye only sends what it sees?" Balofur stretches a little larger. "Then it's time to get to work on gaining our freedom." He shrinks so fast as to disappear.

Traveler enters our cage and regurgitates food we don't yet need, when I notice something tiny spring onto the automaton's back. Balofur. My heart leaps.

Traveler pays no heed to his presence.

Is he really over his grief, or has he found another way to die?

Amber has to leave as Traveler exits the cage. Traveler moves ahead of her, and she whispers behind her hand, "Don't worry, Rumplewing. It's time for all of us to get to work."

Which means I must continue to encourage the dragons, even if they ignore me, and to prove my intelligence to the Collectors.

"Sisters, hear me. We are working on a way to free you. Here are some Watcher words you should know…"

CHAPTER 38

Spies

-1-

Traveler offers nothing but a slippery seat atop its head, seemingly unaware of Balofur's presence. Balofur digs his claws in and still no response from the automaton. They walk from the dragon cells to the elevator. There, Traveler commands, "Ickety wombat. Shaft down."

The door opens. The automaton flies up the shaft to the ground floor. Traveler doesn't command the elevator to rise or close, once they are on the main floor. From his investigations, Balofur remembers it will close automatically.

Traveler points its nose at the exit door and it slides open. The outer world rushes to meet them, with rain-freshened air. Traveler leaps into the sky. Balofur squints into it as the wind blows his fur. Gingerly he backs down, feeling with his feet. And then stops. Traveler's head has no indentation, no third ear. The automaton smells like Collectors' rooms and their aircraft, not at all like something alive. Its scales are not as good as a dragon's. Unyielding. Unfeeling. Balofur bores acid into the top of Traveler's head and gets no response. He talks to Traveler and gets no response.

And Balofur remembers how Traveler led him and Seemor through a wall of flame into the ship. The same with Rumplewing. Balofur will need to find a way to protect himself on their return. If Traveler leads another dragon captive, he could leap onto her and hide in her mouth.

When Traveler approaches a feeding flock of Shining Ones, Balofur screeches a warning to the groombugs, "Tell your dragons to flee. Flee the fake dragon. Flee death."

Before Traveler can get close, the flock disperses. And there goes Balofur's chance of surviving the curtain of flame. But then what groombug would have allowed him to share a dragon? If they had found a dragon without a groombug, as in the case of those enslaved unfortunates, what slave would return to captivity, once she had a groombug?

Balofur tucks the problem away for unconscious consideration and skitters from one side to the other to spit acid in Traveler's ears. Traveler must have sent some type of message. Eventually it lands on an island in a bog, where an outworlder with only a hip covering greets it. Balofur memorizes the outworlder's appearance. Its skin reminds Balofur of his own burned bareness, except this one's skin is softer looking, the color of red soil, with red hairs, heavy on the face and head, shorter on the arms and legs. It has what looks like plugs in its ears. It talks to Traveler, and Balofur drops off to hide nearby to watch it examine the automaton's ears and swab them.

It tests Traveler, sending it out and bringing it back in to adjust the hearing.

"Looks like I'll have to get replacement parts. Meanwhile that's the best we can do." The outworlder speaks into the air and the ear plugs must pick the sound up and send it to the Collector ship.

Balofur leaps on Traveler, who continues on its way, to collect food from the manna belt. Balofur catches manna on his face and in his fur and laps it up. How good to have it fresh.

On Traveler's return, Balofur recalls how it trumpeted as they passed through a curtain of flame. He can't shelter in Traveler's mouth. He skitters to the tail where he could drop off to miss the flames. Problem is, he'll be caught outside. Unless he can come up with an alternative idea. Not enough time. Too soon the door opens, Traveler cries out and enters through flames. Feeling the burn, Balofur drops off.

The ground is cool outside the ship. He lies there, trembling and checking for burns. No blisters. No soreness. His hair, what there is of it, is soft, not singed. Now he must wait for a way in. How long? Hours? A day or two or more?

Why not just shut down? After all Seemor is dead. He, too, should die. Turn belly up, close his eyes, and breathe his last. No more worries.

However…

The world is too alive. A cool breeze teases his hair. Birds call. Grass hisses. A low mumble reminds him of the Great Mother. And how she told Rumplewing to live. How can Rumplewing live without a groombug? And why was she told to live? For a reason, no doubt. A great task. One she cannot perform without a groombug. She needs Balofur. She needs his elder wisdom and knowledge. If he were to shut down, what would happen to the other captive dragons? Would they die? What was that to him? In a simpler time, a time without outworlders to capture and kill dragons, their fate would mean nothing to him, for it was the natural order of things. Now, the natural order is disrupted. Without him and Rumplewing, the fate of all dragons could lead to extinction because there would be no one to stop the Collectors. The Watchers won't stop them. They can't.

The sun has long moved past the center of the sky when the door opens. Out fly a dozen drones, buzzing like insects that resemble giant vultures. Drones. Off to kill and collect animals or plants. They will levitate the pitiful remains back to the ship. Balofur shrinks to walnut size, and as the last drone leaves, he leaps inside. The door closes with barely a shush.

"Shaft down," Balofur commands.

The elevator forms in the floor. Balofur rides it down. How long before it raises on its own? He must make sure. He counts.

"One dragon, two dragon, three dragon…" At sixty dragon, the floor rises until it is even with the main floor.

Balofur repeats, "Shaft down," and it lowers to where dragons— young, old, restless, and resigned—fill the cells. Some, recently captured, are calling for their groombugs. Pleading, getting no answer. Balofur calls in high frequency, careful to let no one see him. No groombugs answer. There are none. It is almost more than he can bear.

Thankful he must return to Rumplewing and make his report, he disappears into a vent into which old uneaten food has been washed.

-2-

Balofur appears from the floor vent and leaps into my third ear. I am relieved almost to tears to see him. I report on my efforts to reach the other dragons.

Balofur's only response is, "I found the spy."

I don't mind his interrupting my monologue. Balofur shares what he has learned, and I feel almost euphoric.

I quiver with excitement and wait for Amber to come. If I'd been in the habit of chewing my claws, my reachable hind talons would have been chewed to the quick. As it is, I pace until at long last she appears, with Hote.

"Balofur is here," I announce after the Collector moves on. Balofur expands atop my head. I can feel his hair flaring, making him visible. "Tell vhat yuh saw."

Balofur describes his adventure and adds, "It had fur under its nose."

"Red hair?"

"Yes. It plugged its ears and talked to the air."

"Baaden," Amber says. "I'm sure of it. Of him. Baaden is a he. He was a Watcher who became a Collector. He was probably speaking to someone on this ship."

"Through earbuds," Hote adds.

"Vhy?" I ask.

Amber pats the side of her thigh. "I suppose because his heart is in his purse."

"Vhat is that?"

"He's greedy for gain. He wants to take what doesn't belong to him."

"What will you do?" Balofur asks.

"We will send word to the Watchers, and they will deal with him. According to law."

CHAPTER 39

The Agreement

-1-

Hote stood with Amber beside the outworlder ship. The Watchers had to go outside to transmit without interference. Fresh air washed over Hote, bringing with it the smells of vegetation and soil. Except for the open door, the ship appeared invisible. He stood close enough to see the dust, the fly specks, and the stuck-on feathers or blood smears of collision kills on its skin. It was enough to tell him of the ship's size. In places it caught the sun's glint and cast a blinding glare. Within a redwood forest, it would allow a bird's eye view of the treetops.

Somewhere unseen, it bore the title, I. D. Express. The ship didn't belong here on the dragon planet, yet here it was, a deceitful presence, unseen while eating away at the planet's goodness like a disease. It was a disease. And to think, Hote had been concealed within its skin, supposedly under his father's care from the time he and Radiant were stolen from their mother just as they left their classrooms at the Academy. He frowned at the ship, frowned at the presence within himself that wouldn't go away.

"Amber, what does I. D. mean?"

"Interdimensional."

"Interdimensional Express. How long has it been here?"

"Oh…" She looked off in the distance, calculating. "It showed up a couple years or so after I got here."

"And it never left."

"2Ray1 has a contract with the Academy. As long as that lasts, he's parked here. The Academy pays him to serve the planet's needs by importing supplies to the launchpad. Anyone who joined the Watchers after I did, arrived on the launchpad. But…" She trailed off.

The Academy was supposed to be a benevolent organization, the alma mater of many. Hote dug at a feather caught in a spot of blood on the ship. "But what?"

"I. D. Express strained the Academy budget. Consequently they allowed 2Ray1 to provide self-support through the harvest and trade of certain items."

"By robotics? Drone harvesters?"

"Supposedly to provide the least interference with planet life."

"So the crew stays inside the ship while they trap, kill, and collect. Like Traveler."

Amber nodded. "Like Traveler."

Hote recalled snippets of conversation he'd overheard because the entity within drove him to eavesdrop. None of it had made sense. Now the pieces were coming together, and he didn't need to ask his mother for more details.

"I wish—"

"What?"

"Nothing," he muttered. He didn't want to get started, afraid he'd never stop. He wished Father would leave, that 2Ray1 had never come to the planet, that he had never kidnapped Hote and Radiant, that she had not left and joined StarCircus, that Hote was free of the entity that kept him out of others' favor. He wished he didn't have to keep his misery a secret. At first he had talked incessantly of being possessed, though Ahmed could find nothing wrong with him, other than he was fixated on a fantasy. After Hote earned the reputation of being unstable, he quit talking of the one within, so members would think of him as different but no longer delusional.

"What do you wish, son?"

"It's just that—" He leaned his face against the craft and sought for a change of subject. *Think of something productive.*

The Watcher crafts were small, but their invisipaint could still account for bird deaths and dragon injuries. Hote felt a need to apologize anew to Rumplewing for having flown the shuttlecraft without permission outside the compound. The marvel was that she held no grudge against him and that she and Balofur recognized that he was indeed inhabited by an entity that could pull him into the void. To them, he was not delusional. Somehow their belief gave him strength to rise above his misery. He would concentrate on improving the lives of those indigenous to the dragon planet. Take invisipaint. The first time he saw it, he had marveled at its pearly appearance that once sprayed onto a surface would bend the light rays so the structure seemed to disappear. The invispaint now seemed a weapon. He patted the I.D. Express's surface.

"Too much invisipaint."

Amber swept her gaze upward over the stained exterior. "Any amount is too much."

"You think Watchers can switch completely to camouflage?"

"I don't see why not." She pulled her visor into place. "Time for a report."

Hote followed suit. With their minds, they opened the Watcher Base band.

"Chief Li. Come in."

Li's image appeared before them. "How is it going?"

They didn't want to reveal too much or talk at length, lest the outworlder ship may have access to the Base band. Amber spoke first. She described the status of the dragons, their numbers, their treatment, and their needs. "We're delaying their deaths. That's all. They need groombugs in order to survive."

The Chief took two seconds to make sure he understood. "That creature in the corpse?"

"Precisely. More detail on that as we learn more." Amber quickly switched topics. "By the way, have you found Baaden?"

"No. 2Ray1 doesn't have him?"

"He's not a hostage, if that's what you're suggesting. Rather, he works for them. Using Traveler."

"You saw him?" The Chief sounded expectant.

"Traveler, yes. Baaden? As far as we know, he's somewhere on the planet, hiding."

"Mm."

"By the way, how did we get him? He seemed never to fit in."

"The Academy hired him from StarCircus, evidently he was recommended by Mr. Star, himself. Star uses a lot of robots in mock battles. Part of the entertainment industry for the wealthy. So Baaden seemed like the best choice because he is a mechanic and a robotics expert. Even the Academy can make mistakes."

The report quickly swung to a recommendation to change from invisipaint to camouflage, with Li agreeing to the proposal.

"Before we sign off, Chief, Hote has something to report."

"Go on."

Hote wasn't sure how much to say. Only that it was important. And that made him feel important. "You know that incident with the ship when the dragon crashed into it. There was something more. It scolded me, in our language. And we found this same dragon here, on the ship."

"Are you saying…?"

"It's true," Amber said.

"Interesting. Very interesting indeed. Carry on."

After they signed off, Amber placed her arm around Hote. "Do you know what this means? Chief Li won't hesitate to pursue a petition for an arbiter's response. We now have a case."

As soon as they returned to the ship, Amber sent a message to 2Ray1.

-2-

When Amber returns to our cage for our treatment routine, she looks more guarded than usual. She pats my shoulder. "Watcher Base couldn't find Baaden."

Balofur walks up my spine and perches on top of my head. "I know where he is."

Amber's eyes flicker. "On an island in a bog, yes, you told us, but it's not likely Traveler would take us there. Not when Baaden controls it."

"Hah dangerous is he?" I ask.

"More dangerous than what we suspected, it seems." She frowns. "Baaden worked in robotics maintenance. He was our chief mechanic and the only one who didn't do research, except perhaps in robotics. Besides research, we work as programmers, cooks, medics, and the like. And each of us is required to learn the basics and history of the overall project. So Baaden would have learned a little about dragons and a little about programming."

She pinches her lower lip. "He was uncooperative from the start, going against protocol, keeping to himself. The Chief and I never told anyone else, but Chief Li ordered him to resign, pending his replacement. Just before he was to be interdimensioned out, he disappeared, along with a set of earbuds and Traveler. With the earbuds he could contact the Collector craft. So, yes, he's very dangerous."

"Hah can ve stop him?" I ask.

Amber rubs my snout. "I arranged a meeting with Commander 2Ray1."

"I will go with you," Balofur says. His tone is final. I wish to go, too, and know I cannot.

Once the Collector arrives to let them out, Balofur springs into her hair.

Left behind, I feel helpless. What will the Commander do to halt the spy who helps him? That Amber and Hote should try to negotiate is absurd. I could drive Commander and his crew away, with a few blisters, providing I wasn't prevented from doing so by being kept in a cage.

So I stew. I snort steam. Pace. Even if I could attend, I'd still have to prove my intelligence. Maybe Balofur will speak out and prove his intelligence. Unlikely. He is too fond of hiding.

Tap, tap, tap. I tap the hard floor with my toes. I breathe against the force field and watch the steam of my breath condense and run in streaks of moisture. It is solid. No holes anywhere.

I gaze at the dragons in the cells beyond. Some glance at me, then away. To them, I am an outsider, to be ignored. Again, I try speaking in a deep base to the dragons. To no avail.

-3-

Hote squinted at Amber's hair. Its bushy grayness easily hid Balofur. He wouldn't have thought it possible for the groombug to squeeze himself to less than half his bulk and go unnoticed. On the other hand, Hote went unnoticed without the ability to reduce his bulk. He moved now with Amber and her hidden passenger from the stairwell into Commander 2Ray1's office. Father was leaning back in his chair behind his desk, arms crossed.

"Amber," he acknowledged.

"Commander," she returned a formal greeting.

His eyes flicked over Hote and returned to her. Hote felt his father's indifference.

2Ray1 gestured toward chairs that faced the desk. "Sit."

Once they were seated, he continued to regard Amber, and his chair rocked slightly. "Getting gray, aren't you."

Amber took no offense. "We all age. Part of life."

His eyes again flicked at Hote. "Hote?"

Hote didn't care to honor Father with a response.

"Still dazed? Not particularly useful, one would imagine."

Amber answered quickly. "He's harmless."

2Ray1 grunted.

He's harmless, she had said. Did she expect him to pretend to be intellectually diminished?

2Ray1 tapped the desk with his fingernails. "You wanted to meet?"

"To discuss certain things," Amber said.

The Commander raised his eyebrows. "It was inevitable. What did you want? To blame a father for the loss of your children? A daughter's escape from you? A son's warped brain?"

Her name is Radiant, Hote wanted to exclaim. Why couldn't 2Ray1 mention the name of the daughter who preferred Father over her mother?

Amber hid her pain well and seemed in a hurry to push it aside. She shook her head. "What's done is done."

Hote didn't want to push it aside. He started just above a whisper. "There is the box."

2Ray1 eyed him.

Hote gradually raised his voice. "It's like a kit. There is a doll that needs assembling. I can't assemble it."

2Ray1 seemed at a loss for words. Or was he simply curious over a demented son?

"It belongs to Radiant."

2Ray1 raised his hand to stop Hote.

Hote would not be stopped. In a louder voice, he continued. "There is a box. It's like a kit."

"Silence your son."

"Hote has a right to speak. After all, he is your son, too."

"There is a doll that needs assembling."

"Stop him or he will be removed."

"I can't assemble it. It belongs to Radiant."

"That's enough, Hote." At last Father had spoken to him, called him by name.

Hote broke from his litany. "Where's Radiant? Has she messaged you lately? Do you keep in touch?"

If 2Ray1 had lost control of his emotions, he regained it with a raised eyebrow. Having dismissed Hote, he again concentrated on Amber. "Radiant left no more messages after that one. It's obvious she wanted to be on her own."

"She loved you," Hote said, voice heavy with feeling. "And she's my twin. Why wouldn't she stay in touch?"

2Ray1 refused to look at him. He raised a palm upward, fingers spread. "That's the way she was. She found her calling."

"At StarCircus?" Amber said. "Then put us in touch with StarCircus."

2Ray1 tapped the table. "It's a huge organization. They don't deal in personal matters."

"How convenient." Amber's lips firmed. Hote felt her anger, the heaviness of it.

The Commander rose. "Not convenient at all. This meeting is over."

Amber raised her hands as if to push 2Ray1 to sit down. "Please, Commander. We didn't come to mull dead issues. We're here to discuss the dragons."

A moment's hesitation and Father resettled in his chair. "Ah. The dragons. You have rescued them from certain death."

"It's temporary. We can't prevent the eventual breakdown of their systems. They need something else."

Hote held his breath. Would Amber mention the groombugs? Balofur was against any mention. Hote slid a sideways glance at his mother's hair where Balofur hid so effectively.

"They are intelligent," she continued, "and undeserving of this slow death you have brought upon them. They need freedom. Only then can they survive."

The Commander again leaned back and recrossed his arms. "No matter. You're keeping them alive long enough before they are sent to their final destination."

Hote clenched his teeth and clasped his hands in a tight fist.

Amber leaned forward. "2Ray1, you must release the dragons. If you don't, you violate the rules laid down by Guiding Congress. You do know the rules, don't you?"

The Commander pursed his lips, looked up. "The planet must be harmless. With proper precautions, the dragons have certainly harmed no one. So even though they appear dangerous, we've been given permission to harvest them, which we have been doing for some time now."

"There are other points." Amber raised a finger. "That we were to work on drugged dragons would suggest that you consider them dangerous. You commanded Hote to wear a protection suit with a gas mask." Actually Hote had refused to wear the suit or mask, and his ushers seemed neither to notice nor care. "I'm glad that at least in my wing you've chosen to allow me to work with dragons that are not drugged." She raised another finger. "Have you taken a census? No? We believe their population is small, that their reproduction is slow. They are in danger of extinction if you continue to harvest them." She raised a third finger. "Finally, they are intelligent. Killing them is murder."

The Commander chuckled. "Lots of animals are intelligent. Until they become members of a governing body, it's pointless to be enraptured over their brain power."

"They can talk."

2Ray1 leaned forward. "Even if they talked like parrots, it doesn't make them smart enough to avoid being collected."

Amber raised her hands to the side, palms down and lowered her head in a bid for calm.

Hote coughed and said nothing. He focused on Amber, careful not to look at Father.

"If you wish," the Commander said, as an afterthought, "we'll stop drugging the dragons, even the ones that threaten us. Hote and you shall take full responsibility by working with them without protective suits."

"They've never threatened us." She took a breath and slowly released it. "Listen, Commander. You already have some products. From unicorns, from certain plants. While replicators have their limitations, I know you can multiply your simpler products. And if that includes things you've already taken from dragons, I'm sure you can replicate them. You don't need to take any more dragons captive."

The Commander listened.

"You're walking on shaky ground, 2Ray1. The rules can be interpreted to exclude you from this planet."

"You'd like that."

"That goes without saying."

"Because you think you married a heartless man? Do you think I kept the children to spite you? Did you know Radiant begged to take her and Hote from you from the first? There was no thievery involved. Only a caring father who is sorry about…" He gestured at Hote. "But it's silly to grieve."

Hote felt the heat in his face. Amber's silence suggested she already knew of Radiant's betrayal. A child's betrayal.

The Commander shifted in his chair, as if he'd reached a decision. "Those rules from Guiding Congress are flexible and allow for compromise. Seated before you is a reasonable man, despite your opinion of a former mate. One who doesn't allow emotions to rule. Unlike some people."

His lips twitched. Hote was sure he had just insulted Amber, although he never considered his mother to be led by her emotions.

"Here is a promise." The Commander raised his finger and locked eyes with Amber. "Here is a promise. We will collect no new dragons. In fact, we will release the dragons you see on the ship."

"How about dragons you've already sent out?"

2Ray1's finger disappeared into his palm. "We have some in the void."

"They are alive?"

"To be used as breeding stock. Before they die of whatever is killing them. Consider them gone. Beyond your control." He stood. "Essentially you win. You can take your dragons and leave, when the time is right. We'll let you know."

They left the room and stumped down the stairs. They were three steps down when Amber spoke. "By your father's reaction, I get the impression the box you keep talking about is important. Where was it?"

Hote had expected her to talk about the dragons instead of a topic she often dismissed as irrelevant. "On the launchpad. It was a prank."

"How so?"

"I thought the doll was real. It scared me and Father forced me onto the launchpad to show me it was safe."

"Safe from what?"

"I don't…I guess…the doll in the box. I guess I thought it was torn up from being transported. And…"

"And?"

"So after being in the void, Father sent me to the ship's doctor. He gave me some treatments which he said would calm me down and make me forget."

Amber stopped him halfway down the stairwell. "He what?"

"He told me it would calm me and make me forget."

"His exact words?"

"Pretty close."

Grumbling she rushed back up the steps, Hote on her heels. She flung the door open, and 2Ray1 looked up from his desk.

"Put me in touch with the ship's doctor," Amber demanded.

"Why?"

"He gave Hote something to erase his memories."

2Ray1 stared at her as if at an irritating child.

"You had his memories erased and probably had false ones planted! If he's delusional, it's because you made him that way. Let me speak with the doctor."

The Commander seemed in perfect control now. "The doctor you refer to no longer works on this ship. He moved on. Where, who knows? It's of no concern."

Amber leaned forward on the desk. "What are you hiding?"

He stiffened.

"What are you hiding?"

"Nothing you need to know. It is time for you to leave."

Amber gave a huff. "This is definitely a matter for an arbiter."

"Is it? Then contact the Guiding Congress immediately. Yes, do that. Now go."

-4-

Amber and Hote return after the meeting, with no Collector to let them in. Caught in the hallway, Balofur leaps off Amber and nestles against the force field, as if Amber had become the enemy. Without a Collector to open the barrier, he can only huddle on the floor.

Hote stands, arms folded over his chest, frowning down at Balofur. Amber shakes her head.

"Vot is it?" I ask from my side of the barrier.

Amber says, "Commander agreed to stop collecting dragons."

Good news. I hold my joy in check until I learn why Balofur is upset. "Vot's bad with Balofur?"

Hote nods at the groombug. "Ask him."

"They can keep the captive dragons they have moved to the void. For breeding. The Watchers agreed to this. Agreed!"

"I'm so sorry." Amber kneels before Balofur. "It was the only way we could get anything in your favor."

Hote remains standing. "I don't blame you for being upset, but those dragons are already gone. They're not here. They're already lost to us, as good as dead. Don't you understand?" He raises his arms. "Look on the bright side. We won. Traveler will no longer be going out to capture dragons. Only to gather manna. We'll make sure you and the others are released. All we have to do is work out a time with Father."

"Why not now?" Balofur says. "Without their groombugs, the dragons here cannot last long."

Amber speaks gently. "We have to do it in a way that appears friendly and respectful of the Collectors."

"How about friendly and respectful of the dragons?"

Amber strokes what's left of Balofur's hair. He lets her, which shows how much he has come to accept her.

"So what if we don't win completely," Hote says. "Since Traveler won't be bringing any more dragons in, the worst they could do is cloak the ship and keep it in the I.D. zone. The void. which means unless it's uncloaked, we can't leave it or transmit from it. But don't worry. Father, being what he is, we were lucky to get this agreement. The dragons on ship will be released. He will let us know the time. Meanwhile we'll continue to tend them and treat their sores."

"Vhen the ship is uncloaked is vhen Traveler leaves to gather and bring manna?"

"At least that. I'm sure they'll uncloak at other times. They have to, so we can communicate with Base. It's been in the agreement from the time we were hired to care for the dragons."

"Too vague." In a huff, Balofur, unable to reenter my cage, hops and rolls down the corridor, away from Amber and Hote.

They start after him. "Balofur."

Balofur rolls away all the faster and disappears through a vent.

"I'm so sorry," Amber tells me. "We're lucky to get what we could, and I know 2Ray1 could make it difficult. It's a personal thing between him and me. He doesn't care who he hurts in the process."

"Ve vill be hurt. The dragons in the void must be freed."

"You don't understand," Hote tries to explain. "It's on the condition that he keep those dragons that the rest of you are freed. He can't really win, because no one can breed them. They're all female, and without groombugs, they'll die anyway."

"No," I insist. "All dragons carry egg inside."

Amber's eyes enlarge. "You mean they're already bred? And they could lay? Would they before they died?"

I doubt it, but I don't want to give them cause to relax.

Hote breathes what seems a sigh of relief. "Even if they did lay an egg apiece, if any should hatch, they'd still be dragons with no groombugs. So they'd all die anyway, and Father still loses."

"No," I said. "Ve lose." I explain something I had to learn from Balofur. That an egg contains both a dragon and a groombug. While the eggs are still covered in their nest with debris and the shells are soft, the groombugs hatch and enter a different egg, to replace the groombug that had left it. There the groombug empties himself of a fluid that bathes the developing dragon. It contains a life enhancing force that the dragon will use at the end of her life to lay an egg.

I don't explain how, when the dragons hatch, each groombug bonds with the one he has anointed, a scene Fetidbreath allowed me to witness. It means I was Tweekie's bond mate. He was the parent of my potential offspring. And I remember Balofur telling me, "You are the future of your race, Rumplewing. My future was spent at hatching." These last parts I keep to myself.

"So…" Amber's eyes remain large. "Balofur is really a dragon, in a different form."

A dragon! Of course. The revelation brings Balofur closer to my heart. And now I see their distress as Hote bows his head into his fists and Amber covers her mouth with her hand. "Oh, my God," she murmurs. "Oh, my God. They can produce shes and hes."

At last they have the urgency I've felt for my kind.

Hote thumps his fist against his side. "We've got to get all the dragons out. Which means they've got to show their intelligence."

I remind him how I spoke to Collectors.

Hote shakes his head. "It's not enough."

Amber eyes her son. "What do you have in mind?"

"We've got to teach the other dragons to speak."

"Ve all can speak."

"Outworlder?"

"Dragon speak."

"Then teach us," Hote cries.

Before Amber can deny him, I beat her to it. "Yuh have no tail, no wings, no fire. Yuh can't change color. Yuh can't learn dragon speak."

Hote neither pauses nor loses his intensity. "Then show us how to teach the dragons our language."

Amber asks, "Didn't Balofur teach you our language?"

Before I can answer, Hote breaks in. "That's right. And he's free to move around. He could teach the other dragons."

This time I shake my head. "No one commands groombug."

"Surely," Amber begins.

"No," I interrupt. "It much dangerous. They have no groombug. They fight over him. Not learn outvorlder speak."

An idea pops into my head. "That thing in Hote. Get pointer. Have it take pointer inside yer hand. Point with yer hand. Point all dragons to freedom."

Amber's jaw drops. "You told them you had that thing, and they believed it? I thought you were past that."

Hote waves his arms about. "They believe because they saw it wasn't my imagination. They saw!"

"Ve saw," I said.

"So…" Amber looks back and forth between me and her son. "Is that possible? Could it take the pointer into your hand? Your flesh?"

Hote almost squeaks in anger. "If it can pass me through walls or pull me into the void, of course it's possible. Except I have no control over it." He turns on me. "I told you that."

Fetidbreath's gentleness comes to mind. I imitate her tone. "Maybe it not understand yer speech."

"It…" Hote pauses, thoughtful. "It understands. Because it's nosey. It likes to listen in on conversations. It likes to poke around. For its own reasons."

"Try make friend vith it."

A smile touches Amber's face, only to be replaced with a look of compassion at Hote's mixture of frustration and doubt.

-5-

Hote paced in his quarters after agreeing to join his mother in fifteen minutes for lunch in the ship's mess. Rather than study the gray metallic walls, he watched his feet, back and forth on the black rubberized floor. He needed only a minute to try something he'd never tried before without the risk of making a fool of himself before others. Try befriending the entity inside him, Rumplewing had suggested. In all the years it had inhabited him, he'd never tried to befriend it. Only in his thoughts had he spoken to it, insulted it. As if it could know his thoughts. Surely he didn't know its. And yet it had listened in on conversations. Therefore, he needed to speak to it aloud. What could he say to make it his friend? First, he must address it in a courteous way. What should he call it? What was it? Hitchhiker? Parasite? Thing?

"Hello, fellow traveler." Yes, that seemed a good start. Did he sense a shift inside? Attentiveness? No. Maybe if he continued he would get a response. "Since we're stuck with each other, we should try to get along. I'm sorry I haven't been helpful. So maybe we can work together."

Surely the entity must be listening. He tried to see from its perspective. "Maybe you can't talk, being inside me and all. You're a captive. Forced to go along with everything I do. Do you hear me? If you do, give me a sign. Maybe let me put my hand into the wall."

Hote pressed his palm against the wall, its metal cold to his touch. Smooth. Unyielding.

"Listen. I know you understand. You like to eavesdrop. You've got to be eavesdropping on me right now."

Hand still on the wall, Hote closed his eyes and tried to relax. He concentrated inward, only to sense emptiness. If anything, the entity seemed to shrink away from his awareness, as if into a void inside.

Hote felt a growing frustration. "Listen. We need to cooperate. In this situation with the dragons, it's important. They're counting on me to help them. And I need you to help. So couldn't we at least be friends? And help each other?"

For all its retreating, Hote didn't feel less insubstantial. As if it could find a hole and pull him in with it. Right now it seemed to have found the hole.

"What do you want of me?" he cried. "What do you want? Why won't you help?"

Hote leaned against the wall. He was useless after all. Useless as usual. *Boxes.* "There is a box. It's like a kit. Inside is a doll. And I can't assemble it." *It belongs to…*

Hote's mouth suddenly went dry.

"It belongs to…"

His heart quickened and he felt sick to his stomach.

"It belongs to…"

He choked. It belonged to Radiant; it was Radiant!

He sank to the floor against the wall. "No! No, no, no! Oh, Radiant, Radiant!"

And then his mother was there, hovering over him.

"Hote, what is it?"

She knelt before him.

"She's gone," he gasped. "She's dead."

Her arms encircled him, hugged him close, her cheek by his ear.

"What do you remember?" she whispered.

"The launchpad malfunctioned. The doll in the box, it was Radiant, in pieces. It had to be. Father tried to tell me it was a robot that needed to be assembled because it was a gift from StarCircus. It wasn't. It was Radiant, dismembered. An accident because the launchpad didn't work properly. And Father made me ride it. In a box. Forced me in. Told me it worked perfectly. Sent me into the void. And…"

Amber rocked him. He felt the tears spill onto his cheeks. And though his mother said nothing, he felt wetness dribble over his ear and down the side of his neck.

For a long moment they held each other and said nothing more.

When they parted and wiped their faces, Amber whispered into the silence. "Why the cover-up? Why would he keep it from us?"

Hote couldn't keep the bitterness from his voice. "He probably didn't want to lose the contract with the Academy because the launch malfunctioned."

Amber shook her head. "Something's not right, here. When did he put you on the pad?"

"I don't know."

"Was it soon after? Or did they take time to repair it? Did they test it before 2Ray1 launched you?"

"I was terrified. I think it was immediately after I saw her."

"Why would he do that? Beam you into the void from a faulty launchpad?"

"I don't know."

"It doesn't stack up."

"You think I'm mistaken?"

She gripped his shoulder. "Not entirely. Something terrible happened that made the doctor erase your memories and perhaps plant false ones. I think you're recalling some of that awfulness."

"Do you believe Radiant is dead? Because I think she is. I think that's why we never heard from her. That-that message she was supposed to have sent. It sounded too much like Father. She's dead."

Amber closed her eyes. Hote saw her struggle for composure. He wiped fresh tears from his eyes.

She started to speak in a hoarse voice, cleared her throat, and tried again. "If she is alive, I should feel it. I have never felt it, even with that message." Her voice trembled. "I have never felt it."

"You think we should confront Father?"

She huffed. "And have him continue to deny everything? He's agreed to see an arbiter. Perhaps an arbiter will look beyond the dragon issue into ours."

CHAPTER 40

Balofur's Discovery

-1-

Balofur's plunge hasn't been intentional. Rather, he rolls so fast, he careens against the wall. Whoosh, down he goes into the waste vent, amid dust, detritus, and debris. Air sucks at him and blows and bounces and buffets him, until he settles at last amid the sweepings. There he catches his breath and brushes the grime from his eyes and from his fur with his tiny hands. Twilight gleams through translucent structure. He's been in this zone before, when he had searched the first time beyond Rumplewing's cell. He had found nothing but dust, old scales, and bones. And dried poop and scraps of outworlder food. Nothing alive down here.

Disgust for the meeting between Amber, Hote, and 2Ray1 has followed him down the vent. The Commander sneered at Amber and Hote and belittled them. And Amber spoke gently. And Hote bit his lip, clenched his fists, and raved, not about dragons but about a lost family member. Radiant, who had gone to StarCircus where dragons were sent to be killed for sport. Radiant is involved somehow. Perhaps working with her father to provide the trade in dragons. Yes, it makes sense. It would be one of 2Ray1's secrets. She may even be killing dragons, herself. And what did Amber and Hote do about dragons? Nothing!

Watchers! Ineffectual and weak.

Because they haven't the dedication for any but their own kind. And dragons aren't their kind.

As for Commander 2Ray1's promise to free the dragons, Balofur has little faith it will happen. He, himself, must rescue them.

Somehow.

It would take more looking around and more learning of the outworlder words. At least the Watchers are useful in explaining words.

He is about to make his way back to the surface when he hears a sigh. Was it the ship's air? Or something else? A small mound draws his attention. It smells of groombug. Fresh. Close up, he blow dusts from it.

It is a groombug. Alive. Quivering. On his back, feet in the air. A youngster, dying. He was washed here after passing through flame with his dragon. His pale hairs are singed. Unexpectedly, he seems to have sustained no further injury.

"Why are you shutting yourself down?"

The youngster moans, and another quiver passes over him.

"Don't meet the gryphon."

He doesn't answer.

"Don't meet the gryphon. You have no reason to." Balofur nudges him. "My injuries are worse than yours, and I survived. Would you leave your dragon?"

Balofur thinks he heard the other speak. He leans in close.

"Already gone."

So that's it. Under normal circumstances a dragonless groombug will slump down, close his eyes, and die. Normally no one will stop him. These are not normal circumstances.

"What makes you think she is gone?"

"Wall of fire."

"That's no proof. You were separated, that's all."

"She's gone."

Balofur hisses at the youngster. "What's your name?"

"Sharpie."

"And your dragon?"

"Blueclaw. Gone."

"Not gone! Separated. Dying would be irresponsible. For sure, you would kill Blueclaw."

"Gone."

"Not gone! Alive!"

Sharpie's voice is clearer. "Blueclaw is alive?"

"If you are alive, Blueclaw must be. How is it you are alive and not burned up?"

"She is alive?"

"Sit up and pay attention. Explain why you are alive."

Sharpie rolls upright and brushes himself off. His fur is pearly gray. Except for being singed, he is quite handsome. How did he manage to survive?

"Blueclaw is a fast flyer. She likes to go fast. Faster than any other dragon. And when she is startled, she'll put on a burst of speed that truly amazes. That's what happened when she hit that wall of flame. It was so sudden, I got knocked off."

Balofur snorts in contempt. "So you assume that because you got knocked off that Blueclaw was killed? You give up too easily. Would Blueclaw give up as easily?"

"If she thinks I'm dead, she will."

Of course Sharpie tells the truth.

"She'll be alive. We can use your help in freeing her and all the other dragons."

Sharpie perks up. "And I can be with Blueclaw?"

"If you do exactly as I tell you. Will you?"

"Oh, I will, I will." Sharpie jumps up and down.

"Good. We will use hyperspeak, so no one else will hear us. Follow me, and do exactly as I say."

Groombugs have a good sense of direction and are seldom lost. Without trouble Balofur trundles through the system.

-2-

I am surprised to see Balofur emerge from the floor vent into my cage. The venting system must be connected throughout the ship. That means he can move anywhere. I am relieved to see him, at first so small as to be nearly invisible—the size of an outworlder's thumbnail. Then he relaxes to palm size, hair raised. If not scarred, he would be beautiful. Actually just seeing him return is beautiful.

"Amber and Hote were worried about you," I say. "They did their best to free us. The Commander makes it difficult because he and Amber are bonded, and they hate each other. So he punishes her by hurting us. Hote is their offspring."

"I must think about this." Balofur hops onto my scales and grooms. I stretch out in ecstasy and sigh in contentment to hear his buzzy song. After he has run a quick once over of my scales and settles to serious grooming, I yawn, smack, and steam in appreciation. And then I dare to gently repeat, "They were worried about you."

Balofur continues to sing and groom.

I venture to continue. "Hote and Amber always worry about you. Whenever you ride Amber, she's afraid you'll fall off and be hurt."

"I could sleep and never fall off."

"That's what I told them. Groombugs never fall off. And if they did, which they don't, they can leap back on. They can leap as high as an outworlder's head."

"True enough."

"When you left, they were afraid you would get lost, injured, or even captured."

"And you said?"

"He can take care of himself." I don't tell Balofur I almost choked on my words. While he has survived impossible odds, it doesn't mean he's invincible.

Then my ears tingle. Balofur is hyperspeaking. Why would he hyperspeak unless—? My pulse quickens.

Balofur scoots to my neck. "I found a young groombug. Sharpie. Utterly young and inexperienced. We'll need to reunite him with his dragon, Blueclaw, as soon as possible."

Another groombug! "We need to tell Amber and—"

"We tell no one."

"We'll need their help. Otherwise, how can we reunite Sharpie and Blueclaw?"

"We'll find a way."

"What if Blueclaw isn't alive? What if she…?"

"Then we don't tell Sharpie. Too many dragons need a groombug."

Balofur's actions and attitude seem counterproductive. For an elder, he doesn't seem to be acting with wisdom.

"Balofur."

The groombug waits.

"Balofur, you can't turn against the Watchers. They're our friends. They're doing their best to help us."

"Not good enough. You know what Amber does whenever she's out among the Collectors? She talks to different ones like they are clan sisters. Calling them by name, asking after their kin or hurts or ambitions. How is such and such? How is that scratch you got when you tripped over your toes? Good luck on your new lessons. Rattle, rattle, rattle. And she mustn't hurt their feelings so that they should do anything to save dragon lives. Just a tiny favor, if they please. I wanted to spit acid. It was worse with Commander 2Ray1. That's his name. He beat her up with words, and she cooed in return. And they talked about a family member's disappearance. An offspring, I guess. Radiant, who kills dragons for sport. I thought they'd never talk about helping us. Hote was useless. All he did was rave and get the visit off subject. Well, at the end, they got back to discussing us, to little effect. Empty promises because Amber has little power before the Commander. And Hote has no substance."

I can't argue. Not with an elder like Balofur, who knows so much and understands it all. Nevertheless, I remark weakly, "They're still useful. We may need them."

Balofur clicks his beak. "You are right. Ineffectual as they are, they are still useful. You can tell them I appreciate their help. You needn't tell them I will not rely on them to get us free."

Balofur leaps to the floor and waddles toward the floor vent. So soon he would leave when I hunger for companionship. "Where are you going?"

"On a problem solving mission. It may take a while."

I am left to soothe the Watchers' concern for Balofur, when I really want to frighten them into helping us escape before more dragons die.

Baaden's Displeasure

"He did what?" Baaden didn't like Stilwell's report. Commander's position was weakening.

"I told you, Baaden. He reached an agreement with the Watchers."

"That's bad. Commander shouldn't have agreed to anything."

Given Amber's ability to charm, she could nibble away at the staunchest resistance until it crumbled. And with the weakening situation amid the Collector ship, he would need to arrange for a continuation of his trade with Stilwell, in case Commander was forced out of business. Could he trust the Communications Officer to deal secretly, independent of 2Ray1? It was a risk he didn't want to take. Not if he could salvage the present operation.

"Listen, Stilwell. Get Commander to stall. This plan of his to breed dragons won't work."

"Why not?"

"Because they seldom breed, and probably won't in captivity. They'll die first. And I just learned something else. They depend on a symbiont in order to survive."

"What kind of symbiont?"

"It's called a groombug."

"How does it work?"

Baaden hissed. "How should I know? Am I a sniffer?"

"Well, you must have overheard something with that bug you planted at Watcher Base before you left."

"That bug is practically useless. It's in the bay, which hardly anyone visits; because I had no choice in where to plant it!"

Stilwell sighed and said nothing.

"Listen, Stilwell, are you keeping open communication with StarCircus? I don't want them to cut me off completely."

Stilwell chuckled. "Well, I am Communications Officer after all."

CHAPTER 42

Balofur Eavesdrops

Balofur rolls and scoots and leaps. He navigates the floor and hides in corners and creases, pulling himself small and flattening his hairs. He lurks on countertops, a shadow or ball of lint among the clutter. He leaps onto Collectors and rides in their hair, on their hat, in their collar, or in the folds of capes. He hitches rides on boots. Careful not to reveal the most visible part of him, his large, soulful eyes, he peeks here and there, listening, sniffing, learning.

Eventually he finds 2Ray1 and rides in his cape all the way to the top floor. 2Ray1 enters his office and sits down. Soon Stilwell enters and takes a chair. "It won't work, Commander."

"Explain."

"I talked to Baaden about our agreement with the Watchers. He says it won't work. The dragons need groombugs. Otherwise they will die. It's just a matter of time before all the dragons we have will die. As for breeding them, they won't produce without a groombug."

Tucked next to the Commander's neck, Balofur wonders how they found out about groombugs.

"What is a groombug?"

"Some kind of insect. Baaden didn't elaborate. I assume they settle in clouds on a dragon and groom it. That keeps it healthy. It takes a healthy dragon to breed."

"So you assume. Ask Baaden for details."

"I did. He doesn't know any more than what he told me."

Commander drums his fingers on the desktop. "How does he know this when he didn't earlier?"

"Because through Traveler, Baaden can tap into a bug that he secretly planted in something he calls the bay. Where he used to work. Where he can overhear conversations. It seems to clarify what little we picked up from Amber's report to Watcher Base."

"Small clarity. One cannot think much of your Baaden. While his use of the automaton has some small value, his judgement inspires little confidence. These dragons here are doing fine under Amber's care. It would be a good idea to hold onto a few, just to see how they fare. You will separate out male from the female dragons."

Stilwell hesitates to reply.

"Well?"

Stilwell's face turns red. "Commander, it's difficult to distinguish. They look alike. In many ways they remind me of a giant bird of prey."

The Commander stands and leans his hands on the desk toward Stilwell, reminding Balofur of a dragon's threat stance. Stilwell's face pales, which impresses Balofur. So outworlders can change color.

"Prove you're not useless."

"Perhaps the largest are males."

"Then select what you think are some, and we'll run tests." Commander 2Ray1 sits and looks down at his knuckles. "You may go."

The Communications Officer rises. Balofur leaps onto his hat. On the way out, Stilwell stops, rubs the top of his hat.

Just ahead of his hand, Balofur slips into his collar.

Stilwell brushes imaginary lint from his shoulders, shrugs, then presses something into his ear. An earbud. He speaks to the air, instructing a Collector to gas certain dragons.

Alone, he strolls the length of the main hall and takes the elevator to the bottom floor where he walks along the cells and around a corner into Hote's wing. He has a pointer. He aims it at a cell of unconscious captives, and the force field dissolves. He moves among them, crooking his neck, squatting, looking, and shying away when a dragon shifts. Supported by his hands on the floor, he cocks his head until his hat falls off and his hair brushes the floor. Here is one whose tail is curled in such a way as to expose its underparts. He can't tell a thing. He tries to compare it with another dragon who is more outstretched. When they begin to stir, he replaces his hat, hastens away, and closes the force field behind him.

"Impossible," he murmurs. "Might as well examine the back side of a bird or lizard."

When the Communications Officer returns to the main floor, Balofur creeps to the back of his neck and spits acid.

"Ah!" Stilwell swats his neck. His pointer hits the floor.

Balofur leaps down.

Stilwell yelps and tugs his collar. "Help! Someone. Get me to emergency."

Balofur hops onto the pointer while nearby workers run to Stilwell's assistance.

"What is it? What's the problem?"

"Something stung me. It burns."

Balofur rolls down the corridor. The pointer is large for him. He doesn't dare hitch a ride on anyone. He must remain expanded enough to roll with the device. And roll he must at top speed, lest he be seen. Until he shoves it into a vent.

CHAPTER 43

Into Rumplewing's Hand

-1-

I am astounded to see Balofur holding a device almost as big as he. He tilts it at me and waddles into my cage. The pointer.

"Where? How?" I stammer.

With a shimmer, the force field closes behind us.

I want to hug Balofur. With my stiff arm, I reach, and he stuffs the device into my grasp. "Keep it hidden. Tell no one."

"How did you get it?"

"The Collector dropped it after I spat acid down his neck. Commander sent him to separate the she dragons from the he dragons."

"He dragons?" My jaw drops. "Are Collectors so ignorant? The only he dragons are groombugs."

Balofur stops.

"Do you realize you're a dragon?" I can't keep the wonder out of my voice.

Balofur gives what passes for a shrug and holds to his topic. "When no outworlder is looking, find Blueclaw and unite her with Sharpie."

At that moment, a pale groombug steps from the waste vent into our cage. He huddles, eyes wide. His pearly hair is so delicate, it would waft away, were it not attached.

"I'm Sharpie." His voice is feathery. "Balofur told me to come here."

Such a pretty groombug. So young. I warm toward him, poor thing. "Hide under my tail. There you'll be safe."

Sharpie zips with surprising speed to my tail.

I flex my digits over the pointer. It feels as smooth as a water-polished rock, but light. I direct it at the wall and watch the air shimmer, disappearing and then reappearing, barely seen.

What a wonder Balofur is! He isn't pretty, but he seems less ugly. He is a force that cannot be dismissed. By contrast, Sharpie seems as gossamer as his hair.

Balofur, the elder. Standing like a leader beside my hand. What a dragon he is! A true dragon. He makes me feel on the verge of elderhood, having this pointer in my grasp, given by so powerful a groombug. I feel unbeatable.

"Why not tell Amber and Hote about this pointer?" I say.

"I don't trust them not to mess up. Not when they're dealing with a stupid commander. They can help, and when the time is right, we will all escape."

He leaps to my third ear just before an escort brings Amber to our cell and lets her in. I can feel Balofur shrink. I don't have to see to know he blends in until the escort disappears. Then he is on my shoulder, and we stand, innocent before Amber.

"I followed Stilwell," Balofur says, face level with Amber's.

Amber looks about, ready to pretend to groom me whenever a Collector passes. As it is, she kneads the muscle of my shoulder while Balofur tells what he has seen, omitting mention of the pointer and Sharpie. "They think groombugs are a cloud of insects. And Commander sent him to separate she dragons from he dragons."

"Really!" Amber covers a snicker with her hand. "I've got to tell Hote. It'll give him a big laugh. Let them have their delusions."

Then she grows serious, looks both ways, and rests her hand on my neck. She leans her cheek against mine and looks into my eye. Her expression displays fondness. And something else. Her eyes are dark, troubled. A dimple forms at the corner of her mouth as she presses her lips together, seemingly reluctant to speak.

"It looks like they're not going to honor our deal."

What can I say? Balofur's report wasn't all funny. I let her talk.

"I know how anxious you must be about the situation. I assure you, we will work to rescue all the remaining dragons on the ship."

"Soon?"

"We understand the urgency. Unfortunately Commander sees no hurry in releasing you because he knows you won't starve. As for keeping the dragons healthy, he still thinks Hote and I can do that. I think we should make it clear to him about groombugs and their necessity."

I chuff a thin cloud of steam. Balofur clicks his beak.

"No," he says. "2Ray1 might hold the dragons here until you bring him groombugs. You could never do that."

Before they say more, I divert them. "Commander punishes yuh by hurting us."

Amber pauses then blurts, "What makes you think that?"

"Balofur saw it at the meeting."

She sighs. "It's my worry, not yours."

"You think ignorance will save us?" Balofur's tone is sharp.

"It's not your problem." She drops her gaze. "Strictly between me and the Commander."

"Vhat happened between yuh and Commander?"

Balofur leaps to her shoulder and bellows, "Tell us!"

My heart wants to shrivel at his tone. Amber looks apologetic, the way Hote did when I blundered into his craft. She reaches to touch Balofur, and he evades her hand by leaping to my snout.

Her hand drops to her waist. "It's a long story. We were both students at the Air Academy where we met. I studied ecology, and 2Ray1 kept changing his major, so he learned about navigation and business." She interrupts her narrative only to define terms we don't understand. "At the time I found him attractive. We married, and too soon found we couldn't agree on anything. I was out to save the world, and he to exploit it. I tried to reach him with my foolish youthful idealism. At times I thought I succeeded. I was wrong. He'd say or do something that…" She shook her head.

"We had two children, a son, Hote, and a daughter, Radiant. Twins. Perhaps our marriage lasted because I didn't spend much time with 2Ray1. Our different professions kept us apart."

When they were together though, Hote sensed his father's coldness and was protective of his mother. Radiant, however, was like him in ways that worried Amber. So after some years she took the children and fled.

Balofur and I listen without comment about a girl who so preferred her father, she secretly contacted him when both children were at the Academy so he could steal them back. He kept them on the ship, not so much in his company as in the care of a tutor.

"During this time, 2Ray1 got a deal for harvesting on the dragon planet. He refused to connect with me until some years had passed. And then it was to return Hote after Radiant was killed in a terrible accident that Hote had seen. It must have involved the transport pad because it frightened him, so 2Ray1 forced him onto it, and Hote insisted he suffered from an interlaunch collision with some entity that entered him. I don't know. Ahmed, our Watcher Base medic, said he was suffering from delusions and fixations."

I don't tell her that Balofur said Radiant is alive and killing dragons. If Hote is mentally off, I wonder how we can depend on him. Amber doesn't dwell on his predicament but turns to ours.

"2Ray1 knows Hote and I are required to report in periodically to Watcher Base. And that we have to go outside to communicate, to avoid static interference. So we depend on Bluemont who works at the launchpad to control the doors, to hold them open long enough for us to connect and then get back inside. Watcher Base knows about the agreement, but not about the latest news. Of the possibility of a broken agreement. Be assured Base is doing all it can to help. They are aware of our need to move fast. I think we might be able to get Bluemont to help us get the dragons out. Once that happens, we can bring them to Base, so we can divvy the dragons among clans where groombugs will share in grooming them."

Balofur snaps out a reply. "That won't work. Dragons leave clans to die. They don't enter clans to be saved if they have no groombug, and there will be no groombugs available."

"What about orphaned groombugs?"

"If a groombug loses his dragon, he will die."

"You didn't."

"I almost did. As you are well aware, our needs prevented it. Don't rely on needs to prevent other orphaned groombug or dragon deaths."

Amber pinches her lower lip. "I've been thinking of another solution. What if they collect groombug saliva and use it to make a cleanser for dragons with no groombugs. Would that work?"

What an idea! Would it work? I feel too inexperienced, too young to answer.

Balofur pauses before saying, "It might. I'll give you some. When can you send it out?"

Amber's lips disappear between her teeth before she answers. "Hote and I can receive supplies from Base. We're not allowed to send anything out."

Before Balofur or I can say anything, she hastens to add, "The groombugs of free dragons might—"

"No," Balofur snaps.

To soften his reply, I say, "Free dragons avoid Watchers."

I feel Amber brace herself. Something hard as rock enters her spine.

"Periodically we requisition the Academy for supplies, which are then beamed here through the launchpad. We can't wait around to sneak anything into a regular shipment. That would take too long. We'll arrange with Base for a secret messenger to take it to them. I think Maximus can swing by, maybe under the cover of trees. And Hote will enjoy a walk outside, once I suggest it to Bluemont. Give me a generous sample, Balofur."

After Amber secures a sample of Balofur's saliva, he whispers in my ear, "Getting that into a cleanser might not speed our release. I think we're hardly any better off. Rumplewing, it's up to us to get everyone out of here."

I know what Balofur wants me to do.

"Amber," Balofur says, hopping onto her shoulder, "I'm going with you to take another look at this launching station."

Once the Collector comes to release Amber, she walks off with Balofur contracted to pea size next to her ear.

After they leave, I hear a deep rumble. The older dragons who had ignored my attempts to speak to them are now catching my attention.

"Rumplewing, the one in green has appeared. He croons to us and soothes our scales. It's just as you say. When will he lead us to freedom?"

My heart swells at their response. How do I answer, though? Trust the Watchers? Don't trust them? Say that I, a youngster, will save these older dragons? Surely we can work together. "Hote will lead you to freedom. He and Amber are working on a solution, along with us dragons."

-2-

Almost immediately a couple of Collectors, one short and one tall, appear at my cell and stare at me.

"Locator shows it's here," the short one says.

What are they are talking about? Evidently they're looking for something. The pointer?

Tall One bobs his neck side to side. "I don't see it."

I stare at them, innocently.

"Stupid dragon's in the way. I wouldn't be surprised if the dumb monster is sitting on it, like it's a piece of gravel."

So it is the pointer. How would they know it's missing? They mentioned a locator, whatever that is. I keep my hand closed over the pointer. Should I slip it down the drain? Balofur could retrieve it.

"How do we get it? Last thing I feel like doing is suiting up to face a gassed dragon."

"Better gassed than frying us." Short One rocks to one side, dismissive.

"Well, pointer's not going anywhere. We can get one of the Watchers to pick it up for us."

That settled, they leave.

-3-

My ear vibrates. The groombugs are hyperspeaking.

Immediately Sharpie is on my back. "I felt you talking to dragons. About the pointer?"

I sense his eagerness. I am eager, myself, impatient to work the device. From the distance of my digits, I examine it. Smooth, oval, featureless.

232

I point it at the side wall of my cell, squeeze, and see a shimmer of the dissolving field. Sharpie trembles.

I could point it at all the force fields and dissolve them. We could all escape our cells. What lies before us, though? Can we hide until we find the way out? Is the ship even in contact with the ground, or is it cloaked in the void? We dragons are two and three times the size of these outworlders. Groombugs can squeeze their dimensions and blend in. We might change our colors to match our surroundings, but I doubt we can blend in. We are too big.

My talons clack over the floor. I reach my nearest dragons. Nine young ones. Whether they have heard my communication with the older ones or not, they may not have recognized me as one of them. They rear up, hiss, and shoot flames at me.

Sharpie emits a squawk, and I jerk back.

"Stop," I yell.

They must think only a traitor can move freely from cell to cell.

"I'm not a traitor; I'm your savior!"

More flames.

I dodge.

Sharpie yodels in terror.

"Don't hurt the groombug," I yell.

The dragons stop their flaming.

"Groombug? You got a groombug?"

Necks crane. The youngsters hitch closer. I back away.

"Where? I want. I want."

Their demands rush at me like a flood.

"It's just one," I say.

"Whose is it? Let me see."

I back until I can back no farther.

"Where's mine? Are you here to free us?"

They surround me, sniffing, eyes prying.

"Quiet," I cry.

Again the rush of demands, the frenzy.

"Listen to me."

Eventually they quiet, but their wings rustle, their bodies shift, their feet and fingers clench and unclench. I don't dare tell them their groombugs are dead, lest they panic and lose control.

All these are dragons near my age. Despite my youth, despite my ruined wings, I will myself to speak with authority. "Which one of you is Blueclaw?" Is Blueclaw even here?

"I'm Blueclaw." She raises her hand, and indeed her claws, her very hands and feet are blue, as is her snout.

I want to handle this with order. It is not to be.

"Blueclaw," a sniveling Sharpie cries out from my third ear.

The other dragons explode into action and tear at Blueclaw with their talons. They whip her with their wings and tails, striking one another in the process. She disappears in a riot of bodies. They roll about, and at one point Blueclaw lies on her back, fighting for her life. As quick as she is, managing to right herself, she cannot fend off the mob.

My cries for them to stop go unheeded. Who am I, after all? Not an elder.

Sharpie puffs himself up to full size, raises his hairs, and pales to white, hard to miss. "Stop!" he pipes. "Blueclaw is mine!"

The activity slows. Blueclaw is pinned down.

"Groom me," one says, "and we'll let Blueclaw go."

"I will groom only Blueclaw. If you kill her, I will spit acid on you and die."

The dragons shrug back. Defeated.

Blueclaw spins free, and Sharpie shoots off my head. In two bounds, he vanishes among Blueclaw's scales.

"Where are our groombugs?" come plaintive murmurs.

"Don't despair," I say. "Protect Blueclaw and Sharpie. And be alert."

To the hum of Sharpie's grooming and serenading Blueclaw, some droop, eyes half closed, chins hanging, their wings sagging. Others hiss steam and clack their talons on the floor or slowly fan their wings. Shall I move Blueclaw and Sharpie into my cell to protect them from the others? Not possible. The outworlders would notice. What can I say to win these prisoners' confidence? "We can escape, providing we work together."

"What of our groombugs?"

"They are not here. That's all I know. It may be they already escaped and we must go to them."

The stirring quiets.

"It's up to us to free ourselves. We can only do it if we work together. It will require patience, knowledge of the outworlders. I know their speech. Because of it, I can learn what will happen." It seems best not to reveal I have a groombug, so I can't give Balofur his due. "We must wait for the proper time when I can dissolve the force field, and we will attack and escape. Meanwhile you need to learn outworlder speech."

"Why don't they learn our speech?"

"They can't make the sounds or color variations or posturing that forms our language. They have no tails to wiggle, no way to puff themselves up, and no fire inside. Theirs is simpler because mostly they speak through their mouth, and we can make most of their sounds, enough to be understood."

"I will teach you," Sharpie announces. I realize he is receiving instruction from Balofur through hyperspeak. "I can explore. I can learn all about the outworlders, and I can teach every one of you." Sharpie's clear voice deepens with sudden menace. "But I won't groom you, so don't ask."

The dragons nod and bow like obedient pupils. The power of groombugs!

"Can you get us a pointer?" Blueclaw asks.

It seems both unlikely and dangerous. I don't have an elder's years that earn proper respect and obedience among dragons. I can't trust them with a pointer. They'd be more likely than Amber and Hote to mess up. I need to mollify them. "I can't get you a pointer. If you promise to stay in your areas, I will permanently dissolve the force fields between our cells. Stay in your areas, and the outworlders will never know."

The dragons readily agree.

CHAPTER 44

No Deal

-1-

With the force fields down, Balofur takes off along the corridor. He is hyperspeaking with Sharpie, listening to the young groombug's report and then telling him what to do.

Hyperspeak has great range, and Balofur keeps in touch as he regards the door Traveler uses to enter and leave the ship. It is closed. He doesn't know how to open it.

Balofur waddles and rolls. In and out of vents, along shelves and in the clothes of crew members. Not far from the launchpad, he finds Amber, deep in conversation with Commander, and leaps unnoticed into her hair. There is an edge to her voice.

"Look at it this way, 2Ray1. We've gone along with your games. I've followed all the paths you've taken Hote and me on in order to win a release for the dragons."

Good. She is talking about dragons.

"What pretense will you use this time to delay us?"

The Commander raises an eyebrow. "When you stop playing your little games."

"I have always been serious. You should know that."

"Really? It's obvious you have resorted to trickery. Or tried to."

"What are you saying?"

"We need groombugs."

Balofur has tucked himself behind her ear where he peers through her hair.

Amber looks away and then back. "It's too late. Each dragon came with a groombug, and you killed them."

The Commander sighs. "Give us groombugs or the deal is off."

"Impossible. The agreement is binding."

"We'll see about that." He pivots, starts to move off.

She matches his steps. "Meaning?"

The Commander doesn't answer.

"Meaning?"

He strides across the floor of workers.

Amber strides beside him. "I would be willing to discuss this before a legal counsel. Would you? I think Bluemont would agree to a legal counsel. Since you dismissed her for following protocol."

Commander stops and faces her. "She's under authority that determines when the ship door is to be opened or closed. Not her. Not you."

Evidently he had just dismissed Bluemont. Hote had stepped outside with a tube of saliva. Did he have enough time outside to hide it and call Base to pick it up?

Amber doesn't back down. "You break your own agreement. You agreed when Hote and I were contracted to work with the dragons that we report on a regular schedule to Watcher Base. She was following that schedule when you dismissed her."

"She was dismissed for improper attention to duties, of which includes fraternizing with unauthorized individuals."

For all the tension, they speak in hushed tones. Workers are too busy to notice them, or at least pretend to be busy while their commander is there.

Amber forces her words through clenched teeth. "We are not unauthorized, not legally. If you don't let us report to Base, they will call in the enforcers. Where will that leave you, holding us hostage? Or should you dismiss us, too? Yes, do. Send us back to the Watcher Base. Along with the dragons. You'll be rid of us."

Good for Amber. Balofur would like to shout a word or two. Instead he keeps himself scrunched small, nearly invisible.

Commander shakes his head as if over a difficult child. He turns his palms upward, raises his brows. "There is nothing to hide. Trust us."

"How can I trust you when you won't share Radiant's history with me? What happened to her on the launchpad? Is she alive or dead?"

"Must you dredge that up again? As far as is known, she's with StarCircus. She chose to estrange herself from you. And don't pretend it is anyone's fault but yours. You always were jealous over whom she preferred. Daddy's little girl, she'd do anything for her daddy."

"Hote has his doubts."

"Has he?"

"He saw something."

"You trust Hote's word? Haven't you figured it out yet? He's delusional."

"He's beginning to remember. Something happened to her. Something you're covering up. Why?"

"You have a need to blame someone for something that never happened. And for what else? The weather? Enough of this rehashing of old events."

Yes, keep on subject, Balofur wants to say.

Amber sighs. "Enough, for now. On to the most pressing. 2Ray1, we need to reach an understanding over the welfare of the dragons."

Commander waves a hand in dismissal. "Haven't we already? No? Very well." He faces her. "Let's meet with an arbiter. Isn't that what you wish?"

Amber regards him, as if in disbelief. "Very much."

"It's in your hands to get the best." He smiles. "Nothing less than the High Arbiter, the shapeshifter, who has the power to dispense justice and offer protection. Nothing less."

Amber's lips firm, as if he has demanded the impossible. She stalks away from him.

Balofur speaks near her ear. "Where is Hote?"

"Inside. Bluemont let him out when we told her he needed to deliver a message to Base. 2Ray1 allowed him to return just before he dismissed Bluemont."

So the saliva sample is placed for pickup. The dragons will get their salve and survive a bit longer.

"What is an arbiter?"

She ambles across the workers' section, away from the launchpad, away from 2Ray1, while secretly answering. "It's a special being who is sent to understand our problem and solve it. Commander isn't worried because it likely won't come."

"Why not?"

She nods greetings to passersby and continues on, her voice lowered. "A long time ago, before I. D. Express captured dragons, I petitioned the Academy for the removal of any harvesting on this planet. I argued that it was so unique, it be kept pristine. I received no response. And then lately our leader Chief Li petitioned with a new argument, that dragons are sentient and cannot survive long without a groombug. This is knowledge new to us, but it may not be enough."

"Why?"

"The petition goes to the Academy, which would need proof. After all, there is the contract between them and I. D. Express, which provides the only porthole to our planet and our needs. If the Academy decides the petition needs attention, they would forward it to the Guiding Congress. If the Guiding Congress agrees, they might send an arbiter to investigate. It could take months."

"Empty actions. Empty!"

"Unless we come up with something."

Balofur leaps from Amber onto a worker who marches in the desired direction. *How ineffectual these Watchers are, being met with more delay! Can the dragons survive another week of this?*

He drops off and scoots over to examine the launch station where the transport platform is. No one is manning it. If only he could work it. There must be a way.

-2-

I return from the dragons to my own area where Balofur greets me with a wonderful grooming. From time to time my ears vibrate. Balofur is speaking with Sharpie, who is probably reporting what happened when he reunited with Blueclaw.

Balofur works up to my third ear, and leaves off grooming.

"You did well," he says. "I will teach Sharpie everything he needs to know. Sharpie's going to be our lookout when he's not with Blueclaw. I know the entire layout of the ship. I know the route Traveler takes. The doors may present a problem."

Restlessness grips me. Escape balances on a thin point.

CHAPTER 45

The Code

-1-

The next day, Balofur is riding Amber's shoulder when she meets Hote returning from the wing where he treated older dragons. Most of them are gone now. Either they have died or were shipped out. Balofur wonders if they are hanging from meat hooks in the lowest deck, or are they imprisoned in the void? No one has said a thing. Crew members look up from their work stations and smile, nod, or wave at Amber, hungry to bask in her warmth. Hote might as well be elsewhere for all the attention he gets. Across the room, the Commander bends over a worker's shoulder. Of all those in the work area, only he seems unaware of Amber.

Mother and son leave the common work area and amble down the corridor.

"Bluemont has been dismissed," Amber says, repeating herself.

Hote shuffles along, head down. "It'll make it tough for us to talk to Base"

"True. Only 2Ray1 can control the launch station now, unless he authorizes another to work it."

"When he gets around to it. He wants us to beg, so he can gloat." Hote sounds bitter. "How am I supposed to pick up the salve? Maximus wants me to hike to the nearest grove where he'll be parked out of sight."

"We need that authorization code."

"So…" Hote's eyes shift here and there.

"It means sneaking into 2Ray1's office."

"I'll do it," Hote says. His abruptness makes Amber pause. She slows and then resumes her pace.

Balofur holds his breath, hoping she won't dissuade her son. Who else but Hote habitually pulls his energy inward, so he can pass others unnoticed?

"You don't have to."

"I want to. I'll go now, while he's down on this floor."

"Go, then," she says. "I'll keep watch."

With a look backward, Hote hustles through the door to the stairs.

Balofur is torn. Should he go with Hote or stay with Amber? Hote will know what to look for. Balofur might better serve by staying behind.

Amber dawdles back toward the work area, keeping the stairwell door in view.

Balofur tries to visualize how soon it will take Hote to reach the third floor and enter Commander's office. Will the way be clear? Or will he have to slip by other officers?

Amber lifts a hand to her hair and touches him. He shrinks. She withdraws her hand.

"Stay where you can see the stair entry," Balofur says. "I'll watch Commander."

Before Amber can reply, Balofur leaps off her and rolls along the edge of the corridor. He zips beneath counters and watches the Commander wander among workers. Eventually 2Ray1 marches Amber's way. He is probably heading for his office. Balofur rolls back to Amber and leaps into her hair. "He's coming."

Amber walks toward 2Ray1 to cut him off. "Commander."

He waits for her to stroll up. Eventually she stops before him.

"What is it?"

"2Ray1, this is hard. It goes against my feelings for you, but…"

"But what?"

"…Thank you."

A slight tilt forms on each side of Commander's mouth. "For what?"

"For agreeing to an arbiter."

"Oh, that." He makes to pass her.

She steps directly into his path. "2Ray1."

He stops.

Amber hesitates as much as possible, rubbing her hands, brushing her sleeves, stopping just short of touching his shoulder. "This time you really are a dear. You outdid yourself."

He chuckles. "Does it surprise you that a ship's commander can be reasonable?"

"Oh, I know you're only too reasonable."

"More reasonable than you, Madam Perfection. Does it still bother you that our daughter loved her father and hated you?"

Amber shudders slightly. "You always were good at finding ways to hurt me."

"You were her shrew, always finding fault."

"Trying to save her from you."

"This conversation is fascinating, but duty calls."

He starts to pass again. Amber grabs his arm above the elbow. Commander looks at her.

She slowly draws her hand down his arm, and pivots so his back is to the stairs. "There was a time you were my shining hero. Until I saw you for what you are. The children were young, naive. It's only natural that Hote would come to despise you. Cooped up on ship, away from nature, away from the warmth of a mother's love. Our little girl should have known better than be enamored of you. Too caught up in appearances, she took after you."

"Why are you going on about this now, of all times?"

Every time he starts to turn toward the stairs, Amber pulls him back. The conversation grows more tense, more painful. "Every time I see you, I think of Radiant and how I may never see her again. Do you know that today is her birthday? Her and Hote's?"

Balofur would have chosen for her to ask 2Ray1 where the dragons in the wing had disappeared to. Instead she chooses the dead past, which has nothing to do with the present emergency.

Hote appears, and Amber releases 2Ray1's arm.

"Radiant made her choice," Commander says. "Let it go."

Hote comes up. "You threatening my mother again?"

Amber places a constraining hand on Hote's arm but her gaze remains on 2Ray1. "You said you really cared for our children. If you really care for Hote, allow him his time off ship. He suffers a type of claustrophobia and feels much better after a walk outside. Will you allow him that?"

"Perhaps." This with a slight shrug. And then a slight smile. "Happy birthday, son."

"Huh?"

"Isn't it your birthday? Or maybe it's the birthday of that thing inside you."

"Amber, let's go."

"Are you still possessed?"

"Yes, and it allows me to pass through walls and find out things about you."

Angry as Hote is, Balofur feels nothing substantial about him.

His father lifts a brow in amusement. "Still deluded, are you. If one blew on you, you'd disappear like smoke." He snaps his fingers in Hote's face, then strides off.

Hote looks after him, until Amber nudges her son and they march in the opposite direction.

"You got it? You got the code?"

He shakes his head. "No."

Amber glances over her shoulder. They increase their pace. "What happened? You couldn't get in?"

"I got in, for all the good it did. The codes are based on brain prints. No two prints are exactly the same."

Amber frowns.

"Sorry."

"Not your fault."

"What are brain prints?" Balofur asks.

They continue along a lonely stretch toward the elevator that will take them down to the dragons. Amber explains how the brain functions on a chemical-electric current, strong enough that with the right techniques the mind can actually move objects. A positive attitude helps.

A positive thought can move objects?

Balofur mulls the possibilities, only to be annoyed by Hote's next words.

"No way can we rescue those dragons. No way."

Balofur wants to spit acid. Are these Watchers giving up so easily? Even if they can't pull the dragons from the void, there are still those on the ship. Didn't Amber just explain mind power?

Balofur's patience is gone. "We will wait no longer. We will leave tonight. We will use our minds to move things. We will think positive."

Amber reaches a hand to her hair. He shrinks to a different place on her scalp.

"Dear Balofur, I understand your anxiety. Of course you need to escape, but we need to dissolve the force fields. We need to get the dragons up the elevator. And then there's the door. The launch station would have opened the door safely and kept it open."

"What would a pointer do?"

"Well…" Amber lets out a sigh. "If it's properly coded, it can open the door, but it's risky. The launch station can override it. And a loud noise can set off the fire curtain, which a pointer can't control. It can't stop a gas release. All that safety lies with the launch station. Besides that, the pointer code can be changed. And the launch station can detect an unauthorized door opening."

"No one's at the launch station now," Balofur reminds them. And adds, "I have a pointer."

"You have a…?" Hote gapes.

Amber reaches up, and this time Balofur leaps into her hand so they face each other.

"I have a pointer."

Her eyes are large. "How long? How long have you had it?"

"Since yesterday."

She speaks fast, in a near whisper. "If it's missed, which it probably is, it may have already been neutralized."

"Neutralized?"

"Made useless."

Balofur's rage spills over. "The force fields are already gone. The dragons pretend they are still up, while they wait for you to help them escape. And you grasp at every reason to give up and think only of Radiant, the betrayer, who is probably carrying on the dragon trade with 2Ray1!"

"That's not true!" Amber cries. She shakes her head, mouth open.

Hote stares, bug-eyed at her and then at Balofur, who has puffed himself up to where he fills Amber's hand. "We've…we've…we've got to do it. I don't know. I don't know. She's d-dead or alive. I don't know. We can't wait."

"Tonight then," Amber whispers. "Tonight."

-2-

Once the escort leaves Amber and Hote at my cage, Balofur leaps atop my head and demands, "We escape now. Not tonight. Now. Before our pointer is neutralized. Before the launch station is again controlled. If we think positive, we can do this."

Now? My heart thrums. Balofur whispers to me to take charge.

I brighten my colors in an effort to show authority I don't feel. I'm too young. Too inexperienced. I try not to stutter. "Hote. Take pointer. Clear all force fields. Start vith dragons in yer area. I speak to them in a voice yuh cannot hear."

Hote strides down the corridor. Amber waits with us. I alert not only the older dragons who are awaiting Hote; I alert the young dragons and Sharpie. "All dragons," I rumble, "the force fields are coming down. Stay in your area. Don't move until I tell you."

Balofur hyperspeaks to Sharpie and then tells us, "I just told Sharpie to practice outworlder speak. Words like 'go', 'go straight', 'go right', go left', follow,' 'safe', dangerous,' and 'stop.'"

"Amber."

She fixes her gaze on me.

"Yuh vill open the door vith pointer."

"If the door does open."

If it does. I feel the blood vibrate in my chest. My hands tingle with impatience. How long does it take for Hote to walk to his dragons, dissolve the cells, and come back?

Then I hear a rumble, telling me the field is down and Hote is headed back. My breath almost quivers.

"Vhen Hote comes, yuh vill go up and open the door."

"If the door does open," she repeats.

"Ve vill say nothing of escape to dragons if door not opens."

She nods.

When Hote arrives, he passes the pointer to Amber. No one speaks. With Balofur in my third ear, I follow Hote and Amber on all fours to the elevator. Had my wings been flexible, I could have proceeded with dignity, striding on two feet, as any dragon would.

We rise to the main floor, where we stop before the exit. Amber points with arm outstretched, as if that gives the device more power. The door hisses open.

"Quickly," she whispers and passes the pointer to Hote. I stand well back of the elevator. Well away from the door.

Balofur drops from my head. "Shaft down," he commands.

He rides the elevator down and will stay with it, to keep it open until the last dragon flies up and out.

I rumble instructions.

First to appear is Blueclaw with Sharpie in her ear.

"Amber and Hote. Blueclaw vill carry yuh out. Yuh vill go first. Other dragons vill follow."

Should the door close, I'll try to reopen it with the pointer, providing Hote hands it to me. Other dragons fly up the shaft and, taking wing, follow Blueclaw with her passengers into the sky. I have instructed them to come quietly, in single file.

-3-

As Hote and Amber rode Blueclaw out of the ship and toward a grove of trees, they saw what looked like a puff of steam rise and form a cloud. It was a Watcher craft lifting off. Hote and Amber raised their face shields. Amber spoke into hers. "Maximus?"

"Maximus here. With Hunter. What's happening?"

"We're escaping, with the dragons. Lead us to Base."

The cloud shifted from white to a blue tinge and took on the shape of a craft. It had turned. Amber said to Blueclaw. "Go straight. Follow."

Hote looked back at a flash of sun from I.D. Express. "The other dragons are following, coming out of the ship one by one and in groups."

Hunter's voice came through the headsets. "Bug juice awaits them. Or dragon spit, if you will. Donated by Hote. Ordered by Li, concocted by Ahmed, transported by Maximus, and delivered by me. Wondered how we'd sneak it to you.

A smile brightened Amber's voice. "We look forward to using it."

-4-

Amber and Hote leave on Blueclaw, along with the pointer. Will the door stay open? We must move quickly. I descend down the shaft past Balofur, who stands beside the elevator counting 60 dragon intervals. All is in order. Cages are emptying as dragons continue to emerge in order, their talons clattering on the floor, their wings half unfolded, their necks outstretched. Dragons are never comfortable when hobbling on feet designed for gripping. The hard floor has produced sores and callouses.

Some of the elders, farthest from the exit, grow impatient and launch into the limited air space. I trundle toward them, away from the elevator to send calming pulses over my scales. They are older than I, unwilling to bow to my guidance. Youngsters continue to disappear into the elevator shaft and fly to the main floor. I follow them into the elevator that Balofur graciously raises to the main floor for me. As I back off, he again lowers it for the remaining dragons. The sky, the land, the trees beckon beyond the open door. I smell the soil, the plants. I ache to flee this ship with its confining walls, its stiff and sterile interior. Others must go first. Something within me urges them to hurry. Hurry so Balofur and I can follow.

An alarm sounds.

A bleat of terror and a thrash of wings erupt. Dragons below rush the shaft and crash against its walls and one another. The klaxon clangs on and on, pummeling my nerves, my control. I think I hear Balofur yell.

"One at a time," I cry. "One at a time!"

The elevator lifts, depositing its thrashing load on the level floor. Balofur has unclogged the elevator of bodies and lowers it. As the young dragons untangle themselves, a curtain of fire, whomph, covers the door. The dragons shy back and stampede down the corridor.

"No!" I chase after them. "Go toward the door! The fire!"

"It's closed," comes the cry.

I feel its heat on my back. "It's open! Go through the fire!"

Soon I'm too far away to feel the heat, too deep into the ship. Is the door still open? I can't tell. Yet I point everyone toward it.

"Hurry!" I cry.

"Hurry!" others cry.

Screams and more yelling. The cacophony reverberates, thumping in my entrails, my ears.

I flap and get some lift. I can't sustain it. My wings are too weak to negotiate the too small area with its dragons swooping by. I collide with flashing wings, land on my side, and slide on the floor.

Older dragons are coming up the shaft now, far from where I try to lead young dragons back to the door. Shouting and the wing beat of stampeding dragons add to the noise.

Workers, some not properly suited, scramble into the corridor. Into the roar of dragon fire.

Workers scream from a coat of flame or its threat. The alarm throbs its message like an ache in my head, my heart pounding in time. Regaining my feet, I lead with my snout. I can't keep up with the fleeing escapees. Panicked, we toss fire at anything that moves, even other dragons.

Hurry!

Behind us, workers in protective suits erect a force field. Our fire cannot penetrate it. We are in a chamber of blistering heat from the fiery curtain and from other dragons. The workers push toward us behind their force field.

The ship is emptying of dragons. The elevator shaft closes. Where is Balofur? Has he been engulfed by flame? I lag behind the last of the dragons. "Balofur!"

The fire extinguishes. I rush forward, only to see the door close a hand's breadth from my face. "Balofur!" Where is he? Where?

The air is hot. The force field intact with workers behind it. How many? Three, four…?

Amber and Hote are gone. The other dragons are gone.

A hiss! Gas! I try to burn it up by belching fire. I swing my tail at the force field. I try too late to hold my breath. The workers yell, until their voices sound like distant thunder. My thrashing about slows, until I can fight no longer. I fade into sleep.

CHAPTER 46

Stranded

Silence.

I awaken from a stupor. Wobbly, I shake my head to clear it. Only to recognize the dim light of a cell, this time with no way out. The silence is deafening. Except for the woosh of pulse in my ears and the zing like the sound of locusts in my head. The air seems empty of life. Stale. I peer up and down the corridor. I look through the transparent walls of my cell into others. There are no dragons. No Balofur. I am alone. Completely alone. Death awaits me. Overdue, actually. I should have died after Tweekie was killed. Instead I lived because an orphaned groombug elder had chosen to live. Likely Balofur is dead, perhaps incinerated or crushed by fleeing dragons. There is no reason to go on. At last I can shut down, aware the others are free. That is some consolation. My sole purpose when the Great Mother told me to live. At last that purpose is met.

So I bow to death, awaiting its arrival. I lie on my side, neck outstretched. I wait the way orphaned groombugs wait, eyes closed, breath slowed, heat cooled, gradually shutting down. A dreamlike state settles. Death will be painless. This body with its damaged wings will be shrugged off. For what? Will I lose all awareness, my parts dispersed throughout forest and meadows, brooks and oceans? Or will my awareness survive in a different form? Will I join the Great Mother? Will I…?

Something is climbing over me.

Balofur?

I lift my head.

He ends on my snout. Balofur! So ugly, so beautiful, so alive. Balofur! Pulsing with intelligence, power, and warmth.

Youth and energy juice through me.

Forgetting my planned demise, I exhale in breaths of joy. "How did you get here? I thought you were dead."

"I dropped through the vents. Everyone escaped. They'll go to the Watcher Base where they will be cared for. They'll be fine."

Balofur, who had little faith in Watchers, now assures me they are trustworthy. Is this to make me feel good?

"What about us?"

"We'll just have to wait and keep alert. To the Collectors, I'm nothing. And you're a mindless dragon on the edge of death. They might toss you onto a dung heap and forget about you."

"Or process me into leather goods and meat. And then—"

"We did good, you must admit that." I can tell Balofur doesn't want me to dwell on our fate.

"Yes. Real good." I release a cloud of steam.

"We mustn't give up. Think positive. Reach for mind energy and power."

"I'm not giving up. I haven't quite figured out how this mind energy works. I just don't know what to do."

"We wait," Balofur says. "Wait for whatever opportunity may arise."

Will those who escaped find a way to rescue us? Or will they consider us dead? Maybe they will provide a nice memorial for us, one with aerial dancing and fire display.

CHAPTER 47

Watcher Base

-1-

Hote and Amber clung to Blueclaw's sharp spine and squinted into the lashing wind, directly behind the Watcher craft. Riding a dragon, Hote discovered, was precarious. The back undulated with the flapping wings, the scales were slippery, and the girth too broad for their legs to get a good grip. The knobs from the spine were just long enough to act as handles. He and Amber could barely squeeze between them. Hote leaned forward against his mother, one arm around her in an attempt to hold both of them steady.

He sneaked a look over his shoulder. Instead of leading the pack, he noticed the other dragons were exploding into the air from the Commander's ship and winging away in other directions.

"Where are they going?"

He almost lost his balance and threatened Amber's. Blueclaw jogged sideways to keep them onboard.

"Follow us!" Amber called. The wind swallowed her voice.

Sharpie must have heard and told Blueclaw, because Blueclaw blazed blue and chirped. Some escapees veered in her direction. Even so, by time they landed with the Watcher craft at the base, only eight out of twenty-eight dragons entered the compound. They clustered on the open field beside the craft pad.

Amber slid to the ground, followed by a sweaty Hote. Sharpie appeared like thistle down on top of Blueclaw's head.

"We can't let them go," Hote yelled at Sharpie. "They'll die if they don't come here. We can save their lives."

Amber sounded less urgent. "Sharpie? Can you call them? Sick dragons? Make sick dragons come here."

The groombug seemed to talk to Blueclaw, who glanced about at the group of tongue-tied Watchers, her wings half folded. She and the other dragons fidgeted in the strange surroundings and communicated in ways Hote couldn't decipher. Possibly they were struggling to understand Amber's request.

A slight breeze wafted Sharpie's hair. He took a moment to survey the scene—the surrounding wall, the open field beside the craft where fellow escapees rested, the knot of Watchers between the building and the craft—before resting his vison on Hote and Amber. "Dragons go. Go other dragons."

Hote thought he understood. "They've gone home."

Amber cast a look at the empty sky and pursed her lips. "Eight out of twenty-eight. It's a start. Shall we begin?"

"My god, they're big!" someone murmured.

"Easy, take it easy." Chief Li appeared at the front of the Watcher group. "Slow and easy."

Hote didn't see Rumplewing right away. She might be hidden among the others. He felt Amber's touch, and together they stepped confidently among the dragons, encouraging the other Watchers to follow their example. Hunter, without a wise-crack, handed the ointment around. After Hote and Amber demonstrated how to use it, workers got busy grooming and comforting dragons, some of whom sprawled exhausted while others twitched and grumbled at those they didn't quite trust. The Watchers assumed they were warnings, based on Sharpie's struggle to explain.

"It's okay," Hote said, not knowing if anyone paid attention to him. "You can relax; they won't hurt you."

Hote brushed his pocket and felt a bulge. The pointer! When had he put it there? He'd meant to give it to Rumplewing before leaving the ship. He tried not to think about it. And failed. She was missing. Had she left with the captives who had chosen to avoid the base? He looked about at the trees within the compound and then at the forest beyond its walls.

The Watchers continued to smooth ointment on ragged scales, bolder with each stroke. Pip's singing rose, somewhat shy but meant to soothe. "Be thou blessed. Let your heart be rested."

After a few phrases, the dragon she timidly stroked rumbled. Pip squeaked and drew back.

"No," Amber said. "Don't pull back."

The rumble was soon joined by the other dragons' and it grew. Hote saw Amber's face open in understanding and appreciation as he felt the vibrations.

"They're singing," Amber said.

Hote waved to catch the attention of the Watchers. "They're singing for us."

Sparky shook her head to create a beat, but the dragon song thinned at the sight of static electricity shooting from her hair.

On one side Hunter grabbed her head to keep it steady. On her other side, Maximus did the same.

"Wha—?" she started.

"They'll toast us," Hunter said.

"Roast?"

"Roast. Toast."

"Look." Maximus tilted his head.

Hote noted the heat waves warping the air about the dragon nostrils. Had he misunderstood the rumbles? Were they warnings after all? If only Rumplewing and Balofur were here to explain. Still the dragons were intelligent, and Sharpie hadn't said anything threatening. So he yelled, "They won't hurt you," and hoped it was true.

Sparky's eyes popped. She tucked her head between her shoulders.

"Sing, Pip!" Hunter called.

"Sing," Amber repeated.

Pip wobbled into song.

The dragon chorus again swelled. This time her voice steadied and became operatic. Other Watchers joined in, without words, in single notes or harmonics. A song not written, a song released, to flow freely, as the spirit led. Pip, Amber, Hote, Reed, Hunter, Maximus, and Sparky with her hands on her head to keep it steady. Joy entered in, with a deep thrum and light trills. It entered the gut, the bones, the teeth, the heart. Rejuvenating. Uniting. It lasted hardly more than a minute. When it faded, there in the distance came what sounded like echoes.

"It's the other dragons," Amber said in awe.

Hote pointed. "Look. They're hanging from the trees outside the compound." He recognized those the forest didn't hide. "Some of them anyway."

"They're celebrating."

"Maybe they'll come in after a while."

After the song ended, the dragons gave in to weariness. Hote wanted to believe they had shown the Watchers thankfulness and trust. But where were Rumplewing and Balofur? Hote fumbled with the pointer in his pocket. He walked to where Blueclaw was reclining. And waited.

Not once did Sharpie leave his dragon. He refused to groom any other. Instead he hummed and polished Blueclaw's scales until she drowsed.

Hote broke in gently. "Sharpie, where is Rumplewing and Balofur?"

Surely they wouldn't be out there in the forest with the few escapees who lingered. The two wouldn't have gone "home", wherever that was.

Sharpie didn't hesitate to answer in his high voice. "Balofur no here."

Hote felt a leap of dread. "Where is he?"

"No here."

"Is he with Rumplewing?"

Sharpie seemed to search for the right words.

"Did they follow the other dragons?"

"No."

"Did all the dragons leave the ship?"

The groombug mumbled.

"Sharpie?"

"Rumplewing no. Balofur no. No follow dragons."

Hote almost choked. He strode among the dragons and Watchers until he found Amber. "Rumplewing and Balofur are still on the ship."

She rubbed her cheek with the back of her salve-soaked hand. "I was afraid of that. I'd been kind of looking."

Chief Li came up.

"We didn't get them all out," Amber told him.

"Then we've lost them."

"We got to go back," Hote said.

The Chief glanced in the direction from where the escape had come. "Chances are they are dead. We have to accept our losses and concentrate on helping those who'll accept it."

Amber nodded and gave Hote's arm a warning touch, so he nodded, too.

When the Chief returned inside to oversee the lab work, Hote murmured to Amber, "What if they're not dead? You think Father would hold them hostage?"

"For what?"

"I don't know; groombugs?"

She curled her lips inward.

Before she could speak, Hote went on. "Not only that, we haven't recovered Traveler. Not that I care at this stage. Above all else I want Rumplewing and Balofur safe."

"Son…"

"I'm going back."

"Don't be rash."

"I'm not being rash. I meant to give Rumplewing the pointer, and I forgot. I still have it"

Amber showed no distress over Hote's retaining the pointer. Before she could say a word, he continued. "One of the dragons might take me on her back. Blueclaw is fast and daring."

"Too risky. We could lose Sharpie."

"So you think we should just let Rumplewing and Balofur die after all they did to save everyone?"

"Of course not. Don't put words in my mouth, Hote. Don't you see? With the dragons gone, the Collectors don't need us to treat what isn't there. We won't be able to get in. They'll have the doors blocked and the pointer code changed."

Hote wondered if the alien inside him would let him pass through the ship's walls. It seemed to be led only by overwhelming curiosity.

"Amber." Hote raised his arms, palms out. "We've got to try."

"Agreed. And we will."

"So I'll go." He half turned away.

She placed a restraining hand on his shoulder. "My dear son, how do you propose to get in?"

If he could arouse the alien's curiosity, he could slip in. He didn't dare suggest it to Amber, which she would take as proof he was still delusional. "They'll have to contact Baaden sometime. He might come in. If I hang around near the Collector site…"

"And if you're caught? 2Ray1 wouldn't hesitate to hold you hostage."

"Amber—"

A ding sounded. "Attention, everyone. The arbiter has arrived."

The arbiter!

Caretakers among the dragons paused at their tasks. Hote and Amber forgot their argument and looked about. A small craft, shaped like a swollen purple flower with many petals, sat on the other side of the Watcher ship, mostly concealed. It had emerged silently from the void.

"The arbiter is here," Amber said as if in disbelief. "At last. The arbiter has agreed to come!"

Hote felt a tentative joy. "So…our troubles…"

"What troubles? With the arbiter here, our troubles are over. Once an arbiter agrees to come, it's binding. 2Ray1 doesn't dare withdraw from his commitment to the meeting. Not from so high an authority."

"Will I get to see?"

Those who had administered to the dragons stood, facing the ship in an effort to glimpse the great personage. Some murmured that it was the High Arbiter, a shapeshifter of the highest authority.

As one of the top employees, Dr. Kelly Amber could meet with governing officials. She gave Hote a parting pat on the shoulder and walked with firm step to greet the visitor. Rather than stay behind, Hote trailed after and saw how Amber brushed imaginary dust from her uniform and ran fingers through her hair. He thought she was presentable enough, considering their previous demands.

Amber continued to the building entrance, where she would meet the one they had seen only in holofilm.

A woman of indeterminate age stood with Chief Li. He barely reached her shoulder. Her hair was a pouf of white beneath a tall hat. A purple robe draped her lean figure. She was taller and more stern than Hote had expected. Like a child before such dignity and power, he hid among the Watchers as a welcoming committee formed before her. Amber appeared self-assured within the committee. Hote felt a flood of pride. When Chief Li started a round of introductions, Amber stepped forward at the mention of her name. She reached and the arbiter took her hand.

Hote edged closer.

"I must speak to you," Amber said.

The arbiter nodded. "After I freshen up." Her voice was cushioned steel.

"Of course."

Give the arbiter room to rest and eat.

Amber pulled back. Hote stepped to her side. "It's in the High Arbiter's hands now," she told him. "The hearing will proceed soon enough. Neither we nor 2Ray1 can change the timing or the place."

"Where do you suppose it will be?"

"Most likely it will convene in the meeting hall on the top floor of the I.D. Express. The involved Collectors will sit together on one side of the room; we Watchers on the other side."

After everyone had eaten, Amber answered a private invitation to the arbiter's room. Hote surrendered to the urge to amble after and stand outside the door. Somehow he found himself enveloped in the wall so he could see into the room, thanks to the nosiness of the entity that inhabited him. Amber sat in the offered chair.

If there had been a preamble, Hote missed it.

"Our problem is with the Collectors. We've tried to deal with them, without success."

The arbiter held up her hand to interrupt. "It is forbidden to feed me opinions that might prejudice me. I will hear everyone's side when I enter the I.D. Express."

Amber raised a hand to her mouth and cleared her throat. Hote recognized her embarrassment. "My apologies. I've been so taken with meeting you that I should have sent you a message before you arrived. I'm afraid they may be inaccessible. The ship may be cloaked. Or its entrance sealed."

The arbiter didn't blink. "I can uncloak it. I can unseal it."

What power! Amber and Hote needn't worry about a thing.

"Who are the opposing sides?"

"The Watchers and Collectors. The Collectors keep abusing the dragons. They are a sentient species."

"Then the case is between the dragons and the Collectors."

"No, it's—"

She cut Amber off. "If as you say they are sentient, they can defend themselves. They need only a spokesperson."

"Me," Amber offered.

"It must be a dragon. It is the only way the Collectors can agree to my counsel. No Watchers allowed."

Hote felt a chill. Didn't the arbiter understand? Surely Amber could explain.

"They accuse us of disrupting their trade, and we can't defend ourselves or even be present?"

Had Father bought the arbiter?

At her stern expression, Amber looked down. "Forgive me my ill manners. I misspoke."

A hint of humor betrayed itself in the arbiter's face. Her voice softened slightly. "Isn't it the dragons who need defending?"

Hote was grateful for the touch of humanity within this steely figure. Amber leaned forward, evidently encouraged. "It's true, but you need to understand. No dragon is qualified, and only one can speak outworlder language."

The softness receded from the arbiter. "Who is this dragon?"

A hollow feeling entered Hote's chest as Amber paused before speaking. "Rumplewing."

Or Balofur, Hote thought. Would they listen to a groombug? Would Balofur cooperate? Were the two even alive?

"I'm not sure Rumplewing is alive," Amber said. "She's the only one who—"

The arbiter held up her hand. "Enough. I will hear no more of your opinions."

Amber's lips curled between her teeth. Hote wanted to emerge from the wall and rage that they were not opinions but facts. He dared not enter the room. Besides, who would believe the crazy boy?

Amber stood.

The arbiter, cold and dismissive, took off one of several rings on her fingers and spun it like a top on the table. On and on it spun, tossing shards of light about the room. The arbiter watched it, as if it could show her things. She had utterly dismissed Amber.

Chewing her lower lip, Amber bowed and backed out of the room.

-2-

The next morning, the arbiter called a meeting of everyone at the Watcher Base, including the dragons. She stood outdoors, so all could attend. She stood, tall and regal in the garden, among bushes, near the pool, and beneath overtowering trees. Hote wondered if she was indeed an alien and what her true form was, for she reeked of power that radiated an essence beyond what her body contained. It made him feel even more insubstantial. Because of his feelings of inadequacy, he would have retreated to the back of the crowd. Instead, Amber clutched his hand and pulled him with her to the front. Whatever inhabited him, also prodded him to the front.

Chief Li introduced the arbiter.

She seemed hardly to pay attention to Li. After he finished speaking, she looked out across the congregation, the Watchers and the dragons, all of whom focused on her. She raised a hand and set a ring to spinning on her palm. As it spun, her attention fell on Hote.

"Step forward," she commanded.

Hote's throat constricted. Did she know he had eavesdropped? Had she heard that he was mentally defective? Would she scold him before the many eyes who watched?

"Hote." Her voice lowered.

He swallowed, couldn't find his voice. What was her title?

"Hote, I am told you suffer delusions. Is that true?"

"I-I don't know…uh…High…uh…Arbiter."

"Do you believe you are deluded?"

"Uh…I just…I just…"

"Haven't you said that an intruder hides inside you?"

"What-what I said was that…I collided with someone who was launched from a platform at the same time I was, but not from the same…platform. We got intermingled in the void. And no one believes me. Well, the dragons do. I think. It happened a long time ago."

Hote's mouth felt dry. He stared at the crystalline ring in her hand that sparkled as it continued to spin.

"When did this happen?"

"I was thirteen."

"And now you're…?

"Sixteen."

Concentrating on the crystal insulated him from onlookers. Nothing else seemed to exist except the crystal and the arbiter's voice. He welcomed the sensation.

"Where did this happen?"

"On my father's ship. The I.D. Express."

"And your father is…?"

"Commander 2Ray1."

"Did your father believe you?"

"No."

"Did the ship's doctor?"

"No."

"How about here?"

"Uh…My mother wants to believe me, but I can understand how hard it is for her. At least she realizes something happened to me because, well, I'm not normal. I do weird things, which I don't realize until it's too late."

"How do you feel about that?"

"Bad. I want to be normal, not different."

"So be it." Her tone, which had been almost clinical took on a no nonsense tone. "Sneech! Come out of him."

Something tensed inside Hote.

Her eyes flared. "Now!"

Before Hote could react, her arm stretched into a tentacle, pierced Hote's chest and snapped back. Gasps and yelps followed the blur of action. Hote grabbed his chest only after he saw what she had dumped in the grass before her. The creature resembled a cross between an ostrich and a velociraptor. It lay curled on its side, gobbling, whistling, and squeaking.

Sneech, she had called it. She enclosed the ring in her hand and placed her other hand on its scalp. It stood. It was a head shorter than Hote and completely naked except for a scaly body. It fell silent.

"I will protect you," she told the alien. "Wait in my ship."

And then the creature was gone.

She opened her hand again, and again the ring spun.

Hote heard mutters from the crowd. He stepped back, and his mother placed an arm around him and hugged him to her side.

"Oh, my son, my son." And kissed his cheek.

He realized he was unhurt. He felt whole, solid, strong. Astounded.

And for a while the arbiter seemed forgotten as a flood of joy rushed over Hote from the Watchers. It felt like love.

He didn't mind that those nearby reached and touched him in compassion and apology. Hunter punched him playfully in the shoulder and quipped, "I always knew you had it in you."

Hote laughed, feeling a warmth at being included, and eager to reward Hunter for it.

No longer did he feel compromised or diminished. He was free! Free! How sweet it felt! He didn't know whether to laugh or cry.

Amber wiped her eyes.

And then everyone's attention returned to the High Arbiter, shape shifter and miracle worker.

"What you saw," she told the congregation, "was a sniffer. This one's name is Sneech. Sadly not all sniffers are valued. While some perform vital services in medicine, law enforcement, and such, Sneech, like most sniffers, earns his livelihood by collecting and selling information. It can be a dangerous business, which is why Sneech hid for so long in this unfortunate youngster. Hote, Sneech meant no harm. He had fled those who were trying to kill him for the information he had gathered. You were his unwilling and unsuspecting protector."

Hote had forgotten how it felt to be so present. He felt too strongly present, too noticed. He was glad when she changed the subject.

"Before I proceed to the Collectors' ship, I have chosen to speak to all of you first. And to listen."

Hote worked his way back until he stood beside Blueclaw and Sharpie. They gave him one glance and turned their attention to the arbiter.

"Dragons, what are your concerns?"

When the largest dragon raised her colors and then her voice, Hote realized the spinning ring allowed everyone to understand whatever language was spoken.

"We are grateful. The Watchers saved us, and Balofur's saliva will help to prevent us from rotting and dying. We can live on with the hope the egg each of us carries matures and can be deposited. Without our own groombugs, we can't be sure this will happen. So we will mourn. His saliva cannot replace our bond mates. Already we miss their companionship. I am not an elder, and we need them to guide us. They may have the answers we seek."

The arbiter's voice displayed empathy. "When all is ready, I will meet with the Collectors and dragons aboard the I.D. Express. Before you, I will set a holo in the round so all of you here or near the outside of the Collector ship shall see and hear what goes on. Justice will be served."

CHAPTER 48

The Arbiter

-1-

They gas me again. I awaken to find my wings bound together at the wrists, my mouth tied shut. Three crew members tug me erect, and I hobble like a three-legged creature as they lead me through the corridor on the main floor.

Where are they taking me? To the platform? To be sent into the void? Or am I being taken to the lower floor, to be processed into products. My hide into boots. My flesh ground for lunch. My…

I choke, try to blank out the images. I can still speak dragonwise with Balofur, who, shrunk to nut size, would appear as a bump on the back of my head. My color has drained, so I am all pastels. I pant against my bound jaws.

"I can't breathe, I can't breathe."

"You can still breathe through your nostrils."

"What's happening? What's going to become of us?"

"We'll find out soon enough. Quit panting. You're leaking steam. Relax and take long, slow breaths."

Outworlders take me into a massive chamber. Balofur explains the scene before me. Collectors sit in rows facing an elevated table behind which a strange outworlder sits on a high chair that raises its occupant above all others. I guess it is a she, tall, made taller by a fluff of white hair, and on it, a tall blue hat with a white tassel. She wears a blue robe lined with white fur that smells fake. They bring me to her right where I rest on my haunches and drool down the strap that holds my mouth shut. I am eye level with her. By the table, almost tucked under her hand, crouches a being that reminds me of the birdlike dinosaurs on our planet. At her left sits what Balofur tells me is Commander 2Ray1, the top of his head even with her table.

What is this?

When the crew members start to bind me further, she raises a hand and says in a crisp voice, "Enough. Take your seats."

All are silent before her, reduced. Even the Commander seems reduced.

"This must be the arbiter," Balofur whispers. "From the smell of that strap around your mouth, I can tell you they bound you with dragon skin. Impervious to fire."

The tall being scans the assembly. "I am the High Arbiter. You will refer to me as such." Her hand rests on the head of the creature crouched next to her. "This is Sneech, a sniffer and my aide." She tilts her head at the Commander. "Introduce yourself."

The Commander stands, speaks with authority. "2Ray1, Commander of the Interdimensional Express, permanently acting as portal to this planet by permission of the Guiding Congress and under contract of the Academy."

"Very well, Commander. Before you sit, open the door to the ship and leave it open."

2Ray1 clasps his hands behind his back. "With all due respect, I.D. Express must decline your request, High Arbiter. This is a closed meeting and must be secured by a closed door."

The arbiter's eyes flash. "It is not a request, Commander."

2Ray1 stands stiffly erect. "Are you insisting—?"

"I am ordering." Again the arbiter pats the sniffer who cringes, ready to slink away.

"Sneech, step inside the Commander and read the door code in his mind as soon as he thinks it."

Sneech's eyes bug at the arbiter. "I can't—"

The arbiter raises an interrupting finger and then nudges the creature toward the Commander.

2Ray1 steps back with a near shudder. "Very well. The door will open and remain so. Be warned however. No member on this ship will be held responsible for any intrusion."

"I'll be back," Balofur whispers to me.

He leaps from my head and rolls across the floor and into a vent. I want to cry out against his leaving, but I don't dare draw attention to him. He said he'd be back. I must cling to that, despite feeling abandoned. Besides, it suggests he has a plan.

-2-

Balofur must hurry. He scoots into a vent and rolls, racing time. The speeches in the hall are amplified, so they can be heard throughout the ship. Voices boom against his ears.

"Why is this dragon bound?"

"No choice, High Arbiter," Commander explains. "It'll attack and spout fire. And we couldn't surround it with a force field here. Besides, we have no need of a dragon's presence. Our intention is to work out an agreement with the Watchers."

"Does it concern the dragons?"

"It does."

"We shall include the dragon."

Commander's sigh is audible. "High Arbiter, it appears the Watchers have misled you by saying this creature can speak. That's nonsense. If you expect it to argue in its defense, you're wasting your time. If you need proof, that's easily done when we show you it is not the intelligent beast—"

"Spare me your opinions. We will proceed."

"Without the Watchers?"

"Without the Watchers."

"High Arbiter, I need to speak with my officers."

"Very well. I give you thirty minutes. No more."

Thirty minutes.

Balofur can waste no time. When he reaches outside, the sound of the proceedings follow him, and he sees an image-in-the-round of the court projected beyond the dirty, smeared air that must be the invisible ship. In what seems a weedy, unpopulated field, the holo shows Rumplewing on her haunches. The arbiter sits at her table, beside that strange dinosaurlike entity. The Collectors mill about.

A soft whir catches Balofur's attention. Beside the holoimage a Watcher craft has just landed, and Doctor Kelly Amber and Hote soon emerge into ankle-tall grass. Hote points. "Look. The door is open."

Before they can react, Balofur puffs himself up and leaps a couple times into the air. "Amber. Hote."

"Balofur!" Amber rushes up and kneels before him. She presses flat the grass around him. "You're alive. What about Rumplewing?"

"Watch the image." Balofur gestures. Hote is already standing before it, his arms crossed over his chest, his mouth set.

"What—?"

"Where is Sharpie?" Balofur interrupts Amber. "I must speak to him, now."

"He is at the base with the other dragons where they are being cared for."

Hote beckons Balofur to follow him into the Watcher craft. "If he's there, we can radio him."

Hote sits in the pilot's seat, connects with Base, and shows Balofur where to speak. Balofur hyperspeaks. "Sharpie, are you there? Sharpie?"

After several calls, a voice comes on the set. "Yes."

"Have Blueclaw fly you to the nearest clans, and tell the elders a representative of each clan must come. Hurry. We need a council of elders at the Collector ship. Come with them."

Balofur hops off the console and out of the craft.

Hote, unable to hear hyperspeak, follows him. "Didn't you want to talk to Sharpie?"

"I just did."

When they join Amber, Balofur explains. "Blueclaw cannot visit all the clans or even know their locations. The elders do. They'll sing at long distance. Others will hear and all will meet together. Blueclaw will lead them to the Collector craft."

Amber again kneels before Balofur and raises a hand to touch him, only to restrain herself. "They won't let any of us Watchers in to defend you."

Hote frowns at the image in the round and shuffles his feet. "I suppose we should be thankful the arbiter set up the scene so we can watch." He snorts. "Watch. Get it? Watch."

Balofur can't help but notice that Hote feels more substantial. No longer is he in danger of being pulled into the void. It was that sniffer, Sneech. Yes, it was Sneech who had been inside him.

Amber cups her palms together. Balofur leaps onto them and fluffs himself out as much as his exposed hide allows. "Does the arbiter know about the council of elders?"

She brings him closer to her face. "I doubt it. None of us Watchers knew."

"The arbiter must know or suspect something," Balofur says. "I'm going back inside."

-3-

The arbiter has set a ring to spinning on the table in front of her. It flashes and winks, casting reflections across faces, uniforms, and the chamber walls. Somehow it translates, so I can understand every word the outworlders speak.

Then I feel a tick on my head. Balofur is back, seated in my third ear. His presence is a comfort. Nevertheless I chaff over my dragon-skin bonds. They couldn't have insulted me more.

"Where are the Watchers?" Commander says. "Surely you know it's vital they attend. This hearing must not proceed without them."

The arbiter is unmoved. "Regardless of your opinions, this meeting will continue. Without them. The necessary attendants are here."

Commander paces. "Very well, High Arbiter. We'll continue under protest. Shortly you will understand why the Watchers must be here."

He paces some more and then stops before her. "Our trade supports many consumers. Thousands, by the latest report. There are industries connected with the lucrative business of arena sport. After the dragons are killed in the arena, their flesh is used for food, their hide and other body parts sold for other purposes. Their inner furnace, with its fuel, can produce enough heat to warm a room. Their talons are used in ornaments. We are not wasteful. The Watchers, by obstructing our trade and breaking our contract, will plunge thousands into financial ruin."

I huff and steam, trying not to choke. Drool drips off my chin. Balofur hisses for me to be calm.

"We are reasonable people. We were willing to compromise with the Watchers. We finally reached an agreement that we would no longer capture dragons. We would keep those we presently have and breed them. But they broke their promise by tricking us. Our desire is that they honor that agreement with the amendment that a groombug be included. Somehow the presence of a groombug stimulates the dragons to reproduce. Surely only one groombug will be needed; we're not greedy. We'll be content then to leave this planet to its wild dragons."

My heart clenches. "We can't let them do this," I whisper to Balofur.

"They won't succeed with their plan," Balofur whispers back. "It's a dead end, and they'd go after more dragons."

"What do you want of me?" the arbiter asks Commander.

"To force the Watchers to agree to our terms, which are just."

"You wish to control the fate of the dragons without giving the dragons a say. Is that it?"

"They are not sentient."

I glare at Commander.

"The Watchers claim they can talk."

I want to cry out that the Watchers have demanded all along that we dragons are sentient and should not be collected. I am proof. Didn't I yell at the Collectors?

The Commander, himself, brings up the incident of my yelling in outworlder speech. "Parroting. Sheer parroting. Just because they can mimic speech doesn't make them intelligent."

The discussion continues like this until the arbiter calls for a recess.

The Collectors rise from their chairs and refresh themselves while I stew in my own saliva and shift about against the slick floor. No comfort for me.

And then the discussion resumes. Periodically I work my jaws and grind the sharp edges of my beak. I drool. Strain at my wrist bonds.

"Listen," Balofur whispers.

Distant clicking. No one notices it at first. As it grows louder and takes on the sound of clattering, a few faces and then more in the audience turn toward it.

Commander stops mid-sentence. Everyone watches now.

Dragons. Elders.

A gasp comes from the audience.

"The council of elders," Balofur whispers.

To avert panic, the arbiter raises a hand. "Nobody move."

Everyone waits, some gripping the edge of their chair. I feel their tension and smell the stink of fear.

The elders stride into view, wings half spread. How brilliant their colors! Every color there is, glistening in the fake light of the chamber. Peacefully they enter and settle on their haunches near the rest of the audience. Among them is Fetidbreath from my own clan. Fetidbreath! I want to cry out, to embrace her, to ask about the clan members. She gives me a brief nod. The elders murmur among themselves but are otherwise silent.

"Identify yourselves," the arbiter commands.

One rises on her feet and her colors brighten briefly. "We are the council of elders." She eases back on her haunches.

"You are welcome here." The arbiter's gaze sweeps the room and settles on the Commander. "It hasn't escaped my notice that these elders have refrained from roasting you with fire. You can safely remove Rumplewing's bonds."

She knows my name. Did Amber tell her? It can only mean she considers me to be important.

"Stilwell." The Commander signals to a man in the audience.

"No." The arbiter purses her lips. "You, Commander 2Ray1, will remove Rumplewing's bonds."

A soft but firm voice comes from the dragon council section. Fetidbreath. "Consider it your first act of kindness, Commander 2Ray1."

The Commander's face reddens. Otherwise he shows no change in expression. Fumbling, tugging, he manages to remove my bonds. The saliva soaked dragon skin drenches his hands. He signals a nearby Collector to give him a cloth wipe. I work my jaw in relief, shake my hands, and rattle my wings.

The arbiter twirls another ring so there are two on the table, flashing out colors. "Dragon, introduce yourself so all may hear. You may speak in your own language."

"Rumplewing." Somehow the rings enable us to understand each other!

"So, Rumplewing, you will speak for the dragons. All the principals are here. Commander, Rumplewing, you are both here for the purpose of reaching an agreement. I will moderate your conversation as needed. You may proceed."

I don't know what to say. I am too young. An elder should speak. Maybe Fetidbreath.

The Commander doesn't hesitate. "Very well, if we must play at charades, then charades it is. Dragon, we know you for a dumb creature, raised in ignorance and controlled by instincts. You are on par with any pet. A dog, a bird." Evidently feeling foolish to address a dumb animal, Commander turns toward his audience of Collectors, steering clear of the group of dragons. "Look at them. Dragons. They don't change their environment. They don't clear forest to plant crops. They don't build cities, pave over land. They don't build crafts to take them to the stars. They don't conquer others. They don't even wear clothes. They have no culture but are as wild animals." I notice the sniffer squirming beside the arbiter. While the Commander speaks, scenes of his world appear in the round, illustrating what he means. The arbiter provides these scenes by spinning her ring. The little creature beside her bows its head, as if humiliated.

I am stunned. Speechless by the complexity of his world.

Balofur speaks furiously in my ear. "Don't let Commander fool you. He is ignorant. Ignorant. And brighten your colors when you speak."

When Commander pauses for a breath, I clear my throat and spew a tiny cloud of steam. And remember to enhance my colors. "This is what I know," I begin. "All creatures change their world in some way. The very ants build massive cities in ways that suit them. They conquer others. Termites build mounds. Deer and squirrels make paths. They do all these things that you say signify intelligence. Do you honor that? If you put them in cages so they can't do these things, does that render them any less intelligent?"

"You are not like us," Commander says. I am surprised he has any answer.

"I agree, we don't look like you. Our needs are different. Those cities, farms, and factories you talk about in your images, you call that progress toward good. I see it as destruction, as an unlivable environment. I don't want it."

"You show your lack of intelligence, your lack of culture."

"That doesn't alter the fact of our intelligence. Because you are ignorant of our culture, which we do have, you take it upon yourselves to abuse us."

"Is I.D. Express on trial here?" The Commander balls his hand into a fist.

I flick a glance at the elders, the arbiter, and the uncomfortable little sniffer. It is utterly ignored. The elders arch their necks and gracefully shift side to side in anticipation. They approve of me and my defense. The arbiter looks relaxed. How that ring renders our speech understandable is a great wonder and an opportunity. I want to understand more.

"Tell me about yourself, Commander," I say. "Why are you here? What gives you the right? Why do you think you are better than us?"

"The Academy provided me the necessary background, with courses ranging from naval training to economics to mercantilism. Not that you would understand any of this."

The arbiter appears about to speak. Instead, she twirls one of the two rings. Clearly she is interested in Commander's answers. I pursue my line of questioning.

"Did you know Amber from before?"

The Commander chuckles. "We met at the Academy, dated, and eventually married. Something beyond your understanding."

Not when the ring is rendering all speech understandable. I don't understand everything it involves, but I understand enough. "Are you still married?"

"Separated."

"Why was Amber at the Academy?"

"Amber majored in ecology with an interest in terraforming and dragons." The Commander's eyes glitter. "She joined the Watchers. They had already terraformed this planet. They created the dragons in the lab. So, you see, you're already a product. You are owned by the Watchers."

"He lies," Balofur whispers.

The dragon council murmurs, then falls silent.

"Which is why," he says with glee, "there is no need to reach any agreement with dragons."

"Oh, but there is." The arbiter bends forward, resting her crossed arms on the table. "Didn't you complain that the Watchers wanted you to cease capturing dragons? Why was that?"

Commander's lips tighten. "They claim dragons are sentient."

"Which would mean?"

The Commander doesn't answer.

"There is a law against the murder and enslavement of sentient species. You know this."

"Yes, High Arbiter."

"If the species is created by others, it can still be sentient."

The Commander's voice is small. "There is the contract."

"With whom?"

"With the Academy, of course.

"Which did not include dragons. You took a sentient species and abused it for sport. That is slavery. You killed it for products. That is murder."

The Commander sounds tentative. "There is another contract."

"With whom?

2Ray1 hesitates. His lips form a firm line.

"Do not fear to answer."

Why does the arbiter say that? Can she detect fear where I can't? Or is she offering him sanctuary if he agrees to talk?

He releases a heavy breath, raises his chin. "StarCircus."

His voice resumes volume. "Mr. Star presented an opportunity to corner the dragon market, not only because it would be lucrative but because dragons are not considered sentient."

"StarCircus. A corrupt organization with whom you signed an illegal contract. Do you claim ignorance? It won't work."

Commander bangs his fist in his palm. "I D. Express is not on trial. We are here to seek an agreement. With the Watchers."

"Since it concerns the dragons, it will be with them." She shifts toward me. "Rumplewing, it is your turn to speak."

My ear is buzzing, which means Balofur is hyperspeaking to the elders' groombugs. No doubt they are whispering to the elders. From time to time I detect whispers.

I decide to speak slowly, giving the elders plenty of time to convey their messages to me. I stand looking down at Commander. "I should kill you."

"I D. Express is not on trial. We allowed an arbiter to come to work out an agreement. We deserve credit for that."

Balofur is trembling, holding back a stream of demands and suggestions, so I will not be overwhelmed. I love him for it. Before I listen to the elders, I need to get rid of Traveler.

"You stole an automaton from the Watchers and used it to capture dragons."

The arbiter speaks up. "What is this automaton?"

"It can be mistaken for a dragon."

"Commander, who stole it?"

The Commander doesn't answer. Stilwell rises. "High Arbiter, if I may speak?"

The arbiter nods. "Go on."

"A Watcher gave it to us after reprogramming it for our use."

"Why would a Watcher do this?"

"He was dissatisfied with his employers."

I break in. "Amber and Hote told me about this. Baaden was a new recruit for the Watchers. Hired to take care of equipment. He disappeared with the automaton."

"Where is he now?"

"Hiding on the planet. Stilwell communicated with him."

Arbiter to Stilwell. "Speak to Baaden. Tell him to come here."

Stilwell inserts earbuds, mouths silently. After a moment, he looks up. "No answer. I don't know where he is."

The arbiter raises her eyebrows. "This automaton will be found and restored to its owners. That is outside the agreement." She focuses on me. "Rumplewing, you are on equal footing with the Collectors. Do you understand what that means?"

Equals. My mind floods with possibilities, all murky. Does it mean we are to build cities and factories and ships to travel to the stars? Or does it mean we can live our lives as we choose? "I'm not sure."

"You must consider what the Collectors did to you. You must consider that you can do the same to them."

I am dumbstruck. Is she saying what I think she is saying?

"You have the power of life or death."

Over the Collectors! I feel the stir among the elders. I hear the intake of breath among the Collectors. Some look ready to leap from their chairs.

"I-uh," I begin. Balofur speaks in my ear, but I can't tell what he is saying. He is half into hyperspeak. I've never heard him so excited.

"I would like to speak to the elders," I say.

A crease suggests itself along each side of the arbiter's mouth. "I will give you time." She closes her fist on the spinning ring. The understanding of languages ceases.

I can make out some words of protest from Commander as I cross to join the elders.

Fetidbreath raises and lowers her talons, uncomfortable with the hard smoothness of the floor. "I bring you greetings from the clan, Rumplewing. It is good that you are still alive."

"How are the others? Are they well?"

"They are. Even Batwing." She chuckles. "No one has taken to her new name. She's getting too heavy to carry about, so she's left to climb trees on her own and to feed mostly on dribbles of manna on the leaves and ground."

I don't want to feel sorry for her and am glad to turn to the business at hand. "I am not an elder. One of you should take over."

"You're doing fine," Fetidbreath says. "Isn't she, my sisters?"

The other elders agree. "You must continue to speak for us because of what you have experienced here. We won't interfere. We will give you guidance if you need it."

And so in the privacy of our language, we and the groombugs toss ideas about. These are truly wise dragons, and young as I am, I fill with gratitude over their presence and that Balofur is one of them. I owe him my life. I will owe these elders the lives of all dragons. Occasionally they ask me questions. Mostly I listen.

"Our young would call for the death of all Collectors."

"We need to concentrate on their leader. Does he deserve death?"

"Yes."

"What would death do? Prevent others from coming?"

"Probably not. We need a way to keep the planet off bounds."

"A live commander can warn others away."

"What of the crew members? Do we punish them for obeying the Commander? Would they be cast adrift without him?"

Eventually the arbiter spins a ring. Our conference time is up. We are again amid a universal understanding of languages. It is time for me to return to my place near the arbiter.

"Are you ready with your offer of an agreement?" she asks.

"If we could have a little more time. I wish to speak to Sneech."

The High Arbiter points to the Commander. "You. Go there, to the far edge of the room where you will be out of earshot. Sit and wait until I call you over."

Chin raised, 2Ray1 slow-marches across the room where he sits as erect as a pine.

Tenderly she nudges Sneech toward us. "Go on."

Sneech creeps, wide-eyed until we surround it, and then it squats, trembling. The dragons croon and subdue their colors, to make the sniffer feel safe. It relaxes enough to stutter, "B-boxes. There are the boxes."

The ring is spinning, so we can communicate with ease.

I voice my surprise at Sneech's words. "Did you make Hote say that?"

"N-no. I would hear him say it whenever he was disturbed."

"You needn't be disturbed."

The other dragons add their comments.

"Don't be afraid."

"You're safe with us."

"Relax."

Sneech's trembling ceases. Nevertheless the sniffer continues to glance from one of us to the other, as if at any moment it would dart away. After all, we are much bigger than a sniffer.

"Why did you inhabit Hote? Why didn't you come out of him and make your presence known to us?"

"I was afraid."

Again the dragons reassure the sniffer.

"Don't be afraid."

"You're safe."

"We will protect you…try to protect you."

Sneech sniffs and whispers, "I know that now."

"Where are you from?" I ask.

"Far, far away."

"Why are you here?"

Sneech seems to mull the question before answering. "I am fulfilling my role."

Balofur peppers my mid ear with questions, some of which are his and some of which come from the other elders. They are kind enough not to overtly intrude in my questioning. And I choose carefully.

"What is your role?"

"To gather and sell the information."

"By interpenetrating people?"

Sneech hitches itself onto its feet, as if suddenly aware of its dignity. "Ordinarily I don't interpenetrate the living beings. Only the inanimate objects."

"As a sniffer you secretly listen to others?"

"I do." Sneech taps its chest. "Sniffers may have a reputation for dealing in the information gathering. Not all do. Many also work in the medicine and security, due to our ability to penetrate the objects. For the example, in the medicine we can implant the healing chips and thus save a life. In the security we may implant a control chip that prevents the recipient from harming the others."

"Can you read minds?"

"No. We may deal with the brain energy, but to precisely read a person's thoughts, no. Nothing that detailed."

But brain waves! Brain energy. It reminds me of brain codes. The brain produces thoughts, and thoughts can control movement.

Soon time is up. The High Arbiter calls Sneech and 2Ray1 back, and I stand again before her.

"High Arbiter, I am ready now. All the dragons are ready."

"Then speak."

I capture Commander in my gaze and feel the volume of his hate. I'm sure he wants to kill me. I want to kill him, to watch him roast to a crisp. The heat in my gut rises. It burns to be released. I hear its rumble. Balofur rests like a knot on the back of my head. He is one of the Wise Ones. I feel his depth, their depth. Their sea of knowledge hides mysteries. I want to be in their society, despite my youth. How would Fetidbreath act? What would she say?

I reach for benevolence, control, and maturity. I reach for coolness. Ah, there. "Contrary to what you may believe about us dragons, we derive no pleasure from killing others, even when they deserve it. We do not come from a killing planet. My offer is that our world be off limits to any who would harvest from it, no matter if the living are sentient or not. Even the inanimate, the rocks, the very soil and water should be forbidden these offworlders."

"That's unfair." The Commander raises a hand, frowns.

The arbiter tilts her head at the Commander. "You are out of order. Go on, Rumplewing."

"You will leave, Commander 2Ray1, and not come back. To seal the agreement, I recommend that you be marked. If you do anything to break the agreement, do anything that threatens the welfare of us dragons and our planet, your intentions will become visible to the arbiter, and the authorities will intervene to stop you."

"This cannot be agreed to."

As I expect.

I ask the arbiter, "Can the planet be cloaked?

"Too large. Protective devices, however, can be placed at the entrance corridors to the planet. This could include such detection devices and defensive weapons that can only be bypassed by a special code."

That is better than I expected. "Any who enters our world must pass dragon inspection and permission."

"And the Watchers?"

I glance at the elders. "We have yet to reach a decision with them. We will speak to them later."

"They shall be notified," the arbiter says. "Anything else?"

Commander speaks directly to me. "You intend to put I.D. Express and its crew out of work. You intend to make us starve."

"We are not as heartless as you." I allow some heat to enter my voice. "I've already discussed this with the elders. We have agreed to be as merciful as possible while protecting ourselves. Arbiter, can you connect Commander 2Ray1 with a business guild that shows him alternatives and assistance for a legal livelihood?"

"I can."

"Commander, you should have no reason to bother us."

The arbiter nods at the Commander. "Will you agree to train for an alternative employment, which will also help your crew members so they are not thrown out of work?"

"As long as the pay is substantial."

"I'm sure it will be. You will also agree to stay clear of this planet and its dragons. Should you find any contraband from this planet, you will report it. That is the law. Do you agree?"

"What choice is there but to agree to what is already lawful?"

"And the other?"

"Agree."

Balofur speaks into my ear. "We can't trust him. He broke the law before. He could break it later. What if he finds a way to get by the protective corridor? The elders demand another guarantee."

Indeed, I hear the elders' deep voices that others would only experience as a vibration.

Would the Commander comply? Would the arbiter think we are asking too much? I open my mouth to show I have more to say. "The Commander can protect us by warning others away."

His features are wooden. We will be getting no protection from this destroyer. I continue. "Does he agree to accept a device beneath his skin?

"To what purpose?"

"So it can release a poison if you, 2Ray1, disobey. Sneech can implant this device that will detect the energy of your intentions."

"Wha-what? That is in invasion of privacy. No one should stand for that."

"Oh, but you will," the arbiter says. "The alternative is loss of life, loss of freedom, or a big fine."

"You put I.D. Express on trial!"

"No, Commander. You have put *you* on trial. Presently you agreed to leave this planet. Since you have shown yourself in the past to be untrustworthy, the dragons have a right to this assurance. Whether you like it or not, it is part of the agreement. You must accept it. You can always ask for an adjustment later." She scans the hall and its many faces. "Is there anything else?"

I don't like the idea of any adjustment. I have to find a way to stop it.

Balofur speaks into my third ear. "There are other dragons. Don't let Commander have them."

I'd forgotten. "The dragons in the void. They were to be kept in captivity for breeding. If they are still alive, they need to be freed."

The arbiter squints at 2Ray1. "How many, Commander?"

"A hundred."

"A hundred!" Her words nearly explode. "How many more?"

"That's it. There are no more."

"Not on any other planets? Not in factories to be processed? Not in arenas to provide sport? Not in cages for public or private amusement?"

"If they are, no one on this ship is aware of it."

The arbiter's voice deepens in disgust. "Bring them back. All of them."

The Commander signals. "Bluemont. To the console."

Bluemont moves quickly. "I'll bring back all that I can. The access code. I need it."

Commander crooks a finger for her to approach and touches a small instrument to her head. It clicks. She returns to the console.

How long have our sisters suffered in the void? Without groombugs, will any still be alive? We dragons stand, watching. Bluemont raises her hands. Presses the icons. We hold our breaths.

A cluster of bodies appears on the platform. Dragons.

Bluemont works the controls. No more captives appear.

Bluemont coughs, ducks her head away.

Then the smell hits us. A stomach-turning stench. Instead of shying back like the outworlders, I draw close and count.

Five dragons. Sickly, festering with sores. I determine not to wrinkle my snout or snort against the smell. These are our sisters.

Of the five dragons, four blink awake. They stagger, only to droop, chins touching the deck. The strongest dragon wobbles with flopping wings, to steady herself.

Behind me come the moans of some of the elders.

I am glad the arbiter seems unaffected by the stink. She rises and asks the strongest dragon, "What is your name?"

"Bigheart. Who…who are you?"

"High Arbiter. I am here to save you. Where are the others?"

Bigheart eyes the arbiter, as if trying to focus. Her breath trembles. Her voice is weak. "Dead. Only we survive. They fed us false food. Polished our scales. Still we died for lack of freedom and the want of the companionship of our groombugs."

The arbiter points at me. "All dragons are to exit the ship. You included."

We need no urging. Immediately the elders and I help the five dragons from the hall, supporting them. Actually with my stiff wings, I can do nothing more than point the way with my snout. Down the corridor we clack.

Out into the sun and its warming caress.

I gulp in the fresh smell of forest and prairie and bog. Of dung and fruits and flowers. The soil, roughened by rocks and slicked by herbs and grasses, is a kiss to our feet. A subtle murmur of the Great Mother welcomes us like long lost children.

Stricken dragons sink to the ground. Elders cluster around them, and their groombugs offer their services. Soon the little groomers are humming and cleaning away the corruption of the flesh. The dragons moan and weep in relief.

A larger Watcher ship, resembling a speckled blue cloud, joins Amber and Hote's craft, so the sick dragons can be transported to Base. A short Watcher who is introduced as Maximus stands in the door to motion them in. Balofur and I fall to translating for the dragons.

"We have medicines," Amber says. "They might not be groombugs, but they worked well enough with the dragons at Base. Sharpie contributed his saliva. They'll work for the five dragons here."

Before we get everyone loaded onto the Watcher ship, Hote points. "Look."

The arbiter's voice interrupts us as the holo reappears. Elders, sick dragons, groombugs, and Watchers pause beneath the sky and listen as the arbiter judges the Commander.

The ring no longer spins. The arbiter directs the little creature to stand before her.

"Sneech!" Hote cries. "That's the one that hid inside me all these years."

Amber raises a hand, as if to shush him. We refocus on the scene from the ship.

"Commander 2Ray1, you are clearly sentient, and I'm sure you recognize the sentience of sniffers, even though they have no need nor desire for clothes. Yet they are valued for the information they gather and therefore make good witnesses. Sneech tells me he was employed by StarCircus, and when Mr. Star had what he wanted, he ordered Sneech killed to prevent anyone else profiting from this sniffer's knowledge. This happens all too often with sniffers. It's fortunate for their survival they can control interstitial space, which allows them to pass through what appears as solid objects. Sneech, it is time for you to share what you know about 2Ray1 and Star."

Sneech cranes his neck at 2Ray1.

The Commander's face is a mix of bemusement and concern. "If it please the High Arbiter, let this continue in privacy."

The arbiter nods. "Very well. Your crew is dismissed. Once they leave, we will continue."

In less than a count of 60 dragons, the room is emptied, except for the arbiter, Commander, and sniffer. The holo image remains outside the ship.

"Speak slowly," the arbiter says.

Sneech looks about the cavernous room, at the Commander, and finally fixes its gaze on the arbiter. "Here is the true report from Sneech, trusted sniffer employed by Mr. Star, the owner of the StarCircus. The StarCircus wanted me to learn all about 2Ray1. Mr. Star's company was competing for the contract to harvest the dragon planet, and 2Ray1 had won. So the StarCircus moved in and demanded the sole purchase of 2Ray1's harvest."

Commander narrows his gaze at Sneech.

Sneech doesn't slow in its narrative. Instead it speeds up slightly. "It seemed agreeable until they demanded the dragons. 2Ray1 did not have permission to take the dragons, nor the means." Sneech looks at Commander. "Shall I go on?"

The arbiter raises a hand. "Shall Sneech? Or shall you tell us. For if you do, be warned. Sneech already knows the truth."

2Ray1 has deflated slightly. "We are capable of speaking for I.D. Express."

"Who is capable? We? You?"

"Myself."

"Good. Then speak."

The arrogance is gone, the dignity still there. Commander's tone is almost intimate. "I.D. Express fully intended to honor its contract with the Academy. Mr. Star had a different plan. He proved most capable in setting it up. The Watchers had a dragon automaton, built by their founder. It appears that when he died, the instructions on how to operate and maintain it were lost. The Watchers were looking for someone to help them, and thanks to Sneech, Mr. Star learned of it. Consequently StarCircus sent their robotics mechanic, Baaden. When he showed he could handle the automaton, the Watchers hired him. But Baaden wasn't working just for the Watchers. StarCircus wanted him to work for I.D. Express because he reprogramed the automaton to capture dragons. We weren't aware of this until Mr. Star approached us with the plan. We turned him down, as it would go against our contract with the Academy."

"Who is *we*?"

"…Myself."

"Continue then, without hiding behind the anonymity of *we, us,* or *our.*"

A line briefly forms between the Commander's brows.

"…Mr. Star seemed to accept our…my…refusal. In fact he was very friendly. He even helped with the children by sending them a tutor. Eventually the children received an invitation to visit StarCircus, which was only just getting set up. Hote was always shy about new experiences, but Radiant begged to visit. There seemed no harm in her going. A day or two after she left the launchpad, a message came from StarCircus. Mr. Star had taken her hostage and threatened to harm her if I.D. Express didn't agree to harvest dragons, thus going against the Academy contract. We didn't believe Star would hurt her, so we refused to negotiate."

"We?"

"I." 2Ray1 shows no emotion as he continues. "I refused to negotiate. Star returned her on the transport pad, dismembered, in a box, which Hote saw. They threatened to kidnap and do the same to him. He was in shock. We…I had to force him onto the launchpad and send him into the void to hide him. I had the doctor give him a memory eraser, to calm him and undo the shock. Then I sent him to his mother where he'd be safe."

"Oh, my poor Radiant! Oh, Hote!" Amber's remark disrupts my attention, and I notice the tightness of Hote's jaw.

Then I'm again caught up by the Commander's finishing statement. "The boy seemed damaged. But then he always was withdrawn one minute and out of control the next. Brain deficient."

"Is he?" the arbiter asks.

Sneech leans slightly toward her, confident in her presence. "No."

"You are safe with me," the arbiter says. "Tell us, Sneech, what happened."

"The true threat to my safety was always Mr. Star. Mr. Star had no further use of me, so they tried to kill me. I was already wounded when I used the transport pad and collided with Hote. It was an accident, but fortuitous. I entered him and hid until you called me out."

The arbiter nods and dismisses Sneech, who follows her pointed finger from the scene.

She refocuses on 2Ray1. "Have you more to confess?"

He seems to take comfort in the belief they are alone. "High Arbiter, your power and authority are great. To everyone's relief, you chose to come and hear our arguments. While this outcome is unexpected and humiliating, there is a certain benefit if you have the power to shut StarCircus down."

"I can and I will. From this moment forth you are freed from StarCircus's demands. Mr. Star will be held accountable."

"If you will, High Arbiter, then permit the commander of I.D. Express to retain his dignity. He…I, that is, pose no danger. With the threat of StarCircus removed, I admit to dragon intelligence. I accept their sovereignty and freedom."

"Commander 2Ray1, consider yourself fortunate that the agreement to save your life has been reached. Your contract to harvest or even enter the dragon planet is hereby revoked."

The image fades.

CHAPTER 49

Assignments

-1-

The holoimage had disappeared. The larger Watcher's ship and the dragons had left. Only Hote and Amber remained while Maximus waited inside the shuttle. Amber stood, looking at where the image in the round had been. Hote stood with her. He could tell nothing from her face. Was she angry over 2Ray1's actions? Or was she happy over his removal from the planet? Perhaps both.

Father had been a prisoner of fear. Hote could hardly believe this man, so self-controlled, would fall into such a predicament. He, who encouraged coldness in his children. He, who approved of Radiant who had stifled her emotion and emulated his arrogance. He, who disapproved of Hote who had emoted against his father's coldness. Yes, Hote had been defiant. "Amber, how could he have allowed himself to lose control to StarCircus?"

She pursed her lips. "Pride."

Hote shook his head. "I can understand now why Father had treated me the way he did after I saw Amber's remains. It was his way of protecting me. Yet it doesn't make me like him. Why don't I?"

"He did it out of duty. Not love. There was a time…" She rubbed her lower lip. "There was a time when I thought I could teach him about love. I never could. He didn't want to learn. He's a man of mystery. After all this time, I still don't know where he came from, who his parents were, or even if he had parents. He never spoke of his past. Not to anyone. And…well, I'm no longer intrigued."

"Do you think he faked that message from Radiant?"

She shook her head, shrugged. "If he did, he didn't make it any easier…for you, for me, for him…" She hugged him with one arm. "It's over, Hote. It's over."

She turned toward the shuttle. "Maximus, take us home."

-2-

When Base came into view, Maximus snapped his fingers and pointed out the window.

Hunter stood, arms folded, leaning against Traveler who sat beside the shuttle pad. When they landed, Hote exited first. He'd forgotten how beautiful the automaton was. A work of art.

"There it is," Hunter announced.

"When did it arrive?"

"Just when the arbiter left."

"How?"

Hunter shrugged. "The High Arbiter did it. Caught it midflight and, zip, zip, zip, deposited it here."

"What of Baaden?" Amber asked.

"There's the mystery. Still hiding. Looks like we'll have to do a bit of snooping on our own."

Nods all around.

Hote was almost afraid to ask the next question, but he needed to know. "So-uh. Who's responsible for taking care of it?"

Amber smiled. Answer enough. Nevertheless Maximus and Hunter spoke in unison. "You are."

Great! Hote needn't ask anyone's permission to approach it, to touch its sides and to pat it. He was the mechanic. "I'll take good care of it."

Amber went on her way. After all, there were the dragons to care for. Hunter sauntered after, and Maximus lingered to watch Hote continue to rub Traveler and brush away dust. "I'll learn how to reprogram it and put it to our good use. I'm sure Chief Li will approve."

"You need help, I'm here. You know that, don't you?"

"Thanks, Maximus. Thanks."

When it seemed Hote was finally alone, he ghosted a glance over his shoulder. Rumplewing stood there, Balofur perched on her head.

"What do you think?" Hote asked.

"Vill yuh make other automatons?"

"You want me to?" Hote hadn't considered that. It would take a genius.

"Others can steal them and make them hurt us."

In other words, Rumplewing and Balofur didn't trust Traveler. Hote needed to reassure them.

"No one's going to steal Traveler. In fact it will be of great use to us."

"How?"

He settled one hand against the automaton and faced them. "For one thing, Baaden is still out there, capable of stirring up trouble. I bet we haven't seen the last of the Collectors' ships. They'll be back as poachers. So we need to program Traveler to patrol the planet and report poachers."

Rumplewing and Balofur said nothing more. Hote was sure they understood and approved.

-3-

Over the weeks, Hote found himself spotlighted, interviewed, and even feted. By the Watchers; by the Academy.

How do you feel after getting rid of that sniffer?

How do you like your new freedom?

What did it feel like to have that thing inside you?

At first he relished the attention, the sense of being accepted. The questions were like a refreshing rain. At first. Later they pecked at him, the same questions repeated ad nauseum.

His answers did not vary. "I feel great. I feel good. I feel free."

Actually he missed his ability to be seem invisible and to melt into walls. If only Sneech had connected intellectually with him, they could have become friends, companions, partners even.

CHAPTER 50

Baaden's Plan

Traveler was long overdue to Baaden's camp. He'd sent it signals and received nothing in return. After pacing about beneath the great trees that overshadowed his camp, he inserted his earbuds. "Stilwell. Stilwell, where are you?"

The answer was immediate. "Baaden? We're heading off planet."

"What? Why?"

"The arbiter came and revoked I.D. Express's contract."

"The arbiter?"

"The High Arbiter."

Baaden plunked onto his camp chair. How did the arbiter find out? How much did it know? How did that affect him? Before he could ask, Stilwell added, "The dragons are now officially intelligent, and you know it's forbidden to harvest intelligent beings."

Baaden felt a stab of dread. "What about me?"

"No one knows about you. I told no one."

"And Traveler. Where is Traveler?"

"Back with the Watchers."

Baaden hissed through his teeth. "So you're leaving me stranded?"

"I never said that. Don't worry. You're safe. I'm safe. No one knows where you are. You and me? We're not the ones in trouble. We're okay."

Baaden leaned back in his chair. His tension melted away. What was Commander 2Ray1's difficulty but a little bump in the road? "...So... What's up?"

"Well, it's this way. Commander 2Ray1 can't come back. He's implanted with a dab that will release a poison if he disobeys the arbiter. He's to undergo training for a different trade."

"Oh? How about you?"

"I never made any agreement."

Baaden heard Stilwell snicker, and he snickered as well. Like Stilwell, he was still employed by StarCircus, and StarCircus was powerful. He had only pretended to work for I.D. Express, just as he had pretended to work for the Watchers. With Commander 2Ray1 gone, the way was clear for Mr. Star to move in and take over the contract. Baaden gazed up the tall trees at the glittering belt in the sky, its colors like jewels, its deposits to the ground sticky, sweet, messy. For a hellish planet, it wasn't a bad location.

He tapped the arm of his camp chair. "So, what's our next move?"

Stilwell paused. "Not sure. The corridors to the planet are blocked. StarCircus is being shut down."

Baaden gripped the arms of his chair. "Shut down? How?"

"By the High Arbiter."

"Hey, how about me?"

"Like I said. You're safe. No one knows where you are. I told no one. Besides, we're not finished, you and me. We can still work together. There's still a market for dragon pelts. What d'you say?"

"What about the blocks?"

Stilwell almost cooed. "I'm sure we can find a way past them if we work together. You have a certain expertise, right? And I know some sources."

"Fine. Good. Get me what I need. Something like Traveler. Or a drone."

"Okay. Just be patient. It'll take a little time."

Business as usual. Or so Baaden hoped.

CHAPTER 51

Baaden

-1-

I flex my wings. Ahmed had applied a sound tool to unfreeze my joints, so now my wings are as good as they have ever been. Never had I thought I would regain full use. How good to bring my hands to my face. How good to stretch my arms so my wings spread to their fullness, not in awkwardness but in grace. I feel released from a long-lasting cramp. In the two months since our escape from I. D. Express, I feel light, powerful, and graceful, capable of flight with a mere shrug of my shoulders.

I stand on a grassy knoll at Watcher Base near what remains of the fence torn down by dragons. Behind me those without groombugs are leaping about in play, batting a ball around with their heads and wings. They have made their home in the trees just outside the base, for here they receive special treatment to keep their scales polished and their bodies healthy. Every few days the elders visit, and their groombugs voluntarily groom each orphan. They have formed a sisterhood, their own clan, for they can never return to their previous homes. As the orphaned sisterhood, they fly together to the manna belt. More than that, they are a force for good for all dragons, because they took to heart Hote's warning about Baaden after I told Fetidbreath, who alerted the council of elders. The orphaned sisterhood travel the planet in search of any encroachers from the outworld.

Along with the delighted Watchers, I had witnessed their fire ceremony. At the time, my wings were healing, so I was grounded. How I ached to join them as they flew in formations and crossed streams of fire in intricate patterns. How I warmed with pride over the beauty and the appreciative cries of the outworlders. I rejoice at the dragons' survival.

Balofur spends a good deal of time teaching them outworlder speech, as do I. Amber and Hote also take turns teaching. But no outworlder can travel to the clans. It is up to us dragons to bring them learning. Lately the quicker learners are visiting more distant clans, giving lessons in outworlder speech.

"Are you ready?" Balofur puffs himself up before me. He, too, has been healed by Ahmed, with the aid of a replicator, a machine that duplicated Balofur's good flesh and used it to replace the scars. How handsome he looks with his gossamer fur floating about his body. It stands on end, thick, glossy with a blend of browns, really quite handsome, with only one hairless scar above his eye. He's chosen to retain that scar as a reminder of our ordeal. He looks young, bright-eyed.

"Hop aboard," I say.

He leaps onto the back of my head and scrunches into my third ear. "Let's fly."

I push off from the ground and am airborne. Oh, the joy of not having to struggle. No searching for high ground from which to launch. No running to build up flight momentum. When my wings were knitting, Balofur encouraged me to exercise them. I did, and where I was weak, I am now strong. I feel like a feather on the wind. The air caresses my face, and I lean into it and gain speed. No one can fly as fast as Blueclaw, but I come close.

Balofur buzzes a melody. So beautifully does he sing. The champion singer of groombugs, I'm sure.

"Don't we make a handsome pair," I cry.

"Indeed, we do. Show me your speed, Rumplewing. Let's see how fast we can reach the manna belt."

Sooner than expected we see the golden arc in the sky, the sun casting prisms of color onto the forest below. Then I see the Shining

Ones. Members of my old clan sail about, circling and herding the droplets into windrows, and swooping the length of a windrow, mouths wide. There among them, Traveler flies. Traveler?

Hote has been looking for Traveler.

On its back is Batwing. She has been given a tireless mount. And she follows behind the others, mouth wide, capturing great blobs of manna.

Fetidbreath has not invited me back into the clan. I can see why. The one who caused my downfall goes unpunished.

"Look at her."

"No," Balofur says. "Turn away. This ceased to be your clan when you left. Like me, you have no clan. We are beyond that. We will visit another part of the manna belt."

The belt splits into other bands so far apart they appear to be separate.

No one in my old clan seems to notice us. We veer off.

The distance will be great, but Balofur encourages me on. Balofur being Balofur lectures. Ever the elder. No longer do I feel irritated by his quirks.

"We are not utterly alone," he continues. "We belong with the rescued dragons who have no groombugs."

After we have been airborne for a while, he buzzes into song. We leave the forest behind and cross the prairie. We sweep over herds of deer, unicorns, and other creatures. We share the air with vultures and tiny birds. I could fly forever, blissful in the knowledge that these fellow creatures will never be harvested. Not a leaf, not a bug, not a rock will leave our planet, thanks to elders. Over Chief Li's objections, they have claimed ownership of the launchpad that opens a porthole to other worlds. Lately he has been objecting a lot, over dragons being dragons. He'd prefer us to be Watchers and to follow Watcher rules. Backed by the elders, I have explained to him that though we are grateful for their help, they are guests on our planet. Watchers govern Watchers. Dragons govern dragons. We are not Li's to order about.

What of the orphaned dragons? On the surface they appear content. They are thriving, involved. When they are older, will the egg each carries mature? Or since they have no groombugs, will it abort? If so, they will feel the absence of a nest. "Balofur, do you think the time will come when I will bear an egg? I could place it with the orphaned dragons."

He ceases singing. "For one thing, there must be at least two eggs, because there must be at least two groombugs. Give it time."

"Maybe Blueclaw and Sharpie might be willing when their time comes. Maybe they would place the second egg."

"Very benevolent, but I doubt it. They've returned to their clan, and Blueclaw's egg would be for that clan. For another thing, we must be bonded."

Yes. Bonded. It will never happen.

"There it is," Balofur says.

Over a scrubby landscape a prismatic glow in the sky brings a welcome interruption to my sour thoughts. Fresh manna. How it glitters and sprinkles colored spots before my eyes like a hoard of gnats. My throat opens. My stomach readies itself to receive. I arch upward, when Balofur taps me. "Look down there."

I slow and dip. An outworlder scrapes at the bushes below the belt, plucking leaves and licking them free of rancid dribbles.

"The Watchers will be interested in that one," Balofur says.

I'd never seen that one, but I know who he is. "Shall we do something about it?"

"Take authority."

The outworlder is dirty, disheveled, his clothes torn. He looks starved. I descend, and he shies at my approach. I settle near him. He acts as if he doesn't know which way to run.

"Greetings. I'm Rumpleving. Yuh have a name?" Let that one introduce himself.

The fellow bends, poised to flee. "Baaden."

"Are yuh enjoying the feast?"

He rubs his mouth with his forearm. "Uh, well. There's not much to eat on this god forsaken planet. Fallen fruit riddled with worms and ants. And if not, then dangerous beasts are after it, like unicorns and bats and tapirs. This is the best I could find in this hellhole."

I hitch closer and he backs up. "I know vhere there's plenty of food for yuh."

"Where-where's that?"

"The Vatcher Base."

He shakes his head, raises a hand outward. "No-uh. I don't think so."

"Then the council of elders. Dragons."

"Leave me alone."

"Come now. A thief like yuh can't live on dribbles."

"I'm not—"

My head shoots forward. I snatch Baaden up by the arm. He pounds my mouth, kicks my neck, and screams. "Aaah! Let me go! Put me down!"

The odor of dragon swims over my tongue, emanating from him. He is wearing dragon skin boots. Their scent assaults my senses. I want badly to drop him.

"Lift him high, and he won't pound you," Balofur says.

I sail high and sure enough, Baaden stops pounding and holds on. But he tests my balance. Higher yet, and I release him so I can gain equilibrium. He screams, whips the air. I swoop and catch his leg. Yes, this is a better hold.

"Don't struggle, or we'll drop you," Balofur says.

Baaden whimpers but doesn't struggle.

I start toward the Watcher Base, only to be interrupted by Balofur. "He thinks our planet is godless and evil. He needs to learn differently, so he can honor and respect us. Take him to see the Great Mother."

Good idea. Afterward I will take him to the Watchers, and they will deal with him.

He hangs quietly in my jaws. Except for the beating of his heart, he could be asleep. The cone rises beyond the forest. We leave the trees behind, and I can see my shadow undulate over the area of black stone, some of it fractured. It is the Great Mother's avenue that points to her broad porch. As we near, I see the steam and smell the sulfur. She is awake. I hear her murmur.

Baaden squirms.

"Be quiet," Balofur tells him.

He cries out and kicks. "Let me go!"

I can't speak with him in my jaws, especially with him thrashing about.

"Put me down!"

The throat of Mother's entrance fills with fiery lava.

"Be still," Balofur warns him.

"No! Get me away from here."

"We will, if you hold on. We want you to see the heart of our planet. To impress upon you its sacredness, to…"

He tears loose and screams. I dive down to catch him, but heat from the cauldron hits me. Baaden doesn't make it easy. He is kicking about, screaming. He strikes my jaws and I miss.

I flail to regain my balance and dive again. My face feels like it's peeling. My wings burn.

"Pull up, pull up, pull up!" Balofur screeches.

Baaden enters a place I cannot penetrate. And his screams stop abruptly when he hits the surface and disappears into Mother's jaws.

"Go," Mother hisses to us. "Go and live."

We lift, my wings beating furiously. When we are far enough away from the heat, I glide.

"Are you okay?" I ask Balofur. "I feel as if my wings are smoking."

I find a thermal and glide in the cool air. A tremble passes through me and is gone.

Not until we calm, does Balofur speak. "…I guess Mother wanted him."

"I guess she did."

-2-

Much of the day has fled during our return. As we near Base. I am surprised to see Fetidbreath on wing. What is she doing, this far from the clan? I am surprised at the cascade of affection I feel for her. Out of all the dragons, she is the one who ministered to me with heartfelt sincerity. Is she flying to meet with the multi-clan elders?

"Tell her about Baaden," Balofur says. Yes, it is proper.

She listens intently as we fly together. I omit nothing.

Fetidbreath maintains a cheerful countenance and agrees it is good I told her. "You have done your part. I will handle the rest of it."

"Should we tell the Watchers?"

"We will let them know, as a courtesy and to ease their fears. Otherwise, it is information for the elders."

"Are you going to meet with them now?"

"Not right away. I'm on my way to the Orphan Clan."

It has adopted that name, and I realize I am not without a clan. I am one of the Orphan Clan members. Besides, I can enjoy her company all the way to Watcher Base near where the clan resides. My mid ear vibrates. Apparently Balofur is talking to Fetidbreath's groombug.

Fetidbreath continues, "I am delivering a groombug to them."

"A groombug?" Who died? I am impressed that Fetidbreath encouraged the groombug to live.

"With the dragon population down, we must do all we can to replenish it."

My third ear tickles enough to make me wince and wiggle my jaw. Balofur is talking excitedly to the groombugs.

"Who died?" I finally ask. It must be someone from my birth clan.

"Batwing."

My wings stutter momentarily in flight. Batwing! Hadn't we just seen her hours earlier on the back of Traveler? And then I know, just as Fetidbreath speaks.

"She fell from the back of Traveler. Broke her neck."

Traveler isn't designed to carry a dragon, especially a fat one like Batwing. I expect to feel joy or at least relief at her death. She was a great nuisance. But then with my ruined wings, I became a nuisance, a useless member of the clan. Any who tried to help me couldn't give me back my wings.

I feel a touch of remorse. I had treated her badly. I had thought evil things about her and had wanted her to meet the gryphon. My remorse turns into self-loathing. "I was not kind to her. I thought I was helping, trying to get her to use her wings, trying to teach her to fly. She couldn't have used them, any more than she could change into a true bat. I was cruel."

"Don't beat yourself," Fetidbreath says. "You were young."

Balofur breaks off his groombug conversation to tell me, "You were afflicted with youth, a condition that will pass. Presently you are gaining wisdom, a blessing that will grow."

Hote would be glad to get Traveler back. I should tell him. "Where is Traveler?"

"Melted. In pieces."

Hote would be disappointed.

Fetidbreath says, "I had to act immediately to keep her groombug from shutting down. Batwing's groombug tells me yours has just encouraged him by telling him he will have the pick of the dragons in the Orphan Clan, and he recommends which will be the best choice."

Good for Balofur.

The sun glints on the Watcher craft as the Base grows in the distance. Fetidbreath soars, and I soar with her, our flight leisurely. She is stretching the time to spend with me. I want it never to end. She gives a wry smile. "I'm joining your new clan."

A swell of surprise and joy take me. How is it possible?

"I laid my egg. I left, but not to shut myself down. I and my groombug will have renewed life as members of the Orphan Clan. There, when the time is right, I will lay another egg. Then I would leave for good, and my groombug will choose to stay."

I am awed. "A new tradition."

"Not really," Balofur says in my third ear. "Dragon tradition is malleable, as the need arises."

At the same time, Fetidbreath says, "Tradition can be bent when necessary. Our numbers must be replenished. In that regard, you have a different groombug."

"Yes. A very wise one."

CHAPTER 52

Final Touches

-1-

Hote continued to the launchpad site where it had been moved from I.D. Express to the border of Watcher Base. The site was open, and an upright disc of air shimmered where the porthole would be. Momentarily the Academy had closed it while Guiding Congress reviewed the dragons' claim to ownership. The Academy had given only Chief Li permission to use it as a practical measure until the matter of its control could be settled. Hote didn't want to think about Li's discontent with the dragons, their lack of interest in abiding by Watcher rules. He loved the dragons the way they were.

At last Hote was alone in the lengthening shadows, free to complete work on his personal project, an artistically arrayed set of boxes that were closed. He slipped a shield over his head and whispered into it. The box tops opened slowly, and out flowed something diaphanous, like tongues of spirit flame. As it emerged, it broke into wings that flapped into invisibility. The movement repeated.

A sniff made Hote look up. A young dragon sat before him. Hote noticed a fuzzy patch on the back of her head. "Is that a groombug?"

"One of the visiting elders left to meet the gryphon. Her groombug chose to stay, and after grooming other orphans, chose me."

"I'm happy for you," Hote said.

"He says another elder is coming with a young groombug for whatever young dragon he chooses."

"Who is he who says this?"

"My new groombug. He's heard the talk from a great distance. I am young. My new groombug is an elder."

Hote didn't know whether the dragon was complaining or simply stating a fact.

The dragon examined Hote's object. "That is art." She must have just come from Amber's lecture.

"Yes. A monument to freedom."

The boxes opened, and the diaphanous flame turned again to vanishing wings.

The dragon had her own opinion. "It means escape."

"It could mean that. I'm setting it up here to mark the location of the launchpad."

She eyed the porthole and its pad. "That is a vay to other vorlds."

"The launchpad. Yes."

"I could visit the Academy."

Hote raised both eyebrows. What would the Academy make of a dragon visitor? Or a dragon student? Could they accommodate one? "Do you want to visit?"

The dragon seemed to be listening to her groombug, an elder speaking to a youngster. After a moment she spoke. "I am not ready."

Hote was glad to hear that. The dragon made to leave, only to look again at the launch. "How does it vork?"

"By mind control. You have to have a special key."

"Who gives the key?"

Hote wasn't sure how to answer. So far the dragons seemed unoffended by problems of control. "Right now the Academy is in charge. They gave Chief Li a key."

She said nothing more and seemed to be listening again to her groombug. A slight nod, and she walked away.

-2-

It is dusk. Amid the seesaw rhythm and popping light of the evening bugs, I find Hote sitting on the grass at the launch site with something that resembles a stack of boxes. They open to release wings of air, over and over again. A moon casts my shadow over him, warm beneath a darkening sky. He doesn't look up, and we settle beside him and watch the performance.

"Art," he says.

"Art," I repeat. He is not the same youth we met on the I.D. Express. He is solid, confident. Healed. Yet still foolish, according to Balofur.

He stops the activity, with a raised hand, and removes a shield from his head. "Have you seen Traveler?" He folds the shield into his pocket.

"Traveler met the gryphon."

"What do you mean?" For the first time he looks directly at me. "Traveler died? How can a piece of machinery die?"

"Traveler is in pieces on the prairie."

"How?"

Hote seems alarmed. I don't want to tell him how the dragons attacked the automaton with fire, beaks, and tails.

Still, "Traveler never served the dragons vell."

"I set it to patrolling the planet."

"Ve can do that."

"I thought maybe Baaden had found it. He's still out there. A danger to us. To you."

"Baaden met the Great Mother."

"What do you mean? Are you still worshipping a vol—? Are you…? You mean…" Hote's mouth remains open.

"Baaden fell in the volcano."

"How could he do that? How can…"

"By being very foolish."

Before Hote can utter another word, Balofur raises above my third ear. "Enough said."

Out of courtesy, we had informed him. The Watchers' worry is over.

-3-

After eating my fill in the company of my sister orphans at the manna belt, I lounge high in a white-barked tree with broad leaves and wide, sprawling branches. My legs and arms dangle over each side. This high up, the breeze is less sultry. I listen dreamily to Balofur sing as he grooms me. There, along my spine to relieve an itch. And then to my elbow. Ahhh.

Still…

I want to be content. Instead the idea of never bonding niggles at me. Until the orphaned dragons lay eggs, we will never know if bonding occurs among them and any adopted groombugs they may gain. A long wait.

For them. For me.

Trembling enters my gut. Bonded from hatchling until death does not apply for them or for me. What will happen between Balofur and me? Will we continue to be together, or until he finds someone more suitable? Or will we both die without descendants?

Balofur nibbles along my neck.

I sigh and try to appear casual. "I'm sorry about Seemor."

"No, you're not." Balofur doesn't hesitate in his grooming.

"What I mean is, you miss her. Just as I missed Tweekie."

"What's past is past. Over and done with. Seemor is dead."

My throat constricts. Balofur sounds hard. He should have died with her. Just as I should have died with Tweekie. Besides that Balofur is right. I am not sorry Seemor is gone.

He continues in that rough voice, somehow displeased with me. "Fetidbreath said there is a dragon clan to the west of us. We could fly there, and you might be able to trade me in for a younger, more handsome groombug."

Bonded from hatchling till death. No dragon would part with her groombug. Besides, "Why would I want an inexperienced groombug, a baby?"

"Have you grown ancient? You could train him to be whatever you want. He would be much prettier, and you wouldn't have to put up with an old rag like me."

"I don't mind old. I don't mind rag. I don't at all mind your wisdom and learning. In fact I prefer it. So unless you're of a mind to find an elder dragon, would you mind so much putting up with me, young and foolish that I am?"

Balofur eases into a song. He was testing me.

"Did you ever have a hatchling name, or were you always Balofur?"

"Balofur is my elder name. My hatchling name was Winkie."

"Winkie." I feel a stir inside, much like a chuckle building. "Like Tweekie."

Balofur drops down to stand on the branch before me, looking handsome and young, and endearing. Learning his hatchling name makes me feel as if I own part of his younger years, fond memories appropriated. Memories that belonged to Seemor.

Balofur looks me in the eye. "It's about time we gave you a new name. What would you prefer?"

"Rumplewing is fine. It'll keep me from becoming overly proud. It'll remind me that I still have imperfections."

"A wise decision. Very wise indeed." After a moment, he says, "You may be foolish from time to time. Not even elders are immune, but you are open to instruction and are gaining in knowledge and wisdom, my bright and shining one. As for young, it should interest you to know that we groombugs can adapt our longevity to the age of our dragon."

I realize I love him as much as I ever loved Tweekie. More, but in a different way. "Then you can be with me for a long time."

"A very long time."

I lift off into the sky, the breeze in my face. How good it feels to stretch my wings to their fullest. Balofur lifts his voice lustily in song. I join in. His voice fades to hear me, then he sings forth louder. I perform a loop, then climb toward clouds. Our duet rises in ecstasy.

Other novels and novellas by Gloria Piper include:

Finnegan's Quest

Train to Nowhere

Emperor's Hostages

Water Pearl

Long Pig

That Other Kind